OUTSIDERS

TAMMY FEREBEE

OUTSIDERS

Cover design by Ilsie Omareva
Interior design and layout by The Book Khaleesi
www.thebookkhaleesi.com

ISBN-10: 0-9966292-0-3
ISBN-13: 978-0-9966292-0-1

www.tammyferebee.com

First Edition
First Printing, September 2015

To my Kayla and Kaden

Without you two, I could've written and published
this book three years ago.
But without you two, life wouldn't be worth living.
You two are my everything. I know I'm blessed
because I get to see my heart
on the outside of my body
every day.

Chapter 1

$\mathcal{I}$'ve never been religious. Never picked up the Bible to read a scripture. Never even prayed.

"Are you nervous?"

Our eyes briefly meet in the rearview mirror.

"Not really," I reply honestly.

"You shouldn't be. Trinity is an amazing high school. I went there myself."

"You told me."

"Decent class sizes, challenging curriculum, welcoming students and staff. I think you'll fit right in."

She's still selling this school to me. A school she's already enrolled me in and convinced herself I'll learn to love.

I push my hair behind my ear. "Do I have to call the teachers 'Sister'?"

"Well, you'll have both male and female instructors. Some might ask to be called Sister, others won't mind being called Ms. or Mrs. whatever their name is. The same goes for the male instructors. They'll let you know what to call them."

I nod and draw a deep breath as Ms. Ward pulls in front

of my new high school. The tan, brick building stands three stories tall. Small, round bushes have survived the cold, and sit on both sides of the wide-open iron gates. Students flocking from all different directions are headed for the front doors.

"Thanks for the ride, Ms. Ward."

"I'll be back here at 2:30."

"If it's okay with you, I'd like to walk."

"It's your first day. You don't know the neighborhood too well."

"It's a straight shot. Plus, you said you have a conference call this afternoon. No need in rushing it."

"I don't know, Jaylen," she says slowly.

Geez, she makes me feel like a seven-year-old as opposed to a seventeen-year-old. I'm almost an adult. I don't think it's too much to ask to be able to walk the short distance to the house without having my hand held.

I ask, "How else will I learn the neighborhood?"

She sighs. "I guess that would be okay." Her tone is an uncertain one. "Just keep your phone on."

"I will."

"And your water?"

I tap the side of my sequined tote. "Got it."

"Have a great first day."

I step out of her Mercedes E550 and walk toward the front doors of a school I am not at all anxious to attend. I pass by groups of students all dressed similarly to how I am, most wearing their unnecessarily expensive navy-blue blazers instead of a winter coat to protect them from the forty-degree cold. Above the front doors stands a huge cross. I pass beneath it and enter the building without making eye contact with anyone.

"Good morning," the chipper secretary says as I enter the main office.

"Good morning. Today is my first day. I was told to stop

by the office before going to my homeroom."

As the bell sounds, she asks, "What's your last name, honey?"

"Hayes."

"First name Jaylen?"

I nod. "Mm-hmm."

"Got your schedule right here." She hands me a sheet identical to the one I received the day I registered. "Your homeroom is on the second floor. Room 220. If the second bell rings and you're not in class, you're late. We start every day off with prayer. Homeroom is thirty minutes, and then the bell will ring again. From there, you'll head to your first period."

"We pray for thirty minutes every day?"

"No. We pray at the start of homeroom. The remainder of the period is for studying, school announcements, Bible reading, whatever the student chooses. Most of the students use the time for last-minute studying or to review their homework."

I breathe a soft sigh of relief.

"But I don't want to give you the wrong impression. We may not pray throughout the entire period, but that doesn't mean we backseat what our school stands for. We offer each of our students an invaluable education in an atmosphere based upon Christian values in the Catholic tradition. We pray at the start of the day, before lunch, and at the end of the day. Our families also appreciate that a lot of our teachers integrate religion into many of the core subjects. Even in Catholic schools, that's not too common."

Clearly, I released that sigh too soon.

"Are you nervous?"

I shake my head. "It's just school."

She chuckles. "Anything else, hun?"

As I pull a folded note from my tote, I explain, "When I registered, my guardian told the school that I have a medical condition that requires me to drink water throughout the day. My guidance counselor said the school needs a note from my doctor describing that. That's what this is. I need to keep water with me at all times."

She takes the note from my hand. "I'm going to make two copies of this. One will be placed in your guidance counselor's mailbox, and the other in the nurse's mailbox. I'll give you the original back. Show it to each of your teachers at the beginning of each period."

As she walks into a small room to make copies, I look out the office window and into the school's main hallway. I watch as my fellow schoolmates rush to their homerooms. I'm relieved at the diversity I see. I wasn't sure how many other African American students I'd be learning alongside in a private Catholic school.

"Nice jacket."

I turn toward the male voice. He stands at least a foot taller than me. His skin, tan. His light-brown hair, swept across his forehead. His navy blazer, folded and slung over his forearm.

"You new here?" he asks before I have a chance to question why he's complimenting a jacket everyone is wearing.

"Yeah. How'd you guess?"

"Never seen you before. Not too many students go here."

"How many are there?"

"I think about four hundred fifty."

My eyebrows rise in surprise. "That's it?"

"That's private school for you."

It's becoming very apparent just how big a transition this is going to be. While I've always been fortunate enough to reside in upper-middle-class suburbia, I'm not at all used to private schools that incorporate religion into their daily lesson plans, let alone being a part of a student body that is literally one fourth the size of the school I came from.

"What grade are you in?" he asks.

"I'm a senior. You?"

"I'm in my sophomore year. That sucks, huh? Having to move in the middle of your senior year?"

I briefly look away from him. "Yeah. It's definitely not fun."

"I'm Josh," he says as he reaches his hand out for mine.

"Jaylen."

We shake hands.

"Nice to meet you, Jaylen. I hate to rush off, but I have to get ready to present the morning announcements. You'll definitely see me around though. Don't be afraid to say hi."

As Josh walks off, I spot a series of photos hanging under a large, wooden crucifix. In a row are four oversized framed pictures, and the second is of Josh. Beneath it is his title: *Sophomore Class President*.

The secretary sweetly calls out, "Jaylen?"

I direct my attention back to her.

"This is yours."

I take my folded note as the second bell sounds.

"Don't worry about that. You won't be considered late today. And if you have any other questions or concerns, your homeroom teacher will be more than happy to address them for you."

I nod once.

"Enjoy your day. I'm here if you need anything. And, of course, welcome to Trinity."

I force a polite smile before heading for the nearest set of stairs. As I slowly walk up the empty staircase, I smooth down my blazer, running my hands over my abdomen across the covered marks that were left behind. Instantly, my mind goes back to the accident. I remember the exorbitant amount of pain I felt that night. I remember wanting to die alongside the woman I was so proud to call my mom.

I stop, pull out my bottle of water, and take a few swallows. Slow, deep breathing helps me to catch my breath before I enter the empty second-floor hallway. I pass lockers, closed classroom doors, and then finally reach my homeroom. Room 220, the last door on the right at the end of the hallway.

I look through the classroom door window. Everyone is on their feet and heads are bowed. As prayer continues, I enter, quietly pulling the door closed behind me. Immediately, my nerves make themselves apparent. Tingles jolt throughout my body. My breathing becomes labored as my eyes move toward the back of the classroom. They meet another set of eyes. She's staring back at me. The feeling is physically overwhelming. My body is twitching.

Looking at this stranger, I feel a closeness, a familiarity, and yet, a feeling of uncertainty as well. My body is involuntarily reacting to her presence. I look at my hands and silently question what the hell is happening as they jitter.

I coach myself to breathe through the trembling before slowly turning to my teacher. I hand her my doctor's note and class schedule.

She whispers, "I was expecting you. Welcome to Trinity. Pick any seat you'd like and bow your head as we continue prayer."

She hands my papers back to me, and I quietly head for an empty desk in the back of the classroom, earning a few curious glances along the way. I place my tote on the floor by my seat and lower my head. As the sonorous voice projecting through the intercom leads the entire school in prayer, my eyes go back to the girl on the other side of the room. She's still looking at me. I look down at the floor. I try to understand what I'm feeling. It isn't love. I'm not experiencing fear, but more so some kind of weird instinctual connection. One she must also feel, unless she's staring at me because I stepped inside the classroom and immediately locked eyes with her.

"In the name of the Father, and of the Son, and of the Holy Spirit. Amen," the class states loudly in unison as they each take their right hand and sign the cross across their chests.

We all take our seats, and I look to the front of the classroom.

"Good morning, ladies and gentlemen. I hope you all had a safe, productive, and very blessed weekend. I want to quickly introduce a new student before the morning announcements begin. Jaylen Hayes is new to Trinity. Today is her first day. After the morning announcements, I hope you will all take it upon yourselves to make her feel welcome here."

I look around at the very small class of students. As Josh's voice plays overhead, I count them. Nine students. In my old high school, I was sitting in classrooms of twenty at the least.

I look back over at the last seat on the other side of the classroom. She's looking out the window as she pulls her long, black hair into a high ponytail. I turn away before she notices I'm staring again. I pick at my nails and then look up at the clock. I just sat down, and already, I'm ready to leave. I'm ready to escape this unexpected bizarreness.

The morning announcements end and students move around the classroom to converse with one another. The girl in front of me swings around in her seat.

"Hey," she says with a smile as she adjusts her thick-framed eyeglasses.

I remember seeing a documentary on Buddy Holly, falling in love with his retro eyewear at first sight, and running to Amazon to order an identical pair. I wonder if she's wearing hers for the same reasons I wore mine—for stylish reasons—or if she really needs them.

"Hey," I say.

"What's your name again?"

I sip from my water before softly answering, "Jaylen."

"I'm Chloe."

"Nice to meet you."

Her smile widens, revealing her deeply sunken-in dimples. "You too. So, how do you like Trinity so far?"

"I haven't seen much of it, but people seem to be pretty nice."

"Can I see your schedule?"

I hand her my folded daily agenda.

"We have sixth together," she says excitedly.

I'm not sure why that's something to get so juiced about. I'm pretty sure that's one of my boring ass AP classes.

"What's that? Physics?" I ask.

"Yup. It's a really small class."

"I figured it would be. At my last school, the classes were double the size of this one, but Advanced Physics had maybe ten students."

She tilts her head and her golden ponytail falls to the side. "Where're you from?"

"New Jersey."

"Why'd you move?"

My mind goes to the accident. Images of her lifeless body flash before my eyes. I can hear the sirens.

She touches my hand. "I'm sorry. I didn't mean to get personal."

I shake my head. "It's okay."

"You don't look like the geek type."

"What do you mean?"

"Advanced Physics, AP English, and AP Calculus."

I shrug. "The classes are actually pretty easy for me."

"Really? Well maybe you can help me with Physics."

"I'll try. The answers just kind of come to me, but I have the hardest time explaining how I get them. I'll try to help, but I don't know if I'll make much of a tutor."

She chuckles before handing me back my schedule.

"Hi."

I look to my right as *she* sits at the desk beside me. "Hi," I return.

"Jaylen, right? I'm Indigo."

"Indigo? Like the color?" I ask incredulously.

She shakes her indigo-colored bracelets at me. "Yes, like the color. Everyone asks that."

"It's just not a common name."

"Neither is Jaylen."

"It's more common than Indigo."

She laughs. Her teeth are Hollywood-white, and her Latina features are beautiful. Exotic. Her dark-brown eyes are almond-shaped and accented by thick, black lashes. Lashes so voluminous, they look artificial at first glance.

"Is that just a nickname?" I ask.

She shakes her head. "It's my real name. Indigo was my mother's favorite color. She died while having me. That's how I ended up with the name."

I couldn't imagine sharing such a personal piece of information with someone I'd just met. I still struggle to share personal information with people I've known for years.

"I'm sorry to hear that, Indigo."

"It's okay. You can't really miss what you never knew. Plus, I love the color."

Hurt flashes over her face as she looks down at her bracelets. For some reason, I feel extremely close to her. I'm taken aback by the feeling because we've just met. Now that she's next to me, I strangely feel more at ease. It's an unexplainable comfort.

Indigo's head lifts. "So, Jaylen. Why'd you look so shocked when you walked in?"

I think on my toes. "You looked familiar. Like someone from my old school."

She grunts softly as though she knows I'm lying, and I

look back at Chloe.

Indigo asks, "Can I see your schedule?"

I hand her my folded list of courses. I watch as she looks it over.

"First period," she says to herself.

"What?"

She purses her lips and refolds my class list before placing it back on my desk. "We have first period together."

"Why'd you make that face? What's wrong with first period Sociology?"

She shakes her head. "Nothing."

I look at Chloe, and she shrugs.

"Okay," I say slowly in confusion.

"Really, it's nothing," Indigo insists. "Just this guy."

"What guy?"

"This guy, Michael."

My eyes move from Indigo back to Chloe.

"He's cute," Chloe informs me.

"And?" I question in the hopes of hearing the point they're taking forever to get to.

"He's probably gonna try to holla at you." Indigo's tone grows serious.

"What makes you assume that?"

"He tries to get at everyone."

I sigh. "Well, I'm not looking to date anyone," I say. "Is he your ex-boyfriend or something?"

"No," she replies hastily. "I just know how Michael is."

I eye Indigo. I assume they must have some kind of history. I turn back to Chloe. She offers a smile. I don't reciprocate.

"I love your jacket," Chloe says.

I look down at my navy-blue blazer. "It was in the uniform catalog."

"Yeah, but that's the new one." She stands. "This is the one we're used to seeing. See? The emblem on mine is smaller and white. The new jackets have gold emblems, and they're much bigger," she says, pointing as she retakes her seat.

"Oh, that makes sense. I didn't even notice. I got a compliment in the office this morning. I was confused because I thought everyone had this jacket, or would've at least seen it. Just my luck." I shake my head. "I was trying to blend in as much as possible."

"I've only seen a few students wearing them. They're pretty expensive."

I look over at Indigo as I can feel her eyes on me. "You all right?"

"Yeah. You wanna walk to first period together?"

"Sure."

"Where's your locker?"

"I don't know. I should probably ask."

I stand and approach my homeroom teacher, who's writing the day's objective on the dry erase board. I scan my schedule. "Excuse me, Ms...."

"Ms. Noonan," she states before I can locate her name.

"Sorry about that. I was wondering if you were given my locker information."

"I'm sorry, Jaylen. Yes, I was."

She walks over to her desk and flips through a few sheets of paper. I wait patiently as she searches for my information.

"Here you are, my dear."

I take the sheet from her hand.

"I'll excuse you about five minutes before the bell rings so you have time to find your locker. That'll give you the opportunity to make sure your combination works before you're given any heavy books. Would you like someone to go with you to help you find it?"

"Sure."

Her eyes move toward the area where I chose to seat

myself. "You've been talking to a few of the girls, right? Do you want to pick someone to go with you?"

Without hesitation, I select Indigo.

Chapter 2

I open my new locker, take a quick look at the unfilled space, and then push it closed.

"You're not gonna leave your bag?" she asks.

"No. I don't want to have to hold my binder all day."

I stand beside Indigo in the silent, empty second-floor hallway. The blandness of this facility is shocking. For a school that collects tuition from each of its students, one would think they could afford to add a little more life to these halls. Every inch of this place is beige. I don't even know what our school colors are.

She pulls me from my thoughts. "So why'd you transfer schools?"

I look away from her. "I don't really wanna talk about it."

I stare down the hall as feelings of missing my old life take away the little happiness I began to feel while walking and talking with Indigo. I knew everyone would be curious as to why I moved in the middle of my senior year, but the question forces my throat to tighten, my heart to ache, to re-shatter all over again. I didn't transfer because my mom got a new job. I transferred because she died. Every time I'm asked that question, I have a flashback of the accident, the blood, her stillness. It's joy-stealing.

"So why aren't you dating?"

I turn to her. "I don't know. I'm just not in the mood to, I guess."

"So there's no boyfriend?"

"No boyfriend," I confirm.

"That's surprising. You don't look like the type to be single."

"I guess that means you have a boyfriend, huh?"

She smiles. "No, but thanks."

"Why is that?"

She scoffs. "The guys here are lame."

"Even Michael?"

Her eyebrows fold in. "What makes you ask that?"

"The way you brought him up in homeroom was kind of weird."

"I mean, Mike's cool. He's just a playboy. I'm just trying to help you not get caught up in his games."

I nod slowly. I get it now, or at least, I think I do. He must've played her.

"But you're free to do what you want, Jaylen. If you wanna talk to him, it's on you."

I can hear in her tone that she would very much appreciate me not talking to Michael.

"Like I said, Indigo, I'm not dating right now."

The bell sounds for us to head to class, and I'm more than ready for this day to be over. I haven't even made it to first period yet, and I've already been asked where I'm from, why I moved, and if I like a school I've barely even seen. I know these questions will be asked again. The idea of sounding like a broken record for the remainder of the day is beyond exhausting.

"It's this way," she says.

As I walk beside her, I notice a bottle of water sticking out of her purse. That reminds me to check how much of mine I have left. I pull the half-empty bottle from my tote. "You can go ahead. I need to refill my water," I tell her.

"I have a bottle in my locker if you want it," she offers.

"Okay. Thanks."

"My locker is right across from first period, so we won't be late."

We hang a right at the end of the hallway and head up two short flights of stairs.

"Hey, Indigo!" a feminine voice calls out as we enter the third-floor corridor.

We both turn toward the girl.

"What's up, Kennedy?" Indigo responds dully.

She holds her hand out. "I need my homework back."

"I didn't get a chance to copy it in homeroom."

"I have physics first period. I have to turn something in."

"Put it in her mailbox during lunch. It's not late if she gets it before the end of the day."

I wait for the girl to demand her paper back, to leave Indigo to figure out the answers on her own. She doesn't. She lets Indigo know that this will be the last time, gives me a quick look-over, and continues toward her class in the opposite direction.

"That was Kennedy," Indigo tells me as she uses her combination to unlock her personal space.

"Mm-hmm."

"She's saving me from failing Physics."

"That's nice of her."

Really nice of her, actually. I'll be damned if I chance getting points deducted so someone else can earn an A. My A.

She pulls her locker door open, and I notice four bottles of water stored on her shelf. My eyes go from the water, to Indigo, and then back to the water again. Other than myself, I don't know anyone else who keeps so much water on hand.

"Stocking up for something?"

She explains, "I have a medical condition."

I grab a bottle of water.

"So what's your story with the water?"

"Same here," I reply. "Medical condition."

She slams her locker door closed, and we step across the hall into first period.

"Sit behind me," she whispers as she heads for her seat.

I walk up to my sociology teacher.

"Good morning, young lady."

"Good morning," I say, my tone much less cheerful than his as I hand him my doctor's note and class list.

"Don't need this," he states as he hands me back my schedule. "Already got you on my attendance roster."

As he reads over my doctor's note, I look around at what looks to be another small class.

"Another one of those."

I turn back to my teacher. "Excuse me?"

"You're my fourth student this year with this type of condition."

"Really?"

"Two more in this class."

Three others with a condition like mine? I've only known one other, and that was my biological mother.

"You're free to drink. Water only. Right now, we're working through chapter eight. We're studying up on social control and social deviation." He hands me a used textbook. "Seat yourself and follow along."

I walk toward the back of the classroom. I take the empty seat behind Indigo and flip to chapter eight. As she copies Kennedy's homework assignment, I search for this Michael she was talking about. No one is standing out, but then again, I don't know who I'm looking for. I sip my water and begin to read through the chapter overview, only looking up as another student enters the room.

The late bell sounds, and I look around trying to determine which student he is. Mr. Bowers stands at the head of the classroom, collecting homework assignments as they're passed to the front of each row.

The classroom door opens, and in an instant, my heart freezes. My eyes meet his, and I suddenly have a hard time catching my breath. This feeling is almost exactly what I felt at the sight of Indigo. Only this time, I can feel the attraction. I want to take my eyes off of him, but I can't. He's gorgeous.

"Mr. Reed!" Mr. Bowers calls out.

I look down at my desk and then up at my teacher.

"What do you think you're doing?" Mr. Bowers asks.

I drink from my water.

He, too, pulls a bottle of water from his bag. "Nothing." He takes a sip. "Just needed to catch my breath. I was running to get here."

Mr. Bower's eyes narrow. "Why are you late, Michael?"

"My locker wouldn't open."

"That seems to be an ongoing problem. I'm going to have to have that looked at for you."

"No need, Mr. Bowers. Fixed it myself."

"Sit down, Mr. Reed!"

As Michael seats himself in the first seat of the second row, Indigo spins around. "What the hell was that?" she asks in a low voice.

I shrug.

"I can hear you breathing."

I bring my water bottle back to my lips and take a few large swallows. I try to get a handle on my breathing. I try to drink away the weird sensation in my belly.

Mr. Bowers starts instructing, and my thoughts begin a dizzying dance. Who are these people, and why am I overwhelmed with emotion while in their presence? What's up with this odd comfort that I feel when I'm close to

Indigo? And why did my heart almost pop out of my chest at the sight of Michael? It's not like I've never seen a hot guy before.

I look at the back of Michael's head. His light complexion and thick, dark-brown curly hair tell me that he's mixed. He turns and locks his eyes in on mine. I break eye contact, looking away from his green eyes, and back down at my textbook.

"Before you guys separate into groups, I'd like to introduce Jaylen."

My eyes quickly move to my balding teacher.

"Today is her first day here. Tell us a little about yourself."

I sit silently. I'm not sure what to say. There's nothing about myself I'm really comfortable sharing with a class of strangers.

"Where are you from?"

I answer my teacher and silently hope he won't get more personal with the questions.

"That's about four hours or so away, right?" he asks.

"Something like that."

"How do you like Virginia?"

"This neighborhood is a lot like my old one. It feels the same."

"First private school?"

I nod. "Yup."

"What's the biggest difference?"

"The class sizes and the uniform policy."

"You didn't have to wear uniforms at your last school?" asks a curly-haired girl from across the room.

"Nope."

Mr. Bowers asks, "How do you feel about the uniform policy?"

"I don't love it. I think it takes away from students being able to freely express themselves through personal style.

However, I think uniforms reduce bullying and help students feel as though they fit in."

"What were some issues surrounding the dress code at your last school?"

"It was violated every single day. The teachers were more like clothes police."

The students laugh.

"There was also more separation. The students who couldn't afford to dress as nicely as the more privileged students were sometimes teased or made to feel left out."

"Let's talk about that," Mr. Bowers encourages. "We've discussed similar topics. I want some opinions. Jump in. Anyone."

Michael says, "That exists everywhere, though. Even here."

"Elaborate," Mr. Bowers insists.

"There's still separation here even though the uniform policy is enforced. Look in the cafeteria. Though we all know each other, look at who people choose to hang with. There's still a more popular crowd."

"But what's that popularity based on?" I ask Michael.

The curly-haired girl jumps in. "Looks. I mean, even though there's very little bullying here, looks still matter just like at every school and everywhere else in the world. The pretty girls rally together and so do the cute guys."

I don't respond.

"You're not going to find the guy who reads the morning announcements at a party thrown by the prom king," she adds.

"But who selects the prom king?" I ask. "The world can't complain about who's more famous, who gets more recognition, and who's more popular when the people who surround them give them that status. The student body votes for the prom king and queen, I assume. Why vote for who's cuter? Why not vote for the guy who reads the morning announcements? Isn't he more dedicated to the school and his fellow classmates?"

"Excellent point, Miss Hayes. So class, let's talk about that. Why does society appoint the more attractive to higher positions of power?"

The class is silent.

"Come on, ladies and gentlemen. There's a reason for this. Indigo!" he calls out. "You're usually very opinionated. What are your thoughts?"

After a little hesitation, she says, "People vote for or select people they look up to. Attractive individuals often receive the most votes because people want to look and be just like them. We live in a world where looks absolutely matter. The attractive celebrities we see on TV every day are imitated by millions. I mean, who doesn't want to be beautiful?"

Mr. Bowers nods. "That's exactly it. Those who are voted for, selected, or appointed are inspiring individuals. They have qualities and characteristics that make others want to be just like them, want to surround them. Sadly, in our society, physicality is more important than what is on the inside. People are more driven by looks than by knowledge. More driven by fashion and style than by the words of the Bible. This is something that isn't at all new. This is one thing that repeats with every new generation. As Indigo mentioned, everyone wants to be beautiful. What many tend to forget and some don't realize is, in the eyes of God, we're all equal, all beautiful, and all incredibly important human beings. If more recognized that they are beautiful regardless of how much makeup they put on, then maybe more time would be spent on education, and more effort would be put into making a real difference in this world."

I look at Michael whose water is nearly empty. He's looking back at me.

"All right, class. Eyes front. Thanks for the input. I

deeply enjoy hearing your opinions on topics like this. Let's get to work on the group presentations, though. After all, they're what you guys are being graded on."

As Mr. Bowers continues to go over where the groups should be with their projects, I tune him out. I daydream about my old school. I think about my old house. About going home to a place where I felt safe. A place where I actually learned to sleep. A place my mom didn't just fill with pictures of us, but with her unbelievably comforting mommy love. No matter where I was in our home, I could feel my mom. I could feel how much she loved me even when she wasn't home to tell me.

"Miss Hayes?"

My eyes meet my instructor's.

"You'll be working with group B, just to even out the number of students in each group. They'll catch you up on what they've done so far and involve you in helping to complete the final project. You will receive a grade for this presentation."

I nod.

"Everyone in group B, raise your hand."

I notice immediately that the curly-haired girl and Michael are in my group. Indigo isn't.

"All right. That's your new group. Move your seats together." He claps once. "Get started."

My group begins arranging their desks into a circle on the side of the room closest to the door. I walk over and pull an unused desk up to fill the space they left open for me.

A blonde with shoulder-length hair introduces everyone. "I'm Elizabeth. This is Ayana, John, and Michael." She points to each of them as she says their name.

I briefly look at Michael. "It's nice to meet all of you."

"You too," Ayana replies.

"I love your hair," I say. "It's naturally that curly?"

She giggles. "Mm-hmm."

"That's a lot of hair."

"Runs in the family."

"Where are you from, if you don't mind my asking?"

"Born here, but most of my family came over from Ethiopia."

"And your name is Ethiopian, too?"

She nods. "Means beautiful flower."

"That's pretty."

After sipping a little more water, I turn back to Elizabeth, who I assume is our group's leader.

Elizabeth offers me a warm smile. "If you wanna take a minute to introduce yourself to the rest of the group, it's okay."

John smiles at me. "What's up, Jaylen?"

"What's up?"

"You liking Trinity so far?"

"It's okay, I guess," I say softly.

Michael jumps in. "Why'd you move?"

My eyes go to his.

"Too personal?"

"I'd rather not talk about it."

He nods. "My bad."

"Did you take sociology at your last school?" Ayana asks.

"Yeah."

"Did you study social control and social deviation?"

"Mm-hmm."

"What'd you get in your class?"

"I'm a straight-A student."

"That's what's up!" Michael congratulates. "Maybe you can help me with my part in the project."

"I'll try. What exactly are we supposed to be doing?"

Ayana answers, "We're just defining social control and social deviation and sharing examples through an informative presentation."

"Both teams are doing the exact same thing?" I ask.

Elizabeth explains, "We have different decades. Our presentation is about the '70s. We also have to discuss what the consequences were for those who chose not to conform to customary norms."

"That's the part I'm working on," Michael says.

"The consequences?" I ask, flipping through my textbook.

"Yeah."

"Okay. I can help you with that. What part should I do?" I ask the group.

"We've all completed our notes. Well, not Michael. But if you want to put together the PowerPoint, that'd be great."

I tell Elizabeth that putting together the presentation wouldn't be a problem. They each hand me their notes and rubric, and I begin bulleting the information to make it easier to add to each slide.

Michael switches seats with Elizabeth so that he's no longer looking across the circle at me. He's sitting next to me. Though I questioned the various emotions I felt after he stepped inside the classroom, without a doubt, I feel comfortable with him beside me. It's that unexplainable ease I felt sitting next to Indigo in homeroom.

"Jaylen, can you read over my notes?"

I take the blank sheet of paper from Michael's hand.

"That's how far I've gotten."

I hand him Elizabeth's sheet. "She listed the social norms for our decade. She also listed how different people from different backgrounds were expected to act. You should research what would happen if these various groups of people didn't act as expected."

"You don't smile very much, do you?"

I cut my eyes at Michael. "I've never been asked that."

"Damn, that makes me feel bad."

"Why?"

"That must mean you smile at everyone else except me."

I so badly want to laugh at his weak game, but because that would mean he'd get a smile out of me, I just refocus on my work.

"Jaylen?"

I look up again into the eyes of who I'm now sure is the most attractive guy I've ever seen. "What?"

He pulls a sheet from his binder and hands it to me. "I was just kidding. I started. Let me know what you think."

I read over Michael's beautifully handwritten notes. While he's heading in the right direction, his answers aren't specific enough.

"This is a good start, but it sounds more like you're talking about right now. Talk more specifically about the laws and the ways society reacted to this behavior in the '70s."

We look at one another. The corners of his mouth rise. His lips part and he reveals a wide, confident smile, showing his beautifully straightened teeth.

Again, I break our gaze. I give my attention back to my work.

"Nice kicks," he compliments.

I peek down at my black, high-top Chuck Taylors.

"Not too many girls here rock sneaks with their uniforms."

I'm not surprised that the playboy I'd heard about before even meeting pays such close attention to the ladies that he even knows what kind of shoes the majority of them choose not to wear.

I shrug. "I wear what I like."

I continue working on my notes. Michael does the same, taking occasional breaks to glance over at me. Though I met Indigo first and I'm sure she and Michael have some sort of history, not talking to him is going to be difficult. He's not just a pretty face. There's a definite attraction here. One he certainly feels, too.

Chapter 3

I place my books on one of the smaller tables in the back corner of the cafeteria. The booth is cramped, providing barely enough sitting room for another person to sit beside me. I pull my sketch pad from my tote and look over a few rushed pieces I put together over the last few days. I then flip to my favorite piece—a picture of my dream house on a hill. An isolated home with floor-to-ceiling windows in every room, an in-home art studio, and a breathtaking view of the bluest ocean.

As I peer down at a piece that's taken me over three years to finish, my heart begins to race. Tingles awaken all over me, and my belly does a series of tiny flips. Slowly, I lift my head, and there he is. Before I can offer him a seat, Michael sits on the other side of the table on one of the backless stools.

"Whatcha doin'?"

I close my sketch book. "Was looking over a few drawings."

"You can draw?"

I nod.

"We're not talking about stick figures, are we?"

I chuckle and shake my head. "No."

"That was kind of a smile. Mission accomplished."

I look into his forest-green eyes, at the chestnut brown flecks that circle his pupils. They're absolutely beautiful. Mesmerizing.

"They're green," he says.

"I can see that."

"Most people still ask."

"Where do they come from?"

"They're not contacts," he states defensively.

"That's not what I meant. Mom or dad?"

"I guess my dad. My mom is black. Dark-brown complexion, like you. Brown eyes like you, too. Only logical explanation would be that my dad is very pale white with green eyes."

As much as I hate to pry, I ask, "You've never met him?"

He shakes his head, his face expressionless. "Never even seen him."

"I'm sorry to hear that."

"No need to be sorry."

I sip from my bottle of water. He does the same. Our eyes are still locked in on one another.

"So, about Sociology."

"What about it?" I ask.

"I thought you were gonna help me with my part of the project."

I prepare to respond, but before I get a chance, two guys walk over.

"What's up, Mike?" the taller one with a caramel complexion greets. "You coming out to the courtyard?"

"Yeah. I'll be out there in a minute," Michael tells him. "This is Jaylen. She's new here."

"What's up, Jaylen? I'm Warren. That's Bieber."

The three of them laugh and I immediately get the joke. It's the haircut.

"I'm just playing. That's Eugene."

I shake Eugene's hand first, and then Warren's.

Eugene asks, "Where you from?"

"Jersey."

"Like the Jersey Shore?"

"Okay, don't answer this fool," Warren interrupts. "Are you a senior?"

Eugene laughs. "Seriously, I wanna know. Y'all were probably thinking the same thing."

I answer, "No, I'm not from the Jersey Shore. I'm from Hopewell. And I'm a senior. You guys both seniors?"

"I am," Warren says. "Eugene's a junior. We play ball together."

I look past Warren and notice Indigo approaching the table. I'm curious to see how she interacts with Michael.

Her eyes run across everyone. "What's up?"

They each greet her the same way. A simple nod.

Indigo slides into the booth beside me. "Warren, let me get your English notes," she demands.

"I didn't even read. I left my book here. Eric is letting me copy his."

"Go copy them then. And then let me see them."

My face scrunches up.

"What?" Michael asks. He never stopped watching me.

I shrug. "This is just surprising."

"What?" Indigo's tone is defensive.

"No offense. I just didn't think Catholic school students copied each other's notes. Curse. Cheat."

Indigo laughs.

"Seriously, I didn't know what I was walking into this morning. I'm not saying I need to be around that. I just didn't think it would feel like regular school."

"That's all it is," Warren explains. "Everything that goes

on in public school, goes on in here. People cheat on tests, smoke, have sex. Don't get me wrong, Trinity's a good school. A lot of students attend because they come from really religious families. But then there are others, like myself, who only go here because my parents can afford to send me."

Michael asks me, "What'd you expect?"

"I don't know. Everybody well behaved, really smart, well mannered. Praying all day," I add.

They laugh at me.

"Outside of the uniform and prayer, this is regular school, Jaylen," Indigo reconfirms. "Just less fights and smaller classes."

"Yup," Eugene chimes in.

"All right, we're out. Nice meeting you, Jaylen," Warren says quickly as a couple of guys call out to him. "I'll give you my notes after lunch," he directs at Indigo.

Michael stands and leaves with them.

Interesting, I think to myself. No words exchanged. Very little eye contact between the two. I'm more than positive that Indigo and Michael have a personal history. I don't know what happened, but undeniably, something did.

"So, how's your first day going?" Indigo asks.

"Okay. Nothing too special about it."

"Meeting me wasn't special?"

I look at Indigo. Her eyes are attentive as she closely watches my expression.

"I'm actually really happy that I met you," I admit.

She cocks her head to the side. "Why?"

"I don't know. You've just made being here much more comfortable."

She reveals a satisfied smile. "Good."

I change the subject. "What are you guys reading in English?"

"*The Canterbury Tales*. Have you read it?"

I shake my head.

"You're in AP anyway. I think you'll be reading *A Prayer for*…"

As she silently searches her brain for the title, I do the same. I say, "*Owen Meany.*"

"Yeah. Have you read it?"

"No. Never heard of it."

Confusion covers her face. "So that was a guess?"

"Sort of," I respond quickly.

Damn it. I should've just kept quiet. I've always been great at hiding most things about myself, but I almost always reveal that my brain unexplainably produces answers to things I didn't know just seconds earlier.

She surprisingly doesn't question further how the answer came to me and instead begins searching through her purse. I scan the cafeteria. I watch those passing by our booth. Immediately, I notice how every passing student glances at the gorgeous girl sitting next to me.

"Got any lip gloss?"

I pull a tube from my jacket pocket. "Popular, huh?"

"What do you mean?"

"Getting a lot of looks."

She looks at the other students as she lubricates her lips and chuckles.

"What's funny?"

"I really don't like people."

I'm sure the disbelief shows on my face.

She nudges me. "Seriously. I don't feel like I fit in with anybody. I mean, even though girls wanna be my friend and guys wanna date me, I don't feel comfortable around a lot of people."

"So why befriend me so quickly?"

"Because I feel comfortable around you," she says genuinely.

I look away from Indigo. I made a personal promise not to allow myself to get too close to anyone. Close relationships all too often end in disappointment. I mean, I've had my share of supposedly close friends, but over time, the more I shared about myself, the more they realized how greatly we differed. In most cases, we still remained friends, but my *weirdness* was always questioned, especially my level of intelligence and my lack of interest in just about every guy who introduced himself to me.

"I see you and Mike are becoming well acquainted."

I don't respond to her comment. I've never been confrontational, and her tone makes it clear that she's not happy about it.

Girls can be so protective of guys. Guys they won't be with for long. Guys they barely know or feel for. Guys who aren't theirs and never will be.

"What'd you guys talk about?" she asks.

"Homework," I respond truthfully.

"And?"

"Not much else."

She touches her hair. "Do you like him?"

Are you serious? I don't know him enough to like him. I don't know you well enough to like or not like you.

"I don't know him," I answer.

"You got eyes, though."

"He's attractive, Indigo."

"And?"

"And that's it," I reply sternly.

She exhales loudly. "Okay, Jaylen."

I take a deep, cleansing breath before taking a few swallows of water. "Look, you just met me," I say calmly. "You don't know me. So I'm letting you know now, I'm not that kind of girl. I don't like drama. I don't fight over boys. I don't play games. This whole Michael thing is really annoying me. It's my first day and you're questioning me about making friends."

She silently eyes me, and then the corners of her mouth

rise into a closed-lip smile. "You're right," she states. "You're free to chill with anyone you want. I just don't want to lose this comfort. I've already lost it once."

I'm not sure what she means about losing it once, but I certainly understand why she's concerned about losing this comfort. I haven't felt this relaxed with anyone since I was four. But wearing my heart on my sleeve was an old habit that died very hard. Unlike many, I mentally note life's lessons, and if there's anything that this life has taught me, it's that people will come into your life for whatever reason, and will at some point make their exit. Some stay longer than others, but at some point, they all leave. Everyone leaves. Friends do, and even parents.

"We're cool, right?"

I make eye contact with Indigo. For sure, this connection we share is one she's been in serious need of. She's by far the prettiest girl I've seen in this school, but us being close is clearly important to her. More important to her than being friends with all the other students who can't help but stare at her, who make small talk with her just to feel like they're friends with the beautiful girl.

"We're cool," I answer.

She smiles, sweet and sincere.

"Where are you from?" I ask before she can throw another unwelcome question my way.

"Here. Born and raised in Virginia, but my family is Dominican. The aunt I live with was raised in Michigan with my mom. They weren't sisters, but grew up so close, she was named my god-mother before I was born. I really don't know much else about my family. I guess they're all in the Dominican Republic. What about you?"

"I told you earlier that I'm from Jersey."

"But that's all you told me about you."

"You didn't ask much else."

"Fine, I'm asking you now. Tell me something about

you, Jaylen."

"I'm not really the personal type. I don't really tell people much about me."

"Why?"

I shrug. "I'm just not very comfortable doing that."

"So what did you talk to your old friends about? The moon?"

Light laughter escapes us both.

"No, not the damn moon. Just, whatever was happening."

"Did you have a boyfriend at your old school?"

I knew that question was coming.

"Mm-hmm," I answer.

"You guys broke up?"

"Yup."

"Why?"

"I didn't want him the way he wanted me so he did the smart thing."

Her eyes widen. "He dumped you?"

"Sure did."

"You cry?"

I tell her, "I don't cry."

"Was he your only boyfriend?"

"I dated one other guy for like two weeks. Ended the same way."

"You wouldn't have sex with him?"

And I knew that question wouldn't be too far behind.

"I didn't have sex with either of them."

"Just not ready?"

"I guess that must be it, because I just don't have those feelings. I've never really had a crush on anybody. I mean, I can visually see that someone is attractive, but as far as constantly thinking about somebody or, you know, having that feeling that everyone talks about, I've never felt that."

She nods. I don't admit that I felt that "feeling" at the

sight of Michael.

"I know exactly what you're talking about," she says, sounding almost relieved. "I don't feel for people the way most people do. It doesn't matter how cute a person is, the chances of me actually connecting with them are slim to none, so I can totally relate."

I look into Indigo's brown eyes. I don't know who this girl is. I sometimes question not only who I am, but what I am. But I'm beginning to realize that we've connected because whatever I am, she is too.

Chapter 4

I head down the front steps of my school. After a long day of repeating the same answers to the same questions, I'm ready to tune out the world and tune into my playlist. I pop in my iPod's earphones and turn my cell on vibrate. Before I get a chance to increase the volume, I feel a tap on my shoulder. I turn around to find Josh standing behind me.

He smiles big. "How was your first day, newbie?"

"It was okay."

"You're not staying after for any of the groups?"

I shake my head. "I have homework to catch up on."

"Already?"

"Already."

"All right. Well, on one of the days you don't have so much to do, stay after. There are a lot of different groups. Prayer groups. Study groups. Well, you wouldn't be studying with us sophomores, but there are things you could get involved in."

"Okay. I'll let you know. Thanks, Josh."

His eyes widen in delight. "You remembered. Cool. I'll

see you around, Jaylen."

I turn the volume up and begin my slow and very chilly stroll home. I notice Eugene chatting amongst a group of others. I wave and continue on my way. As I walk, I silently hope to pass by Michael. Even if we don't speak, I'd like to see his face again.

I move slowly down a long suburban street that'll take me to a house I have to accept as my home for the next five months. As I pass by leafless trees, and two- and three-story homes, I think about Ms. Ward, who is now legally my guardian. The first time I saw her, I was four. She was suited in all black and accompanied by two officers. I've never believed in God, but that day, I thought I faced the Devil. The woman was taking me away from a home I was sure my mother would return to.

After months in foster care, I met Mrs. Hayes. What I expected to be another temporary stay became a home I never dreamed of leaving. I moved past being abandoned by my biological mother and found an irreplaceable joy in calling Andrea Hayes my mom. Losing her put me back in the hands of CPS. I guess I should be happy Ms. Ward got word of the accident and offered to open up her new home to me. The history we share makes this a little easier.

My body quivers. My heart pounds against my chest. A churning, tingling sensation awakens in my stomach. I recognize the feeling instantly. He's close.

I pull out my earphones when I feel him touch my arm.

"Can I walk with you?"

I shrug once. "Sure."

"How far do you live?"

"About a ten-minute walk. You don't drive?"

"Not anymore. Not until I get my grades up. What were you listening to?"

I put my iPod away. "Alicia Keys."

"Thinking about your boyfriend?"

"What boyfriend?"

He smiles.

A car horn honks. The driver waves excitedly and yells a loud good-bye to him. Michael waves back. His wave doesn't come close to her over-the-top level of enthusiasm.

"She one of your girlfriends?"

He laughs. I don't.

"Girlfriends?" he asks. "No. And why add the *s*?"

"I heard about your reputation before I even met you."

He grunts. "You shouldn't trust what girls say."

"Does that mean I should trust what you say?"

"You might be better off taking that route."

I chuckle.

"I'm being serious."

"I bet you are."

I look at Michael and then quickly direct my eyes forward.

"So how do you like Trinity?"

"It's cool, I guess."

I turn around, expecting to find Indigo as my heartbeat begins to gallop, and the hand jitters return. Other uniformed students are on the sidewalk. She isn't.

"Who you looking for?" he asks as he takes a look behind us.

"No one."

"You meet a lot of people?"

"Not a lot, but definitely enough."

"Not a people person?"

"No, it's not that. I've just been repeating myself all day. Everyone wants to know where you're from and why you moved."

"Yeah, I feel you. It won't be like that every day, though."

"I know. Just a long, slow first day."

"Who did you meet that you feel the most cool with?"

"I guess Indigo," I answer without really having to think. He nods.

I ask a question I definitely know the answer to. "Do you know her?"

"Yeah."

"You guys cool?"

"Indigo's cool. We're not best friends or anything, but we're cool. Why?"

"Just asking questions."

"Y'all have any classes together?"

"Homeroom and Sociology."

He shakes his head. "That's why you asked about the girlfriends. What'd she say?"

We stop walking. Michael folds his arms across his chest.

I say, "Nothing."

"Nothing?"

"Nothing," I repeat. "Someone else implied that you're a ladies' man. That's why I asked."

I can tell he doesn't believe me. His right eyebrow is slightly raised.

"She your ex or something?"

"Nah. Not at all."

We continue to walk.

"Why would you assume that she talked to me about you?"

He glances behind us. "I just know how Indigo is."

I silently remember that she said the same thing about him. What the hell are they hiding? I let my frustration come out in a loud sigh.

"What?"

"Did you break her heart or something?"

"How could I have done that? I just told you we were never a couple." He exhales. "She liked me once."

"And?"

"And why are we talking about Indigo?"

"Because I kind of think of her as a friend. If there's any bad blood between you two, it'd be nice to know just so I don't get caught up in any drama. Girls can be weird."

"You ain't gotta tell me that."

"I'd just like to know what's going on around me, especially since I'm new here."

"I can understand that." He takes a deep breath. "Me and Indigo met in ninth grade. We remained real cool up until last year. She confessed a little crush. I asked to take her out. We went out to the—"

"What's up, y'all?" Indigo asks, appearing out of nowhere.

I jump in surprise. So does Michael. I look behind me and then back at her.

"Where the hell did you come from?" Michael asks.

"I was trying to catch up to you guys."

"I didn't hear you," I tell her. "Not too many people can sneak up on me."

"Where you guys headed?" she asks.

I answer, "I'm going home."

"Where you going?" Michael asks her.

"I was gonna walk with you guys. That cool?"

"That's fine. You live up this way?" I ask.

"I catch the bus up here," she explains.

I ask Michael, "You catching the bus too?"

He points behind us. "I'm back that way. I wanna make sure you get home safely. And we need to work out a time to work on the presentation."

"Right."

Indigo asks, "The Sociology presentation?"

I nod.

"It's not hard. What do you need help with?"

"Nothing really. I'm just putting together the PowerPoint. I'm helping Mike with his section." I turn to him. "I'm sorry. I didn't mean to shorten your name without asking."

"It's cool. I'm Mike to everybody. Nobody calls me Michael. Everyone calls you Jaylen?"

"Everyone. I don't like being called Jay, and I hate being called Len."

"What section are you working on?" Indigo asks Michael.

"The consequences."

She sucks her teeth. "What's hard about that?"

He pulls out his phone. "I didn't say it was hard."

This feels uncomfortable. Whatever happened between the two of them definitely left behind a big blanket of tension. I like Indigo. She's the first person I clicked with. But I really like Michael. I'm drawn to him. I met him only this morning, and already I look forward to seeing him and talking to him. I actually wish we could spend this time alone.

"What are you doing today?" Indigo asks me.

"Just homework."

"I was gonna go to the library to work on mine. Wanna study together?"

I shrug. "Sure. I can't go to the library, though. I didn't get permission to go anywhere after school, and I can't call to get it now because she's in the middle of a conference call."

I silently hope Michael asks to join us.

"It's okay if I come over?" Indigo asks.

"It should be."

Michael hands me his phone. "I'm gonna let y'all go ahead. I gotta head back to meet up with Warren. Can I get your number so we can work on the project?"

I key my number into Michael's cell and hand it back to him for saving.

"I'll hit you up later."

I nod.

"I'll see you, Indigo."

"See ya." Her tone is almost pleasant.

As Michael walks in the opposite direction, I can't help looking briefly back at him. Already, I'm anxious for him to call. Anxious to hear his voice again. To get to know the boy I met in first period and haven't stopped thinking about since.

Indigo adjusts her scarf. "So?"

"So."

"Your first day is over."

"Finally."

She giggles.

"It wasn't so bad," I admit.

"Your parents cool?"

"Ms. Ward's nice."

"You don't live with your mom?"

It takes a moment before the word comes out. Then I answer, "No."

I'm sure the pain shows on my face. The thought of my mom hurts me to my core.

Indigo rubs my back. "I know the feeling."

I try to distract myself. I interrupt the painful thoughts of my mom by thinking about my new crush. My very first crush.

"You okay?" she asks softly.

"Yeah, I'm cool."

"You like everybody you met today?"

"Yeah. Everyone I met seemed nice."

"Crushing on anybody?"

I knew that question was coming. "Maybe. Maybe not."

"Warren asked me out after lunch." Her eyes bulge. "I damn sure didn't see that coming."

"What'd you say?"

"I said to let me think about it."

"Are you thinking about it?"

"No. I like somebody else. I just don't want to hurt his feelings. Warren's nice."

"So you're never gonna respond?"

"I don't plan to."

"I'm pretty sure that's worse than saying no, Indigo."

She laughs. I shake my head and smile at my new friend.

"I don't know what to do. I'm still trying to figure out how to tell the person I like that I have a crush on them."

I know she's talking about Michael. She's been talking about him since we first met.

"How long have you liked him?"

"I haven't liked the person very long at all."

"So what's the rush? He probably likes you too."

"I'm hoping they like me. I'm not looking forward to being rejected."

As Indigo and I walk, she goes on about her new crush never revealing the name and I never ask. Once we arrive at Ms. Ward's house, I let us in. I open the door to a place I really don't want to call home, but have no choice but to.

"In here!" Ms. Ward yells after hearing the front door close.

We enter the kitchen. Strawberry halves and banana slices are separated on the cutting board atop the granite island.

"Conference call over already?" I ask as Ms. Ward rinses the blender.

"Yes. Surprisingly, it didn't take long at all." She dries her hands on a paper towel and then reaches out her right for Indigo's. "I'm Denise Ward."

"This is my friend Indigo from school. I'm sorry I didn't call to ask about having company over."

They shake hands.

"It's no problem. I'm happy to see you're making friends so quickly. Do you live close by?" she asks Indigo.

"I live about ten minutes away. Driving distance."

"You drove here?"

"We walked," Indigo explains. "I catch the bus home."

"Oh no. Not today." She smiles and tells my friend, "I'll take you home, sweetheart."

"Thanks. That's really nice of you."

"So tell me about your first day," Ms. Ward excitedly directs at me.

I shrug. "It was fine. Everyone was nice."

"Homework?"

"Yeah. Indigo's gonna help me catch up."

"Good. You're in AP, too?"

"No," Indigo answers. "But we have Sociology together."

"Okay. Well, study away. You're always welcome."

Indigo smiles. "Thanks, Ms. Ward."

We head up to my room.

"Close the door," I tell Indigo as she walks in behind me.

I drop my tote on my swivel desk chair before moving to each of my windows to pull apart the striped curtains. The natural light brightens my room, allowing Indigo to better see the hand-drawn pieces tacked to my walls.

"Damn! These are dope, Jaylen."

I thank her as she continues to look around. She peeks in my very full closet. Runs her finger across the top of my dresser housing all of my hair care products, and then takes a quick look inside my bathroom.

"You have your own bathroom? Dang! This is a nice ass house. What does she do?"

"She works for CPS and is a partner at an adoption agency. That's why she moved back here, to open a separate office for her adoption agency in her hometown."

"You guys kind of look alike. She's pretty. And sweet. How come you don't like her?"

"I don't dislike her," I state genuinely.

"It doesn't seem that way."

"I'm just going through some things. She's done a lot for me. I have a lot of respect for her. I have no reason to not like her."

"You looked so angry while you were speaking to her. The way you kind of just shrugged her off when she asked about your day. I mean, you didn't even smile at her."

"I'm just trying to get used to coming home here and talking to her the way I used to talk to my mom. I'm definitely not trying to come across as rude or ungrateful."

She places her hand on my shoulder. "I'm sorry, Jaylen. For whatever happened to your mom, I'm sorry."

I turn my back and thank her as I hang my jacket in the closet. Indigo's phone beeps loudly. As she checks her message, I remove my shoes.

"You want anything to drink or eat?"

She seats herself on my queen-sized bed. "Water, please."

"You want it cold?"

She shakes her head. "Doesn't matter."

I point at the fresh bottle of water sitting on my nightstand before heading inside my bathroom to change into a T-shirt. As I unbutton my school blouse, I look down at healed cuts. Cuts I received in the accident. Scars that will forever remain.

I walk out of my bathroom and toss my blouse inside the hamper. "Did you let your family know where you are?"

"I'm good on the home front. Warren just texted me."

"He want his answer?"

We briefly laugh.

"You better tell him something."

"I know, right?"

I sit on my window seat, an addition to my room that Ms. Ward surprised me with.

"I've always wanted a window seat."

I laugh inside. When friends used to visit me at my old house, I always got compliments on my window seat. They always asked to sit there, to have their pictures taken in front of my window to put on their Facebook profiles.

"Can I borrow a shirt?" she asks.

"Help yourself. Second drawer."

As Indigo searches through my dresser, my phone vibrates. I look at the screen that shows I have a new text message. I'm sure it's from a friend back home, so I wait to look at it. I'm not in the mood to answer more questions about my first day. If I'm going to sit on the phone answering questions, they're going to be get-to-know-you questions asked by Michael, and I'm sure he won't be calling until much later.

She holds up a gray Mickey Mouse tee. "This one okay?"

I nod.

As she removes her school blouse, I boot up my laptop. I then glance back over at Indigo. Her belly is pierced. *Perfect body*, I think to myself. Not a flaw in sight. I miss the days when I wasn't so self-conscious about my exterior. The days when it didn't look as though Freddy Krueger had attacked me in my sleep.

She notices me watching her and asks, "Yours pierced?"

"Not anymore."

She puts on my tee and climbs onto my bed. I turn and stare out my window.

"So about your ex-boyfriend…"

I don't make eye contact. "What about him?"

"You guys didn't do anything?"

I look at her. "We kissed."

"Did you like it?"

"I didn't feel anything. It didn't do anything for me."

"So, you don't like kissing?" she asks in a disbelieving tone.

"I guess not. It definitely didn't make me wanna take things further. It only reconfirmed for me that we should break up."

"So you've never done anything with a guy other than

kiss?"

"A little ass grabbing, a little grinding at the school dances, and that's it."

Her brown eyes widen. I always seem to shock people when I admit just how inexperienced I am. I'm not sure if it's my looks, my age, or simply statistics that bring about the assumptions, but everyone seems to think getting laid is already a part of my life. Truth is, I've never even come close.

"Why? Do I look like the type?"

"It's not that."

"What about you?" I ask.

"I'm definitely not as innocent as you are."

I try to make her comfortable. "I don't judge."

"Everyone says that."

"Well, I mean it. And you don't have to tell me anything."

"I'll just say that I've done some things. I didn't really enjoy them. Things don't feel to me the way they do to other people. At the time, I was just hoping to feel something. Looking for this connection everyone spends their lives searching for. And I just didn't find it."

I understand her. I don't feel like I've ever understood anyone the way I understand Indigo. I look at her, and I see myself. I feel like my whole life has been a journey down this confusing road to figuring out what I am. I've never been able to understand why my emotions differ so greatly from others, why I never get sick, why I'm rarely physically affected by things that cause others tremendous pain.

"Have you ever kissed a girl?"

Her question catches me completely off guard. "No. Have you?"

"Yeah," she admits.

"So, you're bisexual?"

"I don't check any particular box. I've never caught feelings for anyone because they were a male or a female. I feel for people because of who they are. Not what they are."

I can feel my eyes narrow as I look at Indigo.

"Are you judging me right now?" she asks.

"Not at all. I think I'm just a little taken aback by you."

"Why?"

"You just put yourself right on out there."

"Might as well. Take me or leave me," she says confidently.

I climb onto my bed. She moves to give me leg room. I rest my back against the wall and stretch my legs straight out across the foot of my bed. She sits upright as well with her back leaned against the black, white, and blue striped pillows at the head of the bed.

"Why don't you share anything about yourself with people?"

I sigh. "Because I don't really understand myself. It's hard to share what you're confused about."

"What don't you understand?"

I look down at my manicured nails. I begin picking at them. A nervous habit my mom used to pop my hands for.

I want to confide in Indigo. I want to tell her about myself. How I often doubt that I'm human. How long I can go without adequate sleep. How little I feel the need to eat. I want her to tell me that she drinks water as often as I do, for the same reasons that I do. To confirm that whatever I am, she is, too.

"Jaylen?"

I don't look up. "I'm just not normal," I confess.

"Define normal."

"I hate when people say that. You know what I mean. I'm just too different in too many ways."

"There's nothing wrong with being different, Jaylen."

I sigh. There's so much I want to tell her. I'm sure I feel this close to her for a reason.

Indigo moves to sit next to me. Side by side, we sit with

our backs against the wall, legs stretched out in front of us, with our right ankles crossed over our left ones.

"You should tell me about you, Jaylen. A person can't relate to what's kept secret."

"Then you do the talking. You're more comfortable letting people in than I am."

"Ask me anything."

My phone vibrates again. I assume it's another text message.

I don't move for my phone. I don't ask Indigo any questions. I begin picking at my nails again. I met this girl hours ago. I'll happily listen to any information she offers, but I certainly won't be questioning her or revealing anything about myself. I'm the new girl. I'd rather not be branded the weird girl.

Indigo softly grabs my left hand. "You don't wanna ask me anything?"

"No. I don't think it's fair to question you. Dig to figure out who you are and share nothing about myself."

"You know what I think?" She interlocks her fingers between mine. "I think you think too much. You don't allow yourself to just feel."

As Indigo squeezes my hand, I begin to wonder what her motives are for trying to figure me out. Is she, too, trying to get to the bottom of our connection, or does she feel something more serious for me?

"I do allow myself to feel," I argue.

"Then, what do you feel for me?"

I look at her. She locks her gaze on mine. Her eyes are watchful. Reminds me of how Michael looked at me during lunch. More than just respectful eye contact. Observant.

I look away from her and respond, "I feel like I've made a real friend."

"You met a lot of people today, Jaylen."

"Yeah, but I'm not considering all of them my friends.

I'm not considering *any* of them my friends."

We sit silently. I want to take my hand from hers, but I don't want to offend her. I don't know what this handholding means to her. The last thing I want to do is mislead her.

I ask a question I'm not sure I want to hear the answer to. "What do you feel for me?"

"Like I've met someone I need in my life," she answers without even taking a second to think.

Need? That's extreme. We can count on our fingers how many hours we've known each other.

"How can you say that for sure when you just met me?" I ask.

"Because we both felt the same thing when you walked into homeroom."

I'll never know if I don't ask, so I do. "What did you feel?"

The girl who was so eager to share herself moments ago suddenly goes silent. I want to say something, but I don't know what to say. I pull my hand from hers and return to my window seat. I place my laptop in my lap and log in.

I look over at Indigo. She's still leaning against the wall. Her legs are still crossed. The room is suddenly filled with an uncomfortable silence that I decide to break.

"What are you thinking about?"

"A lot of things. We graduate soon."

"Yup. Five months. What do you plan on doing after graduation?"

"Jaylen." She lets out a loud sigh. "I have no idea. And even if I knew what I wanted to do, I'm not sure I wanna go to college. I'm so tired of being in school, but I don't wanna live with my aunt forever either."

Her phone beeps loudly.

"Somebody looking for you?" I ask.

She shakes her head after reading her message, and turns her phone face down on my bed. I focus back in on my laptop screen.

"What about you? You wanna go to college?"

I open PowerPoint and then answer, "Yes and no. I don't like being in school either, but I do need a degree."

"What do you wanna study?"

"I'm planning to double major. Art history and finance."

"To do what exactly?"

My eyes remain on my screen. "Work in an art gallery maybe. Maybe become an art appraiser. I don't know for sure yet."

"You don't wanna be a sketch artist or painter? Your talent is sick. And I saw a sketch pad at lunch, so clearly drawing is your thing."

I nod. "For sure, but I don't really wanna be trained. I'm going to college because I need the degree to get a job. I need the job to learn the ropes. Ultimately, I'd like to own my own gallery. I wanna sell my own pieces in their raw form, like the ones you were looking at." I point at my hanging art. "And I wanna sell other artists' pieces, too."

"I wish I could see my future the way you do."

I quickly reply, "I wish I were as comfortable in my skin as you seem to be in yours."

"I've just learned to accept what I am."

I pick up on her use of the word *what*. "And that is?" I ask.

She doesn't respond. Instead, she stands and heads inside my bathroom. As I wait for her to return, I check my messages. One is from Liana back home, and one is from an unsaved number. I skip Liana's message, and open a text I learn is from Michael. It's simple, only five words. *Call me when Indigo leaves.* I respond, explaining that I will if it's not too late.

"Do you think it would be too bold of me to just tell my crush that I like them?" she asks on her way out of the bathroom.

"There's nothing better than being honest."

"I don't really crush on people, but now that I am, I feel like I have to act on it. Like I want to put it out there. I'd rather not dance around something we could just enjoy together, you know?"

I think about Michael. As a female, I don't believe in making the first move, but pretending I don't like him is a joke. I don't like school, but I can't wait to go back tomorrow. I'm dying to see him again.

I answer her. "I know exactly what you mean."

"A-ha! So you are crushing on somebody. You said at lunch that you never really had a crush. You can't know what I'm talking about unless you started liking somebody today."

I don't deny that I have a crush on someone. I smile at Indigo and silently think about talking to Michael later.

"You should tell the person that you like them," she proposes.

"I don't see that happening. I feel like it'll become more and more obvious as time passes. I'm not gonna just blurt it out."

"What if they make a move on you?"

"My reaction would depend on the situation, the move that's made, and the timing."

Her expression becomes a curious one. I think she's beginning to realize the name I'm withholding. She expected that he'd like me. She's realizing that I ended up liking him.

"What if they surprised you with a kiss?"

"I don't know." Michael's face comes to mind. "I wouldn't want to be surprised in public. You know, like in the middle of the cafeteria. But because the attraction is there, I can't say that I'd refuse it."

She keeps her fully dilated pupils on me. "When would you want it?"

"If things got to that point, I'd like it to be just us. Alone. I'm not big into PDA."

She takes my laptop from my lap and asks to sit beside me. I move my legs to give her room enough to sit comfortably. I sit on one foot with my back facing the window. To avoid flashing her, I smooth down my pleated skirt.

I expect Indigo to sit on the other end of the window seat, but she sits right next to me. Her thigh presses against my folded knee.

I look forward and into my closet. I expect her to tell me what happened between her and Michael, to give me all the dirt on him, to end this crush just as quickly as it started.

"You know who I'm talking about, don't you?" I ask.

"Why didn't you say anything?"

"Because nothing has happened yet. It's just a crush. A physical attraction. I just don't want things to get weird between you and me. I mean, even though we just met, I would like to still have you as my friend."

Indigo turns my face toward hers. "We can have both."

She moves her face in closer to mine, and I immediately pull back. She looks at me through squinted eyes. No doubt my eyes reveal confusion as well.

"Again, you're thinking too much, Jaylen."

I lower my head. I realize what has just happened. I've been talking about Michael. She's been talking about me. As I suspected, the handholding meant something totally different to her.

"Indigo, you're a beautiful girl. Really, you are. But, I'm not a lesbian."

She defends herself. "Neither am I."

"I think we're misunderstanding each other."

"I'm just reacting to what I felt. What we felt."

I stand and grab the near-empty bottle of water from my tote and finish it. I then turn to face her. "I'm sorry."

Ripples form in her forehead. "For what?"

"For misleading you." I explain, "I was talking about

someone else."

She rubs her forehead and purses her lips. "Who were you talking about, then?"

I take a deep breath. I try not to fuel the fire. I know my strength, what I'm capable of, and I'd rather not hurt someone because of a misunderstanding. I should've let go of her hand the moment I suspected anything more than friendly support.

"Maybe we should just get started on our homework," I suggest.

She quickly shakes her head. "I should probably get home."

"Okay." My reply is soft.

"Whatever wires may have been crossed, whatever I may have misunderstood, there are no hard feelings, okay? I'd just appreciate you not telling the whole school about this."

"I told you at lunch, Indigo, I don't like drama."

She pulls my Mickey Mouse tee off and hurriedly buttons down her crisp, white school blouse.

"Do you want me to walk you out?"

"No, thanks."

I remind her, "Ms. Ward thinks you're taking a ride from her."

"I'll let her know that I'm okay getting home." She opens my door. "See you tomorrow."

I sink back down on my window-seat cushions. I rest my face in my hands before taking a much-needed deep breath. By no means did I see my first day ending like this.

Chapter 5

I shove my wraparound ear warmers inside my coat pocket before hanging it on the small hook. To lighten my load, I pull the two extra bottles of water from my tote and store them on the small shelf. After a quick hair check in my pocket mirror, I close my locker door. I spin the dial and then recheck to make sure no one can come behind me and reopen my personal space. Before turning around to head for homeroom, it comes over me. That now familiar feeling is present. It's Michael. I can tell without even seeing him. My body reacts to both Indigo's presence and Michael's, but when he's near, I feel a strange tingling in my belly. Something happens to my heart. It feels like it swells. Swells with happiness. Happiness I find odd because I barely know him.

"It must've gotten too late, huh?"

I turn toward a face I've been anxious to see since yesterday. "I'm sorry."

"I'm not mad at you. How are you?"

"Okay. You?"

Michael smiles. "I'm looking at you, so I'm good."

"That's what you tell all the girls, huh?"

He laughs. "Not even. Did you start the PowerPoint?"

"I finished it."

Wrinkles form between his brows. "How? I didn't give you any notes."

"I just wanted to get it done. And with Elizabeth's notes, your section pretty much wrote itself."

Not to mention, I needed one hell of a distraction. Focusing on my homework and answering Ms. Ward's fifty first-day questions kept me more than busy, kept my mind completely off of Indigo and her random kiss attempt.

"What am I supposed to show Bowers?"

I hand Michael a folded sheet of loose leaf paper. "Just reword the bullets."

"Damn. I don't know how to feel about this."

"What do you mean?"

"On the one hand, I could smile about this because you just did my homework for me. But then on the other, it's like you really don't wanna work with me."

That's the last thing I want him to think. Ms. Ward was a great distraction, but I would've preferred being distracted by him. She just wouldn't let up. She wanted to know everything, down to where I sat in the cafeteria.

"No, it's not that," I say. "It's nothing against you or wanting to help you."

He slowly reveals an irresistible smile, one I couldn't look away from if I tried. I return the gesture.

Michael pulls my tote from me and places the straps over his shoulder. "Walk with me."

I stroll alongside the pretty boy who my schoolmates can't help but stare at. As we walk, girls eagerly wave. Some playfully push him just to get a moment of his attention. I laugh inside, especially at the nasty looks I'm receiving. He's the one practically ignoring y'all. Give *him* the hateful looks.

"Get a lot of studying done yesterday?"

"Yeah. I'm caught up in all my classes," I tell him. "So what's up with you and not doing your notes?"

"The work isn't hard for me. It just takes me forever to actually sit down and do it. That's why I need a study buddy."

"There are over four hundred other students here. You mean to tell me you can't find anyone to study with? The way these girls are going out of their way to be noticed by you."

"Maybe I wanna study with you."

"Why?"

"Because you're smart."

I side-eye Michael.

"And you're beautiful. I would just ask you out, but I thought with you being the new girl and hearing of my so-called reputation, you might want to get to know me taking the strictly platonic route."

"You're right about that. I don't want you to think I'm one of those girls." I put emphasis on the word "those."

"Hey, Jaylen! What's up, Mike?"

I wave at Josh, who is leaning against his locker.

"If you're not busy today, stay after," he says.

"Okay. We'll see."

"See you around."

Michael nudges me. "So that's your type? You like the nerds?"

"He's nice. I met him yesterday in the office. We just say hi when we see each other. Nothing more. He seems like the type to be that nice to everyone."

"Yeah, Josh is cool. He loves it here. Dude would sleep here if he was allowed to. He tries to get everyone involved in something."

"And what are you involved in?"

"I was playing ball last semester."

"Why not this semester? Grades?" I ask.

"Yup."

"You better get motivated. We graduate soon."

"Yeah, I know. Moms has made it very clear that I'm going to college."

"What do you wanna do?"

"I don't know yet. I need to find a career that'll keep me interested. What about you?" he asks. "You wanna do something artsy?"

I laugh at his word choice. "Yeah, I guess you can call it that."

"That's what's up. So let's do something after."

I ask uncertainly, "After college?"

"No." He chuckles. "School. Today. Let's chill. Talk. Just us, though."

I haven't asked Ms. Ward for permission to go anywhere after school, but I can't possibly say no. I want to get to know this guy.

"Okay. But just talking."

"That's it. Cross my heart," he promises.

"And where do you wanna go to chill and talk?"

"You can come to my place. We can do some homework. Get to know each other."

Get to know each other at his place? He has lost his damn mind.

"Your place? I don't think so."

"Moms will be there. I know you wish she had other things to do, but Jaylen, it's just too soon. It's too soon to have me all to yourself."

A burst of laughter escapes me. He laughs, too.

I don't know how that just happened. His study invitation had me pissed just a second ago and now he has me laughing.

"Seriously, though, is that okay?" he asks.

"I'll have to let you know."

"I'm talking about today."

"I know you're talking about today. I'll let you know after lunch. I gotta make sure I won't get in trouble. I'll call and make sure it's cool."

"All right."

I stand with Michael as he places his books in his locker. I wave at familiar faces— students I met yesterday. I then look at Michael. He closes his locker and throws me another pearly white smile. I've never felt an attraction like this before. I've never felt such pleasure looking into someone's eyes. Every time he smiles at me, my stomach flips.

"I like your hair like that."

I touch my curls and smile inside. "Thanks."

"That's all you?"

I roll my eyes.

"I'm not trying to be rude."

"It's not a weave."

"Good. I like that."

I look at my schoolmates as they pass by. So many waving, smiling, and staring at the boy next to me.

"You miss Jersey?"

I picture my old home. I fantasize about sitting on the front porch for hours of laughs with my mom, my best friend. I miss those times. Every day, I have to stomach the fact that I'll never be able to experience them again. I'll never see her again, hear her laugh again, or spend hours decorating our home for the holidays.

"Yup," I answer. "I miss my home."

He nods as though he understands.

"You from here?" I ask.

"D.C."

"Never been."

"Never? Not even to see the Capitol or White House?"

I shake my head.

"I'll have to take you, then."

I don't respond. I'm well aware of the lies guys tell in the hopes of getting it on, the promises they never follow through on, the suggestions and ideas they throw out just because they sound appealing. I may have never been in a real relationship, but I know how guys work. I remind myself that this is an attraction. Michael is just a boy. I may have never felt this way for anyone else before, but staying true to myself and remaining realistic are the only ways to stay out of the category all of his exes probably fall into.

"What's up with that face? What's going on upstairs?"

"Just thinking," I reply softly.

"About what?"

The school bell sounds, and Indigo immediately comes to mind. I think about yesterday. I hope she doesn't bring up what happened. I hope she doesn't act weird. I hope things feel the way they did when I first met her yesterday morning.

I tell him, "I need to get to my homeroom."

"I'll walk you."

We head for room 220. Michael greets almost every student who passes him.

"So you'll let me know, right? About hanging out after school."

"Yeah. I'll ask for permission during lunch."

We stop at the entrance of my class.

"So, I'll see you later, then?" he asks as he hands me my tote.

"Umm, in like thirty minutes." I remind him, "We have first period together."

"Right. I'm trippin'. Okay, I'll see you."

As he heads for his homeroom, I enter mine. I head for my desk. Indigo's is empty. *Great!* Maybe she's skipping.

"Hey, Jaylen."

I take my seat. "What's up, Chloe?"

"How was your first day?"

"It was okay. Slow start, but after I met a few people, the day started to move along."

Indigo walks in. I watch her as she makes her way over to the other side of the classroom. She turns, and our eyes meet. She smiles, and I send one back her way. As she sits, I continue to speak with Chloe.

Without really being able to control it, my eyes continue to drift her way. I look out for harsh looks, for anger. When I catch her looking my way, I sense nothing but kindness. Sincerity beneath each smile. If anything else is present, it's slight embarrassment when her smiles fade and she quickly looks away.

As we stand for prayer, I bow my head. I think about how to ask Ms. Ward for permission to hang out with Michael after school. I've never been what many call a fast girl, and I'm beginning to realize that hanging out at a boy's house after my second day of school just isn't a good idea, even if his mom will be there. I think of other places to chill as prayer continues. We can very well get to know each other at the library or corner café.

We take our seats after prayer. My eyes look over at Indigo. She's holding a hair tie in between her teeth and smoothing her hair up into a ponytail. Chloe is facing forward and diligently working on an assignment that must be due today. Ms. Noonan offers no instruction before sitting behind her desk. Students take it upon themselves to move around and converse.

"Pssst."

I turn toward Indigo, and she signals for me to come sit next to her. I point at the empty seat next to me. She immediately points at Chloe, and I get it. This is personal, most likely about yesterday afternoon.

I walk over to Indigo and sit at the empty desk next to her.

"What's up, Miss Jaylen?"

"Not too much."

"I was looking for you before homeroom."

"I was putting a few things in my locker. Then I just walked around."

Indigo looks down at her desk. I know she wants to say something about yesterday. I'd rather she didn't, but I can tell she wants to talk about something, and that's all we really have to discuss.

"We're cool, Indigo. I don't know if you're feeling weird about…" I pause and think about my wording. "Yesterday. But seriously, I don't feel weird about being around you. I don't want things to be awkward and uncomfortable," I say quietly.

"Me neither. I just feel like I caught you off guard."

"You did, but it was just a misunderstanding. I don't think that means we can't be cool. You know, be friends still."

"How do you feel about it?"

"I just feel like you felt something that I didn't. You acted based on how you felt, and so did I. No hard feelings."

"Are you sure you're not just stuck on the whole girl thing? The fact that we go to a Catholic school?"

"No, that's not it," I reply. "I'm not Catholic. And if I had felt something, I would've said so whether I was afraid to act on it or not."

She doesn't look at me. I sip my water and face front. My mind is too focused on Michael to really think of other things to discuss with Indigo.

"So do you want to hang out after school today? Hit the mall or something?"

I tell her, "I can't today. I'm doing something after school."

"With Ms. Ward?"

I bite my bottom lip and then reluctantly answer, "With Michael." I quickly offer an explanation. "I told him I'd help him get his grades up. We're gonna study together. I'm gonna help him catch up in the subjects he's falling behind in."

She purses her lips before releasing an unpleasant grunt. "Where at?"

"Not sure yet."

"Just you guys, though?"

"Mm-hmm."

She raises her eyebrows as she lubricates her full lips with pink lip gloss.

I silently sit beside her. As she begins copying a worksheet, I ask myself what it is I'm doing. Why am I so worried about telling her that I plan to hang out with Michael? Why am I so worried about not upsetting her? I can't help that I'm not attracted to her the same way she's attracted to me. I may be new here, but how I act with her now is how she'll expect to be treated throughout this friendship that may or may not even continue.

I stop this game. Without a word, I stand and head back over to my desk. I'll be damned if I go through the next five months feeling bad for being attracted to Michael and for not being attracted to her. This is day two, and already, I'm exhausted. The connection I feel to Indigo is a strong one, but for sure, what I feel for Michael is much stronger. She's making me feel like I have to choose. He isn't.

Chapter 6

I wait at the main entrance for Michael. Headphones in. Music blasting. After an uncomfortable first period working in my group with Michael while Indigo gave him the look of death, and then a lunch period spent in my guidance counselor's office discussing my history, I feel like crawling under a rock and hiding from my entire world.

As students pass, I text Ms. Ward that I'll be studying with friends at a café a few blocks from school. As I wait for her reply, I see Michael and Warren coming my way. Before making it over to me, Warren and Michael separate, and Warren heads back in the direction they were coming from. I remove my headphones.

"So, it's okay, then?" Michael asks.

"We can hang out, but not at your house."

"I told you Moms will be there."

"And I believe you. It's just that it's my second day. Going to your house just doesn't look good."

"You think I told the whole school that the new girl is coming over today?"

"Can we just keep it public? I don't even know you,

Michael."

Disappointment shows in his face. "Whatever will make you comfortable."

We walk down the school's front steps. Students are everywhere, talking with friends, waiting on rides. We pass them by, waving at a few as we go. Unsurprisingly, a few more dirty looks are thrown my way. I keep moving, unfazed by the hate.

"So you wanna study?"

He shakes his head. "Not really."

"What do you wanna do?"

"Let's go for a walk." He points in the opposite direction of Ms. Ward's house. "There's a spot down this way that I hit up when I need to think and get away from people."

As we walk, I ask, "What kind of spot?"

"You'll see."

I look over at Michael. He seemed more relaxed in school. Now, he's more serious. His hands are in his pockets. His posture is straighter. More stiff.

"You nervous?"

"No. You?"

"Not at all, but you seem a little uneasy. Hands in your pockets, looking all over the place."

He chuckles. "I'm good. It's just cold."

"So are you and your mom close?" I ask.

"Yup. It's just us." He explains, "She's more like a friend, though."

"She's not strict?"

"Yes and no. She lets me chill when I want to as long as she knows where. She lets me date. No arguments about that. Her biggest concerns are my grades and how I date."

As he gulps down some water, I say, "So she doesn't want you banging out the whole school. That's motherly of her."

Loud laughter escapes him. "What the hell did you hear

about me?"

"Even if there was nothing said about you, I'd still think it. Not necessarily in a bad way, though. You just have the look of a ladies' man, and the way some of those girls were looking at me when I was with you this morning only confirms for me that you've probably dated most of them."

"You can't say that based on hating looks alone."

"Okay, maybe you've banged all of them."

Again he laughs. I laugh, too.

"Seriously, though, all jokes aside, I don't think anything bad about you. I just feel like I need to be careful around you."

"I would never hurt you, Jaylen."

"Maybe not physically, but there are other ways to hurt people."

His voice lowers. "I know that."

We walk side by side quietly. I begin picking at my nails.

"So what about you and your family? You guys close?"

I take a deep breath. "I don't have any family."

He touches my back. "I'm sorry."

I look down at my hands as I recall the accident. I think about what life will be like five months from now. After graduation, I'll be out in this world alone. I won't even have Ms. Ward at that point. Just me, left to feel like an outsider in this world I've never felt like I belonged in.

"So what do you like to do, Jaylen? I mean, other than draw."

"I read a lot."

"Romance novels?"

I wrinkle my nose in disgust. "No. I don't read romance novels."

"Why?"

"Because they're boring. And they're always in one way or another, exactly the same. Some woman waiting or looking for Mr. Right. This flawless, unrealistic, crazy attractive man, running in the rain to propose publicly and take this woman away from whatever life she's tired of living. I don't read that bullshit."

He laughs. "Damn, you don't just not read them. You hate them."

"They're just not my type of books. I don't reside in fantasy land. Do you read?"

"Sometimes."

"What do you read?"

"I read biographies and autobiographies. I like history. Understanding how the world ended up the way it is today."

Truthfully, I didn't peg him for a reader. I figured if he read anything at all, it'd likely be sports articles or CliffsNotes to get out of reading an assigned novel.

"I'm impressed," I admit.

"So, what *do* you read?"

"Both nonfiction and fiction. I've read a lot of autobiographies. I read more fiction, though. I've been bingeing on Stephen King these last few weeks."

"Why?"

"Because he wrote about things that hadn't been written about yet. There's nothing like originality, even if you know some of the things he writes about just don't exist."

"I've never read a Stephen King book."

"They're pretty good. Some are scary as hell. Some aren't. But they all keep your interest. Well, I can only speak for the ones I've read."

He nods. "So you like science fiction, ghost stories, and all that?"

"I'm picky when it comes to ghost stories. In terms of science fiction, I think I'm just fascinated by the idea that small worlds and other races outside of the human race could possibly exist within this world."

He makes a soft grunting sound. I drink from my water, and he drinks from his.

"So?"

He softly bumps me. "So, what?"

We become quiet again. There's definitely a weird type of nervousness when you're standing next to someone you really like. Being close to Michael, being alone with him, feels good. The same comfort I feel with Indigo, I feel with him. Just, with him, it's a higher level of comfort. A feeling of safety, like I could close my eyes with him. I don't know what's making me feel this way. I'm not at all the trusting kind.

"Where are we going?"

"I told you already. The place where I go to think."

I stop walking and turn to Michael. "I'm serious. Where are we going?"

He melts me with his smile and then offers me a wink.

I realize that we're walking in the direction he told me his house is in. We're not passing shops. I haven't even seen a park. All homes. This boy thinks he's so clever. We're going to his house.

I look at Michael through squinted eyes. That smile never leaves his face. I hold in the one that so badly wants to show on mine.

He touches my arm. "Come on."

Nerves run through my body. I remain beside Michael, certain that we're headed where I told him I didn't want to go. For some reason, I feel like I can trust him, though. Like the comfort I feel with him and Indigo, I feel because we're the same. Whatever we are.

I ask, "So why don't you have a girlfriend?"

"Haven't found what I'm looking for."

"And that is?"

"To feel more than I see."

"What do you mean?"

"Just something more than a physical attraction, you know? It's not hard to find someone you think is pretty, but it'd be nice to feel something along with what my eyes see."

I don't respond in the hopes that he'll further explain.

"Like Warren, for example. He's been feeling Indigo since…" He thinks about it. "Since forever, it seems like. Every day, he tells me, 'Damn she's so pretty.' I mean, you've seen Warren. No homo, but anyone can see he's not the type of guy who has a hard time getting girls. He's not making it official with anyone, though, because he wants her. That need to be with somebody that goes past the pretty face—that's what's been missing for me. I've never talked about anyone the way he talks about her. I've been listening to him go on about her for a hot minute now."

I ask as though I know something. "Was he mad when you two hooked up?"

His eyes widen. "Who said we hooked up?"

I know that I can't lie and say that Indigo said that, because she didn't. I shrug and keep quiet.

"I know that rule. Girls can't date their friends' exes. We were never a couple, Jaylen. If she was ever my girl, don't you think she'd be the first to say so?"

Makes sense, I think to myself.

"We just didn't feel the same way about each other. That's it. We're still cool, though."

"What do you think about her?"

"Indigo's cool. I told you that."

"I mean, as a person."

"I don't know. We were cool for a while. Indigo's one of those people who feels like everything needs to be done that very moment. She's impulsive. She feels, and then boom!" He snaps his fingers. "She acts on it. But as a friend, I kind of feel bad for her. She wants to be in a relationship, but she just can't find that person."

I think about yesterday. Michael, too, must have rejected her. I dig for more. "So you didn't like her?"

"Not like Warren does. She's beautiful, though."

"She's definitely beautiful."

"But you can't force a feeling, Jaylen. If it's not there, it's not there."

I feel sorry for Indigo. For years I've been curious about these crushes people seem to have on one another. Until yesterday, I couldn't relate. It feels good to talk to Michael. To get to know the guy I have a crush on. I used to question why I couldn't feel this. I remember how lonely it felt. I can definitely relate to Indigo.

"Your turn. Why no boyfriend?"

"I had one at my old school, but we broke up not too long after we started going out."

"Why?"

I use his words. "We just didn't feel the same way about each other."

"So why'd you agree to be his girlfriend?"

I shrug. "I guess I thought it would just happen."

"When did you dump him?"

I admit, "I didn't."

"He dumped you?" His high-pitched tone reveals surprise.

"Yeah. I wasn't hurt, though. If he didn't do the dumping, I was going to."

"So what did y'all do?"

"We went back to being friends. I'm not a drama queen. It just didn't work for us."

"I'm talking about while y'all were together."

"Nothing. We went to homecoming together. We went to the movies. An awkward kiss. That's it."

"Really? That's it?"

"Yes, Michael. That's it."

"He was your only boyfriend?"

"One other guy. Same thing," I answer quickly.

"Damn. So you've never really been in a relationship, huh?"

"Nope." I shake my head. "I've kind of wanted one, but

it hasn't been a priority. My focus is on other things."

"Like what?"

"Mainly myself. Just trying to figure out who I really am. Where I'm going."

"I should probably step back sometimes and do the same thing."

"I guess everybody should."

I look at Michael. Those watchful greens look right back at me.

"So what's up with the water, Michael?"

"I have to drink throughout the day, especially if I don't eat."

"Why?"

"I have to. It's a medical thing."

A medical thing. Though I've never officially been diagnosed with anything, that's the only way I can describe my reason for downing water all day long.

As a child, my mom loved that I never begged for juice or soda, but she just couldn't understand how any kid could feel the need to drink water so often. Her concerns led to fear. She was afraid that allowing me to guzzle by the bottle would lead to over-hydration. After several visits to my doctor and several blood drawings, my doctor couldn't diagnose me with anything. Though my unknown blood type had always raised her eyebrows and even prompted her to send samples to institutes, my doctor couldn't ignore the lack of symptoms. Nothing pointed to excessive water intake. I never had any headaches, confusion, blurred vision, nausea, anything. It seemed like a no-brainer to her. She advised my mom to keep an eye out in case any symptoms were to arise, but to continue giving me water, especially since I would complain of extreme pain when I couldn't drink on demand.

For years, I worried that a lab would one day call with crazy results after studying my mysterious blood. Results that would lead to me being locked away and experimented on daily. The call never came. I was so relieved to read that two new blood types were discovered a few years ago, and despite the fact that my blood wasn't a match for either, it proved that unknown blood types do exist. My case is unique, but not unheard of.

I take a sip from my bottle and look around at the large homes as we pass them by. I then look up into the leafless trees, at how quickly the squirrels scramble up them as I walk in their direction.

"Do you have pets?" I ask.

"Nah. You?"

"No. Animals have issues with me."

He lets out a short laugh.

"Seriously. They either run like hell to get away from me or try to attack me."

Michael's eyes show no surprise.

"I think you think I'm playing."

"I don't. You don't see nature trying to be best friends with me, do you? Got the same issue, boo. That's why I walk this way. There's a shortcut that I could take, but there are more dogs down that way. Down this street, they have taller fences. The dogs can bark all they want, but they can't hop over."

I listen to Michael. I compare what he's told me about himself to what I deal with on a regular basis. The need to drink water so often, the response we get from animals, the lack of emotion we feel toward others. Though I don't know what I am, it's nice to know that there are others like me.

Chapter 7

We stop in front of a large, stone-front home. The front door stands beneath a huge, arched window. Garland is still strung along the outdoor columns though Christmas was weeks ago. A wreath is centered between the two white garage doors. Both are closed, and no cars are parked in the driveway.

"So this is it?" I ask.

"What?"

"The place you come to when you need to think and escape the world?"

"There's no place like home."

"Ha ha," I say sarcastically. "Why are you so determined for me to see where you live?"

"Come on. You'll see."

I nervously follow Michael around to the side of his house. He unlocks the fence door, and we step into his large back yard. He pulls the door closed, locking it behind us. The fencing is too tall for both animals to jump over and for nosy neighbors to see over.

"Big yard," I state.

I notice a woman wrapped in a blanket sitting on the deck. She has a book in hand, but her eyes are on us.

"Come meet my mom."

I walk toward Michael's mother. She stands. Her complexion is chocolate like mine. Her height is around mine, give or take an inch. She's beautiful. Her hair stops at the middle of her back. Her face is welcoming. Her smile is soft. Kind.

Being around Michael and his mother is overwhelming and incredible. There's a sense of belonging. A home-like feeling that takes me back to when I was four and in the arms of my mother, the woman who carried, nurtured, and adored me. Though it was so many years ago, to this day, I can still remember how secure I felt. It's something I've always missed. Missed until now. It's crazy to feel it again.

I stand beside Michael and in front of his mother. My breathing becomes labored. Though this feeling is a remembered one, it's still scary because of its intensity.

"I'm Michelle."

I slowly reach out my shaky hand. "I'm Jaylen," I say softly.

"Nice to meet you. Get her a glass of water, Mike."

As he walks inside his home through the sliding patio door, she pulls out a seat for me.

"You okay? You look flustered."

"I'm sorry." I take a deep breath. "I'm fine."

She smiles warmly. "Michael told me you just moved here. Yesterday was your first day?"

"Yes. I moved here from Jersey."

She nods. "And what do your parents do?"

Michael comes back and places a bottle of water in front of me.

My throat swells as I try to answer. "My mom..." I pause. I look down at my hands as I pick at my nails. I can't say the word. It won't come out. "I don't live with my parents," I say.

"She doesn't like to talk about it, Ma."

"I understand." Her eyes are as watchful as her son's. Her tone is sweet. Motherly.

She turns to Michael. "What are you guys up to today?"

"Studying," he replies. "She's gonna help me get my grades up. She's a straight-A student, Ma."

"That's great. And you could definitely use the help. You need to get that GPA up." She turns back to me. "Do you guys have the same classes?"

I shake my head. "Just one."

"You're taking honors courses?"

"Advanced Placement."

"And you make straight A's?" Her tone is a surprised one. "You go, girl."

I smile and then sip from my water.

She looks at me. Looks at me as though she can read me. Michael stands quietly.

"You hungry?" she asks.

"No, thanks."

Folds form in her forehead. "You are eating, aren't you?"

Michael jumps in. "She's not hungry, Ma."

"Take care of yourself, Jaylen. I know moving in the middle of senior year isn't easy. I can see that something's eating away at you."

I drink more water. I try to swallow all of my emotions. I try to bury all that she's seeing deep down so that it no longer shows.

"You need to stay healthy, sweetheart. You don't look like you sleep well."

"Ma!" Michael's widened eyes are telling her to stop.

"I'm a mom," she says, her eyes on me. "I know I'm not *your* mom, but I'm concerned. I'll stop picking at you." She reveals a loving smile. "Know that I'm here if you need anything."

"Thank you."

I pick at my nails. After the accident, I felt so alone. Now I'm here, in Virginia, living with Ms. Ward. She's offering me around-the-clock support. More support than I need. Indigo and Michael have offered me instant friendships, and now, Ms. Reed. She's opening up her heart to someone she doesn't know, showing love that comes across as genuine to a perfect stranger. I don't know how to feel about all of this. It's what anyone normal would want, yet I don't know how to stomach it, how to fully accept it and just enjoy it.

"Come on. Let me show you the house."

Michael takes my hand and, together, we head inside.

"I'm sorry about that," he apologizes.

"About what?"

"My mom."

I shrug. "She's nice."

I scan the room. A black sectional decorates the large space. The wall across from the sectional is home to a large flat-panel TV. Neatly organized photos behind the sectional show Michael's growth over the years. Then, a framed piece of art grabs me. A hand-drawn piece similar to one that I've sketched. A picture that takes me back to the morning I walked into my mother's room and realized she wasn't there. Lying on top of her lavender sheet was a small object resembling a dried cocoon. Gray in color and light in weight. An object I showed to the officers. They gave it a glance and came to the quick conclusion that it was insignificant.

I point at the piece. "What is that?" I ask Michael.

"My father drew that."

"I thought you didn't know him."

"I don't. And I don't want to know him. He left my mother."

"He left you, too."

"Exactly. That's why I don't pay any attention to that picture. And around here, we don't talk about him."

Michael's phone rings. As he answers, I stare at the picture. I question what that is, what it means. I question my connection to Michael, his mother, to Indigo. I run theories through my mind. Theories about what we might be.

Ms. Reed steps in through the patio door. She walks over and places her arm around me. "Mike's father drew that."

"He told me."

"Do you like it?"

"I don't know. What is it?"

"Kind of a memorial for Michael's grandmother."

"What do you mean, 'memorial'?"

She offers a kind smile. A smile I can easily see is forced.

"I feel like I've seen that before," I tell her.

Uncertainty shows in her eyes. "When? Where?"

I look away from the drawing and away from Ms. Reed. I inhale deeply and slowly let out the air.

"It's okay. You don't have to talk about it."

She wraps me in her arms. I hold on to her, my eyes back on the framed piece.

"You are not alone," she whispers.

Michael walks over to us. He plants a kiss on his mom's cheek. "You ready to get some work done?" he asks me.

I gently pull away from Ms. Reed and walk with Michael up their carpeted staircase. Before he opens his bedroom door, he turns to me and smiles. I offer half a smile. My mind is still on that picture.

"Don't get the wrong idea. Talking, and that's it."

My smile widens, and I laugh softly. It's hard to believe that I feel so comfortable with him when we've only known each other for two days.

I step in before him, and the first thing I notice is how tidy his room is.

"Make yourself comfortable."

I place my tote on his bed and make my way over to his bookshelf. My eyes read over two full shelves of autobiographies including Martin Luther King Jr.'s, Malcolm X's, Ben Franklin's, Gandhi's, and one of my personal favorites, the *Narrative of the Life of Frederick Douglass.*

"You weren't lying when you said you like history."

"Why would I lie?"

I shrug and then bend down to look at the titles lined up on the bottom shelf. This is the shelf all readers put the books they know most people will never see the titles of.

"Have you read all of these?"

"Pretty much."

I read over the titles on his bottom shelf. Books about UFOs, aliens, the solar system, galaxies.

I pull out a book titled *Alien Agenda* and sit at the end of Michael's bed.

"No," he states as he takes the book from my hands. "We're not doing that."

"What's up with the UFO books? The alien and galaxy books?"

He slides the book back into the tight space I pulled it from. "They're interesting."

I look at my phone. I open an unread text message from Ms. Ward. Her message explains that she's okay with me studying with friends. She'll be home late.

"Oh, I gave Indigo your number."

I look up at Michael.

"She asked for it," he explains in a hurry.

"When?"

"I was talking to her in the living room while you were talking to my mom."

I suck my teeth. "That's fine."

"Doesn't sound like it."

"Really, it's cool. I don't care."

Truthfully, I do care, but I can always ignore calls from unsaved numbers. I don't have any beef with Indigo, but I can't deal with her attitude and the questions about Michael. I did meet her first, but that doesn't make me answerable to her. They've both made it clear that they were never an item. That means any kind of friendship I choose to have with Michael is within girl code.

"Well, I'm gonna change real quick. You wanna borrow a shirt? Some shorts?"

I nod. "A T-shirt is fine."

He tosses me a white tee. "Need any help with that?"

"You can help me by closing the door on your way out."

He lowers his head and chuckles. "You're cold-blooded."

I smile as I shoo him out of his own room. Once I'm alone, I quickly remove my school shirt, and as I put on his white tee, I breathe in the scent of clean laundry.

I neatly fold my shirt and slide it inside my tote. I look around his room as I kick off my sneakers. A picture of his mother sits upright on his desk. A basketball jersey is tacked up on his wall under a plaque recognizing our school's team as state champions. On his dresser at the end of his bed stands a flat-panel TV. Beside it is a PlayStation 4. Above the TV, a DVD wall rack houses movies. Most of them, I've seen.

As I sit again at the end of Michael's bed, I smooth down my pleated skirt and look at the floor. My mind is questioning so many things. Things I'm tired of trying to figure out on my own. Things I'm hoping Michael can help me understand.

There's a tap on his door. I tell him, "You can come in."

Ms. Reed opens the door. "You okay?"

Oh, please don't have the wrong idea. I am not sitting on your son's bed and wearing his shirt because I'm a fast girl. We should be studying in kitchen. My mom taught me better than this.

"Yeah, I'm fine," I answer.

"Where's Mike?"

"Changing. I guess he's in the bathroom."

"I'm about to head out to work. Things are unusually hectic at the hospital right now, so my hours are a bit irregular this week."

"You're a doctor?"

"No way. I'm too much of a punk to see blood and broken bones every day. I work in hospital administration."

"Excuse me." Michael squeezes past his mom to get through the doorway.

"I'm on my way out," she tells him.

He looks down at her sweats. "You're not gonna change?"

"I'm running a little behind. I'll change at the hospital."

I watch as he hugs his mother. Their close bond is obvious. His love for his mother is so apparent.

"Eat something, get some homework done, and I'll see you later."

"All right."

"I love you."

"Love you too, Ma. Text me."

"Mm-hmm. Homework, Michael. Do it!"

He smiles. A smile that has no effect on his mother.

Her expression is serious. "Keep thinking I'm playing." Softened eyes look my way. "I hope to see you again soon, Jaylen."

She walks away, and I realize I'm about to be alone with Michael. A boy I've only known for two days and haven't been able to stop thinking about since the beginning of first period yesterday.

He turns his desk chair so that it faces the bed and sits. "You okay? You don't need anything?"

"No, thanks. I'm okay."

I move to the head of his bed and sit with my legs closed and stretched straight out in front of me. I look over at Michael. Those watchful greens are on me.

"Now you look uneasy," he points out.

"I just have a lot of things running through my mind."

"I know. You have one of those faces. It tells people how you're really feeling even when you say you're okay."

"I'm not really the open book type."

"I can't force you to talk, but I hope you feel comfortable enough to come to me if you ever decide to open that book."

I decide to run the risk of sounding crazy. The risk of being branded a freak. I have so many questions, but I'll never find the answers unless I ask them. Instead of immediately questioning him about his grandmother's memorial, I go back to what we were discussing on our walk.

"You mentioned earlier that you're looking for a feeling. Something more than just a pretty face. Does that mean you haven't had girlfriends? You said you haven't found it."

Michael slightly bows his head. "I've had girlfriends."

"And?"

"I thought I could find something with one of them even though the feeling wasn't there in the beginning."

"By having sex with them?"

"Some of them." His voice lowers. His hands are now clasped together. "And I feel bad, too."

"I can tell."

It's nice to know that he has a heart, that he cares about people. I can't stand guys who hurt girls and laugh about it, who break hearts and brag like they deserve a high-five.

"I feel like I used them. Though it's always been consensual, I didn't have any type of emotional connection to them prior to doing it. I was just hoping, eventually, I'd feel something. Like what they were feeling."

"Never felt anything?"

"Nothing that would make me want to do it again. And that's all I hear my boys talking about. How they smashed some girl, and it was so good. It's not like that for me."

"Not even the physical part?" I ask in disbelief.

"It's nothing like I'm told it should feel."

I look at Michael. I hope the disbelief on my face doesn't look judgmental.

"Most of the feelings people tell me they have or get from certain things, I don't. I can never relate, because I don't know what the hell they're talking about."

I think about my lack of feelings for others. My inability to emotionally connect with guys past the platonic stage.

"This one girl I used to mess with would always tell me that seeing me gave her butterflies." He looks down. "I used to flirt with her. I can't lie. Hearing that you have that effect on girls is definitely flattering." His eyes meet mine again. "But I never knew what she meant. That feeling in her stomach that she would always describe sounded more weird than anything else." He takes a deep breath, his eyes still focused in on mine. "Until yesterday." He pauses. "When I walked into first period yesterday, and I saw you…" Another pause. "Right then, I felt it."

Right then, I felt it, too. Like him, I've always been curious about the tummy butterflies everyone speaks of. Seeing him for the first time brought on the flutters. Hearing how I made him feel has brought them back, only these butterflies are on speed.

I look down at my nails, briefly at Michael, and then back down at my hands again. "Why can't you feel for anyone?"

"Because I'm not like everyone else."

I look back up at Michael. "What are you like?"

He cocks his head to the side and throws me an expression that tells me he believes I already know the answer to that.

"Really, I need to know. What are you like?"

After a few seconds of silence, he answers, "You."

I fearfully ask a question I've always wanted to know the answer to. "And what am I?"

"You've already found your answer."

"Have I?"

"What do you think all the books on my bottom shelf are about?"

"You're not suggesting that I'm…" I shake my head. "That we're…"

He nods slowly.

"So we're really not human? That's what you're insinuating?"

"Do you feel human?"

No, but extraterrestrial isn't the alternative. It's true that I have gone through life questioning myself, but alien just seems far out. I've never even considered that as a possibility.

"You know, we could just have a crazy genetic disorder. Or we could—"

"Jaylen," he interrupts. "I know what I'm talking about."

"Or we could just be fucking weird. Alien, though? How did you come up with that?"

"I can't imagine how it must sound. For a second, I thought you knew, but—"

I cut him off. "That just sounds ridiculous, not to mention, impossible."

"Listen, I know it's out there. I know it sounds crazy, but believe me, I wouldn't say anything like that if I had even an inkling of a doubt. And don't forget, Jaylen, my mom is a lot older than both of us. She would know. Besides, there are probably more than a few things about you that most people would consider impossible."

My mind goes back to past injuries. I remember how little pain they caused me, and how fast they healed. Then, memories of the night of the accident fill my thoughts. I clearly recall being transported to the hospital, being rushed into a private room, just to shock doctors with the minimal injuries I'd sustained.

"You can toy around with the idea of having a disorder,

but do you think that would make animals react to you the way they do? Think about it."

I lean back against his pillows and look straight ahead at the blank TV screen. I see my reflection. I finally got an answer. Not the answer I expected, but an answer nonetheless. I knew there had to be a reason why I don't have normal emotional connections to humans. There had to be a reason why I rarely feel the need to eat, and yet I need to drink three times as much water as the average human being.

"You okay?"

Am I okay? Not really. It doesn't matter how long I've questioned myself, my strangeness. Learning that I'm some kind of outer space creature, an alien, doesn't make me feel anywhere near okay. I knew I wasn't human, but alien? That's the weirdest thing I've ever heard.

My mind begins to spin crazily. Again, I question how this is even possible. Why haven't I been able to discover this for myself? I've certainly been researching over the years.

"Jaylen?"

"I'm tired," I tell him. "My thoughts are all over the place."

"Take a nap."

"No, thanks."

"Take a nap," he repeats more forcefully. "I got homework I need to work on. I really don't need the help. Like I said before, it just takes me forever to actually do the work. Lay down for about an hour while I get some of these worksheets done. Let your brain rest awhile."

I tuck myself in under his thick comforter and my head sinks into his pillow. As I breathe in the scent of lavender fabric softener, I do something I rarely do when sharing a room with another. I close my eyes.

I'm awakened by the ringing of my cell phone. The number flashing isn't saved, prompting me to ignore the call. I look over at Michael. His legs are propped up on the side of the bed, his desk chair is slightly reclined, and my sketch book is in his hand.

"What do you think you're doing?"

He turns my favorite piece around for me to see. "This is good. Whose house is this?"

"Hopefully mine one day."

"So you designed this?"

I nod. "I've been working on that for years."

I lie quietly as Michael looks over pieces I've never shared with anyone else. Art that I consider personal.

"You really can draw."

I smile. "Thank you, nosy."

He chuckles. "How'd you sleep?"

"Good, actually. Deeper than I usually do. How long was I out?"

"About two hours. You sleep better around your own kind. Comfort 101."

"So that's what you've been doing? Going through my stuff?"

He continues to flip through my sketchbook. "I didn't think you'd mind."

"I do."

He flips to the next page as I slowly sit up in his bed. His television is now on. My mind is back on what we discussed before I napped.

"Back at it again, huh?"

My eyes move to Michael's. He's looking at me over the top of my sketchbook.

"Back at what?"

"What are you thinking about?"

I push my curls behind my ears. "Turn to the last page."

I don't watch him as he flips through my sketches. I look at the television, at the rerun episode of *The Walking Dead* that's playing. Patiently, I wait for him to respond to what he sees. My cell alerts me of a text message. I sit still.

He pulls out a sheet of loose leaf paper from between the final page of my sketchbook and the cardboard backing. "When did you draw this?"

"Years ago," I say, my eyes still looking forward at the widescreen.

He cuts the television off and sets the sketchbook down. A picture almost identical to the one hanging on his living room wall is in his hand.

"Where did you see this?"

I turn to Michael. "When I was four, I found something like that in my mother's bed. Not her. Just that thing."

"Where did you put it?"

"It got lost over time."

Michael sets the sheet down. He grips his hair. His eyes fill with sadness.

"Do you know what it is?" I ask.

He exhales loudly and lowers his head. My heart suddenly becomes very heavy.

"Whoever was in that bed," he says, pointing at my sketch, "this was them."

In a state of shock and confusion, all I can do is look at Michael, though his eyes are no longer on me.

"We don't die like humans." He makes eye contact. "We don't become a breathless corpse or leave skeletal remains. If we die, we dry out."

"How do we die?"

He shakes his head. "Based on what Moms tells me, we only die from lack of water. I mean, that's why we're here, anyway. This is the only planet with enough water to sustain us." He adds, "Oh, and lack of air. We need to breathe. Fire, too. Fire can kill us. Fire can kill anything."

I rub my forehead. "There was no fire."

"Did she want to?" he asks, his voice so low I can barely hear it.

I shake my head in disbelief. "I don't think she wanted to leave me. She didn't seem…" Again, I shake my head. "I don't know! I don't understand!"

He moves onto the bed. "I don't know either."

He passes me a bottle of water. I drink it quickly. Every swallow hurts.

"There's so much we're still learning about ourselves. Maybe there are other ways we can die."

"Your mom is grown. She had parents. She had your dad. She has to know more than what you're telling me. Even if no one told her anything, life had to have taught her."

"You're taking a lot in right now, Jaylen. Calm down."

I scoot out of his bed. "I wanna go home."

He stands as I force my feet into tied shoes.

"I'll drive you."

"I've been confused all these years. I need some answers. Something!"

He walks around the bed and pulls me to him. His arms wrap tightly around me. Sharp, needle-like pains stab through my heart. My head is swirling, trying to figure out so many things at once.

"I'm sorry," he whispers, his lips right at my ear. "I didn't bring you here to put you through even more than what you're already going through. I thought meeting my mom, and having somewhere you can come to and feel safe, would make being here and being one of our kind easier."

I squeeze him back. "It has. It will."

"Why are you leaving, then?"

We separate from our hug. My eyes are on his. My mind is on my mother.

"You don't have to go, Jaylen."

"I need to research."

"And find what?"

I bend down to untie and retie my shoe laces. "I don't know. But I don't think she wanted to."

"To what?"

"Die! I don't think she wanted to. And if she did, why like that? Have you ever gone for too long without water? Do you know how that feels?"

"Please stay and talk to me."

I sit back down on the side of his bed. "I knew," I say out loud.

He sits beside me, our legs touching. His hand rests on top of mine.

"After a few days of not hearing from her, I knew she had to be dead."

"I'm so sorry, Jaylen."

"I felt something when I saw that little cocoon thing lying there, but I kept remembering her always telling me that we were in this life together. So how could she say that and then give up?"

"I don't know. I can't answer that for you."

I rest my face in my hands. "I can't go through any more loss. I've already lost two moms. No dad." My words are spoken into my palms. "I'd rather be an outsider and know that I don't really fit in anywhere and never will, than to feel a part of something and lose that, too."

"I don't want you to go. Not like this."

I take my hands away from my face. "What the hell happens to us? What kind of life are we meant to have?"

"We have to answer that question for ourselves, just like the humans do. I mean, look at my mom. She went to school, she has a social life, and she makes bread. We have no other place to go, so we have to find a way to live here with humankind."

I let out an ugly grunt.

"Don't leave," he begs. "Not yet."

86

I look at Michael. His asking me to stay means more to me than he'll ever know. Though I'm anxious and feel the need to go home to search endlessly for information I'll probably never find, with Michael is where I want to be. Here is where I feel I'm supposed to be. I kick off my shoes again and move back to the head of his bed.

"Want something to eat?" he asks.

"No. I'm never really hungry."

"You should eat a little something. Salt helps the body retain water. Even in us."

"It's hard to eat when your body isn't asking for food."

He sits back down in his desk chair.

"So your mom knows?"

"About you? Yeah. I told her yesterday that I met another one. I told her that I'm feeling you. It's the first time she's heard that, so she wanted to meet you. She didn't say to get you over here today. That part was all me."

I smile.

"She likes you, though."

"She's sweet. You guys share a beautiful relationship."

"I'd like to share a beautiful relationship with you."

My eyes immediately roll. "Mm-hmm."

"Really."

"And what's your idea of a beautiful relationship, Michael?"

"You and me. Now that's beautiful."

We laugh.

I feel so much like a teenager with him. Though I can never pretend that I was a victim of bullying or one of those left to sit alone at lunch, I've never truly felt a part of anything. I'm not alone here. I've connected with Michael. He gets me. And because I know we're alike, I can be more relaxed and enjoy the time I spend with him rather than silently question our differences. With him, I feel almost normal. As normal as an alien on Earth can feel.

Chapter 8

I lock the front door and walk down the empty driveway toward a face I didn't expect to see until actually making it to school. His text did explain that he'd meet me out front. I just assumed he meant in front of our school building. I had no idea he meant in front of Ms. Ward's house. This is beyond sweet. He bypassed Trinity, in the cold, just to escort me to school.

"Well, this is a surprise."

"I missed you."

I smile an all-teeth-showing smile, and ask, "How could you have missed me? We spent all of yesterday together, you brought me home, and then we stayed up half the night texting."

"So, what you saying? You tired of me?"

"I wouldn't say all that."

He puts his arm around me. "Then what would you say?"

"I'd say that I missed you, too."

"Say what?" he asks in a high-pitched voice. "Miss Unromantic missed me?"

I giggle. "Shut up."

We head for school side by side. As he spits cracked shells from his mouth, he shakes the bag of ranch-flavored seeds in front of me.

"No, thanks."

"Remember what I told you yesterday? We need the salt, too. Take a few. You're not used to eating regularly, and that's cool. Start off with snacking. It's good for you."

I take the bag from his hand and pour a few seeds directly into my mouth. The flavoring is not my preference, but this is the best way to get me eating regularly. Baby steps. I can definitely appreciate Michael's approach. No wonder I'm so comfortable with him.

With his arm still around me, he asks, "You feeling better today?"

"Yeah, I am. I just heard something out loud yesterday that I always silently knew. But last night, after we stopped texting, and after I wasted my time pointlessly researching, I really thought about being here. I've never had this. I've never had a place or group that I feel like I really belong in. You gave me that."

"I didn't give you that."

"You did. You gave me that because you're the first person to answer a question I've been asking myself for the last seventeen years. I'll be eighteen soon, and I'm just now finding out that I'm some kind of extraterrestrial."

We continue to walk. His touch warms me in ways I've never felt before. Never have I wanted to be this close to anyone, with a desire to grow even closer.

"Thank you," I say softly.

"Any time."

He kisses my cheek, and butterflies flutter all through my stomach. Happiness fills me, and right at this moment, Michael has my heart.

"So, have you talked to Indigo about it?" I ask.

"You always seem to think I'm lying when it comes to her, but no. She used to tell me how she doesn't feel for people. I told her I can relate. We didn't get into the specifics. She knows, though. What did y'all talk about?"

I believe in honesty and loyalty. I told Indigo I wouldn't tell anyone about what happened between us, so it's only fair that I keep our little secret.

"We just talked about school, my old life, Warren," I tell him.

"Me?"

I shake my head. "Not really. So what's the big secret?" I ask. "Why didn't you and Indigo discuss it? You guys have been friends for years. You can feel the obvious connection."

"Yeah, but we're raised to keep it quiet for the most part. Even around your own, just like humans, you have to be careful. Revealing too much about yourself could hurt you down the line."

"Does it bother you that we're friends?"

"No. I don't care. I have nothing against Indigo. There's no beef. Because you keep asking, you must have heard that there's beef on her end. I have nothing against you being friends with anyone."

I leave the Indigo situation alone and try to find out more about who Michael Reed really is. I can spend time talking about Indigo when she and I are together. From this point on, while I'm with Michael, I plan on keeping the focus on us.

"So how did you end up going to Trinity?" I ask.

"My mother. She wanted me to get the best high school education possible. She put me here because it's a more disciplined environment, and it's the only college preparatory high school in walking distance from my house."

"So, you're not religious?"

"We believe," he informs me.

"In what?"

"God."

I keep quiet.

"Not religious?"

I shake my head.

"So, you don't believe in anything?"

"I don't know what to believe in. Why do you believe in God?"

"My mother raised me that way. Initially, I just prayed because I was told to, but I do believe in a higher power. We're not like humans, but I feel blessed. I never get sick, all I need is water, my cuts and bruises heal just as fast as I get them. I gotta give thanks to somebody for that."

"Give thanks to your mom, then."

His tone is bothered as he asks, "What do you have against religion, Jaylen?"

"I just don't get it. You're telling me I should thank a higher being that may or may not exist for making me a freak? For making me someone—oh, I'm sorry—some*thing* that can't feel or connect to those who surround me? For taking away everybody in my life that I loved or learned to love? I'm supposed to give thanks for that?"

He pulls me closer.

"Maybe things would be different for me if my mother had introduced me to it as a child. Maybe I'd be like you."

"Maybe. But now you're at an age where you can make those decisions for yourself."

"I know, and I still don't get it. I knew a girl at my old school who was raised atheist. She doesn't believe in the existence of any god, yet she's the most loving, honest, and giving individual you could ever meet."

He shrugs. "What's your point?"

"People who believe in that stuff only behave because they want to go to Heaven. She chose not to do wrong because she's genuinely a good person. I don't hurt people. I try to be a good person. None of that matters though, right?

I'm going to hell according to your beliefs, because I don't believe in your God."

He groans. "So why Catholic school, then?"

"This is my foster mother's hometown. She went to Trinity. They have great art classes, and she likes the curriculum."

"She's religious?"

I nod. "She was raised Catholic."

"And your mom? The one who adopted you."

"She was agnostic."

He shakes his head before spitting out a shell. "I think you're just lost. It's not your fault, though. You've been shuffled around. You've been abandoned. Like you said, you just don't know what to believe in. Or who for that matter."

"Do you pray?" I ask.

He proudly answers, "Every day."

"Do you feel something when you pray?"

"Yup."

We step to the side to allow a biker to pass.

"You've never prayed?"

I shake my head.

"Not even for your mother to come back when you didn't find her in her bed?"

"No. I didn't even cry."

His head snaps in my direction. His eyes bulge. "Not one tear?"

"Not one."

Silence.

"Have you ever cried?" he asks.

"I'm sure I have, but I don't remember."

"You will. One day it'll all come out."

I turn to Michael. "Maybe."

"It will. You've been acting like a sponge. But what happens if you don't wring out a sponge? After a while, it absorbs too much, and eventually, it starts to come out on its own. You better stop bottling that shit up. The day it comes out is gonna be a really bad day for you."

I wrap my arm around his lower back and silently acknowledge that he's right. I often want to cry. I often want to scream. But I don't. I force myself to move through life showing little to no emotion, hiding my weaknesses, and forcing myself to remain straight-faced even when I'm in pain. It's becoming more and more difficult to keep things hidden away inside. One day, my feelings will win. My emotions will show whether through uncontrollable tears, screams, or otherwise.

I make eye contact. "I like being with you, Michael."

He kisses my forehead. "I like being with you, too."

When we make it to school, I spot Indigo standing to the side of the front steps. Warren is standing beside her. We head in their direction, still holding each other close. Indigo stops laughing at whatever she found funny the moment she sees us.

"What's up?" Warren greets.

Michael and Warren dap each other up. Indigo and I exchange smiles. Mine is sincere. I'm not sure if hers is.

"So you two are together now?" Warren asks.

I answer, "We're just cool."

"What about you guys?" Michael asks.

"Same here. Just cool," Indigo answers.

"I'll see you in first," Michael tells me.

He and Warren head inside the building, leaving me and Indigo to ourselves.

"I texted you," she says.

"Yeah, I know." I lie, "I didn't see it until this morning."

"We cool?"

I shrug. "Sure."

"Did you guys get a lot of studying done?"

"Not really. We got lost in conversation."

"Must've been a hell of a conversation. You guys looked

coupled-up walking in here."

Here we go again. No matter how hard I try to keep it out of my mind, I can't avoid the fact that Indigo is completely unaccepting of my friendship with Michael. Unaccepting because the feelings I have for him, she wants me to have for her. It's a relief to finally be a part of a group, but this is something I never wanted to be a part of. I never wanted to be caught in between two people who both have feelings for me.

I tilt my head at Indigo. "Is it gonna be like this every day? Every time we talk about Michael, you're gonna throw these slick-ass comments at me with that tone?"

She chuckles. "No. I didn't mean it like that."

"Well, what's up with you and Warren?"

"I don't know. We're going out to eat together."

"Really?" I ask happily. "So you're considering dating him?"

"No. I told you I don't like him like that. But I couldn't say no to his face. Warren's so nice."

As we head inside the building, I tell her, "Don't string him along."

"I'm not trying to. I'm gonna tell him how I feel."

"When?"

"After we go out to eat, I'll send him a text. I don't want to hurt his feelings, especially to his face."

"Indigo, he's not a child. I'm sure he'd rather you tell him now."

She shrugs. "Maybe I'll tell him over lunch. What's up with you and Mike?"

"I like him," I state honestly.

"That's obvious. I knew that was gonna happen. I believe I called it on your first day."

I admit, "You did. I didn't think I'd like him so much, but I do."

"Don't get sucked in."

I wave at familiar faces as I pass them in the hallway, and ask, "What do you mean?"

"The things boys say and promise. Just be careful."

"I will. We're not taking things to that level."

"You haven't really dated, Jaylen. You'd be surprised how fast a guy can talk you out of your panties, especially when you really like him."

"Well, I'll be careful."

"I'm just looking out for you."

"And I appreciate it."

We enter the stairwell. Indigo steps to the side as opposed to heading up the staircase. I move out of the way of others to stand with her.

The right corner of her mouth slowly rises, forming a questionable smile. "So, I need a favor."

"What's up?"

"Physics," she explains as she pulls out a worksheet. "Kennedy isn't here today."

I pull a pencil from my tote. "I'm not sure why this couldn't wait until homeroom, but I'll see what I can do."

She hands me a worksheet that she hasn't even attempted and I place the paper against the wall. I read over the questions, and instantly, the answers come to mind. I write the answers down just as quickly as they come to me. I hand her the worksheet back after having it for a little over a minute.

"Are you serious? Did you just guess these answers?"

"No. They're right. You just have to do the work to prove it."

"How?"

"Plug the numbers into the equations and make it look like you solved them on your own."

"How do you know they're right?"

"Indigo, if you don't trust me, ask someone else."

She speaks quickly. "I'm not saying that. I'm just asking

how you know. The other day you guessed the title of that book you said you never heard of. You just wrote down six answers that you're sure are right, but you didn't use equations to solve them. How do you know this stuff?"

I sigh. "I don't know how I know, but they're right. Okay?"

I start up the stairs and Indigo stays beside me.

"Must be nice."

"What?" I ask her.

"Being so smart."

"I guess. It comes with its negatives, though."

"Like what?"

"I can't explain where this knowledge comes from. In school, teachers don't believe that answers just fall out the sky."

"Well, it's damn sure far from the norm."

"Yeah, I know."

Clearly, it's not the norm when it comes to our kind, either. Both Indigo and Michael seem to struggle with their homework. That's never been an issue for me. Needed information never fails to magically come to me when I need it.

I can feel her stare. I glance over and she smiles.

I ask, "Trying to figure me out?"

"I don't need to. I know why you're the way you are."

"Good."

"Good?"

"One less person I have to try to explain myself to."

Chapter 9

$\mathcal{I}$ sit for lunch in the covered courtyard with Indigo, Michael, Warren, Eugene, two other basketball players I was introduced to, and Mia, a girl I just met today. The laughs have been nonstop. Eugene has been asking the most ridiculous questions about growing up in New Jersey. I wish I could take credit for amusing everyone, but it's his questions that are comical, not my answer, which has been consistently no.

"So do you fist pump?" Eugene asks.

I chuckle. "No," I answer. "And that's it, your final question. I don't fist pump, I hate house music, I've never seen a prostitute, don't know what the hell a juicehead is, and I've never met Snooki. Eugene, stop watching MTV."

Loud laughter escapes the group. I take credit for these laughs.

I look over at Indigo. Her eyes are on me. I smile. She sends one back my way.

"So you wanna hit the courts after school?" Eugene asks Michael.

"I don't even know. Moms is not happy about my

grades."

My eyes move from Michael to Warren. I look at the way he watches Indigo, the way Eugene constantly glances over at her, the way Mia looks at her. She's a show-stopper and she's not eating up one bit of this attention.

My eyes drift back to Michael. It's almost unbelievable to me that he didn't want to be with her. I understand feelings, but Indigo is gorgeous. I've always considered myself to be just an average girl, regardless of how others see me. She has to know she's beautiful.

Indigo motions with her head for me to walk with her.

"I'll see you guys later," I tell the group.

Indigo and I stand and walk to sit alone on the courtyard stairs. We sit beneath the glass canopy as the winter sun shines down on us.

"What's up, lady?"

She yawns. "I don't wanna be here, Jaylen. I'm so tempted to skip."

"Now *that* you'll be doing alone."

She laughs.

"It's a little too soon for me to be missing class."

She looks behind us. "I don't like her."

"Who?"

"Mia," she whispers.

I shrug carelessly. I'm definitely not one to get involved in girl drama. At my old school, during my junior year, I witnessed a fight in the girls' bathroom. Two girls literally fought until blood was shed because of a nonsense Facebook post about a guy neither of them was dating. I've seen girls want to rip each other's weaves out because of dirty looks. I've heard girls address others as fake bitches simply because they had bubbly personalities. I've never understood it, so I keep myself out of the craziness. I don't gossip, I don't instigate fights, and I do my best to not get into any. Female cattiness is one of those things I don't miss and plan to continue to steer clear of.

"You'll end up having your share of drama with her," Indigo says.

"Really? What makes you think that?"

"She messes with everybody's man."

"I don't have a man, so that doesn't sound like a problem I'll be having. That's your issue with her?"

"We were real cool at one point, but because she's a ho, some people thought maybe I was, too."

"Birds of a feather."

"Yeah, I know. I know. But when people would ask her if what was being said about me was true, she wouldn't be a friend and tell them that I wasn't like that."

"So how'd you stop the rumors?"

She cuts her eyes at me, and after a hesitation, states, "Your little boyfriend over there let his boys know that I don't get down like that."

I'm taken by surprise. If Michael was such a big help, then why aren't they still best friends?

"So, I don't like her."

I nod. "Understandable. I'll make sure to keep an eye on her."

"Make sure you do." She pulls out her cell. "We should chill later. You wanna hang out after school today?"

"Sure, but what about Warren?"

She smiles and slowly turns away from me.

"Oh, no, Indigo. You are not standing him up to hang out with me."

We laugh.

"Jaylen," she whines, dragging my name out.

"No," I tell her again.

She rests her head on my shoulder, and I smile. I like Indigo. Whatever may have happened between her and Michael isn't important. I like talking to her. I like having a female friend I can feel this close to. Indigo's desire for wanting love and a relationship were once feelings I had. I want to be there for her. It's not easy wanting something and having to wait around hoping you pass somebody you connect with.

"I'm gonna tell him after lunch. I don't want to think about breaking hearts anymore today."

"All right," I say. "As long as you tell him something." I sip from my water. "So, what do you wanna do?"

"We'll go to one of my favorite spots."

"Your house?"

She grimaces. "That's actually my least favorite spot. The more time I spend away from my house and my aunt, the better. There's actually a lake I like to go to."

"I haven't seen any lakes around here."

"There are a lot. Actually, there are a lot of just about everything here in Virginia. There are at least three other Trinity high schools. I can't even tell you how many lakes. One of the smaller ones is not too far from here. I usually go there to do my homework."

"Oh, you actually do homework?"

She gasps. "Shut up."

I laugh. "It's probably colder out by the water though, huh?"

"You'll be fine in your jacket. It hasn't been as cold lately."

"I have a coat. I didn't walk to school in January weather wearing only a jacket."

I walked home without a coat on my first day. It wasn't freezing, but it was cold enough that I remembered not to forget it again.

"Cool. So, then, we'll go."

I prepare myself. "Is the lake in the woods?"

"We don't have to walk through the woods to get there. There are a lot of trees, though. Worried about being kidnapped?"

"More worried about wildlife."

"You might see a deer or two."

I let out an exasperated sound.

Indigo inches closer to me to allow a few others to walk down the short staircase. "Not a member of PETA?" she asks.

"I don't have a problem with animals. They have a problem with me."

"Welcome to the club."

I look at Indigo before turning to look back at the group. I spot Eugene and Mia. I don't know where Michael, Warren, and the other ball players walked off to. Left alone at the table, Eugene and Mia sit close. She straddles the bench as she runs her fingers through the pink highlights in her hair. That's something I'd never do. I'd never straddle a bench in a skirt, especially one that's been hemmed.

"If you go there often and the animals don't disturb you, I should be fine," I say as I give my attention back to Indigo.

"You will be. You'll like it, too. It's really beautiful."

I finish up my bottle of water and move about the rest of my school day, discreetly texting Michael and looking forward to hearing the end of the day bell ring. After my last class, I stop by my locker to pick up my coat. My nerves awaken at the feeling of him, but strangely, the intensity has died down. That's odd, because my feelings for him have surely grown.

I put my pea coat on over my school uniform jacket. I close my locker door and wait for him to finish up a conversation he's having with another student before I approach him. As I pull my hat over my curls, he walks over.

"That's cute," he says.

"What is?"

He squeezes the pom pom on top of my hat and laughs.

"Don't hate on my hat."

"I just told you it's cute."

"And then you laughed."

Again, he laughs. I suck my teeth and begin to walk. He remains beside me.

"You said in your text that you guys are going to a lake?" he asks.

"Yeah. She said it's close by."

"To do what?"

"Talk. Hang out. I don't know."

We walk through the hallway. As usual, girls go out of their way to be noticed by Michael. I silently laugh at their efforts. His waves are so unenthusiastic. His attention is on me.

I tell him, "I want to ask you something."

"Ask."

"I can feel something when you and Indigo are close to me."

"I know. I can feel it, too."

"Yeah, but it doesn't feel as strong today. Why?"

"That's normal. You're used to being around us. And you know we're like you. It's like putting two animals together. No, we're not exactly like animals, but it's a good example."

"I'm listening," I say as we head down the staircase.

"If you bring a cat into a house that another cat already lives in, instincts tell them that they're alike, but they feel a bit uncomfortable because it's new. There's still a comfort because they're the same species, though. After a day or two, that other cat can sneak up on the house cat. That house cat's aware that another one of them is around and their guard is down. They're more comfortable."

"I get where you're going, so you can stop."

We exit the stairwell and enter the busy, first-floor hallway.

"Stop what?" he asks as he pulls me to the side, out of the crowd of students heading for the exit.

"Earlier, you compared me to a sponge. Now you're on

cats. I can tell your mom breaks things down for you like this."

"You calling me a mama's boy?"

"Your words. Not mine."

The corners of his mouth rise. So do mine.

"I gotta get going, Michael. I told Indigo to meet me out front. I don't want to leave her standing in the cold."

"I'll walk you."

We exit the building and locate Indigo right out front where she said she'd be.

"You ready?" she asks.

"Yup."

"I'll see you guys later," Michael tells us.

As he walks back inside the school, Indigo and I head for the lake. Our pace is slow. The weather isn't even close to warm, but it's not as cold as I expected.

Indigo squeezes the pom pom on my hat. "You look like one of those bomber men."

"From the Nintendo game?"

She covers her mouth and laughs. "Yeah."

"I actually think they're very cute, so thank you for the compliment."

We giggle girlishly and continue down the sidewalk.

"What did you tell Warren?" I ask.

"The truth. That I'm not really looking to date. That going out might give him the wrong idea and I don't want to confuse things."

"I think that was the smartest thing you could do."

"He handled it well."

"Yeah until he goes home and cries."

"You think he's gonna cry?" Her eyes bulge.

"Indigo, I'm kidding."

"I don't wanna do that to him."

"He'll get over it. That's life. Everyone experiences rejection."

"Yeah, but when the person you really like rejects you, you never forget that pain."

I look at my friend. I know beneath some of that sadness, she's reliving our encounter from the other day. I truly never meant to hurt her. Though I've been questioning how anyone could turn someone as beautiful as Indigo down, Michael said it right. You can't force a feeling.

We small talk our way down a short path. The path takes us away from the residential street, across a small bridge, leading us to a gorgeous scene. The lake is magnificent. The greenery surrounding it makes it look straight off of a postcard.

I admire the natural beauty. "This is amazing."

"Isn't it?"

"This is one of the smaller ones?"

"Yeah. Virginia has huge lakes."

I spot a man canoeing, a few runners pounding the pavement, and a pair of dogs being walked on the other side of the water.

She points. "I usually sit down there."

I follow Indigo down to a picnic table only a few feet from the water. We sit on top and rest our feet on the bench.

I ask, "So, you come here alone?"

"Yeah. Most of the time."

"Who do you usually chill with?"

"The people we sat with at lunch. As far as girls go—Kennedy."

I look out at the lake. I think about Michael. I think about how much I enjoy being with him. Being close to him. Having him touch me, listen to me, smile at me. I saw him less than an hour ago, but I miss him. Already, I miss him. I think about kissing my ex-boyfriends. How awkward those kisses were. I think about kissing Michael. How badly I want to and can't wait to.

"So, what kind of stuff do you watch?"

I answer. "I like thrillers and horror movies."

"Horror?"

"Yeah. Scary movies."

"Why?"

"Because they're fun to watch. Someone always does something unbelievably stupid. They're comedies to me."

Her eyes widen. "You laugh at people getting chopped up. Nice, Jaylen."

I shake my head. "No, don't say it like that. I'm not a sadistic psycho."

She laughs and playfully bumps me. "I know. I'm kidding. We all laugh at the idiot who drops the gun, trips over nothing, and passes the unlocked front door to run upstairs."

I chuckle. "Exactly. That's why they're comedies."

"Yeah, horror movies are cool, sometimes, but I actually like to watch controversial documentaries. The ones about how we may or may not have gotten here. Do you watch stuff like that?"

"If I come across it. I like watching movies about history. About powerful people who were once here and no longer are. Seeing their impact, you know?"

"That's sad," she says softly.

"What?"

"How we're here now, and one day, we won't be."

I nod, my eyes on the water. "That's life."

"Yeah, but to be gone one day. To die. That thought doesn't bother you? To know that you're here now, and one day, you won't be? We may not even be remembered after we die. We don't know what happens after death. All we know for sure is that we all expire at some point. Where we go, if we come back—all of that is unknown until it happens."

"Are you afraid of death?"

"Maybe if I were like everyone else, I wouldn't be. I've tried to talk to my aunt about it, but she thinks it's a stupid thing to be worried about. She says it's going to happen regardless, so there's no point spending my time living worrying about dying. I just can't help it."

I understand her fears. I have them, too, though I don't admit them out loud. To be from another place and differ so greatly from humans is terrifying. Humans know how their insides work, know what can kill them, and they have millions of educators, not to mention the internet, that can help them learn more about themselves with each passing day. Here we are, a part of this great, wide world. We blend in, but we don't fit in.

"Jaylen, I'm in love with the thought of being in love."

I quickly turn to her and then look back out at the water. Indigo never fails to catch me off guard. She says whatever is on her mind, no matter how personal, no matter how crazy it may sound.

"I know that sounded weird."

"There's nothing wrong with wanting to love someone and be loved back. By this age, most people would expect that we've fallen in and out of love about as often as we change clothes."

"Exactly. And I want those experiences. I want to look back on breakups and makeups. I want to look back and laugh at dating mistakes that I'll warn my future daughters about making."

I take her hand in mine. "You haven't fallen in love yet, but you will. There's somebody out there for everyone. Even us."

"Yeah, but what if you're meant for a person that doesn't feel like they're meant for you?"

I look Indigo in the eye. "If you're meant to be together, you'll end up together."

"We." Her voice is almost inaudible.

I ask, "We?"

"Don't you mean if we're meant to be together, we'll end

up together?"

Nothing about this is flattering. Indigo hates the idea of hurting Warren. He's someone she cares for, just not romantically. That's exactly how I feel about her. Her feelings matter to me. Having to tell her no is painful for me. I know it pierces her heart. It sucks.

"Indigo, listen—"

"No, you listen. You stopped on the way into homeroom. You felt it. I felt it. And it's okay."

I shake my head. "I felt that we were alike, not what you think I felt."

"Jaylen, I know the difference. I know that instincts take over, and we can feel when we're close to one of our own. I feel that when I'm getting close to Mike, but I know what I felt when I saw you. I still feel it."

As I stare at Indigo, I realize that she doesn't have a little crush on me. She doesn't just kind of like me and want me to kind of like her. She instantly connected to me the way I connected to Michael. The deep feelings I have for him, she has for me.

She moves in closer to my face. I remain still. I allow our lips to meet. Her hand is still in mine. My heart is beating hard enough for me to hear.

I close my eyes as I kiss my friend. She moves her free hand to my cheek. This kiss, a first for us and a last. The feeling I should have if I were kissing my soulmate isn't present. This kiss is almost as awkward as the kisses I shared with my exes.

Our lips part. Our eyes open, and we look into one another's.

"You're so beautiful, Jaylen."

I look down. I feel too ashamed to look her in the eye any longer.

"You okay?"

I shake my head.

"Talk to me."

"Indigo, you're beautiful." I correct myself. "Stunning." I turn to her. "I don't wanna lie to you. What just happened wasn't fair to you. I don't have those feelings for you. I wouldn't tell you they weren't there if they were. I am not enjoying the fact that you're in pain. I shouldn't have allowed that kiss to happen." I squeeze her hand. "I'm really sorry."

She pulls her hand from mine. Her eyebrows pinch together.

"Indigo, I am so sorry. I really do want to be your friend."

She doesn't hesitate to tell me, "I want to be your friend, too."

"Can we be just friends? Can you be comfortable with that?"

"I'm gonna have to be."

I hurt for Indigo. If her feelings for me are anything like what I feel for Michael, her heart must be breaking into pieces as we sit here.

"I'm not angry, Jaylen. I promise. My biggest issue is gonna be seeing you with Mike."

"You don't have to worry about—" I stop dead in the middle of my statement.

"You feel that?" she asks.

"Shh."

An animal is close. I can feel the threat. A terrifying sense of danger ripples through my body when in the presence of any animal. Chills shoot down my spine. My heart thumps so hard, it steals my breath.

I slowly turn around. The sight of a buck instantly makes me jump from the table, pulling Indigo down with me.

She whispers, "We should make a run for it."

"Ain't no way in hell we can outrun a deer," I say softly.

The buck slowly comes around the table. We take slow, even, backward steps.

Indigo trembles. "I'm scared."

The buck stands on his two hind legs, comes down on all fours, and rears up again.

I keep my eyes on him. I prepare for his attack. Running wouldn't be wise. The last time I tried to outrun a dog, I was caught almost as fast as I took off. I can't imagine having better luck with a buck.

He's looking into my eyes. I'm looking into his. He's back on all fours, his head lowered and his antlers pointing right at me.

I breathe slowly. I try not to let fear push me into extreme panic. Panicking will impair my thinking, and for sure, this buck isn't going to back down.

He charges, running his antlers into me. They hit my ribcage, knocking the breath out of me and forcing me to the ground. Before being given the opportunity to roll away or stand, he attacks me with his two front hooves. The strikes are quick, powerful, relentless.

I shriek through clenched teeth while fighting to get out from beneath his large body and away from his heavy hits, but he keeps them coming.

I push him off of me. He quickly comes back. I scream for Indigo, for a passerby, for anybody. There's no response. No help. Just more hits that I try my best to block.

I look up at the buck. As he jumps up to once again drive his hooves into my chest, I take my balled-up right hand and back fist him completely off my body. The hit gives me time to stand. As he staggers back toward me with his antlers lowered, I reach out and grab one in each hand. As he pushes forward, I shake while fighting for balance.

I maintain a good grip on his antlers and twist his head. He grunts loudly as I pull his body right. As he fights for me to let go, I grip even tighter, lift, and swing his body into the tree to my left. His bones break loud enough for me to hear.

My breathing is ragged. My heart races as my mind tries

to absorb what just took place in broad daylight.

When I'm sure the body has no more life in it, I release the grip I have on his antlers. His body is limp, his eyes open, and his bones visibly broken.

I stare at the lifeless animal that tried to kill me just seconds ago. Everything about him is innocent. Yes, he attacked me, but he sensed that something wasn't right about me, just as my instincts told me to watch out for him. How can I hate animals, whether they attack me or not, when they're only doing what nature and instinct tell them to do?

I back away from the carcass. I turn away from the body I ripped the life from and look for my friend. Several feet away, she stands on the path with fear-filled eyes and a wide-open mouth. Steps away from her, with one hand covering her mouth and a cell in hand, is a pregnant woman. The shock in her face says it all. My belly sinks. What I did was witnessed. A human saw me.

Chapter 10

*I*n the back of the ambulance, I sit wrapped in a warm blanket awaiting Ms. Ward's arrival. I listen as Indigo and the pregnant bystander try to re-explain the attack I've already explained to park police. My nervousness has subsided. Initially, I was worried that she had recorded the incident. Nobody pulls out their cell to call for help anymore. I was afraid of possibly being caught on camera, maybe becoming a viral Vine, and being revealed as the nonhuman that I am. Turns out, she actually did call for help without ever touching the record button. I can breathe easy knowing she has no evidence. Without proof, her story is just too wild to believe.

"There was no taunting. I keep telling you that!" the pregnant woman argues. "He approached these young ladies and attacked!"

"Calm yourself, ma'am. I'm just trying to get the facts."

"He stepped on her after he stabbed her with his... his..." She stumbles over her words. "Horny things."

"Antlers, ma'am," the officer corrects.

"Excuse me?"

111

He calmly explains, "They're called antlers."

Her eyebrows lower in anger. The officer tries to maintain his composure but can't hide his growing frustration with her story that differs so greatly from mine.

He looks at Indigo. "You said you ran. Did you see anything that happened before you took off?"

"He attacked us for no reason. He knocked my friend on the ground and I ran to get help."

He turns to his silent partner. "Maybe he ran into the tree and killed himself. The victim said it happened so fast that she can't really explain it."

The pregnant lady jumps in. "She grabbed him and swung him against the tree."

"Ma'am, you're hysterical. I know seeing an animal attack can be scary, but you've come to some very unlikely conclusions."

"I know what I saw. Ask her."

"We did. And she can't explain what happened."

"I'm telling you what happened!" she yells at him yet again.

"Thank you for your help, ma'am." The officers turn away from her and offer me kind smiles. "How are you feeling?" the lead officer asks me.

"Better."

"Did it run into the tree?"

I shrug. "Like I said, I'm just not sure."

"It's okay," he tells me. "That must've been what happened."

His partner finally speaks. "I'm surprised the bucks haven't shed their antlers."

I look at Indigo. Her eyes are caring and sympathetic.

"Did it step on you?" the officer asks me.

"I don't think so. I think I was just knocked down. I feel fine, though."

The pregnant woman stands feet away. Her eyes move

from me to the officers.

"No pain?" the EMT asks.

I shake my head. "Nothing."

I drink from my bottle of water. The fight didn't leave me in pain, but it has left me feeling weak. I'm tired. Exhausted. If another buck were to come at me now, for sure I couldn't repeat what I just did. He'd have me at his mercy.

I hear my name being yelled in a panic. Ms. Ward runs over to the ambulance. "A deer? You were attacked by a deer?"

I shake my head. "A buck just knocked me over."

"I'm taking you to the hospital."

"No," I object. "I don't need to go to the hospital. Really. It just scared me. I'm fine."

"Jaylen, I get it. You're afraid of doctors. You could be hurt, though. You may not feel it now, but you may be hurt."

"I'm not hurt. I'm telling you, I feel fine. I just want to go home."

"I want to take you in to be looked at."

I continue to shake my head. "I just want to get home. If I feel anything in the morning, I promise to tell you and go to the hospital. No debates."

"I want to take you in," she states sternly.

I need her to agree that a hospital visit is unnecessary. I've been injured before. I know that recovering from this won't be an issue. The last thing I need is to sit in the emergency room, have nurses fuss over me, and possibly have blood drawn, just to be told that my type is so rare it doesn't even have a letter. Every doctor's visit, every hospital visit, just forces my heart to beat erratically for the entire stay. I've always feared a doctor learning just how much of a freak I am. I've always feared being placed in a secret government lab and experimented on like a lab rat. So regardless of the circumstances, if there's any possible way to talk my way out of seeing a doctor, I do it. In this instance, preying on her emotions is my best bet.

"Please, Mom," I beg. "I just wanna go home."

Her eyes soften. She glances at the EMT, and then back at me.

"You can take her home if you'd like," the EMT explains. "I recommend taking her to the hospital, but it's your call."

Her eyes are on me. "Any pain, Jaylen, and you better let me know."

I nod. "I promise."

"This is against my better judgment, but I'll take you home."

I hop down from the ambulance with the assistance of Ms. Ward and the EMT. I brush away dirt from my uniform skirt and push my hair behind my ears.

"Do you need a ride?" Ms. Ward asks Indigo.

"No. My aunt is on her way. But thank you."

Ms. Ward puts her arm around me, and together we walk toward her pride and joy. Her treat for accomplishing all of her career goals.

"You sure you're okay?"

"I feel perfectly fine. It was just really scary."

She opens the back door for me, and I step inside. She quickly gets into the driver seat, and we head for her house. As she drives, I respond to Michael's text telling me to let him know when I make it home. I reply, explaining that I'm on my way now and will call him when I get there.

"So aside from the unexpected animal attack, how was your day?" Ms. Ward asks.

"It was good. Yours?"

"Busy. The office is nowhere near being finished. I have files that need to be entered electronically, orientation books that need to be put together, pamphlets that need to be folded."

"Sounds like chaos."

"That it is."

I look down at my phone. Indigo's text message asks me to please call her when I get a chance.

"How would you like a part-time job?"

"At your office?" I ask.

"Yeah. I could use the help. That would give you a chance to save up a little money before starting college, too."

I think about how little time that would leave me to spend with Michael, and then quickly consider the necessary funds I'll need when going off to school. Living on my own won't be cheap.

I accept her offer. "That would be great."

"Good. And I'll pay you under the table so you don't have to worry about taxes."

"Even better. Thanks."

"Not a problem, sweetie." She clears her throat. "So, umm…" Her tone lets me know she's about to ask me something I probably won't want to answer.

"Yes?"

"Liking any guys?"

I fully expected Ms. Ward to squeeze that question in with the two hundred others she asked on my first day. Surprisingly, she skipped it. She lasted three days without asking about boys. I'm impressed, considering she's such a prier.

"I don't know yet," I say dishonestly. "There's one guy that I kind of like, but I don't know him well enough to say for sure."

"What's he like?"

"He's…" I think about Michael and I can't help but smile. "Funny."

"What's his name?"

"Michael."

"Michael," she repeats softly. "Well, you're almost eighteen. You're a straight-A student. You're a very wise young lady. If this Michael ever decides to ask you out, you're allowed to date. I have to meet him first, but you're allowed to go out."

"Okay."

As we pull into the driveway, I try to hide the exhaustion I feel. I maintain good posture and a relaxed expression as I walk inside the house. As I head up the stairs, my phone alerts me to another message. I wait until I'm alone in my room to check it. It's from Indigo, asking if I'm okay. I call her.

"Jaylen?"

"Yeah, it's me."

She asks, "You home already?"

"Just got in."

"Are you okay?"

I lie across the bottom of my bed. "Just tired."

"Drink, Jaylen. Drink plenty of water, and get some rest."

"I will. How are you?"

"I'm okay. I'm just worried about you."

"You move quickly," I tell her.

"What do you mean?"

"You said you ran off to go get help. I didn't see you run off or run back. I just noticed you standing on the path. One minute you were gone, the next you were there."

"I panicked. I hope you're not upset that I left you to try and find someone."

"No, I'm not. I just never knew a person could move so quickly and so quietly."

"I never knew a girl could be so strong."

"What?"

"I saw," she tells me.

"Saw what?"

"The deer didn't run into the tree."

"That's the only logical explanation."

"When I realized there was no one close enough to come help you, I turned back around. I saw you, Jaylen."

I look up at my ceiling. There's no point in trying to argue this lie any longer.

"What else was I supposed to do?" I ask.

"If I had the strength to defend myself that way, for sure I would. I don't care about the deer. Just don't lie to me about things. I understand why you told the cops what you did. Believe me, I do. But you don't have to pretend with me, Jaylen. I understand why you're capable of these things."

I lie silently. My body needs to rest. My mind, too.

"Jaylen, I'm gonna let you sleep. I just want you to know that I know how it feels to have to hide everything about yourself. You don't have to hide with me."

"I appreciate you saying that."

"Get some rest. I'll text you later."

"Okay."

After ending the call, I move sluggishly about my room, removing my school uniform. I enter my bathroom and turn on my shower. I look down at the scars on my stomach. Every injury that I've ever had has healed itself within the day. Some heal within the hour. I'll never stop questioning why these cuts became scars.

Slowly, I step inside my shower. I wash as quickly as I can. I need to down some water and get some rest. I scrub the dirt off of my legs, arms, neck. I let the water run through my long hair, hair that grows almost as fast as I cut it.

As I lather up, my mind goes back to my birthday last year. My mom woke me with her gentle touch, singing the birthday song in her soft voice. That was the last birthday I spent with her. A birthday I cherish more than all the rest.

I rinse the shampoo from my hair as my mom's singing replays in my mind. I turn, allowing the running water to rinse away any remaining soap I may have missed. As the water runs down my body, I silently wish to forget the memories. As beautiful as many of them are, remembering is too painful. If I couldn't recall them, I wouldn't be in pain. There'd be nothing for me to miss.

"Jaylen!"

I shut the water off. "Just a minute," I shout as I quickly pat my body dry.

I don't want Ms. Ward to rush in assuming that I need help. In a hurry, I secure a towel around myself and step out of my bathroom.

"You okay?" she asks from my bedroom doorway.

I nod. "I'm fine. I just wanted to get the dirt off of me."

"That was quick, but I don't blame you one bit. You hungry?"

"No, I'm actually tired. I was gonna take a nap."

"You should. You had quite a scare today."

I sit on the side of my bed.

"Can I get you anything?"

I shake my head. "I don't need anything. It's just been a long day."

"Do you think you'll be okay by yourself for about an hour?"

"Sure."

"I rushed out of the office. I left a few portfolios behind that I need to look over."

"Go ahead. Take your time. Like I said, I'm just gonna nap. I promise to call you if I need anything."

"Please do."

She walks over to kiss my forehead. I force a smile for her.

"That phone call terrified me."

"I didn't mean to scare you," I say apologetically.

"It's not your fault. I just realized today how much you mean to me. When I decided to take you in, initially it was because I felt too sorry for you to place you with a family of strangers all over again. The more time I spend with you, the more I look at you, I see why Ms. Hayes adopted you." She touches my cheek. "You're a beautiful young lady, inside and out. And I deeply care for you, Jaylen. I want you to know that."

I silently look at the floor.

"I know you've been through a lot. I hope you're happy here. I'm not sure how well I'm doing with the whole parenting thing."

"I am happy here. And you've been amazing. A bit overprotective, but I'm truly grateful that you care as much as you do."

Her sweet smile shows that she greatly appreciates hearing that. Now that I think about it, I should've told her that before. Ms. Ward could've placed me elsewhere, the same way she has to with so many others. She decided not to. Her big heart brought me to Michael, to Indigo, to a feeling of security after all that happened. That deserves constant thanks.

"Call me," she says as she leaves, pulling my door closed behind her.

In private, I slowly dress myself as the realization sets in. I called Ms. Ward the "M" word. It got me out of one situation, but what did it get me into? I don't want her to get carried away with her role as my foster mother and to start overdoing it. I don't want her to start calling me her daughter, or worse, expect me to address her as "Mom" from now on.

I sit on my window seat and twist my long, wet hair into a bun as I wait for Ms. Ward to drive off. Though my pillow is calling me, I want to phone Michael. Not only because I told him I would, but because I could use a laugh, a pleasant distraction from the day's events. Who better to deliver? I dial him up. As I wait for him to answer, I take down a bottle of water.

"What's up?"

"Hey." My tone is a perfect match for how I'm feeling.

"You okay?" he asks, sounding concerned.

"I'm okay now."

"Something happen at the lake?"

I watch Ms. Ward back out of the driveway as I explain, "I got attacked by a buck."

"You what?" Fear deepens his voice.

"I was attacked by a buck," I repeat calmly. "I'm fine now. It just scared the hell out of me."

"Where are you? The hospital?"

"No." I yawn. "I'm in the house. I'm gonna take a nap."

"How hurt are you?"

"I took some hits to the chest, but I don't feel it. I just feel drained."

"You're drinking, right?"

"Yeah." I turn toward to my nightstand. "Just finished one. Got two that I'm looking at right now."

There's loud clattering on his end of the phone.

"You okay?" I ask.

"Yeah. I'm just worried."

I get up to grab one of the bottles from my nightstand. "Don't worry about me, Michael. I'm not saying this in a rude way, but I can take care of myself. Really."

Again, there's movement and shuffling on his end.

"What happened to the buck?"

I take a deep breath. "I killed him."

"How? Take me through it."

"No, Michael. It's gonna sound much worse than it really was. I'm okay now. I called to get away from this subject."

"Tell me what happened," he demands.

Clearly, he's not going to stop pushing, so I take Michael through the attack. I stop a few times to drink a little water, and then continue. His voice is uneasy as he questions how I defended myself. His tone becomes terror-stricken as he responds to what the buck did to me. Minutes roll by as I describe an attack that happened too quickly to accurately time.

"What happened to Indigo?"

"She's okay. She ran off to get help, but didn't find anyone, so she came back and saw what I did. Or at least, that's her story."

"What did she say about what happened?"

"She knows we're not human. Like you said, she doesn't talk about it in detail, but she's made it crystal clear that she understands why I'm capable of what I am. So she wasn't surprised."

As I look out of my window, I spot a Camaro similar to Michael's parking across the street.

"Where are you?" he asks.

"I told you, I'm in the house."

"Do you feel okay enough to come down and open the front door?"

As he steps out of his car, happiness shoots through me. "What are you doing here?" I ask.

He hangs up and runs across the street. I slowly make my way down the stairs to let him in. I pull the door open, and before we can exchange any words face to face, he picks me up in his arms. I wrap my arms around his neck and hold him close. His hold on me is tight. His breathing is deep. His care for me is simply undeniable.

"I'm okay," I whisper.

He lets me down easy and steps back. His eyes look me over. "No pain?"

"Not really."

He closes and locks my front door for me. Another yawn escapes me.

"Where are you resting?"

I point up the staircase. "My room."

"You want me to carry you up?"

I suck my teeth. "No. I've experienced worse. Believe me, I'm okay."

"Well, walk in front of me."

"Why? So you can catch me if I fall?"

"You said you're good, so there's no reason for me not to walk behind you and enjoy the view."

I shake my head before turning to head up the staircase in front of Michael. Aches are beginning to sprout in my upper body area. When we enter my room, he pushes the door closed behind us. I immediately climb onto my bed. My energy level is too low to do anything else other than relax.

"This is a big room."

I open a fresh bottle of water and gulp some down.

He points to the slightly opened door. "That's a bathroom?"

"Mm-hmm."

"Can I look around?"

Another yawn. "Feel free."

He peeks inside my bathroom before turning his attention to my walls. As he looks over personally drawn pieces, he beams. "Damn."

"What?"

"You're really talented. These look 3D."

"Thank you."

He points to a framed photo on my bookshelf. "Who's that?"

"My mom. The one who adopted me. Not my mother."

"She's pretty."

I stare at the framed portrait. "Yes, she was."

He carefully removes his Jordans and places them in front of my bookshelf.

"They're just shoes," I tell him.

"Maybe to you. These joints are fresh, though."

"You guys and your shoes."

He points to my closet. "Really? Look who's talking."

I giggle as he moves to the head of my bed to sit beside me.

"You stay on top of the comforter," I order.

"No problem," he agrees. "Like I said before, you sleep better around your own. That's why I'm here."

I hand him my remote. "Thank you for coming."

"Any time."

I lie on my side, facing Michael. As he gently touches my wet hair, my mom's face comes to mind. I miss her smell, hearing her voice, the way she would rub my head this very way.

"I miss her," I say. "I miss her a lot. They lied when they said it'd get easier."

He sits silently, his hand still on my head.

"When I saw her motionless, with her head lying on the steering wheel, and blood running down her face, I wanted to change places. She was so full of life, and seeing her like that killed a part of me. I can't get the image out of my mind."

"I know you don't believe, but you know I do. And I believe she's in a better place."

I continue. "We were driving home. It was late. We were having so much fun, singing along to Michael Jackson and dancing in our seats." I take a deep breath. "She asked me to reach for her charger in the back of the truck. I took off my seatbelt and climbed halfway into the back to search for it. I couldn't find it." I pause. "I guess she turned to take a quick look." Another deep breath. "We ran a red light and smashed into the side of another truck that was making a turn."

"I'm sorry, Jaylen." His voice is low and his tone heavyhearted. Sympathetic.

"I was ejected from the vehicle."

"Ejected?" he asks, sounding horrified.

I nod. "I was thrown clear through the windshield." I turn over and pull paper-clipped articles from my nightstand drawer. "My neighbors started referring to me as 'Miracle,'" I explain as I hand him articles that covered our accident.

He quietly reads them over as I lift up to drink a little

more water.

"I'd call you Miracle, too. To survive being ejected from a vehicle is unbelievable."

"That's when I knew," I state.

"Knew what?"

"I never knew what to call myself, or what to define myself as, but I always knew I was different from those around me. That night put an end to any possible doubt. You see, I didn't just survive that accident, Michael. I didn't break any bones. I just felt extremely sore for a while. And I got cut. But that's minor considering what the scene looked like."

He continues to read through my tragedy.

"I still have marks," I tell him.

"What do you mean?"

"Something got jammed into my side. The EMTs had to remove it. It left two nasty scars."

"Just be happy you're alive."

"I'm not saying it like that. It's just that I've never been injured to the extent where the wounds didn't heal. Well, technically they did heal, but I've never been scarred unless it was due to heat."

"Hmm," he lets out softly. "Neither have I."

"I've been trying to figure out why I have these marks."

"I don't know. This is sad, though, babe. I can't tell you how sorry I am. Two moms. That's hard."

I release a deep breath and relax my body.

"How are you dealing with all of this? This wasn't too long ago."

"I don't know," I admit quietly.

Michael begins to rub my head again. His touch is so comforting. In this moment, it's so necessary.

"I appreciate you sharing that with me. It means a lot to me, Jaylen."

"Why?"

"What do you mean, why? I told you I really wanna get

to know you. I meant that."

I lie quietly, and Indigo comes to mind. Our kiss suddenly overshadows the deer attack, and right now, I'd rather be remembering my encounter with the buck. It's unpleasant to think about how Indigo feels about me. It's far from fun or even flattering to feel caught in between the two people I'm not only like, but feel the closest to.

"Can we talk about something else?" I ask.

"You should get some sleep."

I ignore his statement, and my body aches. "Can I confide in you?"

"Isn't that what you've been doing?"

"Yeah, but I've been talking about myself. I want to tell you something about someone else. I don't gossip, and I try not to talk about other people behind their backs, but I just need to talk to someone about this. You're the only person I feel comfortable telling."

"My lips are sealed."

I sigh and hope they remain that way. "I let Indigo kiss me."

He chuckles in disbelief. "You what?"

"She kissed me at the lake."

"Why'd you let her?"

"We were talking about being different from humans. She went on to tell me that she had feelings for me. She went in for another kiss, and I let it happen."

"Another kiss?"

I lie silently. This is exactly why I don't gossip. Something that was never meant to come out always does.

"She tried once before. I backed away from that one, though."

"What the hell? I didn't expect that to be the secret. Damn. It would've been nice to see that."

"Michael, don't be such a damn guy. I'm confused now."

"About what? How you feel about her?"

"No. If I'm sure about anything, it's that my feelings for her are platonic. I just don't know how to be around her now. I don't know why I let her kiss me. I knew that I didn't have those feelings. I told her that, and still I did it anyway."

"Maybe you just needed to convince yourself that you didn't feel that way about her."

"To kiss someone who you know likes you will only make them think you like them back, even if you say you don't. I mean, look at it from their point of view. Who kisses people they don't like?"

"You."

We both let out soft laughter.

"Really, Michael. I like Indigo. I don't want to hurt her. I don't want to hurt anybody. She said she felt it as soon as she saw me. I didn't feel that for her then, and I don't now."

"She'll just have to accept that, Jaylen. Simple as that."

"I think things are gonna feel weird. I should have never let that happen."

"What do you think she's gonna do? Rape you?"

"You're ridiculous."

He laughs loudly. "I'm just kidding."

"I just hope she believes me. I don't want her to think persistence is gonna get her anywhere."

He flips through channels and tells me, "Just make sure you let her know that. She'll get it. It might take some time to fizzle out, but she'll eventually get it. She won't have a choice but to."

I look up at Michael.

"What?" he asks without looking down at me.

"I don't know. I just like being near you. I like talking to you."

His hand touches my hair again. "You should let me take you out. You know, on one of your better days."

"I'll see what I can do about that. I just took on a part-time job."

"Doing what?"

"I don't know. I'll be helping my foster mother get her office together."

"Which means I get to have you when?" His eyes look into mine.

I smile. "When I say so."

He chuckles. "As bad as I want to take you out, I probably won't be able to for a while. Moms found out that I drove my car to take you home yesterday, and I'm sure she'll somehow find out that I drove it again today. Once I get home from school, I'm supposed to stay in and study. I am not supposed to touch my car key unless there's an emergency or she tells me to." He massages his forehead. "I'm gonna be grounded for the rest of my life. Even if she does give in and let me go out, she's not gonna let me drive. After today, she'll probably start carrying the key with her."

"Now I feel bad."

"Don't." He shakes his head. "You didn't make me drive you home. You didn't make me come here to check on you. You didn't even ask. I wanted to. I want to be there for you whenever you need someone."

His care and compassion literally warm me. His words are like a blanket. They make me feel safe, cozy, protected, like it's okay for me to actually soften.

His eyes focus back in on my television. His hand remains on my head. "Please go to sleep, Jaylen. Get some good shut-eye while I'm here."

I rest my hand on Michael's leg and close my eyes. I enjoy the warmth of being close to the person I feel safest with. I hold on to a feeling I hope I never lose.

Chapter 11

Three months pass me by without notice, and I've completely settled into my new life. What started as a part-time job slowly became a full-time position. After knocking out months of tedious duties that Ms. Ward conveniently left out of the job description, she offered me the opportunity to personally decorate the office walls. I graciously accepted the offer. At only seventeen, I'm designing four large pieces to be displayed in an office for the eyes of strangers and possible future customers to view. I've been working endlessly on them.

I've had little time to spend with Michael. Outside of school, most of our talking is done over text or late-night conversations that we fall asleep in the middle of. Indigo and I have found a place for each other. There has been no discomfort or further advances, and she's become my very best female friend. Almost every other weekend, she spends the night at my house. Though I confide in Michael with my more personal thoughts, fears, and feelings, she's become a needed shoulder for me to lean on. She understands the loneliness I've felt over the years because she still feels it.

Transferring here has helped me to find true friends. Meeting Indigo and Michael has helped me to find myself.

As I sit beside Michael on our very first date, which we both agree is long overdue, I notice that I'm at my most comfortable. Though the feelings are just as intense, and my thoughts of him are less innocent and more mature, I don't feel nervous around him. I'm with my friend. I consider Indigo to be my best female friend, but undeniably, Michael is my very best friend.

His green eyes slowly look me over again. "You look good out of uniform."

"You've seen me out of uniform before. I don't know why you keep saying that."

"Yeah, but you were dressed to chill. Tonight, you're dressed for me."

"Dressed for you? I don't know about that."

"Mm-hmm. You ain't gotta admit it. You do look nice, though."

I smooth back my long, straightened hair. "Thank you."

He inches closer. I cross my right leg over my left.

"So, Miss Hayes."

"Yes, Mr. Reed?"

"Am I making you nervous? I mean, is sitting this close to you okay?"

"We've laid in bed together. You may have been on top of the comforter, but we were behind closed doors. That's more personal than this."

"No. Tonight is different."

That one statement welcomes back the butterflies.

"I don't want to be in the friend zone anymore."

I quickly tell him, "You're not in the friend zone. Never were."

"You sure?"

"I'm positive. I just haven't had time to date. You know how busy I've been. I've been working like crazy at the office.

I'm still going crazy trying to get the display pieces done."

"You excited about that?"

"Very. These will be my first displayed pieces of art. That's huge."

"I'm happy for you, babe."

I ask, "So, what's going on with your college applications?"

"Still working on them. You hear back yet?"

"Not yet. I really want to get into Princeton, but we'll see. I missed the early application deadline."

"And your birthday? What's up with that?"

My mom's face flashes before my eyes. "Nothing as of yet."

"You're about to turn eighteen. You have to do something."

I shrug nonchalantly.

"Let me take you somewhere."

"Where?"

"Let me worry about that."

I smile widely. I like Michael more than I ever expected to like any boy. Everything about him makes me smile. Smile from within. The way he makes me feel makes me want to give myself to him in ways I've never thought about giving myself to anyone. I can talk to him about anything. I can express myself without judgment. He accepts me for who I am, and he's still here. Nothing is more pleasing than that.

Michael stands and reaches for my hand. I give him my left, and he pulls me from the bench. For a second, I forgot we were even sitting in the middle of a town center.

I walk beside Michael, my fingers interlocked with his. I look down at my tee, my skin-tight jeggings, and my platform heels. I check to make sure I look just as put-together as I did when I left the house. Though he's complimented me more than a few times, I want to make sure I deserve the flattery.

"What's up, Michael? On the drive here, we were

yapping nonstop. Over milkshakes, we were still at it. I feel like we're looking for stuff to talk about now."

"I think we're just dancing around the subject we're avoiding."

As we head for the wishing fountain, I ask, "And that is?"

"I don't talk to anyone else as much as I talk to you. I don't think about anyone else before I go to sleep. I miss you when I don't see you. A few months ago, I was late to class daily. I'm on time every day now. I don't think about any other girl the way I think about you, Jaylen."

I squeeze his hand as my heart flips. Those butterflies wreak havoc inside me. No question, I feel the same way about him. Working has helped me to save money, but it has been more than difficult for me to only see Michael at school. We just haven't been able to get our schedules to match up over the last few months. Whenever I was free, he was grounded. When he had free time, work was keeping me busy. I'm so glad we were able to make time for each other tonight, and to make things even better, Michael finally regained his driving privileges. He was able to pick me up and shake Ms. Ward's hand like a true gentleman.

"I feel the same way," I say as we walk, still hand in hand. "I'm definitely not thinking about anyone else."

"You sure? You've been spending a lot of time with Indigo. You still feel the same way about her?"

"I haven't been lying to you. Only friendship. That's all I want from her."

We stop in front of the fountain. The area is quiet, and no one's occupying the benches surrounding the water display.

"Here you go." He pulls a dime from his pocket.

"Cheap wish."

Laughter escapes him.

"Why do you get the quarter?" I ask childishly.

"We can switch."

I take the quarter from his hand, and he takes the dime. His eyes look into mine as he tosses the coin and makes his ten-cent wish.

"You don't close your eyes to make wishes?"

He shakes his head. "Your turn."

I face the fountain, eyes closed, and wish for a happily ever after with Michael. I wish for him to get accepted into a college in Jersey. I wish for him to commit to me and never betray my trust. I wish for him to kiss me and for it to feel as good as I imagine. I wish for him to love me, to be the one person in my life who doesn't leave me.

"Long wish," he comments softly.

I toss my quarter before reopening my eyes. We stand side by side in front of the wishing fountain. My eyes search for our coins lying amongst hundreds of others.

"You wanna make it official?"

I turn to Michael. The happiness I feel won't allow me to hide it. It's taking over my face.

"Is that a yes?" he asks.

I nod.

"Come here."

He pulls me to him, and we hold each other close. I close my eyes and enjoy the satisfaction I feel from just being in his arms. Nothing feels better to me than being this close to Michael.

Our hold on one another loosens. His eyes look into mine. This silence is louder than any words we could possibly speak. Our attraction is far from a normal one. I've waited almost eighteen years to feel this for someone. Anyone. He has, too. And we feel it for each other.

He slowly moves in closer to my face. Our noses touch. Our lips are slightly parted. His right hand rests on my lower back while my right hand grips his left bicep.

My eyelids lower as our lips meet. Our kiss is soft,

endless, speaking of nothing but honest affection, and possibly even love.

My grip tightens. This kiss makes me want to turn my private fantasies with Michael into realities. Every dream I've had of this moment, every silent wish made, just came true.

The fluttering that was once centered in my stomach has moved throughout my entire body. Those teenage urges girls have a hard time resisting now make themselves apparent inside of me. I'm not just in a relationship with someone I find attractive. I'm in a relationship with someone I want.

His lips are so perfectly soft. His touch is so masculine, and still so gentle. My heart feels like it's only a beat from leaping out of my chest.

We slowly pull apart. I look into those green eyes. Everything in me wants to have him. Have him touch me, move me, make love to me.

He moves back in and kisses my lips once more. My eyes are back on his. My thoughts are now bedroom thoughts.

I decide to cut the date short before I rush into a mistake. "We should get going. I have to work on my pieces."

He pulls back as a crease forms between his brows. "Right now? You sure? I do something wrong?"

"No." I grab his hand. "You did—" I stop and correct myself. "You're doing everything right. Too right."

He chuckles and nods proudly.

"Shut up, Michael."

"I'm not laughing at you. I gotta fight the feeling, too. Shit's not easy."

With my hand in his, we head for the car Michael obsessively cleans. I stand at the back door.

"Do you want to try sitting up front with me? I'll go five miles an hour if you need me to. I just want to be able to see you. To reach over and touch you."

I think back to the accident. I think about how it has affected me, how much pain it had left me in. I had never been in so much physical pain in all my life. I'm still emotionally scarred. I prefer walking to riding, and I haven't ridden in the passenger seat since. I haven't even sat behind the wheel of a car, and I'm licensed to drive.

"Can you try? For me, please?"

My eyes move from the back door to the front, and then back again.

"You'll never be able to conquer your fears unless you face them, babe."

Michael pulls the passenger door open. My mind tries to think around the fear and find more rational thoughts. I've been backseat riding for months now. I haven't been in any accidents. The likelihood of getting into one tonight is slim. And if fate should deal me that hand, the likelihood of being ejected a second time is close to impossible.

I slowly step into the passenger seat. As Michael walks around to the driver side, I buckle myself in. I haven't seen the open road from this point of view in a while.

He turns over the engine. "You nervous?"

"A little, but it's about time. Just keep your eyes on the road. Please."

As Michael drives along the dark roads, I look over at him. I can't help but smile. I've briefly dated two other guys. Two guys I had no true feelings for. Two guys I felt truly uncomfortable kissing. I'm now dating someone I feel for. Someone I've kissed and can't wait to kiss again. Someone I think I might actually love.

"You okay?"

I reach over and touch his hair. "What's it like to be you, Michael?"

"What do you mean?"

"You're always digging around in my head, in my past, in my thoughts. I wanna dig."

"I don't know how to answer that."

"What was life like before I got here?"

"Life was all right. I can't say that I was lonely. I knew others like me. I just wanted the same thing you wanted. I wanted to feel that love connection. As lame as that may sound coming from a man."

"And now?"

"Now I feel…" He pauses. "I don't know. I guess normal."

My friend's face comes to mind. "I feel so bad for Indigo."

"Me, too."

"I love how it feels to be with you. I remember what it felt like to not have this. I feel bad that she hasn't found this with anybody."

"She will. He or she is out there."

"I wonder how she's gonna react when I tell her we're actually a couple."

"It shouldn't bother her. You said she's accepted being just friends, right?"

"She hasn't tried to kiss me again, and I do feel totally comfortable with her, but I can see that it upsets her when I talk about you too much. Or if she's sleeping over, and you and I are texting, it bothers her. Sometimes I feel like she might secretly still like you."

"Doubt that."

I shrug. "She's gonna be upset."

"Oh well." His tone is careless. "I want to talk about you. Us. Not everybody else."

His right hand reaches over and rests on my left thigh. My body shudders. I place my hand on top of his.

"Michael, what's wrong with me?"

"What do you mean?"

"Why am I so strong? You're not. Indigo isn't. Why do I have scars? You don't. Indigo doesn't. I feel like the weirdo amongst the humans and amongst our kind."

"We're all different, Jaylen. I tell you this all the time. I

135

swear I've told you as much as I know. I don't know why you think I'd keep something from you."

"I just want to understand myself. That's all. I know I get on your nerves asking the same things over and over again."

"Yes, you do."

I gasp and push his hand off of my thigh. "Shut up. And even if you mean it, don't say it out loud."

We laugh, and again, that hand slides back over.

"Who told you to touch me?"

"You like it," he states confidently.

He's right, so I don't deny it.

"Answer me this, Jaylen. What were some of the things you thought you could be? You know, before I told you what we actually are. If you had never considered alien, what did you consider? I'm sure you had some crazy ideas."

I've run so many theories through my mind, researched so many possibilities over the years. Nothing I found sounded anything like me. I'm grateful for Michael. If it weren't for him, I'd still be searching for an explanation that isn't documented anywhere.

I answer him. "I spent a lot of time researching genetic disorders and human hybrids. I have blood in me, so I knew I was either part human or animal. I thought maybe our race was engineered. Maybe part human, part robot. That would explain my intelligence. I looked up lots of articles on hybrids of all sorts. I never considered mythical beings or aliens. I figured a doctor would've picked up on that years ago."

He turns down a side street. The streetlights provide enough light for me to feel comfortable. There is nothing that worries me more than the creatures of the night.

He shifts into park. "Well, now you know what you are. Not only what you are, but whose you are. Mine."

Those butterflies are back, and they brought friends.

"What are we doing here?" I ask.

He releases his seatbelt and then mine. My nerves are at

their peak. Excitement mixes in with them. He gestures with his finger for me to come to him. My stomach drops as I lean in. Our lips meet. My body again fills with those feelings I'm not ready to act on.

His left hand slowly moves from my cheek to my breast. I quickly grab his roaming hand. He pulls it from mine and moves it to my waist. As much as I want to be touched, I don't want to move too far, too fast. I pull away from lips I'm already so in love with kissing.

"What's wrong?" he asks.

"I just don't wanna move too fast. It's only our first date."

His loving smile shows no anger or frustration with my wanting to take things slow.

"It's hard to sit this close to you and not touch you."

I smile empathetically. "It's hard for me, too. I just wanna be sure."

"I'm not trying to take it there tonight."

"Yeah, but the touching is gonna make me want to."

We look at one another. Everything about him went from cute to sexy. Everything.

We kiss again. My mind is telling me one thing. My body is telling me another. His left hand is back on my waist. My right grips his hair. The middle storage compartment creates a necessary barrier that stops us from getting too comfortable.

I pull away slowly. "We should stop."

Our breathing is heavy as we stare at one another. Our thoughts are likely the same.

He unlocks the doors. "I need some fresh air."

I grab his arm. "Don't go out there alone."

"I need to move around a little bit. Get my blood circulating again."

I pull a bottle of water from my purse. I sip some down before passing it to Michael. He takes a few sips before stepping outside. I watch him closely, keeping my eyes on him as he leans against the front of his car. I watch out for wild animals, for crazies, for any possible danger.

As Michael fidgets with his belt, I notice a man walking toward him. Michael notices him, too. As the man continues to approach, I notice his lips moving. Michael turns toward me, and suddenly, all the doors lock. He then turns back to the unknown man.

I look down at my hands to make sure I didn't subconsciously lock the doors at the sight of a stranger. My hands are still resting on my legs. The keys are still in the ignition.

"What the hell?" I ask aloud.

The man waves at me before walking back in the direction he came from. I unlock the doors, and Michael takes his seat behind the wheel.

"Neighborhood watchman," he informs me.

I tell him, "The doors locked."

"He just wanted to know why we stopped. I told him I just needed to stretch my legs. He said to be careful. There have been black bear sightings and a possible coyote sighting in the area."

Michael buckles himself in. I do too. We pull off.

I repeat, "The doors locked."

"I know."

"But I didn't lock them."

"I didn't know who the hell that was. I wanted to make sure you were safe."

I sip my water. "How'd you do that?"

"Why are you so strong? So smart?"

I nod in understanding. He can do the unexplainable, too.

"I was gonna tell you. Like I said, we're just taught not to say too much about ourselves."

I look over at him. "I'm not mad. A little envious, but not mad."

He chuckles. "You're about as strong as the damn Hulk, and you're envious?"

"I have to physically touch things. You can just move shit without ever getting up. Must be nice."

"It can be. Everything comes with negatives, though."

"Really? Enlighten me."

"Locking the doors is nothing. If I wanted to slam a big ass buck into a tree, I'd be worn out, too. The same things that weaken you, weaken me. I have mental abilities. You have physical. Everything else is the same."

I nod. "Well, how do you feel about me knowing? This is something you were taught to keep secret from everyone."

"Tell you the truth, it's kind of weird. Until now, Moms was the only one to know." He glances over at me. "Now my girl knows all my secrets. It's weird for someone else to know everything about me, but I'm glad that someone else is you. I trust you."

As we wait at a red light, I gaze at it. I think hard about it turning green. I open my eyes wider and then blink hard. Still red.

He bursts into laughter. I can't help but laugh softly at my failed attempt.

"Fuck you, Michael."

"In due time," he shoots back.

As we drive down dark roads hand in hand, I realize how much trust I have in him. We know all there is to know about one another. I've never been so comfortable with anyone. I've never felt so understood. I feel like I've been waiting for Michael my entire life.

I don't know when I'll let him know. Maybe he already knows. I wasn't absolutely positive before, but I love him. I'm in love with my boyfriend.

Chapter 12

I head for my locker with Indigo at my side. Our arms are interlocked as we discuss tonight's spring dance. We've been preparing for this event for weeks. Finally, the day is here, and as luck would have it, it's being thrown on my special day.

She asks, "So what's the plan?"

"Well, Ms. Ward wants to take me out tonight to celebrate my birthday. Then, I'm heading back here for the dance."

"Are you gonna be dressed for the dance at your dinner?"

"Yeah, probably. I'd be cutting it too close if I waited to get dressed afterward."

"You're eighteen, Jaylen!" she says excitedly. "How does it feel?"

"The same. I mean, I haven't done anything to really make it feel official."

"You should buy cigarettes."

I chuckle. "It's crazy to hear you say that because I was going to. I can't wait to use my ID for *something*."

I spot Michael and our crew at my locker, and immediately, a burst of happiness shoots through me. These last few weeks have been filled with meaningful kisses, with flirtatious touching, with all-night conversations about the inevitable.

He greets me open-armed. "Hey, babe."

I hug my boyfriend, and he bends to kiss my cheek.

Indigo asks, "What time are y'all coming tonight?"

"It starts at eight o'clock, right?" I ask.

"Yeah."

"Probably at, like, nine, then. I have to go home, change, and eat dinner with Ms. Ward. I'm definitely not gonna be there when it first starts."

Michael reminds me, "And you have to do my hair."

"Exactly. We're gonna be hella late."

Warren asks, "Who are you guys coming as?"

"You'll see," I tell him.

He guesses, "Jack and Rose?"

"Hell no," Michael answers.

Warren continues to throw out guesses as I put my books away. We didn't initially plan on going to this dance, but dressing up as famous movie couples sounded too fun to pass up. We graduate in the beginning of June, and prom is just a few weeks away. This is our last opportunity to really hang out all together with our underclassmen friends.

"Who organized this, anyway?" Warren asks.

I close my locker door. "The theatre club. They're fundraising."

"I didn't think so many people were gonna go," Indigo admits.

I shrug. "I didn't either, but they're sold out."

We head for the exit. Michael's arm is around me, and mine is around him. We part ways with Indigo and Warren at the front doors. Since Michael and I have been an official couple, Indigo mentions him a lot less and stands as far away from me as possible when I'm within a few feet of him. Though the distance should offer some comfort, it actually creates more tension. If she's near me when Michael approaches, she hightails it away from me like I let out a pungent fart. If he's near me and she's the one approaching, she'd much rather talk to me from a distance than stand close to me like an ordinary best friend would.

"You sure you wanna spend your birthday at some school dance?" Michael asks.

"Yeah. Why not? Everybody will be there. We'll be partying. It should be fun."

"It's not gonna be a party like you think. This is Catholic school. They're not gonna let us touch."

"We can't party without touching?"

He lets out a mischievous chuckle.

We head for Michael's Camaro in the student parking lot. As we drive the short distance to his house, I read through birthday wishes sent from my old friends in Jersey.

"Why are we going to your house? I'm not doing your hair right now, am I?"

"No. Moms left a little gift for you. I wanna give it to you now."

Warmth fills me. I'm in an amazing relationship with Michael, and I'm building one just as great with Ms. Reed. I'm in love with her only son, and she fully accepts me.

"That's really sweet. She didn't have to do that."

"Yeah, I told her that, but for some reason, she wanted to buy your ass something anyway."

"Shut up, hater. Where is she?"

"I told you, she went out of town. She'll be back on Monday."

Michael pulls inside his garage and lets the door down as we step out of the car. I walk around the front of the car and lean against the driver-side fender as he carefully wipes his window.

"You're very clean for a guy."

He cuts his eyes at me. "What's wrong with being clean?"

"Nothing. I just don't see any dirt."

He moves to stand in front of me. "You think I'm crazy? You think I'm wiping for no reason?"

"Kind of looks that way."

His eyes remain on mine as his mouth forms a one-sided grin. I hold his gaze as those butterflies fill the middle of me.

"Happy birthday."

I tilt my head. "Thanks again."

Our lips meet, and the world freezes. Our bodies are close. Our hands are on one another. Our hormones are raging.

My phone sings. We ignore it. We don't separate for even a second. Nothing matters when I'm with Michael. When we're together, our little world is all that exists.

His left hand moves up my right thigh, beneath my skirt. I reach down and grab it.

"Okay, frisky. I gotta get going."

He moves in for another kiss. I back away.

He sighs loudly. "You're killing me, Jaylen."

"Like you said, Michael, in due time. Now come on. I gotta get going."

We enter his kitchen. His house is silent and immaculately clean.

"Water?"

I nod.

He takes a sip before passing me the bottle. I take a quick swallow and then check my phone as Michael eagerly searches through his refrigerator.

"I'm going to dinner with Ms. Ward at 6:30," I tell him after reading her text.

"You got plenty of time to get dressed."

I softly exhale. "That's a relief. Show me your T-Birds

jacket."

We head for Michael's bedroom. His outfit for tonight is hanging across his desk chair. He passes me the faux leather jacket. I hold it out in front of me and look it over happily. I rarely look forward to too many things, but going to this dance with Michael has been on my mind since he purchased the tickets.

"What's his name again?" he asks.

"Kenickie."

"And you're Reese?"

My frustration comes out in a sigh. "Rizzo, Michael. I'm Rizzo, and you're Kenickie."

"That's the one John Travolta played, right?"

"I can't believe you haven't seen *Grease*."

"I don't like musicals."

"I don't either, but *Grease* is a classic."

I watch Michael carefully remove his shoes and align them neatly next to the others. His closet is unbelievably organized.

"And no, you're not Danny," I respond. "John Travolta played Danny. Somebody already selected Danny and Sandy."

"So we're gonna be matching another couple?" Michael's face scrunches as though he just got a whiff of a bad odor.

"We won't be matching exactly."

"What the hell did I let you talk me into, Jaylen?"

"It's gonna be fun. I promise."

"Kenickie," he repeats softly to himself. "And what's my line again?"

"A hickey from Kenickie is like a Hallmark card."

He releases a quiet laugh. "This is gonna be interesting."

I giggle.

"For you, Jaylen. I'm dressing up like someone I don't even know, for you."

"And I appreciate it, Michael."

"You don't ever plan on calling me Mike?" he asks as he

moves about his room.

"Everyone calls you Mike. I'm not just anyone, so to me, you're Michael."

"Okay, Jay."

I sharpen my tone. "Don't do that."

He laughs under his breath.

"So, what's up with the college apps?"

He shrugs unconcernedly as he sits at the end of his bed.

"Michael, what is going on with you?"

He sighs. "I wanna take a break."

I sit in his desk chair. "For how long?"

"A year. I wanna take a break from school until I figure out what I wanna do."

"Yeah, but you can start undecided. You can knock out your cores while you think about it."

"I'm tired of school. It's easy for you, but I actually have to put in the work."

I ask, "Have you talked to your mom about it?"

"Not yet."

"She's gonna be pissed."

"I know." His tone is so careless.

I move to sit by my boyfriend. I know something's bothering him. I've noticed a change in him lately. He's been more uptight. More snappy. Not with me, but I've seen him become aggravated fairly quickly with others.

"Do you ever plan on telling me?"

"Telling you what?"

"Something's been bothering you, Michael."

He lies back. I turn my body and face him. That smile I love is nowhere to be found.

"Please talk to me," I beg.

He exhales loudly. "I don't know."

"You don't know what?"

"I don't know what's been going on lately. I've been feeling the presence of our kind."

"What's wrong with that?"

"I feel their presence, but I don't see them."

I place my hand over Michael's.

"I feel like they're fucking with me."

I push my hair from my face. "What do you mean?"

He doesn't respond. His eyes are on the ceiling. My eyes remain on him.

"My mom felt it the other day, too."

"Felt that someone else was around?"

"Yeah."

"Has anything weird happened?"

He sits back up. "Little shit out of place. Nothing big," he replies quickly. "It's your birthday, babe. Today is about you. We shouldn't be talking about this."

I ignore his attempt to change the subject. "Does their presence feel familiar?"

"I just feel that it's our kind. I can't really tell who is who just by the feeling anymore, unless it's you or Moms. I'm with our kind every day."

We hold hands. I silently question who he could be feeling. There aren't tons of us. If it's not me or Ms. Reed, Indigo is the only one left, but if he were feeling her presence, he'd know because he'd see her.

"I feel threatened when I feel them."

I squeeze his hand. "Are you scared?"

He shakes his head. "Just uncomfortable."

"Do you feel it now?" My eyes search his room.

"Right now, all I'm feeling is you."

I offer my boyfriend a comforting smile as he kisses the back of my hand. His words warm me. His touch melts me.

"Let me get you your gift."

As he steps out of his room, I sip down some water and reply to Ms. Ward. I let her know I'm picking up a gift from Michael's mother and that I'll be home shortly.

He returns with a small box. It's wrapped in silver and

finished with a red ribbon. He hands me my present. I open it carefully as his beautiful green eyes closely watch.

"Give me," he says.

I hand him the gift paper and lift the top from the small box. The sight immediately brings a huge grin to my face. I gasp at its beauty.

"A charm bracelet."

"It's real, too."

I suck my teeth. "I didn't assume it was fake."

I look over the charms: an artist's palette, my first initial, a boat, a heart, a book, a key, and an angel.

"This is so personal. I absolutely love it. It's beautiful."

I hold my wrist out. Michael locks the bracelet on, and I admire the beautiful silver.

"I love it. Thank you."

"It's from my mom."

"I know that. I also know you had to have helped her with the personal touches."

He winks at me.

"She's so thoughtful."

"I'll give you my gift later."

"Why not now?"

"Because it's not really something I can hand you. I wanna take you somewhere."

I think back to our talk in the school hallway on my second day. "D.C.?"

"The place happens to be in that area."

My eyes widen. I'm excited to take a trip with my boyfriend. Alone. Just the two of us.

"You're a genius. Where do you think I'm taking you?"

"I can't read minds, and I can't predict the future. I tell you that every day. Believe me, I've tried, and I'm always wrong."

"Just the facts, huh?"

"Pretty much. I can tell you anything about history, can

solve any math problem you give me, and can define words I've never heard. I can't tell you anything about tomorrow, and I can't tell you what somebody may or may not do." I shrug my shoulders once. "I only wish I could."

He chuckles. "I'm glad you can't read my mind."

"Me too, because it's filthy."

We laugh.

"So what's going on with Warren and Indigo?" he asks.

"She says they're just friends."

"He's taking her to prom."

I nod. "She told me. Lately, they've been acting like a couple at school."

"I've noticed that, too."

"Hopefully things will work out between them. Indigo wants to be in a relationship, and Warren's cute. They make a cute couple."

Michael's eyebrows lower. "Warren's cute?"

"He's an attractive guy." I stand. "And I would like to see her happy."

"I'd like for school to end so I don't have to see her at all."

"Geez. When did you guys start beefing?"

"Like I told you before, I didn't have a problem with Indigo. But now, I'm just tired of her. I'm tired of the looks, the way she acts when you and I are together. It's annoying as hell."

"Maybe I should say something to her about it."

"You don't see it?"

"I definitely see it. I've just been ignoring it. I don't entertain childish behavior."

"I've been trying to ignore it too, but she's not just rolling her eyes at me. She stares at me. She gives me the look of death every time she sees me, every day. Things haven't been awkward between you two?"

I shake my head. "No. When I'm with Indigo, we chill.

We laugh a lot. No drama. We don't talk about you at all. We just hang out."

"What about when she spends the night at your house?"

"Nothing awkward. There was this one time I woke up to her kind of spooning me. I just moved her arm and fell back to sleep. Nothing else really sticks out at me."

"She definitely still likes you," he states confidently.

"Well, I can't do anything about that. She knows I'm with you. She's just gonna have to accept that. If I see the dirty looks tonight, I'm gonna bring to her attention that it makes me uncomfortable."

I hug my boyfriend, and my eyes close. The way he holds me makes me feel so safe. When I'm around him, I feel so loved.

"I gotta go."

His arms tighten around me. "No you don't."

"Yes, I do."

After holding on to each other for a minute longer, we leave, and Michael drops me off at Ms. Ward's house. I walk in and head for her office, anxious to show off my beautiful birthday surprise. Not only does Michael go out of his way to make sure I know he cares, but so does Ms. Reed. The feeling is truly indescribable. They give me such a sense of importance.

Ms. Ward pops up from her executive desk chair. "Happy birthday!"

I laugh at her excitement. "Thank you."

She walks around her desk to hug me. My cell phone alerts me of a text message as I hold on to her.

She steps back. "How does it feel to be eighteen?"

"The same."

Ms. Ward giggles. "That'll change. What did Michael's mother give you?"

I shake my wrist at her.

"That's beautiful."

As she looks over the charms, my cell phone alerts me again.

"What about Michael?" she asks.

"He wants to take me somewhere. That's all he said."

She nods, and the happiness in her face slowly fades.

"Everything okay?"

"It's just hard to believe you're grown. You've got a boyfriend. You'll be leaving for college soon. I've enjoyed these months with you. I've always wanted kids, but I've been married to my career. With you here, I've felt almost like a mother. It's been enjoyable."

I eye my foster mother and then look down at my French-manicured nails. People have always been very drawn to me. I've never understood why. Before moving here and finding others like myself, I rarely hugged anyone other than my mom. I didn't let people know what I was feeling. I kept all of my thoughts silent. And even still, people have always wanted to be around me. I've always found that very unsettling.

She motions for me to sit down. "I want to talk to you about something, Jaylen."

I take a seat. Ms. Ward's pained expression concerns me.

"I know you've been worrying about the things you left in Jersey at your old house." Her eyes sadden. "They're fine. Everything is still in the house."

"Then what's the matter?"

"Because you were still a minor when your mom passed, I made the calls on your behalf to find out what insurance was left to you, if any."

I nod.

"She left you quite a bit. She made sure you would be well taken care of if anything were to happen to her."

"Why is this bad news?"

She forces on a smile. "It's not, sweetie. I've known for a little while what it is you're entitled to, and I've kept it quiet because I didn't want you to run back home and not finish school."

I pull a bottle of water from my bag and take a sip.

"The house is yours."

I stare at her wide-eyed. "The house?"

"Yes."

I find myself speechless. I haven't stopped thinking of my home on Elm Street, my mom's treasures, or my belongings left there. Lately, this place has begun to feel like a home, but I've never felt about any place the way I feel about my home on Elm Street. My mom's love is all over our house. The walls, shelves, dressers, you name it, are decorated with our memories. Pictures and my art can be found throughout. No matter where I turned, there was a reminder that I lived with someone who dearly loved me. Nothing I've ever created or bought for her was tossed out. Not even the horrible gifts I purchased for her during my younger years, like the blue frog ashtray that's still sitting on her dresser. I purchased it thinking it was just something to place keepsakes in, or even small candies. Turns out, the dent in the tongue is there to hold cigarettes and the wide mouth is meant for ashes and cigarette butts. As ugly as it is, it's still there, not matching a thing in her room. Like the rest of the gifts I've given her, no one was ever allowed to use it, move it, or worse, insult it.

Ms. Ward pulls me from my thoughts. "Jaylen?"

"I just can't believe it."

"That's not all."

I sip more water. My heart begins to race at an unhealthy pace.

"She had life insurance." She hands me a sealed envelope. "She named you as the beneficiary, and you're entitled to the proceeds of her policy."

I cover my face with both hands. This is a surprise I never expected.

"What about her sister?" I ask.

"I don't know. I was only able to find out about you, and make sure you received what she wanted you to have. She kept this policy separate from the one that took care of her funeral costs. Her sister may have had leftovers from that one."

I shake my head in disbelief. "This is a lot to absorb."

"I'm sure it is."

I take a deep breath.

"You should be excited, Jaylen. I'm not happy that you'll be leaving soon, but I'm happy that you have financial help for school. I'm glad you didn't have to lose your childhood home."

"I am happy. I'm just in shock. I love that house, but I never thought I'd own it and live in it alone."

"You don't have to. Whatever you wanna do, just let me know. You still live here. Let me help you in any way you need. I hope that even when you move, you'll think of me as a friend. I'm here for you, Jaylen. That's not gonna change."

I stand to hug Ms. Ward. "I didn't plan on leaving for school and never coming back. I would never leave you hanging like that. You've done too much for me. I wouldn't show that kind of disrespect or lack of appreciation."

Her smile returns. "Thank you, sweetie."

I look down at my envelope. My mom said she'd always take care of me. She certainly meant that.

"You excited about the dance?"

I chuckle. "Yeah. It should be fun."

"I can't believe you selected Rizzo. Why not Sandy?"

"Sandy and Danny were already selected. And I've secretly always wanted an excuse to wear the Pink Ladies jacket."

She lets out a quiet laugh. "Your wig came in the mail today. After you finish getting dressed, I'll help you with your hair and makeup."

"Thanks."

"Take your time. You have a couple of hours."

I head for my room with the envelope in hand. My mom's face comes to mind. Her kind voice telling me she loves me nearly makes tears fall. I shake them away. I hold on to the memories, and I fearlessly look out at a future that now looks even brighter. Brighter because of her.

Chapter 13

I call for Ms. Ward after lint-rolling my black pencil skirt. As I wait for her to come to my room, I turn slowly, giving myself a look-over from every angle in my mirror. Though I like what I see, this skirt hugs me so tightly that I'm seriously afraid to exhale.

She opens my door, and I turn to face her.

"Whoa! Can you breathe?"

I smile and respond, "Barely."

"Turn around."

Slowly, I do.

"It's definitely form-fitting, but that's the character you're portraying."

"Is it too much?"

"You're covered."

"You know what I mean. Is the school going to allow this? It *is* a Catholic school."

"You'll be fine, Jaylen. Nothing you wear is going to hide those curves, especially that butt. Now come on. Bring your wig."

I follow Ms. Ward across the hall and into her room. I sit

in her vanity chair. As she begins to pin up my long curls, I breathe in the scent of barbecue. While the smell of food has never forced my mouth to water or my stomach to growl, it's always been pleasing to my nose. That's just another thing I've never understood about myself. How can I enjoy the smell of something so much, but can hardly bring myself to consume it?

"Mmm. Do you smell that?" I ask her.

"Smells good. We might have to stop by the neighbors' for an appetizer."

I giggle.

"So how are things with you and Michael?"

My eyes meet hers in the vanity mirror. "Things are great."

"He seems like a good kid. His mom must really like you."

I nod. "She's really sweet."

"I want to ask you something, but I don't want to make you feel uncomfortable."

And here she goes, crossing a line only my mom would be allowed to cross.

I state honestly, "We're not having sex."

"Whew!" She pretends to wipe sweat from her forehead. "That's nice to know, but that wasn't the question."

"Oh," I say embarrassedly.

Lesson learned. I won't assume I know what Ms. Ward is going to ask ever again.

"I'm happy to hear that you're not doing that yet. My question is actually about Indigo."

"What about her?"

She pins up another curl. "I'm not trying to offend you. I was just wondering if you and her were ever more than just friends."

I didn't see that coming. Instead of assuming the most believable scenario, which is me sleeping with my boyfriend, for some reason, she believes I'm bisexual.

"No. We're just friends. That's all we've ever been," I explain.

"I hope I'm not offending you."

"You're not," I tell her truthfully. "What made you ask?"

"I don't know. It's... it's..." She fumbles over her words. "I guess it's the way she looks at you."

"How does she look at me?"

"I can't really describe it. It's not a sexual look. It's more of a stare, I guess. She watches you closely."

A soft grunting sound escapes me.

"Don't take what I'm saying too seriously. I don't want to make things awkward between you and your best friend. She just looks at you as though she may have a little crush. I have to keep reminding myself that girls are touchier and more observant of one another now than back in my day. I'm sure it's nothing. I was just curious."

I sit silently. I didn't realize that Indigo's feelings for me were so obvious. If Ms. Ward noticed something, how many others have?

She rubs my shoulders gently. "You okay?"

"Yeah, I'm fine. I'm just thinking about the dance."

I continue to breathe in the smell of grilled food as Ms. Ward fixes my hair and assists in applying my makeup. I glance over at the clock and realize we're running late.

"It's almost 6:30," I say.

"I know. Don't worry about the time. We don't have to go far."

I look in the mirror and grin at my reflection. What I see is exactly what I was going for. She successfully transformed me into Betty Rizzo. I expected the wig to do all the work, but the faux freckles, the cherry lipstick, and the darkened brows have really helped me to embody this character.

"Looks good," she compliments.

"I love it."

"Get your Pink Ladies jacket and head downstairs."

I hurry across the hall as Ms. Ward rushes down the steps. I grab my jacket and my stylish, purse-like overnight bag. Before heading down, I take one last look at myself. Perfect. This is exactly how I envisioned myself looking for this dance. The only thing left to hope for is that Michael pulls off the Kenickie look.

I move quickly down the staircase. The silence is worrisome. I call for Ms. Ward. She doesn't respond. I walk into the kitchen. The smoke escaping the grill on the deck catches my eye.

"What the hell?" I mutter to myself. I walk toward the sliding door and pull it open.

"Happy birthday!" Ms. Ward shouts.

I jump in surprise. As I step onto the deck, a smile takes over my face. I spot my boyfriend, Indigo, Warren, and Eugene. Alicia, Ms. Ward's assistant, is holding a lit cake, and a handsome, clean-cut, middle-aged gentleman is working the grill. I have no idea who he is.

I approach my birthday guests. Ms. Ward puts her arm around me as they sing "Happy Birthday" off-key. Laughter escapes me as I look at my friends' attire. Indigo is the sexy version of Sandy. Warren is dressed as the prep school version of Danny. Eugene is dressed almost identically to Warren. Only thing he's missing is the letter sweater. I'm not sure who he's supposed to be portraying. Michael is dressed in rolled-up jeans, a light-blue tee, and his T-Birds jacket. His hair is still undone.

Alicia brings me the cake, and I blow out the candles in a single breath. Indigo and Ms. Ward are the only two who clap.

"Thanks, everybody."

Ms. Ward smiles broadly. "Did I surprise you?"

I nod. "You did. You all did."

"I'll let you chitchat with your friends in a second. I want to introduce you to someone." She leads me toward the gentleman flipping burgers on the grill.

"This is Corey. He's a friend of mine. Corey, this is Jaylen."

I shake hands with Ms. Ward's so-called friend. The name Corey isn't at all unfamiliar. His name has shown up many times on the house caller ID. He's also the only call she has to take in private when her cell rings.

"Happy eighteenth."

"Thank you," I tell him. "Thank you, too, Ms. Ward. This was really nice of you."

"You haven't seen anything yet," she hints with a wink.

I thank Alicia for coming as well before heading over to my school friends. I hug each of them, starting with Indigo and ending with Michael.

I playfully insult them. "You guys look like a bunch of Hollywood rejects."

We all laugh.

"You're blending," Warren shoots back. "So what does that say about you?"

"Shut your mouth, Warren. I look the most like my character." I turn to Eugene. "You guys supposed to be twins?"

"Who?" Eugene asks.

"You and Warren."

"No. I'm Johnny Castle. He's the dude from *Grease*."

I ask, "So where's Baby?"

"I'm meeting Mia there."

Indigo scoffs. "Really, Eugene? You can't do any better than that bitch?"

I clear my throat. "Let's keep this PG, please. Ms. Ward is right there."

"My bad, Jaylen. I'm just saying, the broad can't be trusted. She just can't stop running her mouth."

Eugene smiles. "It won't be running tonight. Tonight her

mouth will be full."

Michael and Warren dap him up as Indigo and I look at him in disgust.

"So, about the dance," I say with my eyes on Indigo. "People are gonna think we planned this."

"I know, right?"

"We're pretty much wearing the same thing. This is crazy."

She touches my store-bought hair. "I can't believe you're wearing a wig."

"Rizzo doesn't have long hair, and I was not about to cut mine for a school dance."

Ms. Ward walks over. "Can I get you guys anything? The ribs and burgers aren't quite done, but the hot dogs are."

As the boys grab plates, Indigo and I head inside. The boys meet us in my room. Michael sits in my swivel desk chair, Indigo lies across my bed as Warren sits at the foot, Eugene cops a squat on my floor, and I relax comfortably on my window seat.

I ask, "So how did Ms. Ward get in touch with all of you?"

"She texted me that she was having a little barbecue for you. She asked me to invite a few of your closest friends from school," Indigo explains.

Michael looks at Indigo. "You didn't invite me."

My eyes move to Indigo.

"Because I figured Ms. Ward would invite you herself."

I look from Indigo to Michael, and then back to Indigo again. His eyes pierce hers, and she coldly stares back, never blinking. They're not even pretending to like each other anymore. They detest one another and don't seem to care who knows it or who they make uncomfortable.

I realize that I really do need to have a sit-down with her. Having a crush on someone and not having those feelings returned is a hard thing for anyone to accept, but being in charge of my birthday guest list and excluding my boyfriend only proves that Indigo is far from ready to let go of those feelings.

The dirty looks were easy to ignore, but this isn't. What would've happened if I had slid open that door and not seen my boyfriend? I may have been able to smile while blowing out the candles, but learning that Indigo was in charge of my guest list and didn't put him on it would've likely resulted in an argument. Indigo is taking things way too far. It's clear. She's lost her damn mind.

As bad as I want to pull her to the side and discuss this, I don't. I hold off and enjoy my birthday celebration, laughing and talking with my friends over the next couple of hours.

After Ms. Ward gels Michael's hair past the point no return, and then overloads her camera with photos of us all, we breeze through the cake and presents, and finally wrap up my birthday get-together at close to nine o'clock.

"Did you enjoy yourself?"

"I did. Thank you so much, Ms. Ward. I really didn't expect this."

We head for the front door, my overnight bag in hand. My friends are already outside.

"I didn't get a chance to ask, but would it be okay with you if I spent the night at Indigo's? She's a little sour about me never going to her house."

"Sure. That's fine with me. Did her aunt agree?"

I nod, but it's a lie. "She said she'd be happy to have me."

"Just keep your phone on and water nearby."

"Always," I reply.

"You riding with Michael?" she asks as we walk out the front door.

"Yup."

"You don't want to ride in something else?"

I chuckle. "Like what? Your Benz?"

"Not a chance." She points to a silver Volvo in the driveway. "Maybe that, though."

My jaw drops. "What is that?"

"Your birthday and graduation present."

I place my hand over my forehead. "Ms. Ward, this is too much."

"It's not. You deserve it. You're going to need reliable transportation to get you to and from school."

"I didn't want you to spend this much," I whisper.

"Are you kidding me, Jaylen? I wouldn't buy something I can't afford. And it's not new. It's a 2010 S-40. Great crash reports. Very safe car. I got a good deal on it."

I walk to my new used car. I look at my friends. Happiness for me covers each of their faces. I then turn to Ms. Ward. She finds it so pleasing to do nice things for me. As overwhelming and as nosy as she can be at times, the love she feels for me is hard to not return.

"This is nice," Indigo says in admiration. "Good-bye, bus."

I open the driver-side door. The new car smell escapes even though the car is five years old.

Michael places his hand on my lower back. "Get in."

I step inside and search the car with my eyes. "I haven't driven in a while."

"It hasn't been that long. Plus, it's like riding a bike. You can go for years without doing it, but you'll never forget how," he tells me.

I ask, "Ride with me?"

Michael smiles. "Follow me home."

He pushes my door closed and heads for his car. I put the driver-side window down as Ms. Ward heads over. She bends.

"Before you say anything, I want to thank you again. I appreciate this, all of this, more than words. I couldn't imagine having a better eighteenth birthday." I take her hand in mine. "I didn't know how today would feel without my mom being here, but you made today beautiful in every way." I take a deep breath. "I love you for all that you've done for me, even the things you did when I was too young to really appreciate them."

She places her hand over her heart. "You don't know what that means to me, Jaylen. I rarely come across people your age who are so grateful and appreciative of the things they receive. You've done more for me than you realize." She hands me a bottle of water. "Have a good time tonight. Call me after the dance and let me know when you make it to Indigo's."

"I will."

She pinches my cheek. "Drive safely. Love you."

As Ms. Ward walks back toward the house, I wave and thank Corey and her assistant. Slowly, I shift the gear into drive. I plan to pull off immediately, but I freeze. I just started riding in the passenger seat again, and now, here I am behind the wheel.

I place my jittering hands on the steering wheel. In an attempt to calm myself, I close my eyes and remember my mom's voice. I recall her words. *You control the car. The car doesn't control you. Anyone can learn how to drive, Jaylen, but it's a personal choice to drive sensibly.*

I reopen my eyes, and as her words replay in my mind, I slowly follow Michael toward his home. Warren, Indigo, and Eugene head for the school.

I pull into Michael's driveway. As he locks his car in his garage, I climb over to the passenger side. He walks toward the Volvo, and I point him toward the driver seat. He questions me with his hands before walking around the front of the car to take the seat I was just in.

"You don't wanna drive your new whip?" he asks, climbing in.

"I already did."

As we take the short drive to Trinity, I ask, "How come you didn't mention the barbecue to me earlier?"

"I was asked not to."

"So Ms. Ward invited you?"

"Yup. Your girl sure didn't."

"I'm gonna talk to her about that."

"Don't do it tonight. No drama tonight. It's your birthday. Let's have a good time. Y'all can discuss that tomorrow."

I move my head in agreement before locking my eyes on my boyfriend.

"What?" he asks.

"You look so cute. Ms. Ward did her thing on your hair. You definitely got the Kenickie look down."

"You look sexy. Do you know how hard it was for me to watch you walk around in that skirt and not touch you?"

I giggle.

"I'm serious. You got a fatty, Jaylen."

"Believe me, I heard that every day at my old school. I think it's too fat."

He shakes his head. "No such thing."

I pick at my nail tips. "Do you like the way I look tonight?"

"You actually look cute with short hair. I like it. I'm glad you didn't pile on the makeup. I didn't know how much dressing up you planned on doing. Just so you know, for future reference, I'll stop looking at you if you start painting your face."

We sit in the school parking lot, my hand in his.

"Are you gonna dance with me, handsome?"

"Dance? Me?"

I lighten my tone. "Please."

"I'm not a dancer, Jaylen."

"Most guys aren't, but you can still try."

"I don't know. We'll see."

"If you don't dance with me, I'm just gonna have to find someone else to."

He lets out a sarcastic chuckle. "Yeah, okay. Come on."

We head for the front doors of Trinity. I walk beside my Kenickie, our fingers interlocked.

"Hey, Jaylen. Hey, Michael," Josh greets.

Michael hands Josh our tickets. "What's up, Josh?"

"You're Jack, right?" I ask. His suspenders and hair are a dead giveaway.

He nods. "And you guys are Rizzo and Kenickie."

I smile. "Yup. Where's your Rose?"

"Inside. I'm just giving Mrs. Delaney a bathroom break. I'll see you guys in there."

We head for the school cafeteria. All of the tables have been moved, and the only available seating is the booths lining the walls. The lights are dim, stars hang from the ceiling, balloons float on each side of a makeshift stage, and students are everywhere.

"What's the stage for?" I ask.

Michael shrugs.

We walk across the cafeteria. As Katy Perry plays loudly, we join Warren, Eugene, Mia, Indigo, and two others: Mark, another basketball player, and Ayana from my Sociology class.

"Happy birthday!" Ayana yells as we approach.

"Thanks, Ayana. I've never seen your hair straight. It's beautiful. So long."

"It took forever."

"I bet. Looks good, though, Pocahontas."

She flips her hair with a smile. "Thanks. Did you guys plan this? You and Indigo?"

My eyes move to Indigo. "No. We actually didn't tell each other who we were planning to dress up as. We just found out today."

Ayana strokes my synthetic wig. "I love the short hair on

you."

I smile at the flattery. "Thank you."

"And I love the old school look on you, Mike. Y'all did it up."

Michael pops his jacket collar at Ayana's compliments.

As we sit and chat, I notice that while I'm comfortable talking to everyone at the table, no words are exchanged between Michael and Indigo, or between Indigo and Mia. It doesn't bother me that Indigo and Mia no longer have a friendship, but I hate the fact that Michael and Indigo aren't on good terms. I'm so close to both of them. The tension between them is always present. It's palpable.

Josh drifts over to our table. "Here are your ballots."

As I read over the names, I spot my name and Michael's. "I didn't ask to be put on here," I tell Josh.

"Your names were submitted."

"By who?"

He looks at Michael.

"I didn't submit anything," Michael says.

Indigo laughs. Our eyes move to her.

"I didn't think you'd mind me entering you." Her eyes on me. "You spent a lot to look like this character."

"Do you want me to pull your names?" Josh asks.

Michael shakes his head. "It's all good."

I read over the names and look around the room for the couples.

"What are you doing?"

I turn to Michael. "I'm trying to be fair. I want to see the other costumes."

He takes my ballot. "Are you serious? Look at yourself."

Michael votes for us before taking our two ballots to submit them.

"Are you mad?" Indigo asks me.

I roll my eyes. "I'm not mad, but I didn't expect to be put on the spot. I hope we don't win. I do not want to stand on stage in front of everyone."

She laughs. "I can't believe you have stage fright."

"I don't. I just don't like unnecessary attention. I don't like all eyes on me. It makes me feel very uncomfortable."

Warren chimes in. "Um, I think that's called stage fright."

We all laugh.

Though I still don't feel as close to humans as I do to Indigo and Michael, I feel so much more comfortable around the friends I've made here at Trinity than the friends I've had for years back home. Michael and Indigo gave me that comfort. I'm not the only outsider here. Because I'm around others like me, I feel more comfortable with myself and can enjoy normal teenage things as opposed to trying to figure out why I'm so different from everyone else.

Indigo stands. "Let's dance."

Ayana nudges me, and I scoot out of the large booth. Mia stands and pulls Eugene up with her. Warren remains seated.

"You don't wanna dance?" Indigo asks her date.

"I'll meet y'all over there. Let me holla at my boys real quick."

Michael sits back down with Mark and Warren, and the rest of us make our way over to a free area on the dance floor. As Calvin Harris sings, we move to the beat. Indigo and I hold hands and dance, all smiles and nothing but sincere happiness.

Indigo motions with her head for me to look to my left. I look over at Eugene and Mia. She is definitely stepping into her role as a dirty dancer, and the song playing isn't even a twerk song. I grab Ayana's hand and continue to dance with my girls. Our smiles are big. My birthday is exactly what I hoped it would be.

We continue to move to the music, only taking breaks to either sip some water or wait for a better song to come on.

Time flies by after Michael, Warren, and Mark join us on the floor. Before we know it, the ballots have been counted, and it's time to announce the best-dressed couple.

"I think we won," Michael whispers.

My voice low, I say, "If we did, it's because all of your fans voted for you."

He kisses my forehead.

I'm nervous as hell. My hand trembles inside of Michael's as I silently wish for another couple to be called.

"Good luck," Indigo wishes me with a smile.

I flip her the bird, and loud laughter escapes her.

"All right, ladies and gentlemen. Calm yourselves." Mrs. Delaney holds a paper out in front of her. "The ballots have been tallied. The wait is over." She holds the paper closer to her face. "Tonight's best dressed couple is…"

My eyes are on my red, round-toe pumps. My nerves are at their peak.

"Jaylen Hayes dressed as Betty Rizzo, and Michael Reed dressed as Kenickie!"

As our fellow classmates applaud us, I slowly walk toward the stage with my hand in my boyfriend's. At this very moment, I want to throw a shoe at Indigo.

Mrs. Delaney asks, "What made you guys choose this couple?"

I take a deep, cleansing breath. "We wanted to be a couple from *Grease*, and Sandy and Danny were already selected."

"So it wasn't the actual characters?"

"No," I answer. "Not at all."

"Good. I'm glad to hear that."

Our fellow schoolmates laugh.

"What about you, Michael?" she asks.

He smiles that smile I love. "Come on now, Mrs. Delaney. A hickey from Kenickie is better than a birthday card."

The room fills with loud laughter.

"Almost got it, Mr. Reed."

Our picture is taken for the yearbook, and we're sent off-stage with large tins full of gourmet popcorn.

"Congratulations!" Indigo shouts.

I look at her through narrowed eyes. "Payback. That's all I'm gonna say."

Her head falls back in laughter.

We head back over to the booth we were sitting in, but none of us take a seat. I place my tin on the table, and Warren quickly grabs it and struggles to remove the top.

I elbow Warren in the side. "Thanks for asking."

"Oh, you're welcome."

He removes the lid. There are three different flavors separated inside. Caramel, butter, and cheese. He digs in and begins crunching away on a handful of cheese kernels.

Indigo asks me, "So what are you doing afterward?"

"I'm going home."

"Can I spend the night?"

"I can't have company tonight. Ms. Ward and I are gonna pull an all-nighter." I think on my toes. "There's some kind of marathon showing, and we're gonna watch it together."

"Bonding?"

"I guess that's what we'll be doing."

As Warren munches away on a prize he didn't win, we move to the beat of the music while conversing about prom. We argue over what kind of limo to get. While I really don't care about the limousine, they're going back and forth about whether or not to get the Hummer or the Excursion.

"Why does it matter?" I ask.

Eugene's face twists. "Because it's prom."

"You're not even a senior. Your input doesn't count."

Eugene laughs and continues to argue his point in the limo debate.

Indigo grabs my arm. "Do you hear that?"

We run in our heels to the dance floor to move to an overly edited edition of Nicki Minaj's "Starships." We've been waiting all night to hear a Beyoncé or Nicki song, though we weren't sure that the school would play any of their hits.

Indigo, Ayana, and I dance and sing loudly to the music. Other students move closer to us to sing and dance along. In this moment, I feel happier than I've ever truly felt.

Our dates walk over to us and begin mimicking our moves. I dance with my boyfriend, and my friends dance with their dates. Nothing could make this night any more perfect. Nothing except spending the night alone with Michael.

Chapter 14

We all exit the building. Michael and I head for my Volvo alongside Indigo and Warren. I had so much fun dancing the night away, I was able to briefly escape the reality that Indigo's feelings for Michael are far more serious than mere dislike. Her feelings have pushed her to take control of things in inappropriate ways. I promised Michael I wouldn't discuss my issues with her tonight, so I won't. They won't be forgotten, though. I will be confronting her sooner rather than later.

"Where y'all going?" Warren asks.

Michael answers, "I'm going home. She's dropping me off and then heading back to her spot."

"You sure you don't need a ride?" Warren asks Indigo.

"I'm good. I'm going to Kennedy's."

"Where does Kennedy live?" I ask.

She points in the direction of Michael's house. "Up that way."

I nod. "Okay. Well, get there safely. Good night, guys."

I hug her first, and then Warren. Michael and I make a quick stop at the CVS to pick up what my boyfriend cannot go without: beef jerky and ranch-flavored sunflower seeds. Then we head for his house.

He taps my leg. "You friends with Kennedy?"

"No. We've actually never even spoken. She's Indigo's friend. Do you know her?"

"Nope. Even when I was cool with Indigo, I never spoke to her."

"I never see her and Indigo hang out. I didn't even see her at the dance."

"I didn't either."

I turn in my seat to make sure I remembered my overnight bag as Michael pulls into his driveway. He shifts my car into park before releasing his seatbelt.

"Did you have fun?"

I nod excitedly. "I had a really good time. Did you?"

"Yeah. It was better than I thought it would be. And I won some popcorn."

I chuckle. "You should thank all of your little groupies for your win on Monday."

He laughs. "I will."

I touch his gelled hair. He grabs my hand and kisses the back of it. Tingles move through my palm and up my arm.

"You gonna be okay driving home?"

I shrug.

He caresses my cheek. "You could always stay."

"Stay and what?"

"Whatever. Talk, cuddle, watch a movie. If you're tired, you can always go to sleep. Whatever you wanna do."

I smile at Michael. His closed-lip smile matches mine.

"Can you park in the garage?" I ask.

No hesitation. He uses his keychain to open the garage door and pulls up beside his much-loved Camaro. As the garage door lowers, we step out.

"Grab my bag, please," I say.

"Bag?"

"Yeah. I need my clothes and stuff."

His smile widens and reveals his beautiful whites. "I thought that was just a ridiculously big purse. So you already planned on spending the night here?"

"I thought maybe I should comfort you."

He grabs my bag. "Comfort me?"

"Yeah. This is a big house to spend the night alone in. Plus, you think you're being stalked by a ghost."

A ball of laughter escapes him.

We head up the stairs and into his bedroom. He places my bag on the floor, and I pull off my wig.

"Damn," he mumbles.

I turn to him. "What's wrong?"

"I'll be right back. I left my phone in the car."

As he heads back down to get his cell, I kick out of my red pumps. I place them in his closet, just as neatly as the rest of the shoes. I then text Ms. Ward a lie. I tell her that I safely arrived at Indigo's. I thank her once again for the party and then tell her that I'll see her sometime tomorrow afternoon.

As I wait for Michael to come back up, I pull a T-shirt, a pair of shorts, a pair of rainbow knee-high socks, and undergarments from my bag. I also pull out my zip-locked bag of toiletries, before covering my pinned-up curls in preparation for a shower.

After minutes of waiting, Michael finally returns. His expression is far from the happy one he left with.

I move to him. "Everything all right?"

"I felt it again."

"The presence?"

He nods.

"Where at?"

"In the garage," he explains as he sits at the end of his bed.

"You okay? Do you feel safe?"

He nods. His shaky smile is recognizably fake.

"You said you don't see anything. Do you hear anything?"

"Nothing."

I begin to feel uneasy. Though I haven't felt this presence he speaks of, his discomfort affects me.

I tell him, "I'm gonna go get a bottle of water."

"I'll get it."

As he stands, I tell him, "We'll get it."

We walk down into the kitchen. I grab an opened bottle of water from the island and take a few sips.

"That yours?"

I shake my head. "It was just sitting here. I assumed it was yours. I don't believe in wasting water."

He takes the bottle from me. "I don't know where the hell this came from. Moms doesn't buy this brand."

I move about the kitchen. Still, I don't feel a presence. I walk toward the door that leads to the garage. I inhale the faint smell of a familiar scent and immediately, I stop.

"What?" he asks.

"I thought I smelled Indigo's perfume."

"You probably smell it on yourself. Y'all danced and hugged all night."

I ask, "Feel anything now?"

He shakes his head. "I'm probably just trippin'. And I probably brought the water in with me from the dance."

I offer him a warm smile.

He rechecks the house alarm and tells me, "There's nobody in here. Don't feel weird, babe. I'm just being paranoid."

I tell him, "I want to take a shower. Is that okay?"

"Yeah. Take yours in the hall bathroom. I'll take mine in my mom's."

We head back upstairs to take showers. As I wash, I think about tonight. I think about losing my virginity. Once it's gone, you can't have the experience back. Once you let someone inside of your body for the first time, your feelings for them are going to skyrocket whether you want them to or not. I question myself. Am I ready to have even stronger feelings for Michael? We don't even know if we'll be living in the same area after graduation.

I dry off and dress myself. My pajamas, far from sexy. After brushing my teeth, I let down my hair. My curls are still defined. I put on deodorant, and moisturize my arms and legs. My goal is to make my way back across the hall and into Michael's room before he does.

I quickly jump into bed and situate myself comfortably. While waiting for Michael to get out of the shower, I flip through channels, instantly stopping at *Beavis and Butt-Head Do America*. I check my phone. Indigo's text questions if I made it home. I answer, telling her I have.

Michael enters wearing navy-blue, checkered lounge pants, no shirt, and with a white towel wrapped around his neck. My eyes go right to his abs.

"You're ripped." My tone reveals surprise.

He smiles his smile. Damn, I love that smile. It's so picture-perfect. So dreamy.

He points at the screen. "Are you really watching this?"

"This is Beavis and Butt-head. Of course I'm watching this. My old neighbor put me on. It's hilarious."

He throws his towel across his desk chair.

I considerately ask, "Do you wanna watch something else?"

He nods. "And I wanna talk to my girl."

As he cuts off his light, I lower the volume on my phone.

"Do you mind if I take these off?" he asks respectfully as he tugs at the waistband of his lounge pants.

"Do you have something under them?"

He chuckles. "Yes, Jaylen. I do wear underwear."

My stomach sinks when he removes his pants. He climbs

onto the bed in his black boxer briefs and lies back on top of the comforter. I lower the volume on the television and turn to my side.

"So, how do you feel?" he asks.

"About what?"

"Today. You turned eighteen. You got a car."

"That was a little too much for me. Ms. Ward is taking this foster parent thing to a whole new level."

"She cares, Jaylen."

"And I can appreciate that she does. I didn't plan on leaving and never coming back, but now I feel obligated to come back more often. I'm sure she didn't buy me a car expecting to see me only once a year."

"That's true."

I sigh. "I'm gonna have to talk to her. As much as I do appreciate and care for Ms. Ward, she isn't my mother. I appreciate her making my senior year much better than it could've been, but I'm at an age where I'm not looking to feel like anyone's child."

"Yeah, you better talk to her, then. If you get into..." He sucks his teeth. "You're a straight-A student. What am I talking about?" He chuckles. "*When* you get into Princeton, where are you gonna stay? In the dorms?"

"No. Even if there's some kind of requirement, I'm gonna find a way to work around that. My mom left me the house." I swallow. "I'm going back home."

"The house?"

I add, "And her life insurance policy."

His eyebrows rise. "Why didn't you say anything?"

"I just found out today. It doesn't change anything, though. You knew I was going back to Jersey."

"That's love right there. Your mom was young. She could've waited to get insurance like most people do, and you would've been left assed out. I'm happy for you. I'm happy you were given to someone like her."

"Me too. I was definitely lucky."

"Blessed," he corrects.

I think back on my childhood. "She wasn't my first foster home, though."

He props himself up on his elbow. "Really?"

"She was my third. My first foster family consisted of a middle-aged couple. They were white. They fostered me even though they already had three kids of their own and one adopted. The adopted one was Asian. They were planning to adopt me if I was ever freed for adoption, but at the time, we were still waiting to see if my mother or any other relatives would turn up."

"What happened?"

"I got into a fight with one of their children. She just kept picking on me. Everything I touched was hers. Everything I did was wrong. One day, she pushed me in front of all her friends, screaming that I wasn't really a part of her family, and I guess you can say that was the straw that broke the camel's back." I briefly pause. "I punched her in her face, and I ended up fracturing her jaw bone."

Michael massages his lower jaw.

"I didn't mean to. I told Ms. Ward that when she talked to me about it. I was placed with one more family before meeting Mrs. Hayes. When I first met my mom, she was married. They were looking to first foster and then adopt. You know the rest."

"No, I don't. What happened to her husband?"

"He left her for another woman. She actually seemed happy about it. He signed away all parental rights. Since I was already adopted, I guess I just became her child. After that, it was just me and her. Me and my mommy. I preferred it that way. Nothing about him seemed sincere anyway."

He touches my face.

I soften my tone as I approach a sensitive subject. "Michael, why don't you talk about your father?"

"Why would I?"

"Because he's your father."

His face tightens. His nostrils expand.

"You don't want to at least know what he looks like?"

"No," he replies immediately. "I have no interest in him and no respect for him. He's a bitch. What kind of man walks out on his woman and child?"

"What does your mom say about him?"

"She says that she's not angry with him about it and that I shouldn't be, either."

"That's it?"

"I mean, she tries to talk to me about him, but I don't wanna hear it. I don't wanna hear my mother make excuses for a loser."

"Maybe you should listen. If your mom isn't angry, your father may not be the monster you think he is."

Michael doesn't respond.

I can understand his anger. He feels walked-out on. Abandoned. Nothing about that pill is easy to swallow. I just wish he'd vent to me, even cry if he felt the need to. The same openness he wants from me, I want from him.

My boyfriend's icy expression forces me to change the subject. Nothing makes Michael turn so cold except the mention of his father.

I look him in the eye. "Can I ask you something about your mom?"

"Go ahead."

"I'm not trying to be rude. I've just been curious."

"What?"

"The picture in your living room. If we dry out when we die, and that's what we look like, why have a picture of someone's remains on your living room wall?"

He lets out a brief laugh. "I ask her the same shit all the time. It's morbid."

"What does she say?"

"She loves it. She says when she looks at it, she doesn't feel pain or see my grandmother. She thinks of my father. She says only an individual with a truly beautiful heart could make death look so beautiful."

"Hmm," I let out softly.

"Plus, she's obsessed with those damn things. They haven't changed over the years, but she still likes to look at them under the microscope, take notes, and—"

"Under the microscope?" I ask, interrupting him. I lift up a little. "You have one of the cocoon things?"

"My mom has a few. She's not a scientist, but she thinks she's gonna learn something by staring at them. Or maybe she's just expecting them to change at some point."

"Why haven't you shown me one?"

"I don't really look at them. I wasn't trying to keep them from you, or hide that my mom has a few. I mean, I do think it's a little weird that she keeps them, but if you want to see one, I'll make sure that happens. I know my mom wouldn't have a problem with that."

"I want to see one."

He gently pushes me back down. "You'll see one. I promise. Just not tonight. I don't wanna spend tonight, of all nights, looking at dead things."

I nod. "Okay. Just don't forget."

"You have my word."

I take a deep breath. "Can I ask you one last thing?"

"Shoot."

"You were grounded when I first started going to Trinity. Your mom didn't allow you to drive. But she knows we run the risk of being attacked by animals. Isn't that kind of like throwing you to the wolves, making you walk every day?"

"She actually thought I was taking the bus. There's a stop right at the corner. My walk would've literally been under a minute every day. I just can't mess with the bus anymore. Not as an upperclassman. Plus, it's not common for us to be confronted. Most animals that we're likely to come in contact with run from us. Squirrels, birds, normal deer."

I laugh lightly.

He chuckles. "I don't know what that buck was on."

"I know, right? I've never been confronted by a deer. A dog, once. No deer. That was scary beyond belief."

"Dogs usually bark at me and growl. I've seen some try to break their leash to come after me, but no attacks."

"Lucky you."

"No. Lucky you. At least you can defend yourself."

"So can you," I reply softly. "I just don't like hurting, or worse, killing animals. I don't even like using my strength. It wears me the hell out. I'm so worried about having to defend myself against some crazy animal, exhausting myself, and then dying, because I can't make it to water fast enough."

He softly touches my hair. "You're gonna be fine."

"Everyone bumps into a mean dog every once in a while, but we always have to have our guards up. No matter where we go, there's likely to be some kind of animal acting out, because of our presence. Most of them do run, but some become aggressive." I think back to one of the scariest moments of my childhood. "After I was adopted, my mom took me to the farm. I begged her to take me to the movies, but she was dead set on taking me to the farm." I shake my head at the thought of that day. "The animals. Michael, I can't begin to describe the fear of being around so many at one time and having them all react so violently. We barely got through the entrance gate, and the madness began. The goats started charging into their fences, a horse threw a child from its back, and one of the damn cows actually broke out of its enclosure. It was terrifying. My mom grabbed me up, and ran me back to our car. Before she could pull off, a damn emu came running. This huge, dinosaur-looking bird started pecking at the window. I screamed until we made it back to the highway."

"Damn, babe. That sounds scary as shit. Moms knew better, so I never went to farms or zoos."

"Oh, best believe, I never went to a zoo. Not another farm, either. My mom never understood why the animals acted that way, but she never pressured me to go near animals ever again. I guess it kind of worked out."

"I guess it did," he says softly.

I reveal a small smile. "Tonight shouldn't be sad or depressing. Sorry to hit you with a story like that, especially after all those questions."

"It's fine. You know you can tell me anything, and you can always ask me anything."

My smile stretches across my face.

"Okay. My turn now."

I grunt unpleasantly. "Really, Michael?"

"You can question me, but I can't question you?"

I whine, "It's my birthday."

"Wrong. It's after midnight."

I suck my teeth.

"I only wanna ask you one thing. I know I dig deep sometimes, but just one question."

"One question, and then we're watching a movie."

"Deal," he agrees. "It's the crying thing. You have to explain that to me again."

"I don't really know how to explain it well."

"Try," he urges.

I look my boyfriend in the eye. "Crying is just really uncomfortable for me. When my mother was alive, I really had no reason to cry. When I found an empty bed, I didn't know what to do. A part of me felt that she was gone, and another part of me believed she was coming back. Since then, I've just held it in because I knew that I was different from everyone else. I didn't want people hugging all over me and telling me they understood when there's no possible way that they could. I had no place I could really fit into until I got here." I draw in a deep breath and release it slowly. "So, crying just feels weird. I want to sometimes, but since I've always felt that I'm the only person who can come close to really understanding me, I just keep it inside. I keep it to myself. It's damn hard to do that, but I've become an expert at just shaking the tears away."

"If you ever feel like crying—and I do mean ever, Jaylen, two in the morning, whenever—call me. I have two shoulders. You can always borrow one."

My heart swells with love.

"I'm serious. You'll never become that famous painter you want to be if you keep holding in how you feel. Stress kills."

"Famous? I never said I wanted to be famous. Just successful. I don't need my picture in the paper and all that. I just want people to enjoy my work."

"You don't want to be a celebrity artist?"

"I don't want to be a celebrity anything."

He sucks his teeth. "Everyone wants to be famous."

I reply quickly, "Not this girl."

"Why not? What do you have against fame? Against Hollywood?"

"Well, for the most part, I like me, and Hollywood would try to change that."

"How so?"

"For starters, my nose."

"I love your nose."

"It's round, though."

"You're black, Jaylen."

"You're missing my point, Michael. I don't give a damn what celebrities do. I don't care who hacks up what on their bodies, but I'm an everyday, average-looking female. That doesn't exist in Hollywood. Fame nowadays is about looks. Talent comes third to your face and body."

"You'll be the exception."

I scoff. "Maybe. I just wanna do what makes me happy. I'm not looking to be on the front cover of magazines. I'm not looking to be judged by the world. I just want to draw."

"So, no plastic surgery for you? There's nothing you'd hack up or change?"

"If I could, I'd have the accident scars removed. I wouldn't change anything I was born with. I'm not changing my face. I don't ever wanna look in the mirror and feel as though I've lost myself or the features that remind me of my biological mother. This is me. Human or not, I look like this for a reason."

"Damn." His voice is low.

"Damn, what?"

"I didn't think it was possible, but you're even sexier to me now."

I let out a soft giggle.

"Too bad more girls aren't as comfortable in their skin."

"Don't get me wrong. I have my insecurities. Everybody does. I just think most girls today have insecurities because of what Hollywood displays. Most girls in high school are flawed. Whether it's a weight problem, acne, or bad teeth, there's usually something. When they turn on the television to watch their so-called idols, they're not seeing reality. They're seeing flawless, overly made-up, size-two girls. This is why these beautiful young ladies out here are starving themselves, making their faces up at twelve, hating themselves if they have a darker complexion, and suffering from depression before even graduating." I catch my breath. "I know that there are some naturally beautiful girls out here. I've seen plenty. I'm not saying Hollywood or magazine companies should hide those girls. They should show the naturally beautiful girls, but they should also hire talented women with flaws. Flaws are a part of reality. Why hide that?"

"So that's why you watch older flicks?"

I nod. "Things seem more real in older movies. I mean, some of them are a little too dramatic for my taste, but for the most part, most of my favorites were filmed in the 80's or before. That's because real talent is displayed in those films. Superb acting was a requirement. Looking hot wasn't enough."

Michael licks his lips. "You're probably one of the realest people I know. I like the way your mind works."

"Oh, really? Funny you say that, because something in my mind tells me to do things before the last minute. Did you get fitted for a tux yet?"

Michael looks at me and then quickly looks away.

"Prom is in three weeks. What the hell are you waiting for?"

"I'll have it. We're still wearing royal blue, right?"

I sigh. "Yes. And you better stop waiting until the very last second to do everything."

"You get your dress yet?"

"Mm-hmm."

"You got the short one, right?"

"Yeah. The long one didn't look right."

My mind goes to my prom dress. I love it. It's simple, just the way I like things. It's a strapless, royal-blue, above-the-knee, pick up dress. Now that I've seen for myself that Catholic school dances can be just as exciting as public school dances, I cannot wait for my senior prom.

"Do you think you're gonna win prom king?"

"I don't know now."

"What do you mean?"

"After your little speech in Sociology, Josh might win."

I crack up. "Shut up. Do you wanna win?"

"I probably will, but I never cared about any of that shit. I'm just trying to graduate."

"You probably will? You know you're gonna get the votes. Stop fakin'."

He laughs. "I don't ask to be voted at any of these things. Girls just throw my name in cause they like my eyes. I swear if I didn't have green eyes, the freshest kicks, this curly shit that I don't even comb, and an old ass Camaro that still looks new, nobody would know my name. It's all about what you look like and what you got. You know this."

I think about prom. There's no question in my mind about who's going to be awarded prom queen. Indigo owns that title. Her face earned her that title probably as early as her freshman year.

"You wanna be prom queen?"

"Do you really have to ask me that foolishness? I didn't wanna win tonight. That stuff is just ridiculous to me. I don't get why so many people take it so seriously. If it's everybody's special night, give everybody a damn crown or tiara. Every girl who's always dreamed about being prom queen, and doesn't earn the title, will forever look back on prom night and remember that she didn't win. I say make everybody a winner or no one at all. I doubt very seriously that prom would be any less enjoyable if they skipped the stupid crowning ceremony."

He softly rubs my cheek. "You claim that you're just a logical thinker. You are, but you're really sensitive, too. You have a big heart, Jaylen."

I silently look over his gorgeous face. Slowly, my eyes move down to his chest.

"What's wrong?"

I make eye contact. "Nothing. I've just never laid in bed with a half-naked guy before."

The corners of his mouth rise. Our eyes are on one another. My heart is in my stomach. My body is yearning for his.

"So, am I on top of the comforter tonight?"

I shake my head slowly.

He eases beneath his warm blanket. Our faces are closer.

Our bodies are only inches apart with no thick cotton barrier in between.

"Warm?" he asks.

"Mm-hmm."

His right hand moves to my waist, then reaches around to grab the softer side of me. My body shifts.

"You're shaking," he whispers.

My voice is just as low. "I'm okay."

"I don't want you to do anything you're not ready to do, Jaylen. I know all guys say that, but I mean it."

I look into his eyes. I look at someone I not only trust, but love. My head and heart are both speaking to me, and I'm hearing the same thing.

"I want to," I tell him.

He doesn't blink. "I love you."

My heart skips a few beats. Though I can feel that he does, I've wanted to hear him utter those three little words that own such a big meaning for a while now.

"I love you, too."

Our lips meet. My stomach knots up in ways it never has. The way he touches me is so manly and still so tender. So soft.

I roll onto my back as I pull him on top of me. His lips move to my neck, and I exhale. I move my fingers through his hair. I inhale the scent of his freshly washed skin. I massage his back.

Michael pulls me into an upright position. As he begins to lift my shirt on both sides, I instantly stop him.

"What is it?" he asks.

"I don't want you to see the scars."

"Jaylen, you can't be serious. I think you're beautiful. Do you really think I care about a scar?"

"There is nothing beautiful about my scars."

"I won't look, and I won't touch them. I just wanna feel your skin against mine."

I've hated the marks since the accident, but in this moment, I hate them more than ever. Everything about Michael is perfect to the eye. Ideally, in this moment, I'd look just as perfect to him as he does to me. I don't care about how the rest of the world sees me, but his opinion counts.

He softly kisses my lips. "You're gorgeous. Perfect to me, flaws and all."

It's almost like he read my mind. Seems like I care more about my accident reminders than he does. No need to make tonight a struggle. I allow him to pull my shirt up over my head.

We lie back down. The feel of his skin is so silky and warm against mine. The way his hands move up and down my body is so sensitive. So seductive.

We kiss again as his hand finds its way inside my shorts. He pauses for just a moment, and then slips his hand inside my panties. My eyes remain closed as I moan, as Michael touches a part of me no other guy has ever seen or felt.

He pulls at my panty line. "We should take these off."

"Do you have anything?" I ask.

"Do I need something?"

"Definitely," I say sternly.

He gently pecks my lips before climbing off of me. As he reaches over the side of the bed, I ease out of my bottoms while still hidden beneath the comforter.

I ask, "Where do you keep them?"

"In between the mattresses."

"Why do you hide them?"

"Because every time my mom sees one, she wants to give me the damn talk."

I laugh and peek over at what will be protecting us from becoming parents too soon.

"Why is it red?" I ask.

"It's flavored?"

I grunt loudly.

"I'm not looking for that. I buy flavored ones because they don't smell."

"Regular condoms really smell that bad?"

He chuckles. "You really are a virgin."

He remains beneath the comforter as he applies our protection. I can feel my body tensing. It's about to happen. After years of wondering how this moment would play out and who I'd be in this moment with, I'm finally living it. Living it with Michael. Not just a cute guy that I kind of like, but a guy I really love. The only guy I've ever loved.

Michael slowly eases back on top of me. His eyes closely watch mine. He reconfirms that I'm okay with this, and then after months of desiring him, wanting him, and most recently craving him, our bodies become one.

His movements are slow, careful, passionate. There's no pain. This isn't just sex. I may be young, but I'm old enough to recognize love. And that's what this is. This is lovemaking.

My nerves slowly fade until they're no longer present. My insecurities become irrelevant. I'm in my love's arms and that's all I can feel; the pleasure of being with him and feeling him inside me.

We move together slowly. What usually lasts all of two minutes when demonstrated on television feels like forever to me. A beautiful forever I don't mind living. Minutes of pleasure pass, and I enjoy every single one.

His lips are right at my ear. "You okay?"

I nod.

He moves unhurriedly. Though this is something we've been talking about and have been anxious to do, this doesn't feel urgent. He isn't rushing. His pace, his whisper, and his soft kisses make this experience everything I want it to be. Everything I need this to be.

He interlocks his fingers with mine. Our lips meet again. He slightly picks up the pace, forcing us both to get louder. The inevitable is near, and I can tell.

As this once-in-a-lifetime experience comes to its end, my boyfriend's eyes gaze into mine. Our breathing is labored. My heartbeat, galloping. My body, completely satisfied.

He slowly climbs off of me. He pulls the towel from his desk chair and turns his back to me to privately clean himself.

I lie silently. I smile inside. I imagined this night several times, and my thoughts weren't nearly as perfect as tonight was.

He lies back down beside me. I pull the comforter up over my bra.

"Do you feel okay?" he asks, his voice low.

I smile, pleased. "I feel amazing. What about you?"

"Better than that."

My smile grows.

"I didn't hurt you, did I?"

I shake my head.

We silently look at one another. Though he sounded like he enjoyed me, I want to know if I felt as good to him as he did to me. I need to know for sure that I was all he had hoped for.

I nervously ask, "Was I okay?"

"Okay?"

"Yeah. Did I feel okay to you?"

He kisses me. "You sell yourself way too short, way too often. You didn't hear me?"

"I just want to be sure."

"I should be asking you that. Was I all you expected me to be?"

I don't hesitate. "You were better."

Relief and satisfaction show in his smile. He asks, "So no regrets?"

"None."

I search under the comforter with my feet.

"What are you doing?"

"I want to put my panties back on. Feels weird lying here

nude."

He quickly reaches down to grab my bottoms.

"Give them to me," I demand.

"No."

"Michael, I'm serious."

He throws them over by the door. "You want 'em? Go get 'em."

I cover my face and laugh. "I'm naked."

"No complaints here."

"You're such an asshole."

He laughs at my playful insult before checking his phone.

"Your mom?" I guess.

"No. My phone has been trippin'. I need to go to Sprint tomorrow."

I lie still and twirl my finger around one of my curls.

"What are you thinking about?" he asks.

"This was a first for you, too, right? You said you usually don't feel anything in sex."

"I mean, I feel something. It's just not like what I felt with you. What we just did, I could do every night. With the other girls, I was just going through the motions. The whole turned-on thing never happened before."

"Maybe because you were giving it to another species."

He chuckles quietly. "That's probably it."

"So," I let out slowly.

"So, what?"

"Can you enjoy yourself?"

"Masturbate?"

I giggle embarrassedly and nod.

"That's something every species can enjoy. But just like anything else, you get tired of it."

"So how often?" I ask. "Every day?"

"What is wrong with you? Hell no, not every day."

I laugh louder.

"Did you ever?"

I shake my head. "Never."

"Damn. I feel like I corrupted you."

I move closer to Michael. Our noses almost touch.

"You haven't done anything that I didn't want you to do."

We kiss.

Michael moves his hand around to my back. He fights with my bra clasp before finally unhooking it. I hold the cups in place.

"I can't see those, either, Jaylen?"

I silently look at my boyfriend. Even though we've already done it, I'm still not completely comfortable with him seeing my naked body. Though my breasts are unmarked, no one has ever seen them, and as silly as it may be, I'm not ready to show them and have them judged just yet.

"I'll tell you what," he whispers. Michael reaches across me for the remote and turns the television off. "Better?"

I allow him to remove my bra in the dark. He tosses it to the floor.

"You're a piece of work, Miss Hayes."

I smile, and just like that, we're back at it again.

Chapter 15

I open my eyes. I'm in Michael's arms. Have been all night. He's been spooning me since I closed my eyes. My back rests against his bare, warm chest allowing me to feel each beat of his heart. The beat helped me to sleep like a baby. I don't think I woke up even once for a sip of water. I've never slept so comfortably.

I try to quietly ease out of the spooning position as my body is begging for hydration. He pulls me back in place, holds me even tighter.

His voice cracks. "Where do you think you're going?"

I take his arm from around me. "To get water. I'm starting to hurt."

"Be still. I'll grab one for you."

I watch as Michael exits his room. As he heads downstairs to grab me a fresh bottle, I quickly put my shirt back on and crawl to the end of the bed to grab my shorts. I slide back inside them before he comes back up. While waiting for him to return, I sit Indian-style as I silently read through belated birthday messages.

"What the hell is that?"

I turn toward the doorway.

He points at me. "That. You know what I'm talking about."

I look down at my shirt.

"Why do you have that on?"

I don't answer. I bite my thumb nail and smile a "please don't be mad" smile at my boyfriend.

He climbs back into bed.

"You going back to sleep?"

He shakes his head.

As I gulp down some Deer Park, Michael flips through channels. I think about starting college. After last night, the thought of being without Michael is too painful to even imagine.

"You okay?" he asks.

I nod.

"Thinking about last night?"

"That, and moving away."

"Second thoughts?"

"No. I'm going back to Jersey. I'm just thinking about us. You know, our relationship. Long-distance is hard."

"I didn't know we were gonna be separated."

My expression asks Michael to explain himself.

"You don't want me to go with you?"

My eyes narrow.

"You don't?" he asks a second time.

"To do what, Michael? I would never selfishly ask for you to come to New Jersey just because I want to be with you. You can't leave your mother here. And you need to figure out what it is you want to do."

"I can't figure that out in Jersey?"

"What about your mom?"

"I was gonna leave anyway. My mom has a life here. I'm not just running out on her. She expects me to leave."

I keep my eyes on my boyfriend's. "What would you

do?"

"Get a job. Maybe intern. I'm definitely not gonna sit in your house on my ass all day. I'm taking a break from school. Not from life. I just want to be close to you. To me, what we have is serious. I want to continue what we've started."

"It's serious for me, too, Michael. You know that. I just want to do things the right way. I don't want you to leave impulsively and hurt your mother." I sigh. "And I don't want things to change between us."

He turns the television off and sits up. "Why would things change?"

I look down. "Because we've..." I don't finish the statement.

He takes my chin in between his thumb and pointer. Slowly, he lifts my face, and our eyes meet again. "Because we've had sex, things are gonna change?"

"That's usually the way it happens."

He takes a deep breath. "Where were you last night, Jaylen? All night, last night, where were you?"

I think about last night, sleeping so peacefully while Michael held me so close.

"In my arms, right?"

I don't respond.

"I would never hold somebody I don't care about. I would never say 'I love you' to someone I don't really love. I wouldn't lie to you, Jaylen. And I would never leave you."

I pick at my nails.

"Are you sure that you feel okay about last night?"

My voice is low. "Last night was amazing. I want more nights like last night. I want to be held the way you held me last night, every night. I don't want to be less special in your eyes because I gave it up. I want you to still look at me the same way, feel the same way, and still want me the way you did before."

He shakes his head. "That's not possible." His eyes stay

on mine. "I want you more than I did before. You're way more special in my eyes. I plan on holding you every night. I definitely plan on having many more nights like last night. Shit, days, too."

I let out a soft, short giggle.

He grabs my hand. "I love you. I really want you to believe that." His face moves in closer to mine. "I need you to believe that."

I tell him honestly, "I do."

He kisses my lips, and I smile. I truly do feel relieved. I love that no matter what I'm thinking, I can talk to him about it. I love that I can always tell him how I feel, and he takes my feelings seriously, addresses them, and finds a way to help me find comfort.

"I need to get home, Michael."

"Already?"

"What do you mean, already? It's almost one o'clock. Ms. Ward texted me. She wants to have my finished pieces framed and hung in the office today."

"Well, because you have a good reason, I won't get mad at you for getting dressed without asking. You never did thank me for giving you your panties and bra back, though. I was seriously gonna burn them."

Another soft giggle. "Thank you."

He winks at me, and I quickly climb off the bed to prepare for my day. After a quick shower, I brush my teeth, brush my hair back, dress, and head downstairs with Michael at my side. Surely I'd much rather spend this day cuddled up in bed with my boyfriend, but I can't push my responsibilities to the side. Life doesn't slow down because you're in love. I can't start slacking off or showing up late. Ms. Ward doesn't know where I am, but I don't want changes in me to reveal anything to her.

"You're going to your house first, right?"

"Mm-hmm."

We walk into the garage.

"You forgot to let the garage door down," I point out at first glance.

"I did let the door down. I remember."

"When you came back down to get your phone, did you reopen the door?"

"For what?"

I grab his hand. "I'm just asking."

He kisses my cheek. "I didn't mean for it to come out like that. I'm pretty sure I closed it, and I don't remember reopening it."

I offer him a soothing smile.

He exhales loudly. "I'm probably the one moving shit, leaving doors open, and all that. I've been paranoid as hell lately."

"I know. I've seen the change in you."

"I'll be all right, though. I don't want you worrying about me."

I place my bag in the backseat. After closing the door, I turn to hug my boyfriend tightly. "Call me, Michael. If you need to get out of the house, if you start feeling something's a little off, please let me know. I'll come back, or you can come over."

He nods. "I'll call you later. I'm gonna meet up with Warren."

"Playing ball?"

"Yeah. Then we're gonna work out."

I open the driver side door, and then turn to ask a question I keep forgetting to ask. "Can you dunk?"

"Hell yeah," he states proudly. "What kind of question is that?"

"You don't look that tall."

He folds his arms and straightens his posture. "How tall do I look?"

I guess, "Five-ten."

"Get your ass in the car."

Laughter bursts out of me.

"How tall are you?" he asks.

I fold my arms. "How tall do I look?"

"You damn sure ain't standing taller than five-two."

I roll my eyes and seat myself behind the wheel.

He smiles big. "Am I right?"

"Shut up."

"Say it. Tell me I'm right."

I suck my teeth. "I am shorter than five-two."

He squats down. "Don't take inches from me because you're vertically challenged."

I turn over the engine. "Whatever, Mr. Reed."

"Take pictures of your artwork. I want to see them."

"I definitely will. Skip your workout. Go find a tux."

"I definitely won't. It's a tuxedo, Jaylen. They're not like dresses. Tuxedos all look the same. I'll have one."

"Royal-blue vest and tie," I remind him.

"I got this."

"You better. If you pick me up for prom looking a hot mess, we're gonna have a problem."

"When have I ever looked a hot mess?"

"Just get the damn tux."

He chuckles. "I'll take care of it."

We kiss before he closes my door. I begin to back out of the driveway when the waiting game feels like just too much to bear. I hit my brake, let down the driver-side window, and motion with my finger for him to come to me.

"Oh, you couldn't drive your ass back up a few feet?"

"Consider it your mini workout."

He bends and rests his elbows on my open window. "What'd you forget?"

"Where are you taking me?"

His eyebrows draw closer together. "What are you talking about?"

"My birthday has come and gone. I want to know. Where do you plan on taking me?"

"You can't wait?"

"I don't want to," I respond quickly.

Michael groans. "Spoiled ass."

"Come on. Tell me," I push.

"Well, you said you've never been to D.C., so I figured I'd knock out two birds with one stone. Whatever the saying is." He chuckles. "I want to take you to the National Gallery of Art in Washington, D.C. After that, I want to take you to the Smithsonian. You said as a child, you never went to the zoo. I never went, either. So I thought we could go to a museum, look at some stuffed animals, touch some fur. You know, pretend to be human."

Pretend to be human. That's our specialty. We do that every day.

My heart melts. His thoughtfulness touches me in a way I couldn't put into words if I tried. There's no way I can go to Jersey without him. I need this love all the time.

"What do you think?"

"You're so sweet, Michael. An art gallery?" I ask excitedly. "As much as I love art, no one has ever offered to take me to a museum. And most museums are free."

"I know. Why do you think I want to take you there? I ain't got no damn job."

Laughter escapes me. He laughs a little, too.

"I'm playing. I wanted to do something special for you."

We uncomfortably hug through the window.

"I can't wait," I tell him softly.

"Don't go home and look it up online. And don't question yourself about the gallery. I want it to kind of be a surprise. No internet, and no brain-searching. I mean it, genius."

"I promise."

He pushes out his lips, and I kiss them.

"This is probably the happiest I've ever been," I say to him. "Like, I'm really happy."

Satisfaction shows in his smile. "I want you to be happy."

"Are we making it a day trip?"

"Nah. We're getting a room." He lets out a naughty chuckle. "You're gonna enjoy D.C.!"

I shake my head. "I'll talk to you later."

"Love you."

"Love you too, Mikey Poo."

His smile fades instantaneously, and I laugh all the way out of the driveway. As I head home, I think about last night. Butterflies fill me as the memories surge. I'm looking forward to more nights spent together. Nights spent together in my house, back home, in Jersey.

Chapter 16

I walk the halls of Trinity, anxious to find Michael. We haven't spoken since I left his house Saturday afternoon. I've been so worried about him. It's unlike him to be so unreachable. Since we first met, we've spoken every single day. It's weird to be out of contact, especially after sharing such a special night together.

"Hey, Jaylen!"

I turn around. "What's up, Chloe?"

"Well, first off, congrats on winning best-dressed."

I smile. "Thanks."

"Indigo asked me to tell you to meet her in the auditorium."

"She just texted me. I'm headed there now." I ask, "Have you seen Michael?"

She shakes her head.

"Okay. Well, thanks, Chloe."

"No problem. See you in homeroom."

I head for the auditorium to meet up with Indigo. I haven't spoken to her since Friday night. The tone of her text messages sounds urgent. I've been concerned about her, too.

I enter the school's auditorium. The large space is silent and looks empty at first glance. I spot Indigo sitting in the last row, in the end seat, to the far left of the auditorium. I walk over to her. As I approach her, she stands.

I immediately ask, "Are you all right?"

Her expression is unnerving. Ripples are formed in her forehead. Her face is flushed. She's shaking.

"Did something happen?"

She looks away from me and scoffs loudly.

I stand quietly. I wait for her to tell me what's bothering her. I try not to be insensitive, though she's treating me as though I did something to her.

"How was your weekend, Jaylen?"

I can hear the knot in her throat. She's fighting back tears and I can tell.

"It was fine. How was yours?"

She ignores my question. "I called your house on Friday night. Ms. Ward said you weren't there."

My stomach drops.

"The crazy thing is, she thought you were with me."

Makes sense now, I think to myself. When Ms. Ward asked if Indigo and I had a good time and I answered yes, she followed up with several other questions. She knew I was lying, and I tried to save myself by covering a lie with many more.

She shakes her head. "I warned you. I tried to be a friend. I warned your ass, and you didn't listen!" She angrily points at me.

"What is wrong with you? You warned me about what?"

"Do you really think he cares about you? Are you really that naïve?"

I try not to let the anger I'm feeling come out. Having a screaming match isn't going to do anything for either of us, except maybe land us in the principal's office, or worse, escalate into unnecessary violence.

"I don't know what your issues are with Michael, but I'm not dealing with this forever, Indigo. What I do with my boyfriend is none of your damn business."

She laughs sarcastically. "Oh. Your boyfriend, huh? Has he called you? Do you still think you mean something to him? You don't, Jaylen!"

I sip from my bottle of water. I try to keep myself composed. I remind myself that he did mention that his phone was giving him trouble. I then silently question why she would ask if I've heard from him.

She chuckles. "I told you."

"Told me what? You haven't told me anything!"

"I told you the first day I met you that I know how Mike is. You're not special. Never were. You're no more special than Delilah, than Constance, than the rest of the girls he's pulled a hit-and-run on."

I take a deep breath and look away from whom I hoped I could have a lasting friendship with.

"Do you think you're more special than me?" Her volume is much lower.

My heart stops. Completely freezes.

"Friends since ninth grade. Look at us now, Jaylen. Mike and I don't even really talk anymore."

I try to drink the shock away, but it's not helping. I feel like Michael and Indigo are performing open heart surgery on me and forgot the anesthetics.

We stand silently. I'm furious. I'm devastated. I want to hit something and have a breakdown all at the same time. I gave both of them the opportunity to tell me this and neither of them did.

I repeatedly take deep breaths. Her "I told you so" expression further pisses me off. Makes me want to knock her head completely off her shoulders. I met her first. I've considered her a friend since day one, even though I wasn't sure that I should. If anyone should have been the first to tell me this, it should've been Indigo.

"How am I supposed to feel about this?"

I can't hold it in. "Who cares how you feel? Don't tell me you were my friend. Why didn't you tell me?"

She stands closemouthed.

My hands tremble. "Huh? Friend, right?"

She moves closer, her finger only about an inch from my face. "Don't fault me because you were dumb enough to fall for his lies. I told you to stay away from him. I don't have to tell you about my past!"

My voice is low. "Get out of my face."

She lowers her finger, and I turn for the door. I tell myself to keep all of my thoughts silent and to head straight for the student parking lot. It's better to skip classes today than to strangle Indigo and kick Michael down a flight of stairs.

She runs to jump in front of me. "I never wanted you to get hurt, Jaylen. You're my best friend."

I fight with my tears. I control my volume. "You're just as big a liar as he is. Don't ever talk to me again."

"Over a boy, Jaylen? Really?"

"No. This is not about Michael. This right here has everything to do with your secret-keeping, lying ass."

I try to walk around her. She blocks my way yet again.

"Indigo, it's taking everything in me not to explode right now. Please," I beg. "Leave me alone."

"Why? So you can run to your boyfriend?" she asks mockingly.

I can't control it. I drive both hands into her chest to push her from in front of me. Before my eyes, Indigo vanishes.

I gasp loudly as my eyes try to dart everywhere at once in search of her. My heart pounds against my chest. My legs quiver, matching my shaking hands.

The auditorium door swings open. My eyes move to

school security.

"What are you doing in here?"

I try to gather my words.

"We were just talking," Indigo states.

I turn in her direction. I then look back at security. I force myself to catch my breath. The fact that she just disappeared before my eyes and then re-appeared has me literally fighting to breathe normally.

"You okay, young lady?"

I nod slowly.

"You ladies aren't supposed to be in here." He holds the door open for us. "Head for homeroom. The bell is going to ring soon."

I exit the auditorium with Indigo only a few steps behind me.

"Don't ever make the mistake of putting your hands on me again." Her tone is a deep, threatening one.

As she heads for homeroom, I head down the nearest staircase. I rub away the tears in my eyes before they're able to fall. A few days ago, I was the happiest I've ever been. The pain I feel right now is truly unbearable. It's knifelike. Heart-piercing.

I walk toward the school's back doors. My intention is to make it to my car without being seen. My plan fails. As I hurry down the first floor hallway to get out of the building, a late Michael and Warren come my way.

As we walk toward one another, I finish off my bottle of water. I silently try to calm myself, but the mental coaching isn't helping. Seeing his smile causes sharp pains to shoot through my stomach, and even more painfully, my heart. I trusted Michael. I didn't think we had secrets. I remember the exact phone conversation we had when he revealed the name of every girl he's slept with. He conveniently forgot to mention Indigo's.

He's wide-eyed and toting a big smile. "We were looking

for you, babe. You forget something in your car?"

I look into Michael's eyes. I know the hurt is visible in mine. His smile has faded.

"You all right, Jaylen?"

I don't make eye contact with Warren. I keep my eyes on Michael.

He nudges Warren. "I'll catch up with you later."

Warren touches my shoulder before passing me.

"I meant to call you, Jaylen. I never made it to Sprint. I ended up chilling with the boys this weekend. I did swing by your spot after my workout, though. No one was there."

I stand silently. I never break eye contact. His lack of communication over the last couple of days is now the least of my concern.

He reaches out to touch me. I step back.

His face scrunches. "Jaylen, you can't be serious."

I breathe deeply. I control the tears. "Don't ever touch me again."

"Because of a phone call?" His volume is loud. His tone is defensive.

My eyes glare into his. "Not because of a phone call."

"Then what?" He lowers his volume. "What the hell is this?"

"You fucked Indigo! That's what!"

A deep furrow forms between his eyebrows. He sighs loudly and shakes his head furiously.

An administrator quickly moves our way. "Excuse me, young lady! We do not tolerate that kind of language in this school."

I keep my eyes on Michael.

"I need both of you to head to the main office."

"Jaylen." Michael's head falls. His eyes look at the floor.

I shake my head. "There's nothing you can say. You're a liar. You lied to my face."

The administrator repeats herself. "I need for both of

you to head to the main office. I'm not going to repeat myself a third time."

"I'm not these other girls out here. You're not gonna play me, and then make me chase behind you like some damn poodle!" I yell. "Don't ever talk to me again. I mean it. Don't touch me! Don't call me!"

I walk around Michael and away from the administrator toward the opened back doors.

"Young lady!" she calls out.

The back doors suddenly close loudly. I don't turn to him. I ignore Michael's attempt to stop me by violently pushing through the locked doors, and then slamming them behind me. I hear the sound of the door window glass falling and crashing against the hard floor. Still, I keep moving. My feet rush down the short flight of stairs and I head for my Volvo. I ignore the security guards calling out to me. I don't look behind me. I don't stop. I speed off before making the mistake of really hurting somebody.

Chapter 17

After sitting in the parking lot of the Dollar Tree for a little over an hour, I decide to head back to Ms. Ward's. She has been ringing my phone constantly, Indigo has been texting nonstop, and Michael has been doing a mixture of both from someone else's phone. I haven't responded to anyone.

I pull into the driveway. I'm taken by surprise. It's empty. For sure, I thought Ms. Ward would be here waiting for me. Again, my phone sounds off. I ignore Ms. Ward's call and speedily head inside.

I slam my clothing into a suitcase. All I want is to be alone right now. All I want to do is go back to my real home in New Jersey, to be surrounded by that special, loving feeling I can only feel there, and be as far away as possible from the people here who have toyed with my heart.

The doorbell rings repeatedly. I move around my bed to look out the window. Michael's Camaro is parked behind my car. A loud, ugly sound escapes me, and I resume sloppily packing my bag.

The front door slams. I can hear his feet hit against each

stair. Before he reaches my room, I kick the door closed and lock it.

He tries to twist the knob. He knocks twice. "Please, Jaylen."

I face the shut door. "Get the hell out of this house!"

With clothes in hand, I watch as the lock on my door moves from its vertical position to a horizontal one. He used his ability in an attempt to stop me from leaving the school, used it again to open my front door when I ignored the doorbell, and he just used it for a third time to gain entry into my bedroom. I need my space. He needs to respect that. I don't want to explode or cause any damage to Ms. Ward's house, but that's likely to happen if he doesn't go.

"Jaylen, listen."

I continue to pack. I can't look him in the face. "Get out."

He drinks from a bottle of water on my nightstand. I continue to move belongings from my drawers into my suitcase.

"Give me a chance to explain."

"If I wanted to hear what you have to say, I would've let you in myself."

"The police are at the school."

"Do you really think I give a damn?"

He sits on the side of my bed to catch his breath.

I yell, "Get out, Michael!"

He remains calm. "I wanted to tell you."

"But?"

"She asked me not to."

I continue to shove my belongings into an overloaded suitcase.

"I'm not saying that her wants are more important than yours, but it happened last year. We agreed never to bring it up again. Indigo didn't want to be known as that kind of girl, and I didn't want her to be labeled that way. We were cool back then. I just didn't feel it the way she did."

I stop moving. I stand, quietly awaiting his next words though my eyes aren't on him.

"She was moving way too fast. She said she needed me in her life, and that this comfort we had, we couldn't lose." He sips my water. "Indigo and I connected because we're alike. I didn't feel for her what she thought she felt for me. I just knew we were the same. I had already had sex with humans and didn't feel it. She told me she liked me, and I thought I was feeling her too. We did it. It didn't feel right."

I jump in. "Did you call her afterward?"

He exhales loudly. "I talked to her in school the following Monday."

"And?"

"I told her the truth. I told her that we should just be friends."

"You seriously want me to believe that you didn't feel anything with her? That's what you're telling me?"

"It didn't feel right, Jaylen. Of course I felt it differently with her than with the other girls I had been with, but I knew I wasn't feeling Indigo like that. I told her that. She was feeling love. I wasn't."

I begin pulling clothes from my closet.

"Where are you going?"

"Home!"

"Why? Why does any of this matter? This was before you got here."

I look at Michael. "Are you serious? You and Indigo were my best friends. I asked you on my first day of school if anything had happened between you two. I told you that I didn't want the drama." I shake my head. "You didn't say anything! Now there's drama!"

He silently looks at me.

"I put my hands on Indigo today."

He stands. "Jaylen."

"Don't come near me. If you wouldn't have kept this secret, I could've pursued this relationship with you with my eyes open. I feel like a fool. I'm over here thinking Indigo has issues with us because she likes me."

"That is her issue."

"That's only one of her issues. Indigo let you inside of her body, Michael. Just like I did. If I had known that, I wouldn't have been confronted the way I was today. I wouldn't be beefing with the two people I'm closest with."

"I didn't know what else to do. If I had said something about that night, I would've been the asshole who banged his best friend and put it on display. She asked me not to tell. You know what it feels like to walk around, hang around, and socialize with others who are nothing like yourself. We already feel like outsiders. Shit, we are outsiders. Why would I make her feel even more isolated?" His tone softens. "I cared about Indigo. She was my best friend for years. I didn't want to make life harder for her."

I shockingly find myself sympathetic, but a big part of me still wants to slap the hell out of him.

"I didn't want to hurt her, and I didn't want to hurt you."

"I don't understand why you wouldn't tell me that." I point to myself. "*Me*, Michael! That's not putting anything on display. That's being honest with your girlfriend."

"All right, then, Jaylen. What would you have done with that information? Confronted her? I'd still be the bad guy. She'd be pissed that I told someone, and you would've stayed away from me."

"I don't know how I would've handled hearing that, but at least I would've known. I don't want to deal with this bullshit. I don't want or need this drama. I'm done playing the middleman. In order to be comfortable around you, I can't be around her. In order to be comfortable around her, I can't be around you. I'm not playing this game."

"I'm not trying to play with your heart, Jaylen."

"Well, right now, it's broken. And I want to be alone. I don't want to be with you. I don't want to talk to Indigo. I don't give a damn what y'all do as long as y'all leave me and my name out of it."

He sits back down. "Don't walk away from what we have, Jaylen. You said yourself that you've never felt anything like this. I haven't either. I don't want to lose this." Tears fill his eyes. "I don't want to lose you."

"Y'all have put me in a position where I have to either cut both of you off or only be friends with one of you." Tears are desperate to fall. "Get out, Michael. Do not call me. Do not talk to me at school. Do not use your abilities to unlock my front door again. If you love me, respect me and my wishes. Stay away from me."

I hear the front door slam. Ms. Ward yells my name.

Michael begs, "Jaylen, please."

"You better go. I'm sure the school called your mom."

"I don't care."

"Michael, leave," I order.

He slowly stands.

I tell him, "And be careful."

"Of what?"

"I'm not accusing her of anything, but I think Indigo may be your ghost. She disappeared right before my eyes."

Before he can react, Ms. Ward charges in. "What the hell, Jaylen?"

I struggle to zip my suitcase.

"Michael, go back to the school," Ms. Ward says. "Your mother is on her way. The police are waiting for you and for Jaylen."

His eyes bug out. "For me? Why?" he questions.

"Because of the damage done to the school's property. That's illegal, Jaylen! What the hell is going on with you?"

Michael quietly slips out.

"First, you lie and tell me you're spending the night at Indigo's. Now you're having public brawls with your boyfriend in the middle of the school hallway. You're damaging public property! What is this, Jaylen? What has gotten into you?"

I continue to fight with my suitcase zipper.

Ms. Ward sits on my window seat. "Jaylen, please tell me what's going on." Her voice softens. "Please. I need to know." Anger tints her brown cheeks burgundy.

I make respectful eye contact with her. "I'm sorry."

"You were with Michael on Friday night?"

I nod.

She leans back and rests her head against my window. "I think I knew you were going there anyway."

"I'm sorry I lied to you," I say earnestly.

"The police want to speak with you, Jaylen."

"I figured as much. I'll pay for the damage."

"And the profanity. You may not be religious, but you can't go around disrespecting—"

I cut her off. "I know." I sit on my bed. "I was so angry, I forgot where I was. I'm going to apologize. I didn't mean to disrespect anyone."

"What the hell is going on with you and Michael?"

I exhale softly. "Nothing. We broke up."

She shakes her head, releases an exhausted sigh. "This is ridiculous. I have clients that I now have to reschedule."

I apologize again.

"And what are you packing for?"

"I just wanna go home."

"Out of the question, Jaylen."

I so badly want to remind her that I'm grown and don't need her permission.

"You only have a few weeks of school left." She points at me. "You're graduating! You're a straight-A student, you're an exceptional artist, and you've come way too far to just throw in the towel because of a breakup. You'd be a fool to go home now."

As angry as I am with Michael and Indigo, Ms. Ward is absolutely right. I can see the finish line. I tell myself to stop allowing my feelings for these people to control my actions. I've always been rational. I can't let them change that.

"We have to go back to the school. I want you to apologize to whoever you disrespected. I want you to offer to pay for the damage. Make this right, Jaylen. A few more weeks is not going to kill you."

I follow Ms. Ward out to her car. We take the short drive to Trinity, and I calmly head inside, though I know there are officers waiting to speak to me. We enter the main office and are immediately directed to the principal's workspace.

My guidance counselor points to a chair. "Have a seat, Miss Hayes."

I sit beside Ms. Ward and across the office from Michael and his mother, Michelle. The principal, two officers, and the administrator I walked out on earlier are all present.

An officer looks at me. "Do you want to explain to us what happened?"

I take a deep breath. "I take full responsibility for the damage."

"You see, it's just hard for us to believe that a young lady your size could slam those heavy doors so violently that it would shatter and break such a thick cut of glass."

"She did it. I witnessed it," the administrator eagerly explains.

"Damaging property that isn't yours is illegal, Miss Hayes," Principal Landry tells me.

"I understand. I didn't intentionally damage anything. I was angry." I repeat to the officers, "I will pay for all the damage."

They look at my principal.

I turn to the administrator. "I'm really sorry about

walking off the way I did. I'm sorry about using curse words, too."

After accepting my apology, she begins to lecture me on how unacceptable my behavior was. I can't help but look across at Michael. His eyes haven't left me since I walked in.

Ms. Ward asks, "What kind of punishment do students typically receive for this sort of behavior?"

Mrs. Landry answers, "She will be responsible for paying for the doors. We've never had a case of property damage, and being that Jaylen Hayes is such an exceptional student, we're having a difficult time determining the proper punishment."

"She's never been in trouble before. She's a straight-A student," Ms. Ward explains.

"We know," my guidance counselor chimes in. "This was as surprising to us as it was to you. Jaylen may be getting into Princeton, has a 4.0 average, and has never been in trouble. Not even a tardy."

Ms. Ward continues to defend me. "We all make mistakes, especially when we're angry."

"Jaylen," Principal Landry says. "I'm not going to revoke your prom ticket. I'm not going to suspend you. You will be allowed to attend your classes. However, I'd like for you to go home for the rest of the day. But," she adds, "because you are such a good student here at Trinity, and your actions affect everyone who shares this building with you, I am requiring that you stay after school every day until your final day of class. You are required to sign on as a tutor and help prepare your fellow classmates for their final exams."

I look at Ms. Ward. After she nods, I turn back to Principal Landry and agree to her terms.

"I'm also requiring that you and Mr. Reed discontinue any communication on school grounds."

Immediately Michael sucks his teeth loudly.

Ms. Reed scoots to the front of her seat and angles her

body to face her son. "Have you lost your mind? Where is your respect?"

He eyes his mother. "Sorry, Ma."

"I'm not the one you disrespected."

Michael's eyes move to Principal Landry. "I apologize for the disrespect, Mrs. Landry." He exhales loudly, and then his eyes find mine. "I understand. I won't talk to her."

Ms. Reed throws out, "They have class together."

"I'll send emails to their teachers," the principal states.

Ms. Ward softly bumps me with her knee.

"I agree as well," I say. "No communication."

After the faculty agrees to allow me to pay for the damage, the officers leave. Ms. Ward discusses the damage with the principal, and I sit quietly as Michael and his mother head out.

I look down at my charm bracelet. I've worn it every day since my birthday, but I haven't had the opportunity to thank Ms. Reed for it. Everything has happened so quickly.

After reaching a figure, we leave with folded documents in hand.

"At least you can still go to prom," Ms. Ward says.

I shake my head. "I'm not going to prom."

"Jaylen, couples break up all the time. Don't let a little argument between you and Michael ruin the best part of your senior experience."

"I'm not going to prom alone, and I'm not going to prom with Michael."

"Do you want to talk about what happened?"

We step inside the car. I sip some water down.

"I'll listen, Jaylen. I won't judge."

"Things are just a mess right now. I don't even want to think about them. I just want to help you today. I want to make up for the time you had to spend away from the office."

She reaches over and grabs my hand. "I just want you to

be okay."

My voice breaks. "I'm not."

"Jaylen. Sweetheart." Her voice is so low. She sounds so caring.

"I will be, though."

As we pull out of the school parking lot, Indigo texts me again. I toss the phone in my tote and close my eyes. Just a few days ago, I was the happiest I've ever been. I fit in somewhere. I had friends who understood me. Friends just like me. Now I'm forced to finish the last three weeks of school isolated from those friends. I felt lost in New Jersey being the only one of my kind. Here, my kind is within reach, but I'm not on good terms with either of them. I feel more than lost now.

Chapter 18

$\mathcal{I}$ sit in the back of the library. Getting through this day without speaking to Michael or Indigo was just as hard as I imagined it would be. Though Michael and I aren't allowed to communicate on school grounds, he hasn't stopped texting or calling. Every text is an apology. Every voicemail, he tells me he misses me. I haven't responded to anything. Indigo hasn't been calling as much, but she's been sending text messages around the clock asking if we can discuss yesterday. I've ignored and deleted each of her messages as well.

"This seat taken?"

I look up at Josh. "No."

He takes a seat beside me. "What are you doing here?"

I shrug once. "Waiting to see if anyone needs tutoring."

"What subjects are you offering help in?"

"Any, I guess."

"I waited here for about an hour yesterday. Not too many students have been coming in lately. My guess is they're waiting until the last minute to cram."

I pick at my manicured nails as I look around at the

shelves of books.

"I heard about yesterday."

I nod. After all, I'm not surprised. Everyone has heard. Warren keeps referring to me as Gangsta Jay—which has yet to make me even crack a smile—Chloe gave me her number in case there's anything I want to get off my chest, and my guidance counselor stole another of my lunch periods to talk about things I'm uncomfortable discussing. Yesterday's incident re-opened the door for her to discuss my mom's untimely death. According to her, my anger and the loss of my mom are directly related. She couldn't be more wrong. Instead of wasting my time, she should've saved the fancy talk and grief pamphlets for someone else. Being betrayed by my two best friends is the only reason yesterday happened. Both of them lied to me, and when I tried to prevent things from escalating by walking away, they both tried to stop me, causing separate explosions that I never wanted to take place.

"How are you doing, Jaylen?"

"Tell you the truth, Josh, not so good."

"Do you wanna talk about it?"

I quickly answer, "No."

Josh places his books on the table. I continue to watch the library entrance doors. I hope they remain closed. I'd rather not waste anyone's time trying to explain subjects I've never really had to comprehend myself.

"So tell me about graduation."

I turn to Josh. "Not much to tell. I'm just so happy that the day is almost here."

"Are you going straight to college? Taking a break?"

"Definitely going straight to college. I got my acceptance letter yesterday."

He loudly congratulates me, unintentionally grabbing the attention of a few students browsing the shelves.

I touch his hand. "Shh."

"That's awesome, Jaylen. Where?"

Unexpectedly, a smile forces its way out of me. "Princeton."

"What? That's incredible."

I laugh. "You're more excited than I am."

"That's where I'm hoping to go."

I tell him confidently, "You'll get in."

"How can you be so sure?"

"You're a straight-A honors student. You're involved in every club in this school. You're on every committee. Your high school resume looks better than mine, and I got in."

He blushes. "So when you graduate, I won't be saying good-bye to you, huh?"

"Nope, because I'll see you soon."

"That's crazy, huh? I was the first person you met here."

"Yup. And even though I'll be at Princeton before you get there, you're kind of my first friend there, too." I think about what I just said. "Wait. That doesn't make sense."

We laugh.

"I know what you mean," he says.

"I'm glad you do, because I'm a mess today."

He rubs my back and I take a much needed deep breath.

"You excited about prom?"

Michael's face comes to mind. "I'm not going to prom."

"Really? They're not allowing you to go because of yesterday?"

"I can still go. I'm just not going alone."

"Things could change. You and Mike might work things out."

"No." I shake my head. "That's not gonna happen."

We sit quietly. My thoughts are of Michael and Indigo together. I wonder if he touched her the way he touched me. I wonder if he said the same things to her that he said to me. It's a sickening thought, and worse, it's my newfound reality.

I completely understand why Indigo's feelings for Michael were so strong. I couldn't stop thinking about him after seeing him for the first time. Since we first met, we've spoken every day. Not speaking at all is hell. Absolute hell.

"Did you buy your dress?"

"Yeah. I have the dress, the shoes, the jewelry, the clutch."

"Just no date."

"Exactly."

Josh taps on the table. He shifts in his seat. His lips part, but no words are spoken.

I ask, "You okay?"

"Maybe I could take you?"

"To prom?"

"Why not? Friends go to prom together all the time."

I remind him, "You're a sophomore, Josh. Are sophomores even allowed to go?"

"Only if a junior or senior takes them."

I sit still, my eyes on the table.

"No pressure, Jaylen. I just don't want you to miss your senior prom."

I make eye contact with him.

"Really, I won't be hurt if you say no."

Josh's smile is just as kind as his offer. I could skip prom, stay home, and allow Michael and Indigo to steal a very important part of my high school experience. Or, I could get my hair done, wear the prom dress I fell in love with immediately and disrobed a mannequin for, and dance the night away with friends.

I nod. "Let's go."

"Really?"

"Yeah. Why not? I don't wanna be forty, look back on my high school years, and remember missing prom because of a breakup."

His smile widens. "Cool. Cool."

I send an appreciative one back at him. "Thanks, Josh."

"What are friends for?"

I show Josh a picture of my prom dress that's saved in my cell phone. As we plan for the biggest dance in every teenager's life, Indigo enters the library. The slight happiness I began to feel dissolves, and anger shoots through my veins.

She sits across from me. "Can we talk?"

Josh enters his phone number in my cell, and then respectfully gives us our privacy.

She nibbles on her pinky nail. "How are you?"

I don't respond.

"I'm so sorry about the way I reacted yesterday, Jaylen. This whole thing should've never affected our friendship."

Silence.

"Jaylen, please."

"I don't know what to say, Indigo."

"Say what you feel."

"I can't do that. I think I've already gotten in enough trouble."

Her eyes move down to her hands. "You're my best friend."

I rest my elbow on the table and my head in my hand.

"I don't understand why we can't still be friends."

"That's exactly what you want, huh? Me and you to stay friends? Me to never speak to Michael again?"

"He's not the person you think he is."

"Well, we're no longer together. So, here's your chance." I ask her, "Who is he?"

She answers, "Mike is a user. That's why I told you that I know how he is. First, he's your best friend, then he makes you believe that he's genuinely interested in you."

"And then?"

"Then it becomes physical. After that, you don't hear from him for a few days. Once you do, it's because he needs to tell you that things don't feel right. That maybe being friends is what's best." She purses her lips, shakes her head at the painful memories.

"So, because he wasn't interested in being in a relationship with you, he can't possibly want to be in one with me? That's what you're saying, right?"

She can't look me in the eye.

"I can't figure you out, Indigo. I laid in bed last night trying to figure out why you do things the way you do. You hate seeing me and Michael together. I don't know if that's because you wish it were you and me in the relationship or because you have leftover feelings for him."

"No," she states firmly without raising her voice. "I have no feelings for Mike."

"Didn't he do you a favor by not telling?"

"Jaylen, don't make me the villain here. If he loves you so much, why didn't he tell you?"

"Why didn't *you*?"

No answer.

"See, that's what bothers me about this whole thing. I can't do anything about the fact that you guys had sex. That was before I got here. I don't like it, but it is what it is."

Indigo sits quietly with her arms now folded.

I continue. "I'm not excusing him for not telling me, but at least he had a reason. I don't like being lied to, but I can appreciate that he cared enough about you not to tarnish your reputation or reveal information that you begged to be kept secret. It's you I don't get."

She drinks from her water.

"If you had told me this right away, wouldn't that have worked in your favor? That definitely would've made me put space between Michael and me. Why wait until after the sex? You waited until we got physical to pull the rug from under my feet. You could've stopped us from ever getting together, but you didn't. I don't understand why you wanted to hurt me."

"I didn't. I never did."

I slap the table. "Then explain yourself, Indigo."

A student studying at a nearby table shushes us. My head snaps in their direction. I whisper an apology for our rudeness then look back across the table at my ex-best friend.

"I..." She sighs. "I just thought you were smart enough to see through the lies."

I ask, "Did you expect that after telling me you had sex with him that I would hate him, and run to you for consoling? Explain this to me like I'm a two-year-old, because I don't get you. I don't understand why you did things this way."

A tear falls from her right eye. "When you first walked into homeroom, I felt a connection to you like I never have for anyone else." She reveals, "I had a girlfriend before you got here. She's our kind. I deeply cared for her. Still do," she admits. "I didn't instantly feel for her the way I did for you. Our feelings just blossomed. After I met you, I couldn't not be around you. I couldn't not talk to you." She cries. "You having with Michael what I feel I'm supposed to have with you has made me do some really stupid things. I didn't think you and Michael would actually do it. There was no point in telling you about my past when I really didn't see you falling for him. With you being a virgin and all, I thought after a few months of waiting, he would just throw in the towel. That's his usual pattern if girls don't jump in bed with him right away. I thought after that, you'd see what's right in front of you. I figured you just needed some time."

I pick at my nails. I don't know why I'm the special one. I don't know why they both connected to me this way. I've never wanted to be a part of a love triangle. I've only ever wanted a real relationship.

She wipes her tears. "I would never purposely hurt you, Jaylen."

A part of me wants to hug her and tell her she'll be okay, but as much as I care about her, she betrayed me. She's someone who lied while looking me in the eye. She's someone who criticized a choice I made out of love. She's someone who questioned my intelligence because I fell in love with a guy who treated me with the utmost respect and showed me love on a daily basis. I can't hug her. I can't comfort a person like that. I'm going to have to get through my pain on my own. She's going to have to do the same.

"Indigo, I need my space."

"What does that mean?"

"Like I told Michael, I'm done playing the middleman. I have too much going on right now. I need time away from both of you. This shit right here is just way too distracting. I got accepted into Princeton. If I need to focus on anything, it's that."

Indigo's sad expression is almost childlike.

"Please respect that I don't want to talk, Indigo."

"Are you still going to prom and the end-of-the-year parties?"

I hesitate. "I'm going to prom just for the experience. I'm not riding in the limo, and I'm not going with Michael."

Slowly, she stands. She opens her mouth to speak but then walks away without saying another word. As Indigo leaves the library, I rest my head on the table. I miss laughing with her already. I'm going to miss the constant company. It's going to be hard keeping my distance from her, but nothing has been harder, or is going to be more difficult, than being separated from Michael.

Chapter 19

I carefully apply my lip gloss. After weeks of separating myself from Michael and Indigo, my prom night is finally here. I never imagined it would be Josh and his mother waiting at the bottom of the staircase to watch my grand entrance. I thought it'd be Michael and Ms. Reed.

After I dab on a little perfume, I exit my room with my silver clutch in hand. My royal-blue pick up dress still fits like a glove, my strappy, silver, five-inch heels have my feet blinging, and my silver nails and toes bring it all together.

As I take slow, careful steps down the staircase toward Ms. Ward, Corey, Josh, and his mother, each of them beams. Their expressions force a smile out of me. Their eyes dazzle at the sight of me. The flattery is warming.

Ms. Ward stands beside Corey. "You look amazing, Jaylen."

"Thank you."

I continue to take slow steps toward Josh. While I wish it were Michael's eyes looking me over, it's hard not to feel special. His wide eyes and partially opened mouth are a direct compliment. He's stunned by what he sees.

"Wow. You look really beautiful."

I take the final step. "Thanks, Josh. You look very handsome."

"You do look wonderful," his mom says. I thank her, and she whispers to Josh, "Give her the corsage."

Josh hands me a beautiful floral piece. The small royal-blue flowers and the larger white roses are so elegant. I couldn't have picked a more perfect piece myself.

I lightly run my finger across the delicate petals. "Wow, so pretty. Where did you find royal-blue flowers?"

His mother answers, "They're delphiniums."

"I love it, but now I feel bad."

"Why?" Josh asks.

"I couldn't find blue flowers, so I just got the white rose boutonniere. It has a blue ribbon, though."

Ms. Ward hands me the boutonniere to show Josh.

"Jaylen, I appreciate it. Guys don't really care about stuff like that."

Josh slides the corsage on my left wrist. Afterward, I carefully pin the boutonniere to his tuxedo jacket.

"You guys look pretty spiffy," Corey compliments.

We smile and pose for pictures. Ms. Ward and Josh's mother arrange us into different poses and snap photos repeatedly. As we turn, smile, turn again, and smile, my mind goes to my ex-boyfriend. Is he doing the same thing with another girl right now? Is Ms. Reed filling her camera with images of Michael holding someone else, freezing their smiles in time, and creating memories he'll go back and revisit? My stomach turns at the very thought.

Josh puts his hand over the camera lens. "Enough, Mom."

"One more," she begs. "Just one more."

Josh's mother snaps two more photos, and then slides her camera inside her purse.

I turn to Josh. "Ready?"

Josh's mother grabs his hand. "Wait, I'd like to say a little prayer before you guys go. It's prom night. We should thank God for our health, for being able to enjoy this night, and of course, pray for your safe return home."

We all join hands, and I stand uncomfortably silent as Josh's mother recites scriptures from the Bible and gives thanks for all we have. With my eyes closed and my head bowed, my mind goes back to Michael. The distance we've been forced to keep between us hasn't made my feelings for him diminish even slightly. I miss him like crazy. Imagining him with another girl disturbs me, rips all happiness from my world.

They pull me out of my head as they each say, "Amen." Josh and Ms. Ward release my hands from theirs.

"You don't have to worry about driving him home, Jaylen. His brother will be there, and they'll ride home together."

My eyes move to Josh. "You have a brother at Trinity? I didn't know that."

"John. We don't really get along, so nobody knows we're related."

"I don't know which John you're talking about. There's about fifty of them at school."

"I'll point him out."

Ms. Ward, Corey, and Josh's mother follow behind us as we walk to my Volvo. Josh opens the driver side door for me, and I step inside. He hugs his mother before taking the passenger seat, and then we pull off toward what's supposed to be one of the most memorable nights in a teenager's life.

"I have something to confess, Jaylen."

"Confess? What is it?"

He mumbles, "Well…"

"Well, what?"

He scratches his light-brown hair. "I can't dance."

I accidentally laugh. He laughs a little, too.

"I'm not laughing at you, Josh."

"Sure you aren't."

"Really, I'm not. I just didn't expect you to say that."

He asks, "Can you dance?"

"I like to think that I can. I can move, and when I do, it's to the beat."

"See, that's my problem." He explains to me, "The beat loses me."

"Are you sure you don't lose the beat?"

We laugh and small talk our way to the luxurious hotel where our prom is being held. After parking, we head inside. On the way to the grand ballroom, we bump into Ayana and her date, Mark.

My eyes widen at the sight of her. "Wow!"

Ayana giggles and does a twirl.

Her floor-length gown fits her snugly. The sleeveless, backless dress has a halter neckline. Silver drop earrings and a silver bracelet are the only accessories she's wearing. She didn't overdo it with gaudy jewelry. She looks perfect. Perfectly elegant.

"You look gorgeous," I tell her.

"You too. I love your hair up like that."

"I can't believe you actually wore white."

"I can't believe it either. I will not be eating or drinking anything colored in this dress."

We all laugh at her statement.

"You look great too, Mark. The white tux is fly," I compliment.

He pretends to tighten his silver-and-white-striped tie. "Thank you, pretty lady." He looks over at Josh. "You into older women, Josh?" He looks back at me. "Jaylen, I didn't know you were a cougar."

I interlock my arm with Josh's. "There's a lot you don't know about me."

We enter the ballroom, and I can't help but stop and

admire the décor. There isn't a square foot of this room that hasn't been decorated. Moving digital stars cover the ceiling and reflect against the gold, hanging stars. Circular tables are either topped with a royal-blue, black, or gold tablecloth. The room lighting is blue, and straight ahead, centered, is a huge, golden Eiffel Tower replica.

As we walk in, we look up at the balloon arch we pass under. The room is spectacular. They've decorated it to look like a dream. It's magical.

"Do you wanna sit together?" Ayana asks.

"Sure, but what about Mark? I'm sure he wants to sit with the other ball players."

"I plan on table-hopping," Mark tells me.

Ayana tells Mark, "Well, I'll be sitting with Jaylen."

Josh, Ayana, and I take a seat as Mark moves around the decorated space to talk to friends.

"Josh, I can't believe you came to this prom. Now your prom isn't going to seem as special."

He grins at Ayana. "It will. Every year, the theme changes. It won't feel the same."

My heartbeat begins to gallop. My nerves begin to feel more alive. He's here. I can't help it. I turn slowly, and there he is. He's standing in the doorway with those I initially planned on sharing a limo with.

"Look at Indigo." Ayana's eyes sparkle at the sight of my ex-best friend.

Indigo is stunning. She's wearing a champagne-colored high-low dress with gold open-toe stilettos. The sweetheart neckline, the beading, the corseted back—all just gorgeous. The skirt of the dress is very dramatic. It's made with basket-weave organza blossoms. She thought she'd shock everyone by not wearing indigo. That's not the shocker. The shock is just how beautiful Indigo really is. She could easily be mistaken for a supermodel. The girl is a vision of flawless beauty.

"That dress is amazing." Ayana sighs. "Now I feel like my dress is so simple."

"It is," I tell her. "Simply gorgeous. And you're rocking the hell out of it."

She smiles as she glances down at her prom attire, and my eyes move back to Michael. Those green eyes are on me. He's wearing the royal-blue vest and tie under his tuxedo jacket. He's dressed almost exactly like my date.

I turn back around in my seat and spark up a conversation with Ayana and Josh. I came here to enjoy myself. I won't if I keep staring at Michael and Indigo.

Chloe walks over to our table. "Hey, guys."

"Hey, Chloe," I greet. "You look pretty."

"Thanks. So do you. You, too, Ayana. And Josh, you look very handsome."

We all thank her.

"Do you mind if we sit with you guys?"

We offer her and her date seats.

"Did you help organize this, Josh?" Chloe asks.

"No. I knew what the theme was gonna be, but prom organization is reserved for seniors only. Underclassmen can't join the prom committee even if they beg. They did a good job, though, huh?"

"Yeah. It's lovely. So, you and Jaylen came together?" Chloe's tone is unsure.

I nod. "Josh and I are friends."

"Lucky you, Josh. You get to go to two proms."

We talk about graduation and college. My eyes just cannot stay away from Michael, no matter how hard I try to remain focused on those at my table. In a perfect world, I'd be sitting next to him and not Josh. We would've never broken up. Indigo would be just as in love with Warren as he is with her. And most importantly, we'd all be happy.

Michael offers me a smile. I turn back to Josh and join back in the conversation.

Josh asks, "Do you wanna dance?"

"Didn't you say you can't dance?"

"That doesn't mean I don't want to do whatever it is I do on the dance floor."

I chuckle nervously. "Okay. Let's see what it is you do."

We all stand from the table and join our classmates on the floor. I sway from side to side as Josh happily begins to move. His movements are much faster than the song playing. His body remains stiff as his arms make wormlike movements.

"Wait, wait, wait. Slow down," I tell him. "Start with something simple. Just move from side to side."

He follows my steps.

"When you're comfortable, you can work your arms. Just don't lose the beat. And if you do, stop for a second, find it, and keep going."

Josh dances in front of me. His arms are still a little wild, but he's close enough to following the beat that it's not throwing me off.

My clutch vibrates. I wait to check my message. I continue to dance with Josh, Ayana, Chloe, her date, and Mark, who finally joins us on the dance floor. This is nothing like the spring theatre dance, but it's not as bad as I thought it would be. I'm still amongst friends, whether they're my kind or not. I'm well, and above all, I didn't miss my senior prom.

The song ends. We compliment and hug other schoolmates we bump into. Everyone looks so beautiful, so different from how I'm used to seeing them.

"You want some fruit? Some juice?" Josh asks politely.

"Water. No fruit. Thanks."

As he heads toward the refreshment buffet, I take a seat back at our table with Ayana. I check my message. It's from Michael. It's simple. Just five words. *You look so beautiful, babe.*

I can hear his voice in my head. I almost want to cry. I so badly want to talk to him. I want to touch him. I want him to hold me. Words cannot express how much I've missed him. I absolutely hate that we're not speaking. It's torture. Daily torture.

I look over at him. His eyes are on me.

"You okay?"

I make eye contact with Ayana. "Yeah, I'm fine."

"I don't wanna get in your business, but maybe you should just talk to him."

I don't reply.

"You're both miserable. Especially Mike. Everybody's noticed."

"What do you mean?"

"He's been really angry lately."

I look back over at Michael. His eyes are still on me.

"I don't know, Ayana."

"All I'm saying is tonight is prom night. Are you guys just gonna stare at each other all night long?"

"It's complicated," I say.

She does me a huge favor by changing the subject. While discussing college again, Josh brings me a small bottle of water, and I immediately take it all down.

"You having fun?"

I force on a smile for my date. "Yeah. Thank you so much for tonight, Josh."

The night moves along slowly. If I'm not conversing with those I'm sharing a table with, I'm on the floor giving dance lessons to Josh or following Michael around the room with my eyes. He hasn't danced all night.

My phone alerts me of another text. This one is from Indigo. The message reads: *Can we talk?* I explain to her that now isn't a good time, and continue on with the conversation being held at my table.

"Can I have your attention, please?"

We all turn toward the Eiffel Tower. Standing in front of the golden replica is Elizabeth, head of the prom committee.

"The time has come. It is now time to crown the Class of 2015's prom king and queen."

Everyone around me applauds.

"Please stand as we announce our prom king."

We all rise to our feet.

She pulls the name from a golden envelope and brings the microphone back to her lips. "2015's prom king is…"

I glance over at my ex-boyfriend.

"Michael Reed!"

The applause is loud. The cheering is over-the-top. I clap much less enthusiastically as he walks toward the Eiffel Tower to be crowned.

I watch Michael closely. That smile is far from real. To me, it's painfully obvious that he isn't happy.

She continues, "And now, the prom queen." Elizabeth opens the second envelope and excitedly announces Indigo as the winner.

I clap softly as she walks toward the Eiffel Tower to join Michael. The overall applause is even louder for her. As she's crowned, I take down some water from a fresh bottle in preparation for their dance. After their photo is taken, Elizabeth requests that the dance floor remain clear except for the king and queen.

I stand silently as Michael and Indigo move slowly to the song. Seeing them together like this, though not by choice, sets my insides ablaze. I want to break something. Hit something. I'm burning inside, and water isn't putting out the flames.

Josh touches my twitching arm. "You okay?"

I nod. "I'm fine."

Cameras are out everywhere. Flashes go off only seconds apart. Neither of them is smiling. Both of them look as though they wish they were dancing with someone else.

I look around at the other observers. If my schoolmates aren't snapping pictures of the two of them dancing, they're staring at me, likely watching for a reaction.

Being watched like this and having to watch them like that forces my internal struggle to come out in trembles. This is too much for me. Watching them dance isn't a requirement. There's no need to put myself through this.

"I'm going to the bathroom. I'll be right back," I whisper to Josh.

As I squeeze through the crowd, eyes follow me. It's no secret that Michael and I were together and broke up in the middle of the school hallway. It's also no secret that Indigo and I were best friends, now ex-friends. Eyes are glued to me because my two exes are being spotlighted in the middle of my prom night. I'm sure everyone's waiting to see if my temper will get the best of me, and another door will fall victim.

While behind closed doors, I close my eyes and take slow, deep breaths in and out. I try to relax. I look at my reflection in the mirror and tell myself that tonight is my prom night. This is a one-time thing. If I waste this night by spending it angry, I'm ruining an experience I'll never have back again. Not only that, but I'll be ruining Josh's night as well. He did me a favor by escorting me here. He deserves pleasant company.

I take my time returning to the ballroom. Fortunately, their dance is over. I sit back down at my table.

"Where did you go?" Ayana asks.

I tell her, "The bathroom."

"We should dance."

I lie. "My feet hurt. I'm gonna wait a few songs."

Ayana heads for the dance floor with Mark at her side. I remain seated beside my date.

"Proms are kind of sad, don't you think?"

I look at Josh. "They're so final."

"Yeah. That's what I mean. After tonight, most of these people will never party together again."

"That's true."

"It's hard to think about."

"Josh, you still have two more years left in high school. Don't think about it too much."

"I'm just glad you let me escort you. Most of these seniors are my friends, too."

I force on another smile for him.

"I'm gonna go find my brother. Find out what he's doing afterward."

"Okay. I'll be here."

I sit alone. Everyone from my table is on the dance floor. I look for Michael. He isn't sitting with his friends. I scan the room and spot him at the DJ table.

The DJ moves in closer to his microphone. "Ladies and gentlemen, we're gonna slow things down a bit. My man Michael Reed would like to send this song out to his lady, Jaylen."

My heart melts as K-Ci and JoJo begin to sing "All My Life." Our classmates release a chorus of "aww" and other expressions of endearment.

Michael drifts my way. Once he reaches my table, he holds his hand out for mine. I look up into those beautiful green eyes, and it's taking all that I have in me to hold these tears in.

"May I have this dance?"

I place my hand in his, and we head for the dance floor.

Michael holds me close. Being this close to him again feels so right. I've missed him so much.

He whispers, "You look so beautiful tonight."

I don't say anything. I continue to sway with him.

"I'm so sorry I hurt you, Jaylen."

Still no words.

"I love you."

I look Michael in his eyes. They're teary. So are mine.

"I really do, Jaylen."

I tell him, "You look nice tonight."

He holds me tighter. "I only came to see you."

We continue to move to the music. It feels so amazing to be this close to him again.

"Why did you come with Josh?"

"Because I didn't wanna miss prom, and I didn't wanna come alone," I explain. "Congratulations on the win."

"I didn't want this shit. I damn sure didn't wanna dance with her ass."

"Regardless, you won."

He lets out a frustrated sigh. "Can we talk?"

I make eye contact with Michael again. "Isn't that what we're doing?"

"I mean alone. Just us. Away from all of this."

"Michael, I'm here with someone. I can't just walk out on Josh."

"Tell him you're stepping out for a second. I need to talk to you."

I spot Josh across the room talking to a few others. I approach him and tap his shoulder. "Hey, Josh." When he faces me, I say, "I'm gonna step out to talk to Michael for a second."

"No problem. I'm gonna hit the dance floor again."

I chuckle. "Don't hurt nobody."

I walk back over to Michael, and together, we exit the ballroom.

"Where are you guys going?" Eugene asks while heading inside.

Michael removes his crown. "To talk real quick."

He nods. "You look beautiful, Jaylen."

"Thanks. So do you." I correct myself. "I mean, handsome."

Eugene enters the ballroom, and Michael and I head for the parking garage.

I ask, "How have you been?"

"How have *you* been?"

"Okay, under the circumstances."

"I've missed you," he says in a hurry.

After a few seconds, I tell him, "I've missed you too."

"I'm sorry. I know I keep saying that, but it's because I really am."

We stop at my car. The garage is full of vehicles. No people are around except for us.

"Is there anything I can do to make things right? I don't wanna continue on like this."

I stand quietly. As much as I want to be with him, I can't stop wondering if there's anything else I don't know. Other painful secrets that might later surface.

"Did you take her virginity?"

He answers hastily, "No. I swear."

"Did you tell her you loved her?"

"Hell no."

My voice lowers. "Did you like it?"

"It was better than what I had before her."

He leans against my car, prepared to answer anything else I throw his way. I initially had a million questions to ask. The questions all seem irrelevant now. When I'm with Michael, things feel right. This is where I'm supposed to be. The anger is no longer present. The betrayal feels much less severe.

"So, you threw your present away?"

"No. I love that bracelet."

"Not the present from my mom. I got you something."

My eyes narrow. "Got me what?"

"Remember when I told you I left my phone in the car? I only went back downstairs to put something in your trunk."

"I haven't been in the trunk."

Michael takes my keys from me and pops my back storage space. Inside lies an oversized bear, dead flowers, and a small gift bag.

I cover my face. "I feel terrible."

He pulls out the starved floral bouquet.

"I had no idea anything was back here."

He hands me the gift bag. "It's cool. I'm not mad at you."

I pull out the small box and remove the top. It's a gift card.

"Blick," I say softly.

"Ever shopped there?"

"Definitely. I've purchased a lot of my art supplies from them."

I slide the box back inside the bag before returning it to the trunk.

"I hope you like it."

I hug Michael. We hold each other close.

"Thank you so much," I whisper to him.

"Not a problem."

I breathe him in. I silently forgive the secret. I can't be without him. I need him. I love him.

We kiss. He has one hand on each side of my face. My hands are on his waist. I tug at his waistband. I need him desperately. I need to feel him.

He pulls me toward the back door of my car. He unlocks it and quickly pulls it open.

I throw my clutch to the floor, and he rips off his jacket. I slide in first, and he quickly follows, pulling the door closed behind him.

He climbs on top of me. My small backseat doesn't offer nearly as much comfort as his bed, but that doesn't stop us.

Michael moves his hand up my dress. I fight to get his pants unbuttoned.

Again, our lips meet. He doesn't have to tell me again. I can feel it. Michael loves me. And without a doubt, not even an inkling of a doubt, I love him more than I could love anybody else.

He pushes my thin layer of cotton to the side, and finally, we reconnect in the most personal, passionate way. His movements are quick. Strong. This is everything losing my virginity wasn't. This is urgent.

Every one of Michael's movements is an apology. Every sound escaping me is my acceptance. I can't do anything about the past, but I don't want to live my future without him.

I open my eyes. The windows surrounding us are all fogged. I can feel the car moving with us. I don't worry about who might hear or see. I enjoy this time with my Michael. With my love.

I hold onto Michael tight. We kiss hard.

"I love you."

My breathing is loud. Deep. "I love you, too."

I look up at Michael. Those green eyes are looking down at me as he continues to please me. As he continues to say so many things to me without any words escaping those lips.

I close my eyes. I moan loud. I let my sounds tell Michael how he's making me feel.

He grabs ahold of the door above my head. His moans are more like growls. Growls he's releasing through clenched teeth.

It's happening. This is ending. Though satisfied, I could never get tired of feeling Michael like this. I can't imagine how anything that feels this right could not be meant to be.

Michael eases off of me. He takes my hand and pulls me upright. I look down at my silver heels. I'm reminded that this is prom night. I left Josh in there all by himself.

"We have to go," I tell him.

"Go where?"

"Back inside. I came with someone. I don't wanna be rude and just leave him hanging."

Michael reaches into my middle compartment for Kleenex and antibacterial hand gel. He hands me a few tissues and we both clean ourselves and sanitize our hands before stepping out of my Volvo.

"How does my hair look?"

He fixes himself. "Looks good."

As I feel to make sure my hairpins are still in place, I ask, "Does it look like I just did it?"

He laughs. "Nah. It looks fine."

I grab my silver slip-on flats from the back floor. He grabs his crown and his tuxedo jacket. Together, we head back inside.

"You sure I look okay?"

He puts his arm around me. "You look fine. I promise."

We re-enter the ballroom. If Indigo's eyes could kill, I would've just died twice. Her eyes pierce mine. She doesn't blink. She doesn't move. She holds her cold stare as if she knows what we've just done.

I wrap my arm around Michael, and we continue to move toward my table. Respectfully, I take a seat beside my date.

Josh asks, "You okay?"

"Yeah, I'm fine. We just needed to talk."

"Talking is good."

I smile. This smile isn't forced.

Michael takes a seat beside Ayana. That smile I love is back. Those perfectly straightened teeth are showing.

I turn to Josh. "So, did you light up the dance floor?"

Ayana answers, "He was doing *something* out there."

We all crack up.

"I just can't control my arms and legs. The music takes me away."

The laughter continues.

"So, are you guys going to the after-party?" Ayana asks.

I briefly look at Michael and then back at Ayana. "I don't think so."

"Why not? It's gonna be fun. They're having a raffle, a

money machine, karaoke. The seniors last year said the after-party was more fun than prom."

I shrug once. "I don't know. Maybe."

I avoid looking over at Indigo as the night goes on. I sit with Michael, Ayana, my date, and some of our other friends. A smile stays on my face as we enjoy the remainder of our prom night. A smile I don't allow to fade, though I can feel in my gut that something bad is going to happen.

Chapter 20

I slip into my flats before making my way toward the exit with Michael at my side. Though an unsettling feeling has been centered in my gut for the past couple of hours, I haven't allowed it to steal my happiness. Michael and I are back together. No feeling can overshadow the joy he overwhelms me with.

Indigo grabs my arm. "Can we talk before you go?"

I head for an unoccupied corner to privately speak with her. I'm really not in the mood to talk to her, but it's only fair that I do. Michael hurt me too, but I listened to what he had to say.

She shakes her head, scrunches her nose. "I'm confused."

"About what?" I ask.

"Y'all are cool, but we're not? I don't understand."

I sigh. "Indigo, I just don't know how to be friends with you anymore."

"What do you mean?"

"I want to be friends with someone who doesn't keep secrets from me. I want a friend who doesn't mind if I occasionally bring up my boyfriend's name." I lower my voice. "I want a friend who doesn't want to be anything more than just friends."

She stands tightlipped.

"Indigo, I don't wanna hurt you. I've tried my best to make sure that I don't hurt either of you."

"I know that, but you're giving him a second chance. Give me one, too. You're my best friend, Jaylen."

"Can we talk about this later?"

"Are you going to the after-party?"

I shake my head.

"To his house?"

"No."

"Can I come to your house and talk?"

"I'm not going home."

Her complexion reddens. It hurts me to see her like this, even though she betrayed my trust.

"I'll pick up the phone, Indigo. I promise. We can talk about it later. Right now, I just need to be with Michael. Please try to understand and respect that."

She does an about-face and rushes for the door. Kennedy speed-walks to catch up to her.

No matter what I decide, I'm taking a loss. If I pursue a friendship with both of them, I'm back to playing the middleman. If I only communicate with Michael, I have to get through each day knowing I left Indigo on her own, left to feel lost and lonely, and I know firsthand just how awful that feels. I wouldn't wish it on anyone.

Michael approaches me. "What'd she want?"

"To talk. She wants to be friends again."

Michael and I head for the parking garage. I grab ahold of his hand and smile up at him.

"What'd you say to her?"

"I told her we'd talk about it later. Right now, I just wanna be with you."

He takes his hand from mine and wraps his arm around me. "So where do you wanna go?"

"I wanna go home."

"Home?"

"Jersey."

He stops. "Right now?"

I nod. "I just wanna get away for the weekend. I miss my old house."

"That's a long drive."

"I know. I just need a change of scenery."

"What do you think Ms. Ward is gonna say?"

"I don't wanna lie to her, but I know if I tell her, she's gonna find some reason for me to wait. I'm not going for good. I just wanna go for the weekend."

"Yeah, but what about the car?"

"She gave it to me. I should be able to go wherever I want to in it."

We continue toward the garage. Indigo passes us on our way, heading back for the ballroom, I assume. Michael and I follow her with our eyes. Kennedy quickly passes us as well, calling out for Indigo.

"What the hell was she doing in the parking garage?"

Michael chuckles. "Let's hope your windshield isn't bashed in."

"That's not funny. Indigo makes me nervous sometimes."

We reach my car. My windshield is intact. We step inside. Michael is behind the wheel.

"Let's go. We're about to graduate. Why not?"

"Really?" I ask excitedly. "What about your mom?"

"Let me worry about my mom. If you really wanna go, I'm down."

I don't need to think about it. "Okay. Let's go."

Michael begins to drive. I sit silently in the passenger seat. I'm not much of a rebel. The thought of heading to

New Jersey without telling Ms. Ward has my stomach doing somersaults. I've already lied to her once, and it caught up to me almost immediately. Though she didn't react the way most others would have, I know she didn't appreciate being lied to, especially after all she's done for me.

Michael peeks over at me. "You okay?"

"Never been much of a wild child. I can't believe I'm crossing state lines without permission."

"You're an adult, Jaylen."

"I know, but—"

He cuts me off. "But if you feel uncertain, you need to tell her."

"I just feel like something isn't right. I don't wanna be here. I need to get away."

"Do what you feel like you need to do for yourself."

I sigh. "I really wanna go."

"I have to make a stop first."

"Don't I know it. Beef jerky and sunflower seeds, right?"

"Look at you, acting like you know me."

I giggle.

Michael reaches for my hand. "I just wanna let you know that there's nothing else about me you don't know."

I hesitantly reply, "Okay."

"You sound unsure, but I'm serious. I swear on everything I love."

"Okay. I believe you."

We pull into the parking lot of the CVS. I wait in the car for Michael as he goes in to pick up his necessities. While waiting, I check my messages. There's one from Indigo asking me to please call her as soon as possible. I ignore it.

I patiently sit tight, though Michael is taking much longer than expected. I send Josh a message thanking him one final time for escorting me to a dance I'll never forget. I went to prom single, escorted by a friend. I left prom hand in hand with Michael. My love.

The driver door opens. "Sorry about that. Long line."

"It's okay."

"I saw a couple of people we know in there."

"Doing what? Buying condoms?"

He laughs.

"So you're up for the drive?" I check.

"Hell yeah. We're gonna get it, but you only live once, right?"

I exhale. "You only live once."

We back out of the parking lot and head for my hometown.

"So, are you gonna introduce me to all your childhood friends?"

"Of course."

"Even your exes?"

I tell him, "They're still my friends. You'll meet them, too."

"Did Ms. Ward get you a GPS?"

"I can tell you where to go."

"I'm sure you can, brainiac, but a GPS will avoid traffic and detours."

"And why would there be traffic at this time of night?"

"Construction. Accidents." He sucks his teeth. "Just look."

I search my glove compartment for a GPS. It's not there. I check my middle console, and then under my seat. "You don't have one?"

"Guess not."

"I'll just use my phone. I do need to swing by my spot real quick, though. I need clothes."

"What about your mom?"

"She's working. Babe, chill out."

The entire ride to his house, I go back and forth about whether or not I should ask Ms. Ward. I still feel bad for lying to her just so I could spend the night with Michael.

Though I'm grown, I don't want to make the last few weeks of living with her uncomfortable.

With one foot out the car, he asks, "You wanna come in?"

"I'll wait. Hurry up, please."

I nervously tap my foot as I look around for Michael's mother's car. Something about this whole night feels off. My stomach is in knots and has been for hours. I've been able to smile through the weird feeling in my belly, but it hasn't let up.

Minutes pass, and Michael returns with a duffle. He tosses his bag in the back and then jumps back in behind the wheel.

As he backs out of the driveway, I ask, "How do you feel?"

"I feel fine. Why?"

"I feel uncomfortable. I feel like something isn't right."

"We don't have to go."

"My stomach has been jacked up almost all night. I just feel uneasy."

"It could be the sneaking off that's bothering you. Send her a text. She might not even care. You're about to graduate, and you got into Princeton. Finals are done. It's not like we have to go back to school. Why would she say no?"

"I just lied to her a few weeks ago so I could spend the night with you."

"True. I forgot about that." He shrugs. "Maybe you should ask. You don't wanna be on bad terms with her. She did just buy you a car."

I send Ms. Ward a text.

"We should probably pull over and wait for a response, huh?"

I tell him, "Just drive slowly."

"You want to stop by the after-party?" he asks.

"No. Do you?"

"I'm where you are."

I impatiently tap on my cell as I wait for her response. Michael continues down the road, driving below the speed limit.

I look at my boyfriend. My stomach is upset, but my heart isn't. Michael means everything to me. Instead of pressing me to leave town so we can spend all of our time alone and in bed, he encouraged me to do the right thing. I don't appreciate Michael keeping the truth from me, but I can't ignore how much he cares about me, and my doing what's right. He's unselfish, and his heart is huge. I'm so happy to be in it.

I reach over and grab my boyfriend's thick, curly hair. "Do you ever wonder why we connected the way we did?"

He shakes his head. "Nope. I'm just glad we did."

"I never really believed in love at first sight. Or even strong like at first sight."

"Do you believe in anything?"

I side-eye my boyfriend. "Shut up. I believed the only thing that could happen right away was physical appeal. And lust. You can definitely want someone right away."

He snickers at me.

"Don't do that. You sound like a creep."

He laughs.

"I just have to say, I'm not flattered by all this attention. Seriously, I only want attention from you. I really wish Indigo didn't feel the same way about me that you do. I mean, as much as I miss her company, I don't really feel comfortable being friends with her."

"You don't have to be her friend, Jaylen."

"But I feel bad for her. I don't want anyone to feel as alone as I did in Jersey. She may know what she is, but being the only one is not fun. It's lonely. It can be scary."

"There are others like us. I'm sure she'll bump into another one if she goes to college."

"There are others?" I turn slightly in my seat. "Really? I know Indigo has an ex who is our kind, but where are the others?"

"I know for sure there are others in Michigan. I'm sure we're all over, though. We're just scattered. Don't fool yourself into believing we're the last ones left."

"This is why I talk to you. I want to know these things."

He goes on. "My mother has a few friends in Michigan. Apparently, that's where most of us are. There aren't millions, but we're present."

"What's so special about Michigan?"

As soon as I ask the question, my brain does the research for me. Michigan touches four of the five Great Lakes. The state has the longest freshwater shoreline in the world.

I say aloud, "But that water is dirty as hell."

"What water?"

"Michigan would be ideal for our kind because we can't survive without water, but who would drink from those lakes? I can't imagine what's in that water."

"I'm gonna pull over. I don't want to keep driving. Ms. Ward may say no."

We park on a non-residential side street across from a large park.

I think aloud. "Well, freshwater would be easier to purify than saltwater. I guess that makes sense. If our kind were ever forced to fight for our survival, we'd have a better chance doing it up there."

"Stop it, Jaylen. There's no reason for us to worry about that right now."

"Why are y'all here if most of us are there?"

"We still need to live. What do we look like? That's what we have to act like. We're here. What other choice do we have?"

"I know you grew up in D.C., but were you born in Michigan?"

"That's where my mom was born."

I think about Indigo. "Indigo's mom was born there, too."

Revolving lights distract us. The police car pulling up behind us audibly alerts us.

I ask Michael, "What did we do?"

"It's probably because we're just sitting here."

As the officer carefully approaches, Michael lets down his window.

With a flashlight in hand, the officer stops at the driver window. I sip from my water.

"Good evening."

"Good evening, officer," Michael responds.

"Are you aware that there isn't a tag on the back of this vehicle?"

Michael turns to me.

I answer, "No, sir. It was there earlier."

"This is your vehicle?"

I nod. "Yes."

"Why are you guys parked here?"

Michael clears his throat. "I just parked for a second to make a phone call."

"Can I see a license from both of you, and your registration?"

I pull the registration from the glove compartment. We both pull out our ID cards and hand the officer the requested identification. As he walks around to the front of my car, Michael drinks from my water.

The officer walks back to the window. "Sit tight for me."

"He's running your tag."

I finish off the water. "I know."

We wait quietly, and I notice a second police car.

"He's just checking to see if he can be of assistance," Michael tells me.

I nod, but I can't help but notice that the second car

hasn't continued on. I don't know what kind of assistance could be needed for a stop like this.

Both officers approach my car. What seemed routine now feels anything but.

"Turn your engine off for me, please," the first officer says.

Michael does as he's told.

"I need you both to step out of the vehicle."

I'm beginning to feel my nerves.

Michael hesitates. "Can I ask what for?"

The officer repeats, "Step out of the vehicle."

We both follow his orders.

I ask, "What's going on? This seems a bit much for a missing tag."

The officer's eyes are on me. "You said you're the owner?"

"Yes."

"The name on your ID isn't the name this vehicle is registered under."

"It's under my foster mother's name. She bought it for me for my birthday."

He tells me, "This car was reported stolen this evening."

My heart stops. Completely halts.

"Call Ms. Ward now!" Michael demands.

"There is no way this vehicle was reported stolen." I ask, "Can I call Denise Ward?"

The officer ignores my question. "Why is there a bag in the backseat of the car?"

"It's prom night. Why would we steal a car on our prom night? Can I please call Ms. Ward? This is definitely a mistake," I explain.

"What's her phone number?"

I recite the number to the officers. As the second officer dials up Ms. Ward, my eyes move to Michael.

"No answer," the officer reports.

Michael lets out foul-sounding grunts.

"I'm going to have to take you both in."

My hands shake. "We didn't steal this car!"

"Calm down, Jaylen. Officer, who reported the car stolen?" Michael asks.

"The owner."

I shake my head immediately. "There's no way. Call her again."

"We're going to have to run you guys in."

"I'm not getting arrested on my prom night for something I didn't do. This is my car. She knows that I have it."

"Looks like you guys are heading somewhere."

"Regardless of where we're heading, we didn't break the law," I argue.

The officer walks toward me. He begins to read me my rights.

I cut him off. "Call her again! This is my car. You're treating us like we're criminals. We didn't steal this vehicle."

"Riding in a car that's been reported stolen is a crime."

"Officer." Michael's eyes are rage-filled, but his tone and voice remain calm. "You don't have to cuff her. Somebody mistakenly called this car in."

"Just like the tag mistakenly fell off, right?"

"I've never stolen anything in my life!" Michael's tone is defensive, his volume much louder.

As wrong as I feel this is, I don't resist. As he reads me my rights, I allow him to cuff me. Michael is cuffed by the other officer. After locking Michael's hands behind his back, the second officer's cell phone sounds off. He steps back to answer the call.

"This is bullshit, man!"

"Michael, calm down. Please don't make this worse."

"This shit ain't right."

The first officer points at Michael. "Watch your mouth."

The second officer walks over to the other. "Denise Ward is saying she never reported this car stolen."

Michael's eyes move between the officers. "Thank you!"

"Michael, shut up," I tell him.

With the phone still to his ear, his eyes dart from Michael to the other officer. He shakes his head. Folds form in his forehead. "I don't know what's going on here," he admits. "She said she never called the station to report anything. She said no officer came by to take a statement."

"Can you uncuff us now?"

The anger in Michael's voice worries me.

The second officer tries to calm Ms. Ward. "Someone called this in this evening. Believe me, ma'am, we're just doing our job. It takes a little more than a name and an address to report a car stolen. Someone with access to this vehicle's information reported it taken illegally and filed the report in your name."

I can hear Ms. Ward panicking loudly. Michael rocks slowly. His nostrils flare. He's near his boiling point.

"Can you please take these cuffs off?" Michael asks again.

The officers ignore him. A third cruiser arrives at the scene.

"Maybe this is some kind of prom prank. She's insisting that she didn't report anything." The first officer shakes his head. "I think we should take them in. The vehicle owner can meet us at the station with the proper identification."

I can hear Ms. Ward. "You can't arrest these kids on their prom night!"

I jump in calmly. "We're not far from my house. If Ms. Ward could come here right now with all the information you need, would you let us go? It's our prom night. I don't want to remember it like this. We are not criminals."

The third officer slowly pulls forward.

"Please," I beg.

The second officer tells Ms. Ward the street we're on and asks how long it'll take for her to arrive. After a few seconds of silence on his end, he hangs up the phone.

"Give her five minutes?" he asks the first officer.

The first officer shrugs rudely. "Five minutes. That's it. This isn't procedure."

As the first officer walks over to speak to the third who's just arrived at the scene, the second officer offers me a consoling smile.

I offer a thankful one in return. "Thank you for being so understanding. I know you don't have to do this."

He nods once.

"Can you uncuff us, please? We're cooperating," Michael says calmly. "It's obvious we didn't commit a crime."

The second officer moves to uncuff Michael.

"No!" the first officer yells. "You can uncuff the young lady. Foul-mouth can wait until the vehicle owner arrives."

Michael looks across at me. "You see this bullshit? Like I don't have the right to be mad."

The second officer frees my wrists, and I promptly move to stand beside my boyfriend.

"Please try to stay calm, babe. Ms. Ward said she'd be here in five. Trust me, she'll be here in three."

"Without that badge, he's still a regular person. He wouldn't want to be cuffed and made to feel like a criminal for some shit he didn't do."

"I understand why you're mad. I just don't want you to get yourself in trouble."

I rub Michael's back as we anxiously wait for Ms. Ward to arrive. We both face away from the blinding, revolving, red and blue lights.

"You kids going to college?"

I make eye contact with the second officer. "Yes."

"She got into Princeton," Michael says.

"Wow. Ivy League. Good for you."

I tell the officer, "He was awarded prom king tonight."

The second officer congratulates Michael before telling us, "We'll get this straightened out. You guys seem like decent kids."

A few minutes later, I spot Ms. Ward's car. Michael exhales loudly.

I point. "That's her."

Ms. Ward steps out of her vehicle. Her hair is wrapped. Her baggy pajama pants hang past her flip-flops and drag over the ground as she rushes over to us. The officer who pulled us over shakes hands with her. The third officer pulls off.

"I'm Denise Ward. I purchased this car. I have the title, my driver's license, proof of temporary guardianship, and the bill of sale." Her chest rises and falls as she breathes heavily. "I did not report this vehicle stolen," she states firmly in a bass-filled voice.

The officers look over the documents.

Ms. Ward asks us, "You guys okay?"

"We're okay," I answer.

"Why are you cuffed, Michael?" She turns to the officers. "Why are you treating them like criminals?"

The first officer insists, "We're just doing our job, ma'am."

"But this young man hasn't committed a crime. Why is he still handcuffed?"

"He's handcuffed because of his mouth."

"They handcuffed me for no damn reason. I'm not about to sit here and smile about this. After they spoke to you, it was obvious that this was some kind of misunderstanding. He told the other cop not to uncuff me."

"Ma'am, understand our position. For whatever reason, this car was reported stolen. It's missing a tag. Waiting for you to come to the scene is not procedure. In any other case, we would've taken them in, and you would've had to come down to the station. I get why he's frustrated, but understand why I didn't feel comfortable releasing an angry young male spewing all sorts of profanity."

Ms. Ward sighs. "Can we just get this straightened out? Let's give these kids a chance to enjoy the rest of their prom night."

The second officer removes Michael's handcuffs.

"What do I need to do to make sure that these kids are not pulled over again tonight?"

The second officer answers, "We'll make sure that the vehicle isn't still listed as stolen. That has nothing to do with the missing tag. They could still very well get pulled over for that."

The first officer hands Ms. Ward her documents back as well as our IDs. He then turns to Michael. "This report wasn't our mistake. I understand that you guys are just as confused about this as we are, but that doesn't give you the right to disrespect an officer."

Michael folds his arms. "I didn't disrespect you."

"Using profanity toward an officer *is* disrespect, or didn't your mother teach you that?"

"Get in the car, Michael. Please," I urge.

Michael turns for my Volvo, and suddenly, the first officer's vehicle backs up full speed, and loudly smashes into the second officer's Crown Vic parked directly behind it.

My eyes immediately go to Michael.

Ms. Ward's hands cover her mouth. "What the hell!"

The officers are stunned. So am I. The impact was so powerful that I could feel it beneath my feet. I can't imagine what it took out of Michael to move something as heavy as a vehicle, and with such force.

The officers call in for help as they walk toward the inexplicable collision. The second officer's Crown Vic is now trunk-first in a ditch.

Michael looks me in the eye. I question him with mine.

The officers are in a frenzy, loudly questioning what happened and searching around the vehicles. I so badly want to ask Michael why he would do that. Why allow someone to anger you to the point that you not only exhaust yourself but use your powers as publicly as this?

Ms. Ward touches my shoulder. "What the hell just happened?"

My eyes remain on Michael. "I have no idea."

The second officer walks back over to us. "What did you see? Did any of you see anything?"

Ms. Ward shrugs with her mouth open. No words are spoken.

I state the obvious. "His car hit yours."

"How?"

"I don't know. That's all I saw."

He hurries back over to examine the first officer's vehicle.

"Can we go?" Ms. Ward asks. "I don't know what's going on here, but I don't want to chance these kids getting hurt."

"You guys can't leave this scene," the first officer explains.

"Why would we stay?" Ms. Ward asks. "We didn't touch your car. You can both attest to that. You had your eyes on the three of us. We're not going to be blamed for you not shifting your vehicle into park."

The officers stand dumbfounded. I remain hushed. Michael does, too.

"I'll wait," Ms. Ward volunteers. "I'll give a statement or whatever it is you may need. We can all agree that no one touched the vehicle. There's no reason to hold the kids here any longer."

The second officer agrees, and tells Michael and me that we're no longer required to stay.

"I don't think you should head to Jersey tonight," Ms.

Ward tells me.

I agree with her.

"I want your phone on all night."

"Okay."

She looks at Michael. "Why don't you let Jaylen drive? That'll allow you to calm down."

Michael silently walks around to the passenger side.

"Thank you so much for rescuing us tonight, Ms. Ward. I didn't mean to interrupt your evening with Corey."

"Corey? Really, Jaylen? This is what I'm here for. You can call me any time you need anything. I'll always come and get you. No questions asked."

I hug Ms. Ward before stepping into the driver seat. As I slowly pull off, I order Michael to buckle up. He does.

I ask softly, "How do you feel? Do you want me to take you home?"

He doesn't answer me.

His anger saddens me. This was supposed to be a good night. Prom nights are not supposed to end like this.

I stop on another side street not too far from where we just were. Though the police just bothered us for doing this, I want to talk to Michael. I want to calm him, at least figure out where he wants to go from here.

I caress his cheek. "Do you wanna talk about it?"

"What's there to talk about, Jaylen? You wanna talk about the asshole with the badge treating me like I have a record?"

"I'm worried about you, Michael. I'm not your enemy."

Michael gets out of my car, slamming the door behind him. Before following him, I slide my clutch under the passenger seat and turn the car off.

He paces. "Why do you think all of this happened?"

"Michael, you need to relax and drink some water."

"You don't think Indigo leaving the parking garage had anything to do with the tag being removed from the back of your car?"

"We can't worry about that right now. I need you to worry about taking care of yourself."

"That bitch reported your car stolen. Who else could have enough of your information to do that? Ms. Ward damn sure didn't."

I reach out to him. "Michael—"

"Jaylen, we almost went to jail tonight! This is not a joke. There's something wrong with that girl. She'd rather you get locked up than spend the night with me."

I completely understand why Michael is so furious. I'm just as upset about what happened tonight. We're lucky that we aren't sitting at the police station right now.

Michael stops pacing, and walks away. I move to catch up.

"I know you're having a hard time seeing past your anger. What happened tonight was unnecessary, and the way that cop treated you was wrong." I grab his hand. "You need to drink some water and let me take you home so you can rest. Indigo's done enough to us for one night. Don't let your anger distract you from taking care of yourself. Your body is weak."

He looks me in my eye. "I'm sorry."

"For?"

"The cop cars. I'm too old to allow my anger to control my actions."

I sigh. "I'm not happy that you did that, but you don't have to apologize to me." I lighten my tone. "It wasn't *my* car."

He chuckles, and I smile. It's a relief to see half a smile on his face.

"Let me take you home, Michael. And if you don't wanna go home, tell me where to take you."

He pulls me closer. "Where are you spending the rest of your night?"

I tilt my head. "Is that really something you need to ask? I'm wherever you are."

We kiss. We find comfort in the love we share, though we both know we're dealing with something that's far more serious than we initially assumed.

Michael abruptly pulls away from me. His eyes are wide and alert.

My heart begins to hammer against my chest. My instincts take over. "Feel that?"

He grabs my arm. "An animal is close."

"We should go back to the car."

"It's walking on the passenger side of your car. I can see the shadow."

We dash off into the wooded area. The presence isn't as strong.

Michael breathes thickly. "I'm thirsty. Hopefully, it's just something curious and will go away."

"What did the shadow look like? A buck?"

The presence feels stronger. It's moving toward us.

I pull Michael farther into the wooded area. I move speedily through the trees, but can feel that something's following us. The bluish-white glow of the nearly full moon offers just enough light for me to see where I'm going, but not enough to make me feel safe. Anything could be hiding out here. I hope to hit a side street or path. Michael needs water. We both need to find safety.

We're stopped by a river. I begin to panic. An animal is following us, Michael is worn out, and we're away from access to any help.

I scoop up some water in my cupped hands and hold it to Michael's lips. His breathing is still deep. His face is visibly worn.

"Drink it."

Though it's far from clean, he gives his body what it needs. Thunder makes us both jump, and small, scattered raindrops lightly fall upon us.

The animal is closer. My eyes are fully expanded as I look out for our opponent.

As Michael bends to drink more of the water, my eyes lock in on our stalker. I initially hoped that it wasn't another buck. Now I wish it were.

The intimidating beast is completely black. Curved claws stick out from its paws.

I gasp. "A bear."

Michael stands straight. "Don't move."

I whisper, "*You* don't move. I can take a hit. You can't right now."

"Throw something at it. They say black bears are just curious. If you make noise, they'll go away. They're afraid of humans."

"We're not human," I remind him.

I stare at the bear. The large mammal stands very still.

"Don't look at it, Jaylen. Don't make eye contact."

I lower my head.

"Go away, bear." Michael's voice is low and calm.

The rain comes down heavier.

"Shut up." My volume is almost inaudible.

His voice remains calm and low. "This is what you're supposed to do, Jaylen. I'm not trying to get us killed. You want the bear to know you're human. Don't make it feel threatened. Don't look it in the eye. Don't run."

I stand perfectly still, though I'm absolutely terrified. It's not how we look to this animal that concerns me. It's what its instincts are telling him about us. It's how we're making him feel that worries me.

The bear walks closer to us.

"Back up, babe." Michael's voice is a whisper.

I carefully step back. The bear takes another step forward.

"Michael, what the hell?" I ask in a panic.

The bear makes jaw popping sounds and huffs loudly. He stands, and fear overcomes me, forcing my teeth to chatter. His height is nearly Michael's.

"Don't run, Jaylen. He'll chase you."

I breathe in and out slowly. I talk myself into calming down. This could end a few different ways. One way this won't end is with Michael hurt.

The bear comes back down on all fours and charges me. I fall, and deafening screams escape me. Michael's attempt to help fails as he's slapped across the chest by the animal's paw. The second I see him hit, my strength takes over. As Michael collapses, I push the large, wet animal from off of me. I stand and take off. My goal is to distract the attacker from Michael. It works.

The bear follows me and slaps me across my back. I hit the ground again. My screams for help are much louder.

I turn over, kicking crazily and trying to block my face. His claws slash me on each side. I glance at the bear through my arms covering my face. As his mouth opens to bite, I pull back a fist and jab him in the nose. The hit doesn't move the bear the way I hoped it would. It doesn't even knock him completely off of my body.

I kick and stop screaming to conserve the energy I have left. The downpour is damn near blinding. Thunder rumbles, shaking the ground beneath me.

The soaked animal shows all of its teeth once again. I fight with my hands. Screams return.

The bear slaps me again and releases a monstrous growl.

Fear and the need to survive give me the strength to kick the ferocious animal off my body. Freed from his body weight, I quickly crawl into the body of water and swim toward the middle. The water is not nearly as deep as I thought it would be.

I take a huge gulp of the foul-tasting water and watch as the persistent, predatory mammal comes toward me. As he swims, I submerge myself in the chest-deep water and swim beneath the surface, around the animal, in the direction I entered.

I stand. The large raindrops are louder than my ragged panting as they plop into the water. The bear continues in the direction he initially saw me fleeing.

With the bear's back to me, I quickly wrap my left arm around his neck and try to wrap my legs around his back.

He takes me under. He's fighting for me to release him, and I'm fighting to hold on.

We resurface, the bear only on two feet.

I reach around the top of his head and grab his nose. The moment his mouth opens, I reach in and grip his top row of teeth. I reach from under his jaw with my left hand and grip his lower row.

He's fighting, and we go under again. I don't let go. I pull with determination.

We resurface once more. Still, I'm pulling as he tries his hardest to close his jaws. His wiggling is causing me to lose my position on his back.

I pull as hard as I can. I use all that's left in me. I scream through clenched teeth until his jawbone snaps. Until I have pulled the mouth of this beast completely apart.

The fight stops instantly. The bear's limp body weighs much more as I'm now holding a majority of its weight.

I let go of the animal and allow the water to steal the little life left inside of it. Slowly, I head back toward solid ground. The pouring rain is still heavy. I'm fighting to see through it.

"Michael!" I yell.

My breathing is labored. My body is incredibly weak. As tired as I feel, nothing is going to stop me from helping Michael survive.

"Jaylen."

I spot him. He's lying on his back. His mouth is open as

rain falls in. There's little blood, but the wounds are visible. Through the four parallel rips in his shirt, I can see where the claws tore his skin.

I gently stroke his cheek, and his eyelids lower. He exhausted himself by using his abilities to move the cop car. Now, he's suffering from injuries that wouldn't be nearly as big of a deal if his body wasn't already weakened.

"I have to go get you help."

"I've already called. They know the street. I told them to look out for your car."

"Can you walk?"

He shakes his head.

"I'm going back to the car. Did you pack water in your duffel?"

"Of course."

"I'm gonna go get it. I can't just stand here and watch you suffer."

I leave for help. Though I'm moving at a turtle's pace, this is as fast as I can go. I can feel another presence near. My kind. I try to move more quickly, but my legs give way, and my body thuds against the ground.

"Jaylen!"

I recognize her voice. "Indigo! I'm here!"

Her footsteps grow closer. As I lie completely drained, breathing unevenly, I think of Michael. *Fight, babe. Please hang in there. Breathe. Please, be okay.*

Indigo drops down beside me. "What happened to you?"

I take the bottle of water from her hand and gulp half of it down.

"I saw your car," she says.

I point toward the area I just left. "Michael's hurt. A bear attacked. Go give this water to him."

"I'm not leaving you, Jaylen. There could more animals out here."

"Please, Indigo," I beg. "He's dying. He needs it. I know

I look bad, but believe me, he's worse off."

"You need it, too."

"I'll be okay." My breathing is still sporadic. "Indigo, I'm begging you. If I ever really meant anything to you, please do this for me."

She leaves me with the bottle of water in her hand. I look up into the trees. The rain is much lighter now.

"Jaylen!"

I turn toward the voice. I don't see anyone. I assume I'm hearing things.

I look back up into the trees. I spot something dark moving. I focus through squinted eyes, and I realize it's a baby black bear. It hits me immediately. That wasn't a predatory male. That was a protective, territorial mother.

I hear footsteps. My eyes move toward them.

"Jaylen, are you okay?"

It's Kennedy.

"What happened to you?"

I breathe in and out slowly. "A bear," I tell her.

She gulps down water from her bottle. Her gulps are loud enough for me to hear.

"I want you to be still, Jaylen. Be quiet, and be very still."

There's no fight left in me to do anything different. I lie motionless as Kennedy places her hands on me. I close my eyes and lie silently.

Tingles begin to move throughout my body. I begin to tremble uncontrollably. Something is happening to me. Something weird.

I turn to Kennedy. "What the hell are you doing?"

"Shh."

I keep quiet as my body shakes all over. Seizure-like shakes.

Kennedy is perfectly silent. Her eyes are wide and on me. She doesn't blink. She doesn't move her hands.

I look down at her hands and then move my eyes back

up to her face. I question what she's doing. I question why my body reacts to her touch in this way.

She calmly pulls her hands from me after about a minute has elapsed, and sips more water down.

Moments ago, I felt too weak to move. I look at my arm where the bear had slashed me with its claws. There's nothing. No gashes. No blood.

"Need help sitting up?"

I ease upright.

She asks, "You feel okay?"

"How did you do that?"

"One of my many talents."

"But you're human. You're not like us."

"Human? Me?" She chuckles sarcastically. "Far from it."

I remember walking into first period on my first day of school. Mr. Bowers said there were three others with a similar medical condition. He was talking about Kennedy. This is why she and Indigo have remained so close. She, too, is our kind.

"How come I can't feel your presence?" I ask.

"That remains a mystery. I can feel yours, though."

"So you knew about me?"

"Mm-hmm. I can feel our kind. I can feel animals. You guys just can't feel me."

"So you don't pose the same threat that we do to animals? You're like a human."

"Something like that."

She finishes off her water, and I eye Indigo as she comes back our way.

"Is he okay?"

Indigo helps me to my feet.

"Is Michael okay?" I ask again.

"He's fine."

I don't trust what she's saying. Michael would be looking for me if he were really all right. He'd crawl if he had to just to make sure I'm safe. I start toward my boyfriend.

"Where are you going?" Indigo asks.

"To make sure he's all right."

Loud sirens fill the street. The three of us turn toward the flashing lights. As I hear the voices of EMTs in the distance, my eyes move to Indigo. I think about where I'm standing. We're in the woods, nowhere near the after-party, in our prom dresses, on prom night.

I ask, "What are y'all doing out here?"

Kennedy looks at Indigo. Indigo's eyes are on the ground.

"It's prom night. You both had dates." I ask again, "Why are you out here?"

"I saw your car," Indigo answers.

"You're lying, Indigo. You just happened to be driving down this street?" I take slow backward steps. "You followed us from Michael's, didn't you? You ripped the tag off my car while it was parked in the garage, and you reported my car stolen to the police department."

Kennedy briefly looks at me before her eyes move down to her hands. That look confirms everything I'm saying.

As EMTs and officers call out, I head for my boyfriend.

"Young lady!"

I turn toward the officers.

"What are you kids doing out here?" the officer asks.

"My boyfriend called."

"Are any of you hurt?"

"No," Indigo answers quickly.

"Yes!" I shout. "My boyfriend is hurt. He was attacked by a black bear. He's down by the water."

The officer sends the EMTs down with another officer following behind.

"What happened to your dress, young lady? Were you attacked as well?"

I forgot that I, too, was attacked. Kennedy took care of

me, but not my dress. Slits from the bear's claws have been left behind, revealing that something violent occurred. I'm soaked. Brown mud is all over me.

"I'm okay," I reply, though my appearance says the opposite.

"Why are you all out here? Looks like prom night."

I explain, "My boyfriend and I just stopped for a moment to talk. He was angry so he walked a little to calm down. We saw a bear sniffing around the car. We only stepped into this area to hide. We didn't think the bear would follow us."

The officer addresses Indigo and Kennedy. I can't hear anything they're saying. All I can think about is Michael. About him suffering alone on the ground without enough strength to even stand. About him waiting for me to return to him.

"Young lady?"

I look at the officer. "Yes."

"You all right?"

"No. Can I go to him?"

"The EMTs will take care of him." He points. "So that's your vehicle parked up there on the street?"

"Yes."

He turns to Indigo and Kennedy. "How'd you ladies get here?"

Before they respond, an EMT heads back up. "There's nobody down there," he informs us.

"He's by the water," I explain.

He addresses the officer. "We didn't see anyone. Officer Perry is walking farther down to see if perhaps the young man found the path and exited that way."

I take off back down to where I left Michael. I can hear the officer chasing behind me. I call out for Michael as I move swiftly. The other EMT grabs me. I push out of his hold and look around the area. Michael isn't here.

I grab my hair at the scalp and scream for him.

The officer grabs me. "Young lady!"

"He was here!"

I search the area with my eyes. I spot the empty bottle of water. Just no Michael.

"There's nobody here."

"He was here," I argue.

"Maybe he found his way back to the main road."

I ignore the officer. "Michael!"

He shakes me. "There's nobody out here. We need to get you ladies out of this area. If your boyfriend was confronted by a bear, we could be in danger. I'm sure Michael is okay. Officer Perry probably found him."

I look around the area where I left him. My heart is beating out of control. My mind is thinking the worst.

"Walk with me." The officer speaks to me kindly.

I search the ground. Tears fill my eyes. I don't shake them away. Inside, I can feel that something is wrong. Really wrong.

My eyes scan the wet ground. I look over the wet leaves, the broken twigs, the rocks. My eyes move slowly, and then focus on something that knocks the wind out of me.

"No!" I scream.

I spot what looks to me like the piece tucked in the back of my drawing pad. Like the drawing on Michael's living room wall. The object is wet, but absolutely familiar.

"Michael!"

I pull away from the officer. The tears stream down my face. This pain is the worst I've ever felt.

The officer grabs me and begs for me to calm down.

"She did it!" I continue to fight. "I don't know what she did to him, but she did it!"

He holds onto me. "Young lady. Please!"

I fall to my knees. I call on a God I've never talked to. I bawl, each falling tear, a painful one. I scream through closed teeth. I curse myself. I call for Michael. I scream in agony. I hit the ground in anger. I grab my chest in regret, as I'm the one who sent Indigo down to him.

Chapter 21

I sit in the passenger seat of my car with my head resting against the window. More tears fall as I watch Kennedy speak with the officers. They allowed Indigo to leave the scene before I was given the opportunity to confront her. Everything in me wanted to pull away from them and get my hands on her, but I couldn't. Kennedy gave me my strength back, but seeing that cocoon lying there instead of Michael drained me in every way. I had a hard time finding the strength to even walk.

My driver door opens. "Jaylen, I told the officers I would drive you home."

I don't respond to Kennedy.

"If I don't drive you, they plan on transporting you to the hospital. They don't feel comfortable with you operating a vehicle."

Tears continue to slide down my cheeks as I nod slowly.

Kennedy briefly chats with an officer before sitting behind the wheel of my Volvo. As she pulls off, I stare out the window. I look out at the place I had my last kiss with my boyfriend. His face comes to mind. I can still smell the faint scent of his cologne.

"You okay, Jaylen?"

My voice cracks. "Why?"

"It may not have been what you thought it was."

"Why did you guys do this to me?"

"Jaylen, I've never had anything against you or Michael," she says, sounding almost apologetic. "I don't know either of you to have any issues."

"You were with her when she did this. You were both in the parking garage. You've been driving her around all night."

"I didn't know what she was doing in the garage. I never went any farther than the entrance. I heard something hit the ground, and she walked out with a number written on her hand. You saw me chasing after her. I wanted to know what was going on. And I've only been driving her around because she was so worried about you."

Yeah, I bet she was worried. I wipe my face and call Michael's phone. The call goes straight to his voicemail, and I can't help but let additional tears fall. I'm lost right now. Deep inside, I always knew Indigo would never be completely okay with Michael and I being together. Though I knew she'd never truly accept it, I never imagined her hurting anyone.

"Where am I going, Jaylen?"

"Drive to your house. I can take myself home."

"Someone's at your house, right? You're... You're..." She trips over her words. "You're not feeling like doing anything to yourself, are you?"

I sit silently. That thought is the furthest from my mind.

"Just keep in mind that we don't know that Michael isn't okay. There's a path that leads to a parking lot. He may have found it."

I think about my boyfriend. There's no way he would be okay and not let me know that. That's completely out of character for Michael. If he were strong enough to stand on his own, finding me would have been his first priority.

"I'm sorry, Jaylen. I swear that I didn't go to prom tonight intending to hurt anyone."

"I didn't think you did."

"I didn't directly, but I've known for a while now that Indigo has had it out for Michael."

I cover my face with my hands. This entire situation feels like a complete nightmare. I'm sure Michael never thought that being in a relationship with me would cost him his life.

"They hooked up once," she tells me.

"So I heard."

"She never really got over it."

"Neither of them told me about that right away."

"She told me about it. They swore never to bring it up again. Michael didn't want the relationship, and Indigo didn't want the reputation."

"What did she say to you about it?" I ask, expecting to learn something new. There has to be something I don't know.

"I hope you're not under the false impression that Indigo just sort of liked Michael. She definitely loved him. They were super close for a while. Then she wanted to take things further. I guess it got awkward because they weren't nearly as close after that."

I wipe my eyes. "What do you think about the whole thing?"

"I've always been Indigo's friend. I was never Michael's. But with that being said, Michael never tried to hurt Indigo. She'll never even try to understand that because he broke her heart. I can respect someone for not jumping into a relationship for the wrong reasons. She can't see past her emotions, so her thinking is far from logical."

I take a deep breath. "So what about you and Indigo?"

"We were secretly together for a while."

"She told me about a girlfriend but didn't say a name."

"Yeah. Indigo's great at that."

I look over at Kennedy. "Great at what?"

"Giving tidbits of information. Taking you in damn circles."

"You guys aren't still together?"

Her volume is almost inaudible. "No."

"Why?"

"She met someone in January."

I turn back toward the window.

"I'm not mad about it, Jaylen."

"So Indigo has in one way or another hooked up with all three of us?"

"It sounds worse than it really is. Were there any of our kind at your old school?"

"I haven't been around our kind since my mother died when I was four."

"You've never felt another presence at all?" she asks in disbelief.

"Not until I got here."

"What was that like?"

I exhale. "Lonely. Scary. Extremely confusing. I knew I wasn't like everybody else, but there was no one who could tell me what I was for sure."

Kennedy drives on in silence. More tears fill my eyes at the thought of Michael, at the thought of what he may have endured. My heart hurts. There's a stinging in my abdomen. I feel so guilty.

I need to know what happened to my boyfriend, but that's not something Kennedy can tell me. She was with me while Indigo was supposedly aiding Michael. That doesn't mean she can't tell me why it happened. Though I'll never believe he could've done anything horrible enough to cost him his life, something did push Indigo over the edge. I think Kennedy knows what that is. If I keep her talking, she'll likely let it out.

"So, you were saying," I remind her. "It sounds worse

than it really is."

"Oh, right. Indigo just wants to be in a relationship. She wants what she sees humans our age have."

"We all do."

"The way my father tries to explain it to me is that we're kind of like animals in a sense. We don't look like them, but we have incredible instincts and can sense things that a normal human just can't. An animal wouldn't be sexually attracted to a human. I know dogs hump legs, but that's not the same thing. How animals feel about humans is how we feel about humans. We can learn to love them, we can learn to live in their environment, but given our choice of family, we're more comfortable with our own."

I listen. I don't speak.

"We don't have the luxury of picking from hundreds of guys. Only four of us attend Trinity. From what Indigo told me, she felt something really strong for you when she first saw you. She didn't feel that for me or for Michael. With us, it was a friendship she hoped would go in another direction. The reason I said it sounds worse than it is, is because we're the only three people that she really could have anything with. It only sounds bad because we're all kind of connected. We all sort of know each other."

"How did she find out about you?"

"I told her. I wanted to be friends."

My mind goes back to Michael. I think about his last moments. I wonder if he was angry with me. Angry with me for sending someone who harbors so much hate for him to his rescue.

I ask Kennedy, "What do you think Indigo's capable of?"

She shakes her head. "I've learned to just believe that anyone is capable of anything."

I push her. "You've known Indigo longer than I have."

"I know that she loves you. I know that she loved

Michael. To see you two together is hard for her. It's made her do some crazy things. The two people she fell in love with fell in love with each other."

I wipe the tears from my face. "The day I get my hands on her…"

"Jaylen."

"Indigo better not assume that this is something I can forgive."

"Don't start thinking crazy thoughts, Jaylen."

"Her ass is gonna be sorry for taking—" I cry hard. "For taking the only person I had left away from me."

She passes Michael's house, and I can't bear to look at it. I think about how Ms. Reed is going to handle this. Her son left to go to prom. I'm sure she never thought that would be the last time she'd ever see her baby.

"I've never needed anyone in my life the way I need him. The thought of him hurting makes me want to kill her."

"Don't even think like that."

Kennedy pulls into her driveway. Her house is completely dark.

"You want to come in?"

I shake my head as my misery continues to pour out of my eyes.

She grabs my hand. "I'm so sorry, Jaylen."

"I'm lost right now."

Kennedy sniffles. "I understand if you hold me responsible, but please believe that I would never purposely hurt anyone." She weeps. "I didn't know Indigo hated Michael that much. I want to believe he's fine, but I think it's obvious that something happened."

"I don't know what I'm gonna do, but if I stay here, she's dead. That's it. If I see Indigo, it's over."

Kennedy pushes her brown hair from her face. "You don't know what kind of hell you'd be starting if you did that."

"She started this hell. Not me."

She wipes her face. "Stay here?" she offers again.

I rub my forehead.

"Jaylen, I'm not just asking you to stay for you, but for me, too. I feel so guilty, and I'm so nervous about everything that's happened."

"I keep thinking I should call his mother."

"No!" she blurts out. "Don't call. You don't know for sure, Jaylen."

"I know that something happened out there. I know Michael isn't all right. The police asked if anyone was hurt. Indigo said no. She didn't want anyone to go down and check on him. If she didn't do anything, why was she so anxious to leave the scene?"

"I'm not defending her, but she was anxious to leave for the same reason the officers wanted her to go. Nobody wanted you to confront her."

I grab my chest. "It hurts. It hurts so bad."

She grips my hand. "We'll sleep on it, Jaylen. You'll stay here, get some rest, drink plenty of water, and then we'll face tomorrow."

"What's tomorrow?"

"We'll go to Michael's house. We'll ask his mom if she's heard from him. If she has, we'll go from there. If she hasn't, we'll go back to where you last saw him tonight. We'll make sure that what you think you saw was actually there."

I eye my newfound supporter.

"And I'll call Indigo," she says.

"Why?"

"Because I feel involved in something I never wanted to be a part of. This is serious. I have a right to know why she took things so far tonight. I have a right to know exactly what happened between her and Michael. I deserve an explanation." She adds, "And I need my car back."

"It just doesn't feel right to leave his mother in the dark.

That's her child. She should know that he may not be okay."

"I just don't want you to tell her something you only think happened. You can't deliver that kind of news unless you're positive. If you tell the woman her son is—" She suddenly stops. Tears fall from her eyes. "Dead," she says in a low voice. "You have to know that. You can't deliver a shock like that without being certain."

"I'll just tell her that we were confronted by a bear in the woods. I'll tell her that Michael got hurt, I left to get help, and when I returned, he was no longer there. I'll tell her that I've been calling his phone." My voice breaks terribly. "I'll let her know that I haven't heard anything from him."

I turn toward the window to clean my face. I then search through my phone's contact list for Ms. Reed's cell number. The first call rings all the way to voicemail. The second does the same, but I prepare to leave a message this time.

I clear my throat. "Ms. Reed, this is Jaylen. I'm sorry to call so late." The tears come back. "After prom tonight, a few things happened. Michael ended up getting very upset after an incident with the police. He walked around a little bit to cool down." I clear my throat again. "While trying to calm himself, we ended up getting attacked by a black bear, and Michael was injured." More tears. "I went to get help and grab water from my car." I release a deep breath. "Cops and EMTs had arrived by this point. They went back to where I left Michael, and he wasn't there." I sob into the phone. "I haven't seen or heard from him since. This was all maybe an hour ago. An hour and a half at most." I sniff loudly. "Please let me know if you've heard from him. I'm really worried. And if you haven't, I'm so sorry to be the bearer of bad news."

I end the call, and Kennedy reaches over for a hug. Though I rarely lean on people I don't really know, I've never felt so low in my entire life. I'm facing a harsh reality, a sad pattern. Everyone I love, I lose. First, the mysterious death of my mother, then the fatal car crash that claimed the life of my mom, and now the murder of my boyfriend. The losses are getting more and more tragic.

"Tomorrow, we'll get some answers, Jaylen. I promise."

I squeeze her back. "Tomorrow."

Chapter 22

I wait for Kennedy to get out of the shower. I've tried Michael's phone repeatedly, and over and over again, I hear the same recording. I'm told that the number is no longer in service.

Kennedy enters her room. "Anything new?"

I shake my head. "Nothing. It's still saying the phone has been disconnected."

As Kennedy blow-dries her long, brown curls, my mind works overtime trying to figure out how I received a call from Michael's phone while I was asleep. Though I can't feel Kennedy's presence, I slept just as comfortably next to her as I do when I share a bed with Indigo. I slept heavy the entire night.

"Have you tried his mother again?" she asks loudly.

I nod. "No answer."

"Do you wanna wait here while I walk down to go get my car?"

"Absolutely not. I wanna see Indigo."

"Jaylen, we agreed to talk to his mother first."

"I'm going, Kennedy!"

She shuts off the blow dryer. "I don't know about this."

"This what?"

"I don't feel comfortable bringing you when I know you're looking for a fight."

"I want to hear what she has to say. You deserve an explanation, but I *need* one."

She restarts the blow-dryer, and I step out and into the bathroom. I stand behind closed doors by myself and look into the mirror. I quickly turn away from my reflection. This time yesterday, the reflection I saw was of a person still broken-hearted, but not looking to bring harm to anyone. Today, I'm a different person. I'm seeking satisfaction. Michael is no longer with me. That hole in my heart, that deep wound, may never heal. That pain may, and will likely, always be present. That, I can't change. That, I can't fix. I can, however, make sure justice is served. The police can't do anything for me, because there's no body. That doesn't mean Indigo got off easy. I won't be satisfied until the person who took Michael from me is no longer living. If he didn't deserve to live a full life, neither does she.

I leave the restroom and step back inside Kennedy's room.

"You okay?" she asks.

"Just needed a minute."

"The clothes fit."

I look down at myself. "A little snug up top, but the sweats are comfy. I appreciate them. Thanks."

"You still going by his house to see if his mom is there?"

"Yeah. And then I'm gonna drive to where everything happened."

"Mind if I tag along?"

"I thought that was the plan."

"Just making sure. It's your car. Your gas."

I keep my eyes on her. "Why are you being so nice to me? I thought you were friends with Indigo."

"Well, clearly, Indigo isn't being too friendly."

I point out, "She hasn't done anything to you."

"That doesn't mean that I'm even slightly okay with what she's done. Or, may have done." She sighs. "I feel like I owe you, Jaylen."

"You don't," I reply in a hurry.

The room becomes silent. I question Kennedy's sincerity. I befriended Indigo fairly quickly with few questions asked, and look where that's gotten me. I question Kennedy's motives. Is guilt really why she's interested in holding my hand through this?

"What's your deal, Kennedy?"

"What do you mean?"

"You've been Indigo's friend all of this time, and now, because you think Indigo may have hurt someone, you're suddenly my supporter. You've never spoken to me before. Why the hell should I trust you now?"

"Why would I talk to you? My girlfriend dumped me for you. And you don't have to trust me, Jaylen. That's your choice. All I can do is tell you that I'm sorry for what happened, and that I care enough to not want to see you go through this alone. If you want to, that's on you. But seriously, Jaylen, who else do you have? Who else can you tell about this? At this moment, who else can you be you with?"

I lower myself onto the side of her bed. This whole situation is bringing me down more and more by the minute.

I make eye contact with Kennedy. "Where's your dad?"

"Working."

"I felt his presence last night."

"Yeah. It's very strong when he's home."

"Is he your only family?"

"I'm the only child. My mom passed away when I was nine. My father has a couple of relatives in Canada, though."

"I'm sorry to hear about your mom."

"Sorry to hear about yours. Indigo told me you never

found out what happened."

"It's funny that she has no problem sharing my information. She didn't even tell me you were one of us."

"I asked her not to."

I groan. "I guess your secrets are more important than mine."

Kennedy looks through her phone.

"What are we, Kennedy? Why the hell are we here?"

"I think we all have those kinds of questions swirling around in our heads. We all want to know where exactly we're from, and what we're called."

"There have to be stories passed down. Something. Michael gave me bits and pieces, but it's unbelievable that no one knows more."

"My dad was told that our ancestors had no choice but to get us here. Earth had the resources."

"How are we capable of doing the things we do? How are our bodies able to heal the way they do?"

"We've all been blessed with the ability to recover quickly, but we don't all have what my dad considers gifts. I call them our blessings. Whatever you have supposedly came from your parents. My father was capable of healing others by simply placing his hands on them. That's why he became a doctor. He's been recognized several times for what he used to be able to do. After I was born, nothing. His injuries still heal fairly quickly, he still needs water, still has a powerful presence, and like most of our kind, is stronger than the average human, but he can't do what he once could." She sips some water. "But I can."

"Michael told me most of us are in Michigan."

"Yeah. Michigan and Canada. Not really sure why there of all places, but my dad says in certain areas, the presence of our kind is just overwhelmingly apparent."

"Do you ever wish you were just a human?"

She nods. "Sometimes. That is until I get injured and feel

little to no pain, or I see someone sick or badly bruised."

I touch my stomach. "I have scars."

"What do you mean?"

"I was in a car wreck. I was impaled, and it left scars."

"Really? I've never been scarred. I've been burned. No other marks other than those, though."

I lift my shirt.

Kennedy's eyes carefully look over my midriff. "Where?"

I look down. I look to the side of my abdomen. I feel my skin with my hand.

"Where?" she asks again.

I look at Kennedy. "They're gone."

"Gone?"

I pull my shirt down. "That must've happened when you did that thing to me last night. They were definitely there when I dressed for prom."

"Well, that's not a bad thing, is it?"

I let out softly, "No. Not at all."

"I'm gonna ask my dad about your scars. I thought only burns could flaw us."

I sit wordlessly with my eyes on Kennedy's floor. I silently wish that Kennedy had reached me first. I wish that Kennedy had been the one to go down and assist Michael.

I admit aloud, "I feel so guilty."

"Don't, Jaylen."

A tear drops from my left eye. "I miss him so much."

"What was it like?" she asks softly.

"What?"

"What you felt. You know, whatever it was you felt when you first saw him."

I wipe the tear away. "I felt the connection. I felt the closeness," I tell her. "His presence was stronger than Indigo's. Much stronger. And the sight of him was heart-stopping. Almost like I loved him at the sight of him. I mean, I didn't. I needed a little more time to fall, but what I felt right away was serious." I think back to my first day at Trinity. I remember watching him waltz into class so casually after the tardy bell had already sounded. "From the very first moment I laid my eyes on him, I couldn't stop thinking about him. And there have been times when I've tried to stop, just because I felt for him so intensely. It never worked, though. I knew from day one that I absolutely belonged with Michael. The thought of him with someone else, or leaving me, or anything like that, mentally drove me insane. The time I spent not talking to either of them was so painful." I shake my head. "Kennedy, it was so hard to see him and not talk to him or touch him. He owns so much of my heart." More tears fall. "I love him. I really, really do."

She holds her chest. "You just scared me."

I eye Kennedy. "How?"

"Because that's how she feels about you."

I cover my face with my hands and breathe into my palms.

"Love can make a person do crazy things."

I lower my hands. "Who you telling?" I stand and grab my keys from her dresser. "You ready?"

I drive down the street to Michael's house. The driveway is empty, and the garage is closed securely.

"Doesn't look like anyone is here."

"They rarely park in the driveway," I explain.

We both exit my Volvo and take slow steps toward my boyfriend's front door.

"How do you think she's going to react?"

I ring the doorbell. "How would you if someone were giving you this kind of news?"

We both stand nervously. After about a minute of waiting, I ring the bell again.

"I don't think anybody is here, Jaylen."

I notice that I don't feel her presence at all. I definitely don't feel Michael's. We haven't heard any movements.

Kennedy's right. Nobody's here.

Kennedy walks ahead of me back to my car. I move slowly. This is certainly disappointing. I was sure I would've heard back from her by now. She isn't home, and she has yet to respond to my message. I have no idea what to think.

We head back to where all of the horror took place last night. My emotions begin to overwhelm me. I gulp down a few large swallows of water to calm myself and to help me take control of the involuntary jitters.

"You okay?"

I shake my head. "Not really."

I continue to drive as Kennedy directs.

"Last night, you were parked on a side street. We're gonna park in the parking lot so we can walk down the path. It's gonna be too muddy to walk down to the water from the side you parked on last night."

"I want to be on the side we were on last night."

"The path splits. Bike riders stick to the concrete path, and take the bridge to get to the other side. We're gonna take the path and head down the split that turns into the dirt trail. That'll lead you right back to where you were last night, minus the small incline."

I follow her directions and park in a small parking lot already occupied by three other vehicles.

"Got any Mace?"

"No," I answer.

She pulls defense spray from her purse and hands it to me.

"What's this for?"

"Just in case another bear approaches. I can't believe you don't carry protection."

I take the spray from her. "Well, until I moved out here, I never went in the woods."

We head down the trail. This area looks so much more pleasant in the daylight. The bright sunlight dances on the water as kayakers paddle in groups. A family of four fishes from a pier I didn't even see last night. Beautiful, green trees cast their reflections on the water, and lily pads float near the shore, though my presence has scared away the frogs.

"You nervous?" Kennedy asks.

I sigh. "I don't know what I'm feeling."

We head down the dirt trail. The ground is still wet. I watch my step as I'm walking in borrowed shoes.

We walk alongside the river. It's hard to believe I was standing in and drinking from that filth last night. Though the beauty of this place cannot be denied in the light of day, the water is far from clean. It's brown up-close.

"It's a little farther up," she tells me.

I grab her forearm. "You feel that?"

"Maybe it's Michael."

I state positively, "That's not Michael."

My heart rate elevates. My insides heat up at the sight of her. The empty water bottle is still on the ground. We're where everything occurred last night, and so is Indigo.

Kennedy whispers, "Jaylen, please stay calm."

My hands clench into fists.

Indigo's eyes move to Kennedy, the ground, the water, her hands, but never to me.

"Hey."

"Hey, Kennedy." Indigo's voice shakes.

"What are you doing out here?"

She looks around. "Last night was crazy. I just came out here to…"

She pauses in the middle of her sentence. I watch as she rubs her hands together. She nervously touches her hair.

"To what?" Kennedy asks.

"I don't know." She shrugs. "To… To…" She stammers and shrugs once again. "I just came out here to look around."

Kennedy moves toward her. "Are you okay?"

She reveals a shaky smile. "I'm fine."

"Indigo, what happened last night?"

She shakes her head. "I don't know."

My fists tremble. I want to grab her. I want to beat her face in. I want to kill her. *You don't know? Bullshit, you don't.* Only two people know what happened last night, and one of them isn't here to tell.

Kennedy turns to me and then back to Indigo. "What happened between you and Michael?"

Indigo's eyes briefly look into mine and then quickly move back to the ground. She stands silently.

"You told the police he wasn't hurt," Kennedy reminds her. "Jaylen said he was really weak and lying on the ground when she left him."

I watch Indigo closely. Something's eating away at her. She can't keep her head or eyes up.

Kennedy's tone is gentle. "You can talk to me. Us," she corrects. "You can talk to us. We're your friends."

I don't comment. I don't attempt to comfort Indigo. The only reason a person would look so guilty is because they did something wrong.

"I have to go," Indigo says. "My aunt is waiting for me."

"Answer her question!" I demand.

"I don't know what you guys want to hear me say."

I step toward her. "Say what you did! What did you do to him?"

"Get the hell away from me, Jaylen." She steps back.

"I know you did something." I point at her. "You psychotic bitch."

Kennedy grabs my arm, but I pull away.

"I didn't do anything to your boyfriend that you didn't send me to do."

I snap. I grab Indigo by the shirt and throw her to the ground. I place both hands around her neck. As I squeeze the life from her body, I violently slam her head repeatedly against the wet ground.

"Jaylen, get off!" Kennedy shouts, trying to pull me from Indigo's body.

Indigo kicks wildly, but I hold firmly. As I look at her, at what I'm doing, tears run from my eyes. As much as I hate her for whatever she did to my Michael, this is a person I used to love. This is someone I spoke to daily, laughed with regularly, and cared for deeply.

Indigo's face turns beet red. She's suffocating, and all I can think about is Michael. All I can imagine is his misery. His pain. Pain she caused him.

"Jaylen!" Kennedy cries out.

I'm yanked from Indigo's body and thrown to the hard ground so quickly and with such force that I'm not sure even a second elapsed.

I look up at the woman who just grabbed me. The long black-haired woman's electric-blue eyes pierce mine. I can feel her presence now that I'm no longer focused on Indigo. She's definitely our kind.

"You stay the hell away from her." Her voice is deep. Threatening.

I look at who must be Indigo's aunt, at a woman Indigo has always described as cold and never wants to be around. She keeps so far away from her aunt that I've never even met her.

Indigo's aunt doesn't look Dominican in any way. Her blue eyes are large. Her skin is very pale. Vampire pale. Her legs look like they go on forever. She towers over Indigo and Kennedy.

"Did you hear me?"

I stand. "Don't ever put your damn hands on me again."

"You better never come near her again."

Indigo lies on the ground, gasping for air. Her aunt kneels down beside her. She pushes Indigo's hair from her face and offers her bottled water.

Kennedy steps closer to me. "Please, Jaylen. Let's go."

"You don't know what you just started for yourself, little girl."

I look at Indigo's aunt. "Your niece doesn't know what she started. How the hell can you defend a murderer?"

"You have a problem with her, you have a problem with me. I don't care what she did. I'm not going to sit back and let you kill my child."

"Then we have problems." My eyes move to Indigo. "If Michael couldn't have his life, you won't have yours. This is so far from over! I don't give a damn what this woman says!"

"You be careful. If my niece's life is in danger, so is yours."

I move toward her aunt, and she hurriedly stands.

A passerby grabs our attention. "Hello. How are you all doing?"

Kennedy responds, "We're well, and yourself?"

"Oh my Lord." Her eyes are on Indigo. "Is she all right?"

Indigo sits upright. "I just fell. I'm fine." Her voice is strained. She massages her neck.

As Indigo's aunt and the passerby help Indigo to her feet, I turn around and head back for the path. I can't look at Indigo. If I remain in her presence, I'll end up putting my hands on her again, which will lead to her aunt jumping in for a second time, and the passerby calling the authorities. We're lucky no one saw what just took place. The last thing I need is to deal with the cops again.

"Jaylen, you almost killed her," Kennedy says in panicked breaths as she catches up to me.

"Get away from me, Kennedy," I order.

"What?"

"Go get your car from Indigo, and stay away from me. I'd rather not have my problems become yours."

Kennedy stops walking, and I continue to my car. The anger darts through my veins. The reality sets in. Michael is gone. I'm alone. Alone and facing problems I may not be strong enough to handle on my own.

Chapter 23

There's a soft knock at my bedroom door. I don't move to answer it. I don't respond to her. The reason I've stayed in here behind closed doors is because I want to be alone. Unfortunately, she won't just leave me be.

"Jaylen," Ms. Ward calls out softly.

I don't turn toward her. I lie silently, holding on to the oversized birthday present that remained inside my hot trunk for weeks.

She walks over to my bed. "Can you please eat something?"

I stare at my wall. My eyes hurt from all the crying. My heart is in pieces because I miss Michael so much. Not just him, but my mom as well. I've never needed her so much. While she wouldn't be able to make the pain go away, she'd be able to offer me that one-of-a-kind comfort. That comfort one can only receive from their mom.

"Jaylen, please. Please, tell me what to do."

My cell rings. I ignore it.

"This has gone on for three days now. I don't know what to do, but I can't just let you lay here like this. You've put me in a position where I have to do something. You're not eating, you're not talking, you won't answer your phone. I don't know what's going on."

A tear escapes my eye.

"Jaylen, I know as a teenager, ups and downs are normal, but this is extreme. You won't leave this room, you won't open your blinds, you're not even nibbling anymore. This isn't healthy."

I bury my face in the bear.

"What is it that you need?" Her tone becomes an impatient one.

I shriek into the stuffed animal. "I need Michael!"

She snarls, her frustration mounting. "I think you need to speak to someone. High school breakups shouldn't bring you down this far. You haven't known the boy that long."

"Leave me alone."

"Your relationship with him isn't healthy."

"You don't know what you're talking about."

"First that incident in school that ended with you damaging school property. Now this. Three days in the bed, cut off from the outside world. This doesn't sound like the typical fairy tale to me, Jaylen."

Anger fills my tone. "You have no idea what you're talking about."

"Then tell me! Tell me so I can understand why you're acting like this."

"I don't wanna talk about it."

"You're going to talk to someone about it. If not me, I'm going to arrange for you to see a therapist. Your way of dealing with problems is not normal."

"I'm not talking to a therapist."

"Then who, Jaylen? I'm not gonna let you sit in here like this for three more days. I don't feel comfortable going to work knowing you're just lying in here sulking."

I remain silent.

"Maybe you should call Indigo. Would you prefer to talk to a friend?"

I instantly respond, "Not her."

"Then who, Jaylen? Give me something."

I rub my forehead. I'm beyond annoyed. "I'll call my friend, Kennedy. I'll talk to her."

Ms. Ward stands mutely. I can feel her eyes on me, but I don't look her way.

"I thought we were closer, Jaylen. I thought if you were ever in need, you'd come to me."

I sniff loudly. "I just can't talk to you about this. It's not something you'd understand."

"Try me."

"I'd rather not."

She sighs loudly.

I truly feel bad. I never wanted to hurt Ms. Ward. I have the utmost respect for this woman, and I appreciate everything she's provided me with and helped me through. This situation just isn't something I can talk out with her. Ms. Ward thinks our insides match. If I were to die, she'd have no understanding as to why my body couldn't be boxed and buried like hers. If I were to tell her that I believe Michael's dead and explain to her why, she'd skip calling a therapist and take me to a psychiatrist. I can't talk to a human about what I'm going through. The concept isn't one they could fathom.

She shrugs. "Well, call her, then, Jaylen. Call your friend and talk things out. I'm not asking you to just get over whatever it is you're going through. I'm just asking you to face it in a healthy way. I don't like to see you in pain. It hurts me to see you suffer."

She leaves my room, pulling the door closed behind her, and I immediately pick up my cell to do what she's asked of me. I'd prefer to be alone right now, but at this moment, it's more important for me to know that Ms. Ward isn't sitting around worrying about me. She's done too much for me. It'd be unfair to leave her in distress.

"Hello?"

My voice is low. "It's me."

"Are you okay, Jaylen?"

"I'm fine."

"I've been so worried about you. Where have you been?"

I clear my throat. "In bed."

"Well, why haven't you answered my calls?"

"To say what, Kennedy? I haven't felt like talking to anyone. The person I want to talk to, I can't."

"About that, have you heard anything?"

"Nothing. I've checked his Facebook. He hasn't been on. I've called. The number is still out of service."

"No word from his mom, either?"

"Nope," I tell her, "I'm sure she's listened to my message. She must be dealing with this the same way I am. Alone."

"You don't have to go through this alone. I'm here if you ever wanna talk."

I lie still.

"Jaylen, did you hear me?"

I ask her, "You wanna come over?"

"Now?"

"Yeah."

She hesitates. "Umm, okay. Sure."

"If you don't want to, you don't have to."

"No, I want to. I want to talk."

"Okay," I reply softly.

"I'll come now. Text me your address."

I end the call with Kennedy and text her my location. I then place the phone beside me and lie quietly next to my oversized bear as I wait for her to arrive.

As I wait, Indigo's face comes to mind. Not the beautiful face I saw on my first day at Trinity, but the face of someone I didn't know, standing in the wooded area, looking more than guilty on our prom night. I can't get that face out of my mind. I didn't recognize that girl. That was not the same person I originally met and spent almost all of my free time with. I loved that person. I miss that person.

I give it another shot and call Michael's cell. As the recording starts, I end the call. I don't need to hear it again.

I bury my face in the bear again and close my eyes. I think about Michael holding me. I remember his touch, his smell, his kiss. I keep my eyes closed and spend time in my memories. Beautiful memories I'll forever hold on to.

The shaking makes me jump. My eyes spring open.

Ms. Ward pushes my hair from my face. "You have company."

I turn toward Kennedy.

"I didn't know you were gonna take a nap. I would've come by later."

I yawn. "It's okay. I didn't mean to fall asleep. I guess I just dozed off."

Ms. Ward steps out, closing Kennedy and me in my room alone.

"I don't wanna make you feel worse, Jaylen."

"What?"

She sits on my window seat. "You look terrible."

"That's how I feel."

She smiles kindly. "I know you're probably tired of hearing me say it, but I'm so sorry. I don't think I've ever seen anyone in so much pain."

I tear up. "I think about him all the time."

"Have you spoken to Indigo?"

"Why the hell would I speak to her?"

"Just asking."

I ask, "Have you?"

"After she gave me my keys back, her aunt told me to stay away from her unless I want trouble."

I release a frustrated sigh. "Kennedy, maybe we

shouldn't hang out. I don't want you to have beef with anyone just because I do."

"I don't think that means we can't be friends." She lowers her voice. "It's hit me. Michael isn't here anymore. I can't associate myself with a murderer."

I remind her, "I almost killed Indigo."

"You were emotionally driven, Jaylen. You were hurt and angry."

"I wanted to kill her."

She shakes her head. "I don't believe that."

"Kennedy, what do you think would've happened if her aunt hadn't arrived in time?"

Our eyes look into one another's. I can see that Kennedy so badly wants to hear me say that I wouldn't kill anyone, but saying that would be a lie. Last week, I could've said that and meant it. Today, with only emptiness inside me, all I can think about is justice. Justice for Michael, which means an eye for an eye.

"Don't be like her, Jaylen."

"I don't want to be. I really don't. But Kennedy, if Indigo is left to walk around as freely as she pleases, what did Michael die for?"

"It's out of your hands now."

I look at my wall. I think about how much this situation has changed me. How different I've become.

"You okay?"

I admit, "I've been praying."

"So have I."

"But I'm not religious."

Her eyes widen. "You go to Catholic school, and you're not religious?"

"Never have been. Never been to church. Never prayed or been saved. None of that."

"I don't understand. What do you believe in?"

"Life. We live and then we die. That's what I believe in."

"So you just started praying?"

I nod. "I don't know if I'm doing it right. I don't know if I'm saying the right things." I turn onto my back. "I drove here and took a shower right after the incident with Indigo's aunt." I shake my head. "I didn't even realize what I was doing at first."

"How did it feel?"

"It was a desperate plea. I'd do anything to have Michael back. Anything at all. I begged to have him back."

"But did you feel anything?"

I shake my head. "I don't think so."

"I'm sorry to dwell on the subject, but what's it like for you to be in an environment like Trinity? Every morning, there's prayer. A lot of the teachers incorporate religion into their lessons."

"It was uncomfortable at first. I have my own issues with religion, but I try not to disrespect other people's beliefs. Personally, I'd much rather skip the subject. I don't usually talk about it, and I prefer not to debate or listen to opinions about it. I've always been comfortable being an atheist. As far as I'm concerned, people can believe in what they want, do what they want, and be what they want. Don't disrespect me, and I won't disrespect you."

Kennedy's mouth turns downward as she shoots me a disapproving look.

"Are you judging me right now?"

"I'm trying not to."

"You're Catholic?"

She nods.

"Your dad okay with you being a lesbian?"

She scrunches her face. "I'm not a lesbian."

"You said you dated Indigo. Doesn't that make you a lesbian?"

She opens her mouth to speak, and then slowly, her lips close.

"I'm not trying to make you uncomfortable, Kennedy. I'm just asking."

"Sometimes, I wonder if I only dated Indigo because there was no one else for me to date."

"Why didn't you pursue Michael?"

"Because she liked him."

I look away from Kennedy. It frustrates me that each of us allowed Indigo to control so much of the relationships we shared with her.

"What do you plan on doing, Jaylen?"

"What do you mean?"

"Where do you go from here?"

For the first time since everything's happened, I remember that I'm about to graduate from high school. I'm going to Princeton in the fall. I have a house waiting for me in New Jersey.

"I guess I'm going home," I answer.

"Home?"

"Jersey."

"Who's waiting for you there?"

A knot fills my throat. "No one. There's no one waiting for me anywhere."

"You going to school?"

"Princeton. You?"

"Seton Hall."

I ask myself where that is. Seconds later, I realize she'll be attending a Catholic university in New Jersey.

"You're following in your dad's footsteps? You wanna be a doctor?"

"Absolutely. I would never have a gift like this and not share it."

My eyes meet Kennedy's. I questioned this person's sincerity, but I'm realizing that she's truly a beautiful individual. Unselfish. Someone who cares for others.

"Good for you, Kennedy. More people should be that

way."

"I learned from the best."

"Daddy's girl. That's cute."

She smiles sweetly.

I turn to my phone. I tap the screen to view the text message that just alerted me. Instantly, I sit up.

Kennedy jumps up from my window seat. "What? Who is it?"

I turn the phone around for her to see.

"His mom? Jaylen, this is what you've been waiting for! What address is that?"

"I don't know."

"Call her."

I press send and the call goes straight to Ms. Reed's voicemail. I end the call without leaving a message.

"Went straight to voicemail," I tell her. "An address. Just an address. What kind of message is that?"

"Charles Town, West Virginia? Has Michael ever mentioned any relatives out there?"

I scoot off the bed. "No, but I'm going."

"You're gonna drive to West Virginia right now?"

"Yes."

"Are you serious? You don't even know what's at that address."

I grab a pair of sneakers from my closet. "I'm gonna go see."

"Jaylen, think about this."

"I am."

"Think about what that address could mean."

"Kennedy, I've been lying here crying, praying, cursing, and thinking all kinds of crazy ass thoughts. I've been losing my mind. I haven't heard anything from Michael or about him. Finally, his mother contacts me, and you expect me not to go?"

"Jaylen, that address could mean anything."

"Like what?"

"She could've sent you the text by mistake. Or that address could be for a ceremony." She whispers, "His family could be gathering there for his memorial service."

I stare at Kennedy. Those words are painful to hear and even harder to digest, as that's a definite possibility.

"You should really think about this. Maybe you should wait until you touch base with his mom."

I shake my head. "I've waited as long as I can. I have to go."

As I step inside my shoes, Kennedy types away on her cell. "That's a little over an hour away," she informs me.

"I'm fine with that."

"And you're going like that?"

I stand in front of my mirror. Dried tears have stained my face. My hair is undone. The T-shirt and boxers I'm wearing are definitely not outside attire. Kennedy didn't lie. I look terrible.

"Go clean yourself up and get dressed. I'll take the drive with you."

I push my hair back. "Are you sure?"

She nods. "I wouldn't feel right letting you go alone when you don't even know where you're headed."

I step inside my bathroom to quickly shower and dress. I prepare myself for the worst. I have no idea where I'm about to go, but I'm definitely ready to take this ride.

Chapter 24

I ride silently in the passenger seat. The past hour has turned me into even more of a wreck. I can't get a grip on my emotions. My head is spinning, and I have no control over it.

"Feeling any better?"

I wipe the tears from my face. "I'm so emotionally overwhelmed and confused."

"Do you want to try calling her again?"

"I've been trying. All I can do is assume that she wants me to come out here."

"Sure seems that way. I still don't know how I feel about going to a random address, but she's making sure you can't reach her. Whatever is out there, she must want you to see."

We continue to drive. The destination arrival time and the time on the clock are almost a match. We're close, and I don't know how to feel.

"I think the address is for a house," she predicts.

As we pull down a long street with huge houses sitting on plush seas of green, I begin to pick at my nails. I truthfully don't know what frame of mind to be in right now. I want to be hopeful, but I'm not sure what to hope for at this point.

Kennedy cuts off the GPS and points. "It's that one right there."

We park at the very end of a long driveway that leads to a large but charming home. The house looks like it could easily be featured in a Country Living magazine. The front porch reminds me of my home in Jersey. It's furnished with a wicker conversation set similar to the one my mom and I used to sit on while sharing hours of laughs.

"Maybe you should try to call one more time."

I remove my seatbelt. "I think I'm just gonna walk up and knock."

"And say what, if someone you don't know answers?"

"Hopefully, I'll figure that out before I get to the door."

I step out of my vehicle. Momentarily, I stand and look at the front of the house. I scan the yard with my eyes. The lawn is freshly mowed. The floral bushes are perfectly trimmed and colorfully bright.

"I can go with you," Kennedy offers.

I don't turn to face her. "It's okay."

The front door opens. I take slow steps toward Ms. Reed. Tears so badly want to fall. I have no idea how to talk to this woman. I lost a boyfriend, but she just lost a son. A son she'd still have if I didn't send his biggest enemy to his rescue.

She stands in the doorway, and I breathe deeply. I briefly stop walking to regain control of myself, and then resume taking small steps. My hands shake. My eyes fill with tears. My heart pounds so hard that I can feel it in my throat.

About halfway up the driveway, I stop. My body trembles all over. I feel him. I'm sure of it. I turn to look behind me. Kennedy's standing on the passenger side of the car. I turn back to his mother. She's still patiently waiting for me. I close my eyes and take a deep breath. I try to make sure I'm really feeling what I think I am. I reopen my eyes. The feeling is still present.

As his mother steps down the porch stairs, my eyes move to the side of the house. A door opens, and my eyes focus in on what I hope isn't an optical illusion. The sight of him makes me sprint. I run and jump onto him, wrapping my arms tightly around his neck and my legs around his waist. With my eyes closed, I cry loudly. If this isn't Michael, I don't want to see that it isn't just yet.

I hold on to him. My tears are full of pain, relief, anger, confusion. My head is spinning right now. There's absolutely no other place I'd rather be in this moment, but I can't understand what the hell is going on.

"I'm so sorry," he apologizes.

Ms. Reed rubs my back. "Jaylen?"

I don't let go. I don't want to chance letting go and finding out that I'm imagining this, even though I can feel him. The mind can play tricks. I already feel like I'm going crazy. I don't want to face the reality that I really might be.

"Jaylen? Sweetheart?" Ms. Reed's voice is so sweet.

I loosen my hold. I lower my legs until I can feel the ground beneath my feet again. Then, I open my eyes. I look into Michael's. I don't know how it's possible that I'm standing before him right now.

I place one hand on each side of his face. A tear falls from his left eye as I stare at him.

"It's me. I'm really here, Jaylen. I'm okay."

I snatch my hands from his face. Slowly, I back away.

He steps toward me. "Jaylen, listen."

"Why did you do this to me?"

Ms. Reed reaches out to me. "Listen to me."

My eyes stay on Michael. "Do you have any idea what I've been going through?" These tears are from anger. "Why the hell would you do this to me?"

"I disconnected his phone, Jaylen."

Ms. Reed's statement grabs my attention.

"That girl tried to kill my son. The only way I knew to protect him was to make her think she succeeded. At least until we figure out what to do."

I wipe the fallen tears from my cheeks.

"I wanted to call you. I've been going crazy here knowing that you thought I was dead," he explains.

"Who did—?" I clear my throat. "Who did I see? I saw the dried-up thing."

"I put that out there," Ms. Reed confesses. "I've held on to the people I've lost. Luckily, I had that one with me at work. I was taking a look at it under the microscope during my break." She continues, "Michael called me right before he called the cops. I shoved it in my pocket, and got out there to him as quickly as I could just in case another bear was nearby. I didn't think I'd need it, but—"

Ms. Reed stops speaking mid-sentence and focuses in on something behind me.

I turn toward the sound of approaching footsteps, and then back to Michael and his mother. "This is Kennedy," I say. "She's a friend."

Michael and his mother eye one another.

I tell them, "She won't say anything."

Michael reaches his hand out for Kennedy's.

"What's going on here?" she asks. She never extends her hand.

He tells her, "We can't really discuss that with you."

"I was there that night. I already know what you feel like you can't discuss."

"What do you think you know?" Ms. Reed asks her.

"She's, umm. She's like us," I reveal.

Michael's eyes move to mine. "Like us how?"

"I can feel you guys. You guys just can't feel me," Kennedy explains.

"Kennedy healed me that night after the attack. That's why I sent Indigo to you with the water. I collapsed. I was so exhausted."

"She's Indigo's friend, though, Jaylen."

"First of all, I didn't even know you were still alive," I say. "The address sent to me didn't come with instructions."

"And I'm not Indigo's friend," Kennedy makes clear. "I can't even go anywhere near her."

Ms. Reed asks Kennedy, "Why?"

"Because Jaylen thought Indigo killed Michael. She went crazy and almost killed Indigo. She would have, too, but Indigo's aunt intervened. Threats were thrown, and now this situation is way out of control."

Ms. Reed shakes her head. "This is a damn mess."

Michael reaches out to me. I push his hand away.

Creases form between his brows. "Jaylen?"

"I've been falling completely apart. I need a minute. I need to absorb this."

Ms. Reed touches my back. "You guys come on in. I was just making a little something to eat."

As we head inside, Michael grabs ahold of my hand.

Kennedy pauses at my side. "Wow. Do you feel that?"

Without even stepping inside the house, the presence of others can be strongly felt.

I ask Michael, "Who lives here?"

"Friend of my mom."

We walk in and head into the large kitchen. Sitting at the island is a guy with short, black hair and brown eyes. A smattering of freckles covers his nose. He looks to be around our age.

He stands. "I'm Ethan."

Kennedy shakes his hand. "I'm Kennedy."

He looks her up and down. "Nice to meet you, beautiful." He reaches for my hand. "And you must be Jaylen."

I shake his hand. "Nice to meet you, Ethan."

"I wish we were meeting under happier circumstances,

but it's nice to meet you, too."

Michael opens the fridge. "Where's your mom?"

"Firing up the grill," Ethan tells him.

Ms. Reed leaves the kitchen.

"Don't forget to finish up in that room," Ethan says to Michael.

Michael passes Kennedy and me bottles of water. "I won't."

"Michael, I want to apologize if I was rude outside," Kennedy says.

He smiles kindly at her. "It's okay. No hard feelings."

As we all sip down some water, I look at Michael. His face has never looked so beautiful. This is a face I never thought I'd see again. It's a face I've missed.

Michael tosses his empty bottle into the trash can. "I wanna talk to Jaylen alone. You guys mind?"

Ethan responds for the both of them. "Not at all."

Michael pulls me up the stairs and into a bedroom. I look around the space. The room is as clean as his room at home. The space smells of Michael and fresh paint.

I point toward a hole in the wall. "You did that?"

"I'm gonna fix it."

I sit on the side of the bed. Michael pulls over a chair from the corner of the room and sits in front of me. We look over one another.

"It's weird seeing me, huh?"

"I'm happy to see you," I tell him. "I haven't stopped thinking about you."

"I wanted to call you. It's been killing me."

I pick at my silver nails. "What exactly happened out there that night? Did Indigo do something to you?"

"She didn't physically attack me. When I saw her, I asked her what the hell she was doing."

I imagine the situation as he talks. I continue to pick at my silver, gel nails. Several are missing. They popped off during my fight with the bear.

"She told me you sent her down to give me some water."

"Did she?"

"First, she took a sip. Then, she wished me luck before she poured it out right in front of my face."

For a brief moment, I had felt bad for attacking Indigo. After learning that Michael isn't dead, I thought for a moment that maybe I'd made a horrible mistake. I didn't. I didn't wrongfully accuse her. She just didn't succeed at what she attempted.

"And then what?" I ask.

"She hit me with the empty bottle and walked off. I called my mom back. She was already on the path trying to find me. She stayed on the phone with me and I told her what Indigo had just done. Once she found me, she helped me up. She had just missed seeing Indigo walk away."

Indigo was lucky Ms. Reed didn't see her that night. Michael is her baby. Who knows what Ms. Reed may have done at the sight of her. No matter what Indigo may have been feeling, or how much he may have hurt her, pouring his water out was downright disgusting. Indigo's one of us. She knows how important water is. She knows we can't survive for days without it like humans can. Even in good health, a couple of hours without water can leave us in the worst pain. If we're hurt, and without it, every second is excruciating. We can feel our bodies drying out. It's an indescribable pain that only worsens until death relieves us of it. These are facts Indigo knows, facts she's shared with me.

It's hard to believe anyone could be so cruel. Indigo saw Michael lying on the ground, groaning in pain. She took a sip of what his body was in dire need of. Just a sip. She poured the rest out. To her, the dirt was more deserving of that water. Clearly, his life means nothing to her.

He sighs. "I'm just glad it rained that night. The rain is what kept me alive. As close as I was to the river, I just couldn't get there. I was so weak, and in so much pain, and that girl didn't give a single fuck." He shakes his head as he recalls that night. "You should've seen her face. She didn't care. I've seen Indigo mad before, but she didn't look angry that night. Just stone-faced." He exhales. "But anyway, once my mom pretty much dragged me to the car, she drove me straight here. The whole ride, we fought. I wanted to call you, but she didn't want Indigo to be tipped that I was alive. She knew no humans would believe I was dead, because there was no body, so she wasn't too concerned about them looking for me. She was only worried about Indigo."

I take my boyfriend's hand. "I guess if I look at it from your mom's point of view, she did what was best for your safety. I wouldn't have told, though. You being all right was the only thing I cared about."

"I know that. She does, too. She's thankful because you saved my life. Without you, that bear would've killed me for sure."

I sigh. "Michael, I can't begin to tell you how hard these last three days have been. I've been feeling so guilty." I try to blink the tears away. "So lost."

He moves in closer. "You can breathe now."

"I've been praying for you. I've been crying."

"Praying? You?"

"It just comes out."

"I've been praying, too. I think that's what brought us back together."

I shake my head. "I don't know about that. All I know is, without you, I almost felt like I couldn't go on. I would never kill myself, but the pain…" I shake my head again. "I can't explain how bad I hurt. I couldn't conceal it." I squeeze both of his hands. "I remember you telling me that one day, it'd all come out. You weren't lying. Everything came out. One second, I'd be crying for you, and the next, I'd be crying uncontrollably because I miss my mom so much. I tried to tell myself that I could pull through, that I have to pull through. Then I'd get an earful of what the universe was making clear. That I'm meant to be alone. That in my life, love won't last."

"You'll never feel like that again."

I stand as my emotions force shivers out of me. "Michael, please just hold me."

He takes me in his arms. He holds me close. He whispers, "I love you."

I cry. "I'm so glad you're okay. I'm so glad I didn't lose you, too."

I exhale in the arms of my love. I keep telling myself that this is real. He's alive. He hasn't been taken from me.

"You tried to kill Indigo?"

We slowly separate.

"Yes," I admit softly. "I choked her."

"Kennedy said her aunt jumped in."

I picture Indigo's aunt, her blue eyes, her jet-black hair, her long, slim figure. "That woman is so strong. She grabbed my ass up and threw me down like I weighed nothing."

His voice deepens. "Y'all fought?"

"No. We would have, but a passerby saw us. I just left after that."

"What did she say?"

I try to remember exactly. "She told me I started a big problem for myself. Then she pretty much threatened me. She said if Indigo's life is in danger, so is mine."

He shakes his head. "Moms is right, then. We're not really left with a choice. We're gonna have to take her out."

"Kill her?"

"Would her killing you be better?"

I shake my head. "I don't think they're going to retaliate."

"But how am I supposed to feel safe? I'm not afraid of Indigo. At this point, I'd knock her ass out with no problem.

But she can disappear. How am I supposed to protect myself from someone I can't see? This broad has been in my house. She tried to kill me. I don't have a choice." He adds, "Plus, y'all got beef now. You tried to kill this girl, Jaylen. Her aunt is in the same position my mom is. They have to protect their kids. They don't know I'm okay. For sure, they think you're not gonna stop coming at Indigo. This isn't gonna just go away. And we can't involve the cops. We have to handle this on our own."

"Michael, I want you to be safe. When I thought you were dead, killing Indigo didn't seem so hard. Now that I know you're fine, I don't see myself being able to walk up to her door, kill her, and then get back to my everyday life. I agree with everything you've said, but I don't think I can take part in that."

"I'm not asking you to do anything. I would never ask you to kill somebody for me. I have to protect myself. That's what I'm gonna do."

I wish. I so wish I could wave a magic wand and make this entire situation go away. It's a relief to know that my Michael is okay. It's frightening to imagine what the near future holds for him. For him and for us. He's being forced to defend himself. He's being forced into violence. In a situation like this, we don't have the law on our side. If he called the cops and reported that someone tried to kill him by pouring out his water, they'd laugh him off the phone.

"I have to do what I have to do. And if I don't, Moms is gonna feel obligated to. She doesn't want me back at the house. She doesn't trust what Indigo might do if she finds out I'm still alive."

"This whole situation is growing out of control. This is really tearing me apart." I whisper, "I'm scared."

"Don't be."

"You should be, too. You have no idea what could happen. You're planning to take her out. Keep in mind that's there's always a possibility that things could go another way."

"I know that."

I touch Michael's face. "Also know that if you're serious about this, as much as I'd like to, I'm not going to be able to sit home silently hoping you return to me. I'm gonna feel like I'm supposed to be there for you in case you need me."

"I'd rather you stay out of it."

"I wish I could."

"You can, Jaylen. And I want you to."

Ms. Reed steps in. "Can we talk?"

"Sure, Ma."

The three of us sit in private. Ms. Reed and I sit next to each other on the side of the bed. Michael's seated in the chair in front of us.

She turns to me. "Jaylen, I don't want you to think I've enjoyed knowing that you've been suffering. I thought about you every day and every night. I was just as worried as he was." She grabs my hand. "I couldn't chance anyone knowing he was okay. I didn't want her to panic and feel the need to try and finish the job."

"I understand. You had to protect your son."

"That's all I've been trying to do. Mike told me that Indigo had given you water and that you sent the rest down to him, so I knew you were alive and okay. The only reason I left anything behind is because Mike called me a second time and told me he could feel himself drying out. I could hear my son suffering, crying on the other end of the phone. When he told me what she did, the idea just hit me." She snaps once. "I knew if I left it there for her to see, she'd believe she killed my son, and she'd no longer have a reason to sneak around my house. I've held onto my loved ones for years, but I'd rather fully let go of someone I've already lost than to give her the impression that Mike's okay, just so she can invade my home again. I didn't want her looking for him or planning anything. Indigo is clearly unstable and unpredictable. I couldn't take chances. I needed to keep my child safe."

"I know. I can't be mad about that."

She squeezes my hand. "I thought allowing Mike to text you from my phone was the right thing to do. I saw my son going crazy in here. Punching walls, cursing, disrespecting somebody else's home." She catches her breath. "I realized that not contacting you was hurting him more than what she did to him. Right now, he needs a clear head. That's why I let him text you. I can't have him thoughtlessly reacting because he misses you."

I look at Michael and then back at his mother.

"But now, I feel like I made a mistake. Or maybe he should've said come alone."

"I didn't know where I was going or what I'd find here. That's why I brought her with me."

"Who is this girl?"

"She was initially a friend of Indigo's. She's been feeling pretty bad about what happened. She's been nice. Helpful."

"Do you trust her?"

I think about how little I know about Kennedy. Just because she doesn't agree with Indigo's actions and seems nice, doesn't mean I can trust this girl. A few days ago, she was a stranger to me. She was a friend of Indigo's who never spoke to me. She was with Indigo the entire night everything went down.

I shrug once. "I don't know."

"I don't want this girl blabbing to Indigo. I don't want our time figuring things out to be interrupted. We don't need surprises right now."

"I understand."

"We're going to be staying here. I've contacted a few friends in Michigan. We're trying to figure out the best way to go about this without the situation turning into a family-against-family war."

Michael jumps in, "I'm not staying here."

"You're not going back to the house," she states firmly.

"I'll go to Jersey with Jaylen. She's got a house there. I'll head straight there from graduation."

"You're not going to graduation."

"What? Yes, I am. It's like a week and a half away. For sure, we'll have something figured out by then. There's no reason why I should miss out on walking the stage with friends I've had for years."

"I thought the goal here was to keep you hidden. To make sure she doesn't find out about you," Ms. Reed states.

"I thought I just needed to hide out until we come up with something. I'm not staying in West Virginia. Graduation day, I'm going to Jersey. She's not gonna attack me in front of people. And once I leave, she won't know where I am. She doesn't know where Jaylen's house is. I'll be safe." He touches his mother's knee. "I want to graduate, though. And don't lie, Ma. You know you wanna see me walk."

I look at Ms. Reed. Her eyes are on her son.

"Ma, what do you think she's gonna do if she sees me? Most likely, seeing me is gonna scare the shit out of her."

"Watch your mouth, child." She looks at me. "You going?"

"I have to. Ms. Ward would lose it if I didn't."

"Are you scared?" she asks me.

"I'm scared of how much bigger this could get. I'm not afraid of Indigo. I'm much stronger than her. Her aunt, however, is a whole different story."

"So she's got strength, too?" Ms. Reed asks.

"When she pulled me from Indigo, the force behind the pull was insane, and hitting the ground was no joke. It happened so fast, I don't think I even blinked. And I definitely felt it when I got home. Not exhaustion. Not achiness. Straight-up pain."

"She have any other family?" Michael asks.

"Not that I know of. She only mentioned an aunt, but

I'm learning through Kennedy that Indigo is very good at telling little about herself but making it seem as though she's telling you everything."

"I think we should do it now. I mean, think about it, Ma. Let's not give them time to call anybody."

"It's been days, boy. Do you really think she hasn't let her family or friends know Jaylen's out to kill her? Get real. That's why we're thinking about this carefully. We're not experienced in something like this. I don't want you hurt because you're acting on impulse."

"So, what do you guys plan on doing?" I look at Michael. "How do you plan on, you know, getting rid of her?"

He looks at his mother and then those green eyes look into my brown ones. He smiles sweetly. "You know what, Jaylen? I think we should chill today. Let's try to enjoy this. Everybody's okay. Nobody knows where we are." He stands. "Moms is right. We got a lot more thinking to do, but we don't need to do it today. You definitely don't need anything else to worry about. Let me worry about Indigo."

Ms. Reed stands. "I think you're right. Let's take a day off and relax our minds a little. At the moment, standing where we are, she's not a threat. Let's not let this girl control us any more than she already has."

I sit silently.

"I'll give you guys some more time. Come out to the deck when you're ready."

"Ma, send up Ethan and Kennedy, please."

Ms. Reed leaves us alone, and Michael sits beside me. He lifts my legs and places them over his bent right knee. He rests his face against my neck. I'd give anything to be this close to Michael forever.

"You smell nice," he compliments softly. His lips gently press against my skin.

"I've missed you so much. It's gonna be hard to leave here later."

"It's gonna be hard to watch you go."

"You'll be able to call me, right? I mean, the big secret is out now. I know you're alive."

He sits up. "Yeah. For sure. Every day."

I take a deep breath. "I need to know something."

"What?"

I stare into those eyes. "Do you forgive me?"

"For what?"

"For sending her to you. For putting your life in jeopardy."

He takes my chin in between his thumb and forefinger. "I never blamed you. Never."

"I love you, Michael."

Our lips meet. They meet again after what feels like forever, though in reality, it was less than a week.

Pain ceases to exist when I kiss Michael. My worries fade away. Happiness returns.

A loud knock forces us to jump apart.

Ethan peeks through the hand covering his eyes. "Y'all invited us up here to see this?"

He and Kennedy step in and close the door. I look at Kennedy. She smiles. I return the gesture.

"Was that a smile?" Her eyes bulge.

I giggle as I bury my face in Michael's shoulder.

"And a laugh?"

I turn back to Kennedy. "Thanks for bringing me out here."

"I'm glad I did."

"It's been tough, huh?" Ethan asks.

I tell him, "Worse than that."

"She was a mess." Kennedy looks at me. "No offense, Jaylen." Her eyes move back to Ethan. "She looked horrible. Sick. Her eyes were bloodshot. She wouldn't get out of bed. The room was dark. There were water bottles and snotty tissues all over the place."

Michael holds me close.

"Breathe, Jaylen," Ethan encourages. "He's fine. We'll get this thing worked out so life can get back to normal."

"We're not talking about that today," Michael tells him.

Kennedy asks, "Because of me?"

"No. I just don't think it'd be right to fuel a new fire of worry when she's just beginning to feel some relief."

We all become silent. We all look at one another. The room suddenly feels uncomfortable.

"Awkward," Ethan says, dragging out the word.

We all let out small laughs.

Michael lies back on the bed. "So, Ethan. I saw you peeping Kennedy downstairs."

Ethan blushes. "Just a little bit."

Michael presses him. "You like her, don't you?"

"She's a beautiful girl."

I look at Kennedy. The embarrassment shows in her cheeks.

"You know she's one of us, right?" Michael asks.

"Duh."

I turn to Kennedy. "Oh, so you told him?"

She shakes her head. "No." She looks at Ethan. "How did you know?"

"I could feel it. Especially when I shook your hand."

"Nobody's ever been able to feel my presence."

Ethan throws her a wink. "I can."

We sit together and talk. After about thirty minutes of taking the time to get to know one another, we finally head down for the deck. Ethan's mother is beautiful. Her presence is incredibly strong, much stronger than Ms. Reed's. Her light, hazel-brown eyes are probably some of the kindest eyes I've ever seen. They're compassionate. Caring. And like her son, freckles decorate her nose.

"I'm not angry at Michael. I'd just prefer that he take his frustrations out on the punching bag. That's why I bought one. Ask Ethan what happened to him the first and last time he damaged a wall in my house that he pays no bills in."

We all laugh. Ethan's mom's personality matches Ms. Reed's. They're both strong women, but have fun enough personalities that their sons feel like they can actually talk to them. They're both so warm, but their open arms don't give the false impression that they can be walked over.

"I promise, Ms. Housley. You won't even be able to tell that the wall was damaged," Michael assures her.

"So you're headed to Princeton, I hear," Ms. Housley directs at me.

I drink some water and nod. "This fall."

"You staying on campus or home with family?"

"I'll be off campus. No family."

"I'm sorry, darling. I forgot. Mike did mention that."

"I'll be out there, though," Michael says happily. "I can't wait. I wanna gamble."

Ms. Housley asks me, "You live near Atlantic City?"

"My house is in Hopewell. That's about an hour and a half away from Atlantic City."

"Gamble?" Kennedy asks Michael. "You're too young to gamble. You have to be twenty-one to even go inside a casino."

"No, I don't."

"Yes, you do," Ms. Reed confirms. "And what are you supposed to gamble anyway? You ain't got no money."

Laughter bursts out of each of us.

"Do you feel that, Jaylen?"

I ask Ms. Housley, "Feel what?"

"This is family." She smiles warmly. "Don't say you don't have family. We're right here."

Michael kisses my cheek.

"You're not the only one facing this nasty situation. We all are. I hadn't seen Michelle in years before she called Friday night. I haven't seen Mike since he was little. He didn't even know who I was. But when she said she needed me, I was there. It'll be that way for you, too. If they love you, so do I. Going through this, and the rest of your life alone, is just not something we're going to let happen."

I smile gratefully at Ms. Housley.

"Same thing goes for you, too, Miss Kennedy."

Kennedy smiles gleefully.

"Look at my son. He hasn't stopped looking at you since he's been out here."

Michael corrects Ms. Housley. "He ain't stopped looking at her since he first met her in the kitchen."

We all make fun of their blushing. They even laugh at themselves.

I sit with my hand in Michael's. The thought of him killing Indigo makes me uncomfortable. It scares me. My mind jumps back and forth, trying to determine whether or not this is something that should be done. Is this our only option? If he kills her, that'll make her aunt want to retaliate. The feeling surrounding us today is peaceful. It's loving. It's beautiful. Like Ms. Housley said, this is family. A family of people I don't want to see hurt due to our actions sparking up a full-on war.

Chapter 25

I stand before my mirror. The royal-blue, asymmetrical, one-shouldered, ruffled dress looks much more appealing on me than I thought it would. On the hanger, it looked more like an eighth grade party dress. With the black pumps, everything came together quite nicely.

I exit my room and walk across the hall.

Ms. Ward smiles. "Beautiful."

I look down at myself. "I like it a lot. Thanks."

She passes me my yellow cap and gown. "How do you feel?"

"More than ready to walk that stage."

She grabs her purse. "You said Michael isn't going?"

"I don't think so. There's been a lot going on in his family. They've been out of town with relatives."

"That's unfortunate. I'm sure no one wants to miss their graduation."

"Yeah, he wants to go."

"I'm sure he does, but the diploma is still valid. That's what's important."

We head down the stairs. Kennedy and I have been

texting all morning. Our goal was to leave and arrive at the same time. I failed on my end big time. She's already left her house. I haven't.

Ms. Ward grabs two bottles of water from the fridge. I look around. I won't be coming back here for a while. Straight from graduation, I'll be heading back to Jersey. Ms. Ward is under the impression that I'm going to grad parties tonight and then hanging out in Jersey to re-organize the house and visit Princeton's campus. She has no idea I'll be shacking up with Michael and hiding out there to avoid any unexpected attacks from Indigo and her people.

"Do you have everything you need?"

I nod. "It's all in the car. I'll be back to get the stuff that's still upstairs."

"No rush. I don't need the room." She hands me a bottle. "And you'll need things for when you come back to visit me, right?"

"I will be back, Ms. Ward. I promise."

"It's going to be quiet around here now."

"No, it won't. You still have Corey."

She gasps. "And just what are you implying?"

I smirk. "I never bought that 'just friends' lie you tried to sell."

She giggles in embarrassment. "So what, smartass. Yes, I still do have Corey, but I'd like to still have you over sometimes."

I laugh. She does too.

"I'm gonna miss you, Jaylen. Really. I felt kind of like a parent. It felt nice to have more than just a career. I've been married to my job for a long time. As corny as it sounds, that marriage brought you to me. I kind of thought and wished you'd want to stay here."

"Everybody has to leave home at some point."

"So this was a home for you, right? It wasn't just another temporary foster stay?"

I'm taken by surprise that she'd even have to ask that.

"Absolutely, this was a home for me. And it wasn't just the room additions that made it feel that way. You made this feel like home."

Tears fall from her eyes.

"I mean it, Ms. Ward. That's why I can't be the only person making visits. You have to come spend time with me, too."

We hug. She holds me securely. The way she took me in and embraced me is something I'll never forget and will forever hold on to. If she and Corey are really in it for the long haul, she'll truly make one hell of a mom. The love she has for kids, the work she's done for years, makes her one the most special individuals I've ever known. She's dedicated her life to taking children out of troubled environments and finding them a place of peace. I was not in love with her when I first met her, but without a doubt, everything I've had and still do have is because of this woman.

I whisper, "We better get going."

She slowly releases me. Her eyes are pink from the crying.

I wipe her tears. "Stop it. You're gonna mess up your makeup."

"Oh God. I forgot about my makeup!"

I laugh quietly as she frantically pats the tears away.

"I'm gonna leave you," I threaten.

She turns to me. "Let's go graduate."

We leave quickly. I follow closely behind Ms. Ward the short distance to the school. I wasn't at all excited to hear that the ceremony was going to be held outside, but fate dealt a beautiful hand. The temperature is in the upper seventies, and the occasional breeze offers the right amount of cooling to keep me comfortable on such a warm, sunny day.

I line up with my cell in hand. I text Kennedy. She's already in line. I haven't seen Indigo, and Michael hasn't responded to my texts. I guess he agreed with his mother and decided it best to stay hidden. Though his absence is disappointing, I'm not too saddened by it. I know he's safe, and this evening, we'll be together. That's satisfying.

The line moves slowly as we take the white seats in the order we'll be called. My small senior class of only 115 looks so much larger when we're seated like this. As the parents and extended family members take their seats behind and to the side of the senior class, the feeling of a presence grabs me. It's not Michael's.

I watch as she sits three rows ahead of me. She's uneasy, and that's quite obvious. She shifts in her seat. Her eyes look everywhere, but even when she looks behind her, Indigo makes for certain that her eyes don't meet mine.

Kennedy texts me. *Keep your cool, Jaylen. Remember, he's fine.*

I respond immediately. *I'm good. I ain't thinking about her ass. I'm just ready to walk.*

I sit patiently. I avoid looking at Indigo in order to hold on to the joy surrounding this day. Though more than anything, I'd love to see Michael walk the stage and vice versa, graduating is an amazing accomplishment no matter who's present. I'm not going to allow my hate for Indigo or missing Michael take away what this day means to me.

As the remainder of the students move in an orderly fashion to find their seats, I shudder at the feeling of another of my kind. I turn in my seat. Her large, blue eyes pierce mine. Indigo's aunt stands beside another woman, a woman with hair so platinum-blonde that it shines white in the sunlight. Both have their arms folded. Both sets of eyes are locked in on me. I turn away from them. Without even looking their way, I can still feel the chill of their icy glares.

Kennedy texts me again. *I can feel more of our kind.*

I text back, *Indigo's aunt is here. She brought a friend. They're both staring me down as I'm texting this.*

She responds, *Well, don't look at them. Don't look at Indigo.*

Focus on what's important. Graduating!

After reading Kennedy's text, I place my phone in my lap and turn my attention to the podium. The ceremony begins the same way each day of class does, with the signing of the cross. As I normally do, I sit still as those who surround me pray.

The girl sitting next to me sniffles, pulling my eyes her way. As she dries her tears, I look around at my schoolmates. This is likely the last time I'll ever see these people I've shared classrooms with for the last few months. While graduating is an amazing celebration, there's also a very sad undertone. Today is definitely bittersweet.

The valedictorian is called up to the podium by Principal Landry. He adjusts the microphone and begins to deliver a heartfelt speech. Without being able to help it, my eyes move to the back of Indigo's head. As those around her glance at her in admiration of her beauty, I look at her in disgust. I still don't agree that killing her is the best and only answer, but she deserves some form of punishment. No one capable of killing another for their own selfish reasons deserves to walk free, let alone be admired. I just can't seem to find an answer to what should be done with Indigo.

The applause steals my focus. I join in and clap, though I was too distracted to hear his words. The reaction from the others indicates that his words were touching. Some of the faculty members have lowered heads. Some have teary eyes. I'm sure their emotions have a lot to do with the size of Trinity. With a school this size, teachers can't help but grow attached to most of us. There's a great opportunity to know your students more personally in such a small and close-knit environment.

Elizabeth from my first period steps up onto the stage. Initially, I assume she's going to speak, but then the music starts and pre-recorded background vocals play. I listen as she beautifully delivers a slower version of Christina Aguilera's

"Soar."

There are voices that bring a smile to your face, and then there are voices like Elizabeth's that literally take your breath away, that force you to remember to breathe.

I look back at Indigo's aunt. She's watching the stage. I turn back around in my seat and continue listening to Elizabeth. I rarely find myself afraid of anyone, but without a doubt, there is something about that woman that shakes me to my core. Her eyes tell a story, and I don't believe it's fictitious. They say that anyone who plans to get to Indigo has to go through her, and that fight will be the most difficult one of their life.

We all stand and applaud. Whistles and loud cheering are directed at a deserving Elizabeth, who just belted that song as though it were her last.

She bows. "Thank you so much. I love each of you, and I'm never going to forget the time we spent together walking the halls of Trinity."

We clap for her once again as she takes careful steps from the stage and returns to her seat.

Principal Landry steps back up to the podium. This is the part of the ceremony all seniors look forward to. Before anyone's name is called to accept their diploma and walk the stage, I text Michael. *I'm about to walk. Cross your fingers. I hope I don't trip. Thinking about you. Love you. Wish you were here.* I sign the message with a heart before unzipping my gown just enough to secure my phone in my bra.

As each of my fellow schoolmates takes that unforgettable walk across the stage, I clap. I watch each of them, and then it hits me. I'm graduating from high school. I'm graduating and my mom isn't here to see me. Michael isn't here to see me. Though tears want to fall, I shake them away. This occasion is a bit painful for me, but I refuse to spend it with sadness covering my face. Someone is here for me: Ms. Ward. And though we haven't seen eye to eye on everything, she loves me.

Indigo's row heads for the stage. I watch her closely. I continue to clap, though my feelings for her are unchanged. Michael being alive will never change the fact that I despise her. I'll never forget what she tried to do to him.

I watch Indigo graduate. I watch Warren, Kennedy, Ayana, and rows of my senior class take their walk before my row is told to stand. We slowly walk toward the stage. It's almost my turn.

Principal Landry holds out her hand to the student before me. "David Harrison."

Everyone claps, and I take a deep breath. As he's photographed receiving his diploma, I scan the family seating areas for Ms. Ward. I spot her sitting next to Corey, and I smile. She's not my mom and never will be, but I'm so happy she's here with me today. Her support is undeniably needed.

"Jaylen Hayes."

The crowd roars, and Ms. Ward's voice is louder than everyone else's. I smile wide as I accept my diploma. I know for sure if my mom were here, she'd be just as loud and just as proud.

"Congratulations, Jaylen."

I know the excitement shows in my face. My cheeks are pushing up my lower eyelids. "Thank you, Mrs. Landry."

As I exit stage right, the feeling of graduating from high school with honors and a 4.0 GPA warms me. I'm so proud of myself. Though my super intelligence played a huge role in my academic achievements, I could've easily slacked and given up after I lost my mom. I'm glad I stuck it out. I'm glad that I didn't give up on life just because my mother and my mom both lost theirs. This is what they both wanted for me.

I pass by Warren on the way back to my seat, and he holds out his fist for me to pound. Though he's not like me on the inside, I'll miss him. I'll miss Eugene, and I'll also miss seeing Ayana.

I take my seat as the remainder of my senior class receives their diplomas. The feeling of my kind's presence intensifies. I quiver and search behind me to see if perhaps Indigo's aunt invited others to stand beside her to give me the evil eye. Beside her still stands her one friend. Again, they're both eyeballing me. I face forward. I clap as students continue to collect their diplomas. As another row of seniors head for the stage, butterflies awaken inside me. My heartbeat takes off like a runaway train. Michael is here. My eyes try to dart everywhere at once in search of him.

I find him. I light up at the sight of my boyfriend approaching the stage. I swing around, expecting to see his mom standing behind our senior class, but I don't.

"Patricia Ramos," the principal calls out.

We clap, and the hugest smile takes over my face as Michael prepares to be called next. Having him here and knowing he saw me walk touches me and fills me with happiness. Pure joy.

"Michael Reed."

I try to stay in my seat, but I can't. I stand and shout for my boyfriend. His mother congratulates him even louder. I follow her voice and notice that Ethan and Ms. Housley came along with her to share in this experience.

Ms. Reed videotapes her son cabbage patching across the stage. Everyone laughs. It's something that can't be denied. Michael is just a funny and loveable individual.

As I sit back down, I look at Indigo. She's turned in her seat. Her eyes are on her aunt. Neither of them expected this surprise.

A text from Kennedy alerts me. *I think Indigo just pissed herself.*

I respond. *Lol. You're probably right. Did you see who came with Michael?*

She responds with the blushing emoji.

I send back, *I think I smell love in the air.*

The final seniors in our class walk the stage. I watch Indigo from behind. She fidgets and repeatedly turns to look at her aunt. I can't imagine what must be going through her mind right now. For the first time, I actually wish I could invade another's thoughts.

Principal Landry dabs the corners of her eyes. "Ladies and gentlemen, it has been an absolute pleasure to see you grow over the last four years. Our time spent together at Trinity will forever remain in my heart. I am so proud of each and every one of you. Every enrolled senior is sitting in front of me. We did not have one student fail to meet the necessary requirements to graduate with their class. Give yourselves a round of applause!"

We do. We cheer for ourselves and so do the families and faculty.

"Will the graduating Class of 2015 please rise?"

We all stand.

"We have reached that time, ladies and gentlemen. It is time for each of you to signify the completion of your high school years here at Trinity. Please do so by moving your tassel from right to left."

As we follow the time-honored tradition, our families loudly express their delight.

"Congratulations, Class of 2015! Are you ready?"

Without waiting for her to give the order, we scream and toss our caps into the air. Royal- blue and yellow caps hit the ground as we hug our classmates and celebrate our achievement. This is a day we'll never forget.

I don't waste any time. I squeeze out of my row and make my way over to Michael. I wrap my arms around him.

He lifts me. "Congratulations."

"You, too. I can't believe you're here."

Kennedy approaches us. "Congrats, guys!"

We group hug.

"Can you believe it?" Kennedy asks excitedly. "We're

done. High school is over."

I shake my head. "It's crazy. We're grownups for real now."

She grabs my hand. "I want you guys to meet my dad."

I pull Michael as we squeeze past friends trying to get our attention.

Kennedy hurries into her father's arms. The resemblance is uncanny, and his presence is the strongest I've felt from any of our kind.

"Damn," Michael says. "They look just alike."

"Watch your mouth," I scold.

"Dad, these are my friends, Jaylen and Michael."

I shake her father's hand first, and then Michael does.

He hands his daughter a bouquet of roses. "Congratulations. I'm proud of all of you."

Michael and I both thank Kennedy's father.

"You guys can go ahead and mingle with your friends. I'll hang here."

"No way, Dad." She grabs his hand. "Come with us. You have to take pictures anyway."

"Oh, I do?"

Kennedy giggles. "Yes, you do."

"Aye!" Warren yells at us.

Michael and Warren dap each other up.

"Where you been at, son?" Warren asks. "Your phone has been off. You ain't been on Facebook."

"Been on punishment, bro. Moms had me on lockdown."

"What's up, Miss Jaylen?"

"Congratulations, Warren."

We hug.

"Thanks. You too, Princeton." Warren turns. "Kennedy," he says, smiling broadly. "Congratulations."

I didn't realize they knew each other, but I now understand. Kennedy wasn't a stranger to everyone. The reason Michael and I didn't have a relationship with Kennedy is because she went out of her way to stay away from us.

Warren extends his right hand. "How are you, sir?"

Kennedy's father shakes hands with Warren. "Very well, thank you. Congratulations."

We all head toward Michael's mom. Ms. Reed's eyes are full of tears. As Michael walks her way, he holds his diploma above his head. Their hug warms everyone standing around them. She is so proud of her son, and Michael is ecstatic about pleasing his mother.

"I told you I was gonna graduate, Ma."

"I knew you could do it," she cries out. "And I am so proud of you, son. So proud."

We all hug. After accepting cards from Ms. Reed and Ms. Housley, I excuse myself to go find Ms. Ward. I locate her speaking with faculty members.

She opens her arms. "Congratulations, you."

I embrace Ms. Ward tighter than I ever have.

"How does it feel?"

"I can't explain it." I let her go. "I didn't think the ceremony would be so moving, but being here in my cap and gown, accepting the diploma, and walking the stage…" I place my hand over my racing heart. "I'm really proud of myself."

"You should be."

"It feels amazing to graduate from high school. I can't lie. I kind of want to do it again."

We laugh, and I hug her again.

"Thank you for everything, Ms. Ward."

"Thank you, Jaylen," she says softly.

"Can you take pictures of me and my friends?"

"Yeah, of course."

I look around. "What happened to Corey?"

"He needed to use the bathroom."

We carefully walk in our heels toward Michael and his

family.

"Oh, there's Indigo." She points.

I grab her hand. "No. We're not talking to her."

"We're not?"

"No."

"Okay," she lets out uncomfortably. "I won't even ask."

I rejoin the group alongside Ms. Ward. I introduce her to everyone, and she individually hugs and congratulates each of my friends. No one's face is missing a smile. This occasion may have a sad undertone, but it's a wonderful occasion, and we're all filled with elation.

"I'm gonna go find my mom and dad," Warren says.

As he steps away, Ms. Ward excuses herself as well to go look for Corey.

Ms. Reed pulls me close. "You all right?"

"Mm-hmm."

She asks quietly, "Which one is the aunt?"

"The one with the long, black hair."

We turn in their direction at the same time. Indigo's aunt and her platinum-blonde friend look right back at us. Our faces aren't housing anger. Theirs are. Indigo won't make eye contact.

Michael moves in closer. "This is gonna be a problem."

Ms. Reed whispers, "Maybe not Indigo, but you can tell that this aunt of hers definitely feels threatened."

We turn back around. Ms. Housley smiles at me. I throw one back her way.

"We'll be back," Kennedy tells us.

As she and her father step away, Ethan, Ms. Housley, Ms. Reed, Michael, and I all gather closely.

"The hot chick tried to do you in?" Ethan asks.

Michael sucks his teeth. "She tried to kill me, Ethan. She ain't so damn hot."

Ms. Housley speaks softly. "I'm not too worried about the girl. She looks terrified."

"That's what I was telling them," Ms. Reed says.

"What are y'all talking about?" Michael asks. "Indigo only looks like that because she's in shock. Don't forget what she did. Don't forget what Jaylen did to her."

His mother looks into his eyes. "Look, Michael. No one is saying we don't have anything to worry about. We're just pointing out that her aunt is going to be more of a problem than she's going to be."

"I agree," I remark.

"Then we'll prepare ourselves to deal with her, too."

We look back over at Indigo's family. The three of them are looking back at us. Indigo's eyes are no longer on the ground. They're on me.

"I can't even look at this girl." Michael turns away. "I just wanna walk over there and knock her out."

I rub his back. "Calm down."

"No! Moms has to drive over an hour to go to work because she doesn't feel comfortable going home. I can't be in my own house. All because of this broad!"

"Shh." Ms. Housley moves closer to Michael. "Calm down. Nothing public."

"And I'm not afraid to go home, Michael. I just don't want *you* there," Ms. Reed states.

"You're not gonna stay at the house by yourself, Ma!"

I touch Michael's arm. "Shh."

Ms. Reed tells her son, "I didn't say I was going back home, Michael. I said I'm not afraid to."

"This is blowing me, Ma. I'm letting this girl run me out of Virginia. We're letting her run us out of our home."

"What else can we do right now?"

Ms. Housley asks, "Is she going away to school?"

I shrug once. "I don't know."

Ethan opens his ceremony program. "They listed where everyone plans to go to college. I saw it."

Ms. Reed reads aloud, "Montclair State University. She's

studying fashion."

"Where the hell is that?" Ms. Housley asks.

I ask myself the question.

Michael turns my face toward his. "What's wrong? What's with that expression?"

"She's going to Jersey, too," I reveal.

Ms. Reed panics. "What?"

"Montclair is a little over an hour away from Hopewell. If that program is right, she won't be too far from us."

With our eyes on Indigo and her family, we immediately realize that we're facing a new issue. I was looking forward to the safety we'd have by moving out of state. I was looking forward to having Michael with me, away from Virginia, in a place where Indigo couldn't get to him, and he couldn't do anything to her in a moment of anger. I don't know what to look forward to now, and unfortunately my super intelligence can't help me to see what's next. All I know for sure is that my unpredictable, dangerous ex-best friend and my vengeful boyfriend need states in between them. Indigo's college choice doesn't provide the necessary distance.

My heart was overflowing with happiness just minutes ago. It was racing with joy. Now, it's throbbing. It's painfully throbbing because of the unpleasant reality I must now accept. The problem I thought Michael and I were temporarily getting away from is following us.

Acknowledgements

There are so many people who played an important role in helping me publish this novel. Each of you mean so much to me.

First and foremost, I must thank God for all the blessings he has bestowed upon me. My faith is my strength. It has given me the courage and confidence to break rules and really trust myself in my writing.

I am grateful to Thierry "T" Arnoux for supporting this project from the very beginning. I have been bouncing ideas off of you for years. Not only have you been honest about the storyline, but you've been an amazing website designer. You're truly my ace!

Kahina Haynes, my Bubbs, my crazy sister, you deserve a special thank you as well. You are the first person I discussed the topic of this book with. I remember the exact day. We were driving to Ross to go Christmas shopping and I told you that I wanted to write something totally different from all of my other stories. You said to run with it. I did! Thank you for being so supportive, being an amazing beta-reader, and even helping me edit the first few chapters.

Victoria "Vick" Epie, I appreciate you as well. You read the entire first draft and provided me with helpful feedback. Your support means so much to me. I knew if I wanted the truth I needed to talk to book fanatic. It means the world to me to have you in my corner.

Evelyn E, there isn't enough space on this page for me to fully thank you. You have been the world's greatest mentor. You're brutally honest, direct, but never hurtful or unkind. You've been so supportive, and like a mom to me. Having you in my corner means so much. I love you!

Christina Frey of Page Two Editing, you were so amazing to work with. You were the first professional editor I'd worked with, and I was so nervous, but you were thorough, kind, and provided the most helpful notes. Developmental editing can be frustrating, but you made this step less stressful for me. I truly enjoyed working with you.

M Leigh, my line editor, and Thomas Shutt, my first proofreader, I appreciate your time and helpful notes.

Amber Drappier, my second proofreader, your notes were so helpful, and there were still a lot of mistakes left behind that you helped me to catch. Thank you.

Laura Hicks, the final editor to read over my manuscript, thank you. After making a few last minute changes, I wasn't sure if another editor would be needed. I'm so glad that I decided to go with my gut and hire you. You were prompt, thorough, kind, and you caught things we all missed. I loved working with you, and I'm excited to work with you again on future projects.

Ilsie Omareva of Wonderburg Creations (http://wonderburg.format.com), working with you was an absolute pleasure. I love my cover, and appreciate how patient you were with me. Not only were you patient, but you went above and beyond to help me find something I could be proud of, and then you created marketing materials to match. Everything you created was beautiful, our professional relationship is one I often talk about, and I can't wait to work with you again in the future. Thank you!

To my amazing beta readers, Denis Elena Nicolae, Silje Johnson, Arabelle Johnson, and Charlotte Woollock, your feedback was so helpful. You all took the time to read the work of someone you didn't know, and provided very helpful feedback. I can't tell you how much that means to me.

Last, but certainly not least, I have to thank all of my family and friends. Thank you for the love and support.

Thank you all for helping me make my dream come true!